P9-AQM-833

HOME BY STARLIGHT

HOME BY STARLIGHT

Jerri Corgiat

A SIGNET ECLIPSE BOOK

SIGNET ECLIPSE
Published by New American Library, a division of
Penguin Group (USA) Inc., 375 Hudson Street,
New York, New York 10014, USA
Penguin Group (Canada), 90 Eglinton Avenue East, Suite 700, Toronto, Ontario M4P 2Y3, Canada (a division of Pearson Penguin Canada Inc.)
Penguin Books Ltd., 80 Strand, London WC2R 0RL, England
Penguin Ireland, 25 St. Stephen's Green, Dublin 2, Ireland (a division of Penguin Books Ltd.)
Penguin Group (Australia), 250 Camberwell Road, Camberwell, Victoria 3124, Australia (a division of Pearson Australia Group Pty. Ltd.)
Penguin Books India Pvt. Ltd., 11 Community Centre, Panchsheel Park, New Delhi - 110 017, India
Penguin Group (NZ), cnr Airborne and Rosedale Roads, Albany, Auckland 1310, New Zealand (a division of Pearson New Zealand Ltd.)
Penguin Books (South Africa) (Pty.) Ltd., 24 Sturdee Avenue, Rosebank, Johannesburg 2196, South Africa

Penguin Books Ltd., Registered Offices:
80 Strand, London WC2R 0RL, England

First published by Signet Eclipse, an imprint of New American Library, a division of Penguin Group (USA) Inc.

ISBN: 978-0-7394-7115-9

Printed in the United States of America

To LaMae Enstrom Rundle Brainerd and E. Byron Brainerd, who have taught me about uncommon strength

Acknowledgments

This book was written during a time when personal events turned life upside-down. I owe deep gratitude to my *remarkable* friends—among them, Ann Handelman, Nancy Phillips, Jill Meradith, Pam Cyran, Sarah Buechel, Sharon Handler, Diana Rhodes, Karen Brichoux, Libby Sternberg, my sister Lynne Ruf—and all the people who showed up to help (are you listening, Mary Enstrom? Arlene Hershorn? Bobbie Whitfield?) They had unending patience whenever I needed to rant, weep, or gnash my teeth! You all inspire me.

I also want to thank Karen Brichoux for supplying me with chicken lore, and Joe Benedick for tossing me nuggets on broken ankles, unfortunately mined from his personal experience, and also for causing a stir in the Versailles, Missouri, Wal-Mart! Thank you, too, to writer Mary Beth for her donkey tales, and to Sandy Cahill for giving up an afternoon to share her love and knowledge of weaving. And, as usual, thanks to Marcy Posner and Claire Zion for your friendship, expertise, and support. Your gifts are never taken for granted.

Chapter 1

The ground beneath her feet had shifted when her oldest daughter had left for college just over a year ago. And—to her bewilderment, because what did it have to do with her?—it had tilted again when the St. Andrew's choir director had run off with the Wal-Mart pharmacist.

But the day that she slipped, fell, and broke her ankle, that was the day Patsy Lee O'Malley's life changed forever.

She was thinking about tomatoes at the time, though, so of course she didn't know it had changed forever. Up until the moment when she skidded on a patch of soap bubbles spilled on the sidewalk in front of her in-laws' rambling old house and landed flat on her back, it had been a very pleasant day. Actually, a special day, because of the wedding.

Despite the bride's choice of a Friday for the nuptials (to satisfy her desire for a weekend honeymoon package in New York), a good chunk of Cordelia, Missouri, had still spilled into Zinnia and Pop O'Malley's backyard this morning. In Zinnia's early October garden, bursting with cinnamon and harvest gold chrysanthemums, they'd seen the O'Malleys' youngest daughter wed to her childhood sweetheart.

But special or not, it wasn't the kind of day where

Patsy Lee would have expected fate to step in and turn her life upside down. Although the way she'd felt lately, someone needed to.

Catching the breath she'd lost to the initial burst of pain that had now subsided to a throb, Patsy Lee rose on her elbows. Her hair, thick and dark except for a few strands of silver that she'd had Betty Bruell at Up-in-the-Hair highlight red, swung loose and brushed the ground. She'd worn it to her waist until not long ago, when she'd made Betty clip it to her shoulders in a matter-of-fact nod to advancing maturity.

Not that a new hairstyle, however age appropriate, had stimulated whatever hormones it would take to make her feel mature. Most of the time she felt like she was picking her way through a tangled warp, no more certain of anything in life than when she was a girl.

And, for the last year, less. She'd hoped to get some questions on her mind cleared up this weekend in Columbia. But, looking at her right foot, she knew the trip was out.

In fact, given that her ankle had already swollen to twice the size of one of Zinnia's award-winning eggplants and would soon be as purple, it was a safe bet to assume a lot of things were out. She edged off her pumps before the Jaws of Life were required, then looked around for help.

And saw none. Even though the O'Malley family was the size of a small town (partially populated by her own brood of four children), for one of the first times since she'd married Henry O'Malley, she was alone. The wedding guests were gone. They'd left an hour ago, once the champagne was drained, the brunch eaten, and the bride and groom cheered off in a cloud of Tootsie Toy Bubbles. The front yard was silent under a coverlet of maple leaves. The porch yawned across the front of the house; a swing covered in faded rose upholstery creaked back and forth in the breeze.

She resigned herself to wait. The O'Malleys were rarely still; somebody was bound to come out soon. She wouldn't call out—her voice was softer than theirs—and she wouldn't crawl to the porch steps; the rust-colored duster and dress she wore had to last at least through the Christmas pageant at St. Andrew's.

She lay back. If they even had a pageant this year. The choir director's flight had left the event in a fix, which had left Preacher Phelps wringing his hands (not the least because the choir director was his wife). The scandal would provide grist for the Cordelia gossip mill for months. She pitied the preacher's wife and her paramour their notoriety.

Almost as much as she envied them.

She stared up through leaves the color of pumpkins. The sky was hard, cloudless, and sharp blue, the kind of blue that presages a first frost, the kind of hard frost that would ruin the last of her tomatoes if they weren't picked today. She no longer relied on her truck garden for income like she had during her marriage, but she hated to see her tomatoes go to waste. She hated to see anything go to waste. Poor Henry crossed her mind.

It was moments like this when she thought it would be nice to have a husband to impose upon. Not that Henry O'Malley had ultimately proven up to the task. Even before his death almost a decade ago from a genetically bad heart while she was pregnant with her youngest, she wouldn't have called her husband terribly reliable. More like terrible at reliability. But that had just been Henry. Since any romantic whimsies she'd once harbored had drowned under a deluge of responsibilities a long time ago, her single state rarely bothered her, but sometimes . . .

Sometimes, like when she'd heard about the latest

scandal, she wondered what it was like to be so much in love, you didn't give a hoot or a holler about anything else.

She stirred. She'd never used to wonder about things like that, but in the past year, she'd found herself entertaining unfamiliar thoughts. Uncomfortable ones, even. Insane ones, occasionally.

"What have we here?"

A male voice came from the direction of the porch. Recognizing it, Patsy Lee didn't turn her head; she closed her eyes. Of all people . . . the voice belonged to Zeke Townley, her unexpected (unwanted) houseguest, just arrived this morning. Zeke was . . . cool. Her kids would roll their eyes at her use of the word, but there really wasn't another way to describe him.

Footsteps sounded. Then stopped beside her. Knowing she looked like an idiot with her eyes closed, she still didn't open them. *Cool*—a word that had never been used in the same sentence as *Patsy Lee*—flustered her, almost as much as the fact she hardly knew him. Even though Zeke dropped down to Cordelia every time he traveled from his home in San Francisco to foreign places beyond, with a regularity that had her mother-in-law treating him like a member of the family, he always stayed with her sister-in-law, Lil O'Malley Van Castle, and Lil's husband, Jon, his best friend. Except this time.

This time he'd made such a last-minute decision, the guesthouse on Lil and Jon's estate was already promised to wedding guests. Lil had begged her to house him. Begging hadn't been necessary; she never refused Lil a thing. Although this time she might have had Lil asked her to play hostess for the several months Zeke planned to stay in Cordelia. Why that long, she hadn't asked, too relieved to find out her hospitality was required just for the weekend.

Seconds had turned into a minute. Regrettably,

Zeke Townley apparently wasn't going to leave her for dead. She opened her eyes and looked up. Way up. Zeke was as tall as he was lean. Beneath black hair brushed with silver, and black eyebrows arched in amusement, a pair of black eyes looked back.

She untied her tongue. "I think I broke my ankle."

His gaze went to her feet. "Damn. I think you're right." He hunkered down, one hand dangling a plastic flute of champagne, forearms on the knees of his white pants. She rose on her elbows again and they both stared at her ankle.

"Hurts like hell, I'll bet." He paused, then sighed. "The O'Malleys will be beside themselves. And they've already been beside themselves more than a man should have to take in a day."

He winked. She smiled. And for the briefest of moments, he looked unsettled. She rather liked the expression on somebody else.

"Unfortunately, I can't think of another option. Let's get you inside."

Before she could protest, in one fluid movement, he set down his glass and scooped her into his arms. A sound escaped her, and she clung to him, blinking.

Straightening, he frowned. "Sorry if I hurt you."

"You didn't." He had. "But—"

But what? But I might hurt *you*? She was short. But not svelte. Definitely not svelte. She was what her mother had termed healthy, what Henry had called curvy, and that added up to what fashion magazines indicated was at least two sizes over par.

"Never mind." Forty-three-and-four children-old was a bit late to worry about her girlish figure.

When he moved, pain shot up her leg. Biting her lip, she concentrated on the white button on the white collar of his very white shirt, and wondered how anyone could travel all night and arrive here this morning looking like he'd just come from the dry cleaner's.

And the barber. His cheek was smoothly shaven, shorn of the beard he'd worn when she'd first met him nearly a decade ago. His hair was trimmed to a razor's edge just above his collar.

He carried her like she weighed nothing. He didn't even grunt with effort.

"Although you wouldn't, would you?" she murmured.

"Wouldn't what?"

She felt herself turn all shades of red and bowed her head so he couldn't see. "Nothing." She fastened her eyes on the general region of her belly button and swore to keep them there. *Never mind. Nothing.* What witty repartee.

She rued the genes that had not only made her blush long past an age when blushing was cute, but had bestowed on her a pair of tilted round eyes that, along with the sprinkle of freckles across a turned-up nose, made her look about as self-reliant as Bambi. It hadn't helped that her mother had saddled her with the name Patsy Lee, either, or that she'd developed a habit of blurting her thoughts. She suspected early dementia.

Although maybe she could be forgiven for feeling addled. Not only was her ankle broken, but she was being borne about in the arms of a celebrity. A hunk of a celebrity Okay, he was a hunk if you were her age—she risked another look—or maybe even younger than her age. Until her brother-in-law Jon Van Castle had disbanded his country music group, a band that had rivaled the fame of Alan Jackson and Diamond Rio, after Jon had married Lil O'Malley some eight years ago, Zeke Townley had been one of the most famous bass guitarists in history. She supposed he wasn't as famous anymore. And without the beard, very rarely recognized. But still very . . . well, *hunky*.

He glanced down. Blushing anew, she furiously worked to replace whatever fever might show on her face with a look of bored sophistication, a look she rarely (never) adopted. His mouth spasmed. Honestly, she was pathetic.

When they reached the top of the porch steps, Lil stepped through the door. Now, there was an example of svelte. At thirty-nine, her sister-in-law was lovely, blond, confident, willowy, successful, and everything else Patsy Lee wasn't.

Next to Lil—actually, next to any of the three O'Malley women who made up her trio of sisters-in-law—Patsy Lee faded right into the wallpaper. Not the least because she was dowdy next to the eldest Alcea's renowned golden beauty, and dull as a dishrag next to the younger Mari's redheaded exuberance, not to mention nearly a foot shorter than any of them. She was her mother-in-law's height, although Zinnia would never get overlooked the way Patsy Lee often did (preferred).

Lil's exclamation brought Zinnia hustling. "What's all this commotion?"

"I slipped on some soap bubbles. My ankle . . ."

As she explained, Pop O'Malley stepped out behind Zinnia. Pop had changed from his one good suit into green overalls and an orange corduroy shirt, reminding Patsy Lee of carnival squash, although his shape was more zucchini—tall and slightly bent. He sported a shock of white hair and toothbrush eyebrows.

Gray curls corkscrewing around a plump face red from the exertion of hostessing a wedding and now turning redder at the plight of her daughter-in-law, Zinnia turned to enlighten her husband. ". . . And I should have thought to hose off that sidewalk, now shouldn't I? I swear, with all the details . . ."

"Don't you go blaming yourself, dear." He put a

hand on her shoulder. Ever since Zinnia had undergone heart surgery last spring, he'd grown protective, uncharacteristically exercising his will, long rusting after more than half his seventy years of dealing with four women that had various quantities of steel in their spines. "You've had too much on your mind as it is, and—"

"And now isn't the time to worry about—" Lil's voice had gone soothing.

"I'm not blaming myself, I'm just saying—"

While they jabbered, Patsy Lee gave another glance at Zeke, unafraid he'd notice her look, since his gaze was resting on Lil. (See? Wallpaper.) Pop was responsible for her visitor. While Pop hadn't murmured any protest over Zinnia's intentions to direct the wedding in their home—he was a man aware of his limitations, after all—he'd insisted she not burden herself with overnight guests, as well. Hence Lil's full guesthouse. Hence, Patsy Lee's houseguest.

"What's up?"

Jon Van Castle pushed open the door, dark brows arrowed over topaz eyes. Those eyes, combined with a lion's mane of tawny hair, now cut short and salted with white, had once been his trademark, just as his bass guitarist's penchant for black-and-white attire and a *GQ* crease in his trousers had once been Zeke's. As Jon slipped an arm around his wife's waist, Patsy Lee saw what looked like envy flash across Zeke's face. She averted her eyes, feeling like she'd intruded.

"Patsy Lee slipped on some—" Lil started in.

"I should have gotten one of the kids to—"

"—and now she's getting herself all excited over—"

The screen door bumped against Jon's back and he stepped aside so Patsy Lee's quartet of children, Jon and Lil's two, and Alcea's one could spill out. The youngest had a school holiday today for parent-teacher conferences; the oldest had skipped classes to come home from college. The explanations began anew and the clamor increased. Zeke and Patsy Lee went largely ignored.

Zeke shifted. "Much ado about nothing," he murmured.

" 'An infinite deal of nothing,' " she agreed. She'd just finished reading *The Merchant of Venice* for the literature class she was taking, the only one of her night classes that she enjoyed. The phrase had lodged in her head for reasons she didn't want to examine.

A corner of his mouth hitched and he looked at her with—yes, he did—with appreciation. "Sorry I made light of your situation."

"That's okay." She sighed. "At least you remember I have one."

His smile grew.

Zinnia's voice cut through the chatter. "What are we doing, standing around? We need to get this gal to the hospital and then we need to figure out how to help her manage. From the looks of things, she's gonna have a time of it."

Suddenly, Patsy Lee wished Zinnia *hadn't* recalled her situation.

"Don't you worry, honeybunch. Once you're all fixed up, we'll have a meeting."

No *wish* about it. She groaned, this time not with pain. The O'Malley Family Meeting was Zinnia's version of a national summit. Patsy Lee last featured as its primary topic (target) when Henry had died. The ultimate result had been security for her family at the cost of her pride.

She wondered what she'd need to swallow this time, and flushed with irritation. Then felt guilt at her annoyance. Then anger at her guilt. Finally, having thoroughly confused herself about how she felt about anything, she offered no objection at all.

* * *

Five hours later, as dusk settled on the windowpanes, the family meeting was getting underway in Zinnia O'Malley's kitchen, a bower of wallpaper cabbage roses climbing up wallpaper purple trellises. Stacks of china and piles of silver, along with Tupperware containers bulging with wedding leftovers, decorated the counters under casement windows that were nearly obscured by a bounty of greenery.

Jon signaled Zeke to take a seat at the scarred oak table. But Zeke decided—undying friendship and complete loyalty aside—there were some things a man must face on his own.

Giving his best friend a sweet smile, he ignored the desperation shading Jon's handsome mug and headed in the opposite direction, walking a straight line—damn straight, really, considering the champagne he'd consumed—through a dining room where lace hung from the windows, into the parlor at the front of the house where more lace graced the arms of a sofa.

With the sigh of a man who had just outwitted fate (or at least Jon Van Castle), Zeke settled around the lumps, setting his champagne flute under a beaded lamp on the table beside him. Through the dining room, he could see Lil and Jon, Zinnia and Pop, arranging themselves at the table where Patsy Lee already sat, angled sideways so she could prop up her foot.

Under Zinnia's supervision, Lil and Jon had delivered their patient to and from the regional hospital after Zeke had deposited her in Jon's SUV. When they'd returned, Jon had helped her to a chair while Lil explained that they'd spent most of their time waiting. An orthopedic surgeon had finally set Patsy Lee's ankle, "a partially displaced fracture of the right fibula," in one quick motion. "Almost knocked her out," Jon said, despite a dose of Percodan. The doctor's assistant had splinted her foot, but it wouldn't be cast until Monday, giving time for the swelling to subside.

"She can't put weight on it for at least seven weeks. No driving," Lil said.

"And crutches might be a problem, because"—Jon grinned at his sister-in-law—"sorry, darlin,' but you're a klutz."

"Jon!" Lil had frowned, and Patsy Lee had given Jon what started as a glare but whimpered into a grimace.

Zeke leaned forward to thumb through magazines fanned on a coffee table. No need to wonder why she hadn't put her foot down. And it wasn't because of *that* kind of pain. Considering the traits Zinnia O'Malley shared with his own mother, Patsy Lee undoubtedly knew objecting would be a complete waste of energy.

Good Housekeeping, Field and Stream, Better Homes & Gardens . . . sighing, he hitched an ankle up on his knee and pulled *Field and Stream* into his lap. Ah, *trout.* When was the last time he'd held a fishing pole? Oh yes. That would be never.

Far from the first time, he questioned his sanity in deciding to visit Cordelia for a few months. He was already restless after only one day, shorn of the city bustle and culture he was used to. What in the hell would he do with himself?

But if he left . . .

Well, what in the hell would he do with himself?

He rubbed a hand over his face. From the kitchen, he heard Patsy Lee broach the idea that she could manage with her children's help. And only her children's help.

Absolutely she could. Zeke's own mother had proved it. She'd run her brood of five with laughter, love, and the discipline of a general, afraid, he suspected, that otherwise they'd end up poster children for the idle not-quite-rich. Her only son (him) had been her sergeant at arms. Especially after the laughter had died.

"Well, let's take a look at that possibility, honeybunch."

He smiled wryly. Zinnia's tone told him she wasn't looking at anything.

Zinnia ruled out Patsy Lee's eldest daughter's help. "Not only does Daisy need to get back to college Sunday, she's . . . oh, you know I love her to pieces, but our Daisy, she's just not *reliable,* if you know what I mean."

He did. There was self-expression . . . and then there was self-expression. Anyone looking at the college coed's explosion of blond curls, turquoise eye shadow, earrings to her knees, and yellow leather boots (somewhere a poor cow spun in its grave) wouldn't attach *reliable* to her name.

Of course, his opinion just *might* be colored by an encounter he'd had with her earlier. She'd fixed him with wide blue eyes and commented, "You were famous once, weren't you?"

He picked up his champagne, suddenly thirsty.

"What about Bebe?" Lil asked.

He didn't know who in the hell Bebe was. He took a sip and thought back. Nope, nobody he'd met among the wedding crowd today.

"She's like a mother to you. She'd—"

"No, not Bebe." Patsy Lee's voice had taken on an edge. "I couldn't ask—"

"Of course she can't. Don't you remember, Lil?" Zinnia's voice. "Don't blame you if you don't. We haven't seen Bebe in eons, but she's a professor of—what's she a professor of, honeybunch?"

"She teaches textiles. Did anyone call—"

"She can't just drop everything and hie down here to help out. We'll make do with—"

"Did anyone call to tell her I can't go to Columbia tomorrow?" Patsy Lee pushed her soft voice between Zinnia's words.

"Rose did," Lil said.

Rose. He studied the half-full flute in his hand. According to Jon's tortured explanations of the family tree, the second of Patsy Lee's three daughters. Sharing ninth grade and friendship with Jon's son Michael. She had serious brown eyes and wheat-colored hair as thin and straight as she was herself.

"God love her. That child always thinks of everything. But we can't ask her to take on the responsibility of taking care of you and keeping track of Hank and Lily-Too, as well. Bless their hearts, but their heads are always off in the clouds. Besides, Hank isn't driving yet, so he wouldn't be much help. Funny thing, that. At sixteen, most boys can't wait to . . ."

Hank was Patsy Lee's sole boy. Tall and lanky and tan: tan hair, tan eyes, tan jacket and a perpetually strained expression. Probably all those sisters; Zeke could relate.

Daisy, Hank, Rose . . . and Lily, recently rechristened Lily-Too. Daisy had explained the name change to Zeke over wedding cake while he was still fascinated, not appalled, by her outlandish apparel. (This would have been before the *famous* remark.) Her cousins had grown tired of the constant confusion caused by Lily-Too sharing the same name as her godmother, Lil.

His eyes were drawn to the kitchen, where Lil and Jon sat side-by-side. Like Lil, Lily-Too was enchanting, with hair the color of sunshine and eyes fired with a sheen like fine blue porcelain. But she was shy, barely able to give voice to her age (eight).

He remembered Patsy Lee had been pregnant when Jon and Lil had met. But what he remembered most was his friend had ended up with a life that Zeke had then scorned, but now thought he envied. Who'da guessed? He took another drink, a bigger one this time.

When the talk moved on to the logistics of handling the family's routine, he got lost somewhere between son Hank's astronomy club, daughter Rose's drill team and additional class load (apparently, she hoped to graduate after her junior year), young Lily-Too's school hours, Patsy Lee's night classes, her work as manager of Merry-Go-Read, the children's bookstore that Lil owned (among several), her home's remote location in the countryside, and her animals. . . . Animals? Good God. Would this meeting never end?

He turned his attention back to the magazine. Last night's flight, the day's events, and the champagne were creeping up on him. He wanted to crash. Even in some flea-bitten motel.

Or rather, cockroach laden.

Despite Pop's visible dismay, although he said nothing (Zeke didn't blame him), Zinnia O'Malley had decided that Patsy Lee and her children would stay here tonight—"I just wouldn't rest easy, honeybunch, if she wasn't where I could keep an eye on her." Which left Zeke without a room at the inn. She'd ruled out Patsy Lee's farmhouse ("too far to drive tonight"), Jon and Lil's guesthouse ("still plum full till tomorrow"), and her eldest daughter, Alcea's, home.

She'd bobbed her gray curls at Zeke. "She and Dak left this afternoon on the fall trip they take every year so he can research those books of his. Did you meet her husband? He's an author. But old Julius—the mechanic from Cowboy's Tow and Service and just like a grandpa to Kathleen (their daughter, you know)—is putting up there to keep an eye on things. He's using their bedroom. And Kathleen's home from college and using the other. But don't you worry."

Brain tired from trying to follow her, he hadn't, although he should have. She'd ultimately finagled a room through Helen Tidwell, proprietor of the Cordelia Sleep Inn. Even though the inn had sold out for the wedding, Mrs. Tidwell had reluctantly said he could stay in the one room that had remained unleased until exterminators came, because "well, because somebody said it had cockroaches. As if! Why, no bug, I don't care *how* big it is, would stand a chance against Helen and her mop. Cleaner woman I never have met."

He flipped a page, unsure that it was the idea of cockroaches that was, uh, bugging him. He suspected it was being alone. Again. As usual. He'd hoped to ease that loneliness against the collective shoulder of Lil and Jon, something he admitted only to himself a little less grudgingly than he did his envy, but looks like that wasn't going to happen. . . .

He frowned. It had been stupid to come here. To . . . run away here. If he'd wanted family, he had enough of his own. Three of his sisters had scattered to different corners of the country, but Teresa, the youngest by a decade, still lived in San Francisco, as did his mother.

Of course, if he heard his mother give one more mournful sigh over how his life was wasting away, he'd shoot himself.

He sighed. Mournfully. Then crossed his eyes at himself. Your baggage came with you whether you wanted it to or not. Tomorrow, first thing, he'd check flight schedules. Then he'd make his excuses and get the hell out.

But for now, he'd revel in the wonders of fly fishing. He uncrossed his blurred gaze on a photograph of a fisherman. Specifically on the fisherman's expression, which wasn't unlike the look on the groom's face this morning. Pure bliss. Envy pricked him again. He examined the feeling, thinking he must be wrong: The fisherman was wearing *hip boots,* for cryin' out loud. But, no, there it was. Envy. It seemed everyone he'd encountered today had a place and a purpose. Or at least an interest. Everyone, that is, except . . .

God. He'd had *far* too much to drink.

But he might as well. There was nothing else slated for the day. Or for his life. He slapped the magazine on the table, picked up his glass, and raised a toast in the direction of the kitchen, where O'Malleys shifted around the table in their usual state of unrest. He'd been this way—maudlin, mawkish, just a downright sentimental sap (and maybe, just maybe, a little too caustic)—since his breakup with Christine six months ago.

After fourteen years. Fourteen years ago, on a visit home between gigs, he'd fallen for Christine, Teresa's favorite gal pal since they'd met in the private school he'd paid for. At twenty-two and newly accepted into law school, Christine was a true blueblood; she swam in rarefied circles where his family only waded. His dad's income—substantial enough—had been invested in his children. Music, private schools, sports, travel. Not in the trappings that surrounded Christine.

But it hadn't been her wealth that attracted him. (Although it hadn't hurt.) She had beauty, intelligence, and as much overarching ambition as he had. He dazzled her with his rising fame. They'd seen each other intermittently during those first years, but once she graduated, passed the bar, and hired on at a law firm with no less than a dozen names on its letterhead, they set up housekeeping in the same vast town home where he still lived.

Not that they'd been there much. Their focus was on their careers; marriage and family just distant thoughts. She'd been the perfect room at the inn when he came off the road. And he'd given her a reason to avoid the distracting business of forging a new relationship as she climbed the career ladder with a speed that would have left Jeff Gordon eating her dust. There had been love there, but he suspected they'd largely found each other convenient, and—let's be honest—worthier of each other's affections than lesser mortals.

But once he'd decided his road trip was over, she'd chafed at his constant presence, then grew chilly at the possibility of wedlock, then downright cold when he'd mentioned children, a whim that had surprised him, too. She'd finally ended things entirely not long after they'd returned from the one visit she'd ever taken to Cordelia with him eight months ago.

Actually, forget Christine. To be completely honest, schmaltz had grown on him since the breakup of the Van Castle Band eight *years* ago. After that, a solo act put together by his former agent had filled some months, travel some others, and Christine a few more.

The solo act was best forgotten. There was no more Christine. Travel bored him. *He* bored him. San Francisco, despite his mother and sister—or maybe because of his mother and sister—seemed stifling. Several weeks after he'd received an invitation to Mari O'Malley's wedding, weeks when he'd fingered the missive in indecision, he'd finally and impulsively called Lil and Jon. Undoubtedly zeroing in on his loneliness with that sixth sense she seemed to have inherited from her mother, Lil had urged Zeke to sojourn in the country. "Stay as long as you want. In fact, we'd love to have you through Christmas."

And Jon, undoubtedly zeroing in with that sixth sense *he* seemed to have for ferreting out his wife's feelings, had joined her exhortations. "Do it, bud. We can work up a remix of old recordings à la Lennon and McCartney for charity. Lil's been after me to toss in some coin on one of those causes she adopts like so many stray puppies. I could use your help."

The comparison to the Beatles' songwriting duo had made Zeke feel as ancient as Zeus, but he'd accepted in a brandy-induced fit of longing for the warmth the couple generated, a warmth he remembered from his childhood before it had faded to glowing embers just shy of his sixteenth birthday when his father had died.

He put the champagne flute to his lips. He'd made a mistake. One he should have remedied upon his awakening the morning after said phone call, with the thought that there was a reason why he'd once shunned alcohol. But he'd reconsidered. Jon had a hefty amount of rural real estate. A comfortable guest-house. A state-of-the-art recording studio. Fresh air was supposed to be beneficial, and God knew he needed to clear his head. So he'd purchased a ticket and boarded a plane.

"And now it's time, my man, to get thee back on one." He drained the flute.

The voices from the kitchen intruded on his thoughts, and he looked through the doorway at the family seated in the gold circle of light that spilled from an overhead lamp with copper fittings.

Then he looked at the empty glass in his hand. He pushed himself up to find more.

Chapter 2

Patsy Lee eyed a bottle of uncorked champagne sitting on the kitchen counter and wished she had the energy (nerve) to demand a glass, even though she knew that once its initial effects wore off, it would only add to the headache that had blossomed along with the throbbing in her foot as the Percodan faded. She rubbed her temple, trying to follow the conversation around the table. They'd made her life sound so chaotic.

"I'm amazed I can keep track of it all," she said to nobody in particular.

And nobody in particular listened, even though she was rather proud of how she managed to wedge everything she had to do within six days a week. Well, to be honest, six days plus some hours on most weeks. She tried to save Sundays, when all the stores on Cordelia's town square, including Merry-Go-Read, were closed for family time. But since she'd started studying to get a business degree through Central Missouri State's satellite campus four years ago, she hadn't had much success in keeping the day entirely free.

She worried she was shortchanging her children. Especially Lily-Too. Since starting third grade in September, Lily-Too had fallen behind in class and often ended the day in tears.

Patsy Lee's headache intensified, thinking of her conference with Lily-Too's teacher, Mrs. Sherlock, early this morning. "The witch."

Zinnia frowned. "What's that, honeybunch?"

"Oh, no. I was thinking of—I didn't mean you."

Zinnia eyed her, then turned back to the rest of the table.

Pop's mouth twitched around the unlit pipe perpetually stuck between his teeth since he'd quit smoking years ago. He sat at the head of the table, although nobody doubted who really held command; Patsy Lee sat at the other end, her foot propped on another chair.

She glanced right, knowing she'd get a sympathetic smile from her brother-in-law, despite that earlier crack about her clumsiness. Jon's chair sat near hers, probably a precaution so he could catch her if she toppled sideways, which wasn't unlikely given the way her head swam. Opposite him, Zinnia had angled her own chair, too. But only so she could pin Patsy Lee in her gaze, still a bright blue, despite sixty-nine years and her smudged glasses.

Right now that gaze was busy elsewhere. Patsy Lee picked up a spoon resting in a bowl of vegetable soup, growing cold, that Zinnia had insisted on serving her since her stomach had felt too queasy for the leftover wedding food the rest of them had eaten for supper. She hated canned soup. She forced down two swallows, let the spoon drop, and pushed the bowl a few inches away.

Without missing a beat, without even looking, Zinnia pushed it back. "Even if we could find a way to transport those kids all over kingdom come, it makes me plum uncomfortable to think of Patsy Lee all on her lonesome during the day. If something should happen . . ."

Situated on five acres that were all that was left of

an original farmstead, most of its pastures now returned to woods, she and Henry had fallen in love with the old place shortly after they'd married. Correction: Henry had fallen in love while she'd held her tongue against the reservations she'd felt. Wild roses frothed in a pink waterfall over the fence he'd never fixed out front, the peace of deep woods cradled three sides, and red hawks arrowed over the Ozark mountains in a sky so blue you wanted to chew on the view when you sat on her porch.

It *was* a wonderful setting. But the farmhouse was a money pit, she didn't have time to sit on the porch, not with all the chores the place required, and, situated half an hour from town, it wasn't what you'd call convenient. Sometimes, it was even downright lonely.

For quite a while, she'd thought it might be time for a change, but since a place in town—at least this town, where gossip was served up with the local diner's home fries—hadn't enticed her, either, she'd done nothing about it. Now, unable to drive and Hank without his license and herself at Zinnia's mercy, she could kick herself for dragging her feet.

Still. "I do have a telephone. Or maybe I could change my hours at the bookstore; let Mr. Stuart work more." Although the fussy little man who worked for her part-time would likely object. "Or maybe I could drop my classes. The semester isn't that far underway."

"But you've worked so hard and we're just so proud. Why, we can't let a little thing like a broken ankle stick a spoke in your wheel. We'll figure something else out," Zinnia said.

Lil frowned—and still looked pretty. As she'd grown older, Lil's skin hadn't grown lined; instead it had taken on the patina of fine china. Not that she was fragile. "You're not really planning to work, are you? The doctor said you should rest at home."

Unless the doctor planned to pay her bills, he didn't get to vote. "That's only because he doesn't want me moving around that much. I can still do storytelling hours and the bookkeeping, maybe some of the ordering."

She kept a grimace off her face. She usually left all that to Lil; she liked the storytelling hours, but not any of the paperwork.

"True, but I know you, sweetie. If someone doesn't sit on you, you'll end up doing too much. Since I have to divide time between this store and the ones in Sedalia and Kansas City, I can't be there all the time to be sure you don't. In fact, I don't want to see you at the store for a while. Mr. Stuart, me, and the part-timers can juggle things for a month."

"A month? Lil, I can't—"

"You'll still get your salary. We'll call it disability leave. The store can afford it."

She knew the financials as well as Lil. Henry had owned Merry-Go-Read before Lil had bought it after he'd died, and now Lil gave her a percentage of the profits in addition to her salary. The store could not afford it.

But Lil and Jon could. The Van Castles had enough money for twelve lifetimes. They both avoided wild displays of wealth ("I want the children to grow up grounded") but never hesitated to spend it on family. At least the ones who couldn't stop them. Which included her, and on more than one occasion. She wondered if there would ever be an end to it.

Although Lil's lips and eyes were smiling, a certain hardness to her chin said she wouldn't brook an argument.

Still she had to try. "You've done so much for me already—"

"Don't be silly. I know you'd do the same for me if our positions were reversed."

At a movement in the doorway, the table fell silent. Waving a hand in a don't-mind-me gesture, Zeke wandered into the kitchen.

"That's settled," Zinnia said. "But we still need to figure out . . ."

Mentally, Patsy Lee threw up her arms in defeat. The O'Malleys had always been a stampede she couldn't control. She tuned out and watched Zeke. It was hard not to watch Zeke. He possessed the same magnetism as Jon Van Castle, the magnetism that had helped their country band top *Billboard*'s charts and fill arenas. Even now, they still commanded attention in the same way they'd once commanded a stage.

She thought about what she'd read long ago about the famous bass guitarist in the pages of *Country Dreaming*. He'd grown up with money, but his family had suffered a reversal of fortunes, they'd called it, when his father had died in a car accident when Zeke was fifteen. Drunk driving, if she remembered right. His dad's. A lawsuit had followed, the lawyers and verdict exhausting the family's savings and insurance. Zeke had dropped out then, gone to work to help at home; then at eighteen, he'd chased an oil rig job in the south. On a trip to Nashville to indulge a country music hobby, he'd met Jon Van Castle. The rest was history.

Undoubtedly, she mused, having money, then losing it, had fed his ambition. It had also probably fed the air of urbanity he carried, as well as the *GQ* fashions that he wore with the ease of, well, a superstar.

Zeke moved to the counter, picked up the champagne bottle, studied it, then turned it upside down. Only a drop fell out. He frowned.

A snort escaped her—just a little one. "And what a superstar." She realized she'd spoken out loud and turned beet red. Accustomed to her . . . dementia . . .

Lil and Zinnia continued their conversation uninterrupted, but Jon choked.

And Zeke raised a brow. "A *thirsty* superstar, I'll have you know. But I don't"—he lowered his voice to a stage whisper—"need a drink as much as you probably do."

High color fading, she smiled; he smiled back.

"I'd love a glass," she said, but her voice was lost in the clatter of footsteps down the back stairs.

Seven children spilled into the room. Four were hers, two were Jon and Lil's, and Alcea could claim one. Although she supposed the three eldest, all students at MU in Columbia, could no longer be called children. Alcea's daughter, Kathleen, with the blond elegance of her mother, Jon and Lil's Melanie, slender and slight with large dark eyes under brown bangs like her younger brother, Michael, and her own Daisy, now busy wrapping a scarf in a striped succession of eye-popping hues around her neck, were young women.

Even though they could still behave like they were six. Along with the others, they bumped, jogged, and joshed with each other as they pulled on coats. Except for Lily-Too. Pale hair tucked into a pink hat with a pom-pom, she'd stepped out of the way, not far from Zeke. He'd set down the bottle and leaned against the counter, apparently hypnotized by Daisy's scarf.

Jon eyed the horde. "And where are you hooligans off to?"

"Patsy Lee's," Zinnia answered. "I told them to get the chores done, collect clothes, and hightail it back."

Patsy Lee made sounds that maybe she should go, too, if only to supervise.

But Zinnia shook her head. "Tomorrow's soon enough." She looked at Hank, who slouched with his hands stuffed in his pockets. "And don't you forget to pick those tomatoes and anything else left in the garden. There's gonna be a frost."

Resigning herself, Patsy Lee settled back again and managed a wink at Hank, but he only looked away. She sighed, watching him as he followed the others out the door. He'd always been a loner, more interested in animals than people, but in the past year he'd grown moody, as well.

Once the children left, Zinnia pulled them back on topic. "I think the only way we can manage your family, you, and your menagerie is if someone stays out there with you. Lil's out. She'll have enough on her hands at the store. And at home. We've got to think of Michael, too."

Michael and Melanie were products of Jon's first marriage, both adopted by Lil and loved as though they were her own. Last year, Michael's birth mother had died and the fifteen-year-old had taken it hard, causing trouble both in and out of school. After a summer at a camp for troubled adolescents, things were finally on the upswing, but Lil and Jon still kept a watchful eye and weekly counseling appointments.

Patsy Lee felt compassion for what they'd endured but was thankful for what his experience had taught Rose. Her daughter was more determined than most fourteen-year-olds to avoid the teenage pitfalls her friend had experienced. She was a much easier child than Daisy had been. Than Daisy *was*. She wished she could say his cousin's example had taught Hank as well, but . . .

Patsy Lee's eyes wandered back to Zeke, who had poked his head into the refrigerator. He pulled out a bottle and wrestled with the cork. She marveled. Zeke even looked unruffled with his tongue poked out between his—of course—very white teeth.

"Jon's out, too," Zinnia continued. "He's busy with

that work he's doing up in Kansas City at Vreeley Home." The organization had sponsored the camp Michael had attended. Since then, it had become the beneficiary of Lil and Jon's charitable efforts.

The cork exploded from the bottle, zipped over their heads, and hit the wall. Lil bit her lip, Patsy Lee the inside of her mouth, and Pop made a business of fiddling with his pipe.

Zinnia glared at Zeke. "Put that champagne away, Zeke Townley, and sit down before you fall down."

Grinning, Jon pulled over another chair. "Rest your bones. You heard the woman."

Looking agreeable, Zeke set the bottle aside, but not, to Zinnia's obvious disgruntlement, before filling a flute. When he reached the table, he slid the champagne in front of Patsy Lee, then took his seat slightly behind her and stretched out his long legs. If she looked down, she could see the sharp crease of his pants and the high sheen of his shoes. The Percodan (and a sudden desire to align herself against Zinnia's usually unquestioned authority) scattered any concern she might normally have about mixing alcohol and medication. She only hesitated an instant before she picked up the flute and took a large swallow. Zeke's foot twitched.

Shaking her head, Zinnia moved the flute out of her reach. "So Lil and Jon are out. Alcea is, too, since she's gone. And Mari. That leaves—"

Beside her, Jon said sotto voce to Zeke, "I think you should volunteer. You've been grousing how you've got nothing to do."

"My man, I may be drunk. But you are out of your freakin' mind."

Choking down a laugh, Patsy Lee glanced back. Zeke's dark eyes were on her. He winked. Her heart fluttered. Which alarmed her. Fluttering hearts at her age usually signaled a coronary event. Then she remembered the Percodan—that must be it—and relaxed.

Zinnia frowned. "Things seem to be getting out of hand. If you could all contain yourselves for a few more minutes, we can get this settled."

They'd better. Between exhaustion, drugs, (crummy vegetable soup), and a gulp of champagne, she couldn't last much longer. To prove the point, she swayed. Behind her, a hand reached out to steady her. Carefully, she straightened. The hand on her shoulder stayed put.

Zinnia opened her mouth, her expression turning triumphant. Patsy Lee sensed what was coming and her heart fell into an increasingly roiling stomach. Now that the wedding was over, Zinnia wanted another pet project and she was it. "Looks like I'm the only one who can spare the time to—"

"Oh, no, you don't." Pop took the pipe out of his mouth. Everyone stared.

"But—"

"You've already worn yourself out on this wedding."

"I agree with Pop, Mother." Lil leaned forward. "You hardly gave yourself time to recover before you were up to your elbows in wedding plans."

"Pish. I'm fit as a fiddle and—"

"It was just this morning you were complaining about angina." Pop said, chin thrusting out in an expression Patsy Lee had only seen him use recently.

"I . . ." Zinnia flushed.

This time Patsy Lee couldn't stifle the snort. The angina Zinnia had experienced had come on the heels of an argument with the bride over Mari's changes to the place cards set at the bride and groom's table. And had immediately subsided once Mari had changed them back.

But Lil didn't know that. She stared at Zinnia, who

was glaring at Patsy Lee. "Your chest was hurting, Mother?"

Patsy Lee looked away from Zinnia. She hadn't been able to help the snort, really, she couldn't; the champagne had gone straight to her brain.

"Mother, you just can't do this. I didn't say anything when you planted fall flower bulbs at St. Andrew's with the ladies' auxiliary, or when you signed up for the Oktoberfest bake-off, or even when you told Mari you'd host her wedding. But obviously you've been doing too much. And this—" Lil was truly upset; her hands, as usual carefully folded on the table in front of her, had grown white-knuckled. She looked at Patsy Lee. "I'm sorry. Taking care of you is one thing, but you know she'd get in a fuss over Hank and Rose and Lily-Too. Even if you all stayed here, it would be too much. There's your house and animals and the drive back and forth."

"Lil's right, she can't manage," Pop said.

Zinnia stared at him, then her eyes softened.

"Jon and I can hire someone—" Lil continued.

"Oh, no." Patsy Lee's amusement fled. She tried to cut through Lil's words. "Lil—"

"—To help you out. We just can't allow Mother—"

The hand squeezed her shoulder. "I'll do it."

There was a beat of pure silence.

Then heads swiveled toward Zeke, none faster than hers.

He blinked, as if surprised the words had come out of his mouth, but repeated, "I'll do it. It sounds like all Passy—*Passy* L—" He frowned at Patsy Lee, then enunciated carefully. "Your name is really a mouthful, you know."

He was snockered. She wasn't so sure she wasn't, too. She ignored everyone else, who still sat stunned. "I don't care for it, really. But it's a family name."

"Ah. Your mother's?" he inquired politely.

"My grandmother's, and then my aunt, who died young. And . . ." She stopped and considered. "You know, I've actually always preferred Patricia." Although Patricia wasn't even on her birth certificate. (Although not as conspicuous as the absence of the name of her father.)

"Patricia. Patricia Lee." He rolled the sounds out with the slowness of the very inebriated. "A beautiful name, shorn of local conventions."

Patsy Lee smiled. She'd floated the name before, but Zinnia had always shot it down, saying it just didn't sound natural.

Zeke nodded sagely, then looked around the table at the others. Seeing their puzzled faces, he frowned. "You know, local conventions? Ida Mae. Joe Bob. Etta Lou . . . Patsy Lee."

Jon suddenly found something worthy of intense interest on the tabletop.

Zinnia shook her head. "I think you're three sheets to the wind."

"Or insane," Zeke agreed. "But let's let the lady decide. I'm sensing she'd like to make a decision about herself . . . *By* herself."

Zinnia went mute again. As did everyone else.

Zeke didn't seem to notice. He leaned forward to whisper to Patsy Lee, although his voice was hardly soft enough for secrets. "If all you require is a chauffeur and someone who can pick you up if you happen to fall down, I'm your man."

He looked so sincere, so earnest, so . . . drunk, Patsy Lee struggled to contain the imp that wanted to accept just so she could see him try. But she knew the ruckus that would raise. Nobody would take his suggestion seriously. Not only was it ridiculous, but he'd riled Zinnia. Although, come to think of it, if she could really have a choice between skilled hired help and unskilled Zeke . . . drifting into a drug-induced haze, she gave the chiseled planes of his face some serious study: the aquiline nose, the arching dark brows, the high cheekbones, the black eyes. . . . She cocked her head, gaze sharpening. Those eyes rested on Lil, moved to Jon, then back. And in the back of his gaze . . .

Oh, no. So that's where the wind blew.

Zinnia spoke up. "You realize, don't you, that you'd have to stay there until she no longer needed you? I don't want stopgap solutions."

Patsy Lee's eyes whipped to her mother-in-law. "You can't seriously be considering—"

"I do," he said.

"Have you both completely lost your minds?"

Zinnia and Zeke ignored her.

"This may be just what the doctor ordered," Zinnia said. "Seems to me, Zeke Townley, you've been up to next to nothing for a good long while. It's about time you made yourself useful."

Zeke frowned. "Do you know my mother?"

Zinnia ignored him. She turned to Patsy Lee, an odd light in her eyes. "And it'll be a good thing for you, too."

Watching her mother, Lil's expression had grown thoughtful. Her gaze slid from Patsy Lee to Zeke and back, then exchanged a look with Jon. The same speculative look that was on Zinnia's face spread over theirs.

They were *matchmaking?* "I—he—you can't—"

"Not a bad idea." Jon said.

She looked at her brother-in-law. *Et tu, Brute?*

"It'll be okay," Jon assured her. "Believe it or not, he could compete with Mary Poppins. He helped raise four sisters, all younger than Rose at the time. He can handle your quartet."

"A quartet," Zeke repeated as though he'd just remembered she had children. He looked at Zinnia. "I didn't really raise my sisters."

Jon sighed. “I knew you weren’t up to the challenge.”

So had she.

“You think I can’t do it?” Zeke eyed Jon.

“Jon.” Patsy Lee glared at her brother-in-law.

But he didn’t even look her way. “You won’t last a week.”

Patsy Lee saw her mother-in-law clamp down on a satisfied smile. Oh, no. “Please. This is ridiculous.”

Zeke glanced at her, appeared to consider her words. Her hopes rose; then looking back at Jon, he shook his head. “No, I’m certain. . . . I can last a week. Much more than a week. Put your money where your mouth is, my man.”

While the men made their odious bet, she slumped. Zeke didn’t have a clue what he was getting himself into. She thought of her children. Her farmhouse. Her animals . . . and Zinnia O’Malley.

He really didn’t.

All he’d provide was another person for her to take care of.

She opened her mouth, but before she could get a word out, Zinnia slapped the table. “Done. Welcome to the family, Zeke Townley. Now, let’s see. . . . You’ll fix the children’s supper.”

Looking smugly at Jon, Zeke agreed. “I’ll fix the children’s supper. Actually, I’m a good cook.”

“And their breakfast.”

“And their breakfast.”

“At six.”

“At”—Zeke tore his eyes off Jon and stared at Zinnia. “Six?”

“Six. The high school bus picks up at seven. Lily-Too’s comes just after.”

Jon snickered.

Zeke gave his friend a hard look. “A hot breakfast.” He drew a breath. “At dawn.”

"Zinnia," Patsy Lee interjected. "They aren't babies. They can certainly fix—"

"And you'll help with the chores, of course." Zinnia continued.

"Of course."

"At least, most of them. Rose will help Patsy Lee with her bath."

Patsy Lee covered her eyes.

"And Hank will show you the ropes for the rest. He'll likely do most of it, but you'll have to keep after him or he'll forget Dowdy and Dharma."

"Dowdy and Dharma . . . I don't remember children named—"

"Not children." Jon's voice was strangled. *"Donkeys."*

"You won't need to do much with the chickens, though," Zinnia continued, "Lily-Too takes care of them."

"Chickens." Zeke's voice had grown faint.

Although her alarm at heart flutters had faded in her very real fear that she would die from embarrassment, Patsy Lee uncovered her eyes and twisted to look back at Zeke. "Please. You don't have to do this. I can—"

"Patsy Lee's right. We've had our fun, and I'll rescind the bet." Standing up, Jon slapped Zeke on the back. "We won't blame you if you're—what is the word I'm searching for? Oh yes. Chicken." The smile he gave Zeke was pure evil.

Zeke narrowed his eyes at Jon, then looked at her. His gaze softened. "Dowdy, Dharma, and chickens notwithstanding, I'd like to help."

In response, all she could manage was a sickly smile. The drugs and champagne had gone from making her loopy to making her nauseous. "Okay."

But it wasn't okay. Without warning, she suddenly upchucked vegetable soup all over his shoes.

Chapter 3

Early the next evening, keeping *Pride and Prejudice* bookmarked with her finger, Patsy Lee pushed to a sitting position on the sofa in her parlor, parted the drapery covering the bow window behind her, and peeked out for the umpteenth time in the last hour. She didn't want Zeke's arrival to surprise her. Last night, following her shining performance, Lil and Zinnia had hustled her off to bed and Zeke off to the Cordelia Sleep Inn before she could recover enough to apologize. Tonight, she was determined to greet him with decorum and dignity, just to prove she had some.

From the hollow of her lap, Blinken, one of her trio of cats, gave her a look of annoyance from blue eyes and jumped down. Patsy Lee ignored him as he stalked off, black tail sticking up stiff as a bottle brush. She peered down the slope that led to Red Hollow Road. In the last rays of sunlight, the maples standing sentinel on her front acre were orange starbursts against a violet sky poised to blanket the Ozark hills. The long drive up to the house was empty.

She let the drapery drop and looked around the room, seeking distraction and not finding any at all. The scene was as familiar as her own face. Sometimes that comforted her. Sometimes it felt stifling. Usually it felt stifling. Today in particular.

The parlor had been the first room she'd refurbished after she and Henry had bought the place, but it certainly hadn't been the last. Over the past two decades, she'd painted, stripped walnut moldings, sanded some floors, tiled others, laid carpeting, and squeezed out money now and then to pay for repairs to roof, plumbing, and wiring, and last year, new tile backsplashes and counters in the kitchen. She'd furnished it all with rummage sale finds, curtains she'd sewn herself, and the upright piano that had once graced the O'Malley's parlor.

Lil was an accomplished pianist, and Henry had also played. The only one of his offspring who had inherited their talent was Lily-Too. Lily-Too didn't just play; she sang. Boy, did she sing. Every once in a while, they'd gather around the piano, although they hadn't done that, or anything like that, lately. Not since Patsy Lee had gone back to school.

Her gaze stopped on a large fabric sculpture hung over the stone fireplace. She'd woven the fabric, executed the sculpture with Bebe's help. It, too, was something else she never did anymore. She studied the intermingling of threads, a mix of pale yellow, a green the powdery shade of Russian olive trees, and one heavily textured yarn of bold cranberry. She'd patterned the scheme in this room in those colors. She liked color, had a good eye for it, really, and she'd doused her home with it.

Much as she'd doused Zeke's shoes last night. The room's distraction value evaporated and she closed her eyes.

How had she landed in such a pickle? Why couldn't she just state her own intentions and stick to them for once in her gutless life? She continually allowed herself to be guided (railroaded) by the O'Malleys, most notably her mother-in-law, although Lil, despite her generosity, was little better. She thought back to her conversation with Zinnia earlier today. This time, she'd admit that at least Zinnia had a method to her madness, and, considering how much she owed Lil, Patsy Lee felt helpless to do anything else except go along.

Just after she'd opened her eyes this morning, at sea in the middle of the four-poster bed in Lil's old bedroom, just after she'd thrown the blankets over her head, as memories had flooded in, and just after she'd formed the intention of taking a stand against this cockamamie scheme, following a full three seconds' worth of profound thought, the door had opened.

She'd peeked over the edge of the blanket, saw her mother-in-law, and took a deep breath. "Zinnia, I know you mean well, but I just can't let—"

"How's the ankle?"

"Fine. I mean, not fine, it hurts like crazy, but we need to talk about—"

"I know." Handing off a glass of water and a pain pill, Zinnia sat down beside her. "I know this is an uncommon situation we have here, but—"

"Uncommon?" She cupped the pill, not wanting to addle her senses again. "I don't think—I mean, I wouldn't call it uncommon. It's—"

"Outrageous. I'm sorry I pushed Zeke off on you. But he can't stay out at Lil's. Take your pill."

A Seth Thomas clock ticked time on the end table. Hesitating, Patsy Lee finally swallowed her pill, then set down the glass. "So you saw."

"I did. I'd wondered sometimes. He's in Cordelia often enough, that's for sure, but I never worried about it; thought I was imagining things. Or maybe his guard was down because he had more than his fair share of the bubbly. I've never seen him drink like that."

"But we don't need to worry. Lil loves Jon. She'd never—"

"No, she wouldn't. Not ever. Nor do I think Zeke Townley would do anything unseemly himself. He has a good heart and knows right from wrong. But if we're right and that's how he feels about her, it's only a matter of time before Lil and Jon catch on, what with him staying here until after the holidays and all."

"But if he wouldn't do anything and Lil wouldn't do anything, then there's no need—"

"Yes, there is. Jon and Zeke are best friends. They've been together for years; scrapped to get Van Castle going when they weren't much more than boys. Even with the distance between them, they rely on each other like brothers. And Lil . . . Lil loves him, too. In a different way than Jon, naturally, but he was there at the beginning, rooting her on when she almost lost Jon to his own stubbornness early on. There would be a world of hurt all the way round if Jon or Lil guessed he felt what we think he feels."

She shouldn't have taken the pain pill. She was getting confused again.

"They couldn't ever be on their old footing again. No, we've just got to help him keep his distance until his time here is over."

"Why couldn't he just stay with you?"

"You heard Pop." Zinnia's smile was indulgent. "Unusual for that man to put his foot down the way he did, but he's made it a habit since my ticker gave me trouble. Not to mention that I don't have an excuse like you to hold him here. What am I supposed to tell Zeke? Us old folks are lonely?"

"But . . . I need to think of my children. Especially Lily-Too."

Zinnia frowned. "You can't think the man's a pervert."

"No! It's . . . it's just *unseemly*. People will talk."

"I'll give them what for if they do. But I don't think they will."

Of course they wouldn't. The whole idea of Zeke Townley and Patsy Lee O'Malley was utterly ridiculous. She sank down.

Zinnia guessed her thoughts. "I meant, if I tell them he's strictly helping out at the house, they'll believe me," Zinnia said with the utter conviction of a pillar of the ladies' auxiliary. She patted Patsy Lee's knee. "Don't give yourself such short shrift. You're a good-looking woman."

She sank down further. Sure. For someone like Rusty Peterson, the local cop she'd briefly dated a year ago. But not for Zeke Townley. It wasn't that she wanted Zeke; that wasn't it at all. It'd just be nice if her fantasies were rooted a little bit in reality instead of completely out there in the ozone.

"I'll get Daisy in here to help us get you dressed and then we'll have you back at home before you know it. This is best for everyone. You'll see." Zinnia stood up.

For one wild moment, Patsy Lee thought what was left of her spine really had turned to putty in her mother-in-law's hands. She straightened to make sure it still worked. "Two weeks." She picked an arbitrary time. "I'll do it for two weeks, but no longer."

But Zinnia had already closed the door.

"Not *months*. No way." Stomach churning, Patsy Lee had pulled the blankets back over her head. "And call me Patricia," she'd muttered.

"Two weeks," she said again now, peeking out her front window again. Nothing stirred in the gathering twilight except some leaves in the breeze. "Two weeks and that's it." She wished she could sound that firm when there was someone around to hear it. But now that Blinken had left, the parlor was empty.

When Pop and Zinnia had delivered her here a few

hours ago, Pop had started a blaze in the fireplace, Zinnia had fussed in the kitchen, and Daisy had leaned her mother's crutches against the stone hearth and had thwacked the sofa pillows into submission before she'd disappeared upstairs to her room, muttering about homework. Patsy Lee's other children had likewise scattered after her in-laws left.

Now the fire needed stoking, her stomach was rumbling, her crutches were out of reach, and the pillows could use more thwacking.

She looked up at the high ceiling, vibrating under the assault of rock music pounding in Daisy's room. Her eldest was obviously *not* hitting the books, despite her promises to do so since she'd skipped her Friday classes for the wedding.

Patsy Lee shook her head. Daisy needed to get serious about school if she wanted to make the exorbitant amount it cost worthwhile. She owed it to her aunt and uncle, who had loaned Patsy Lee the tuition. She owed it to Patsy Lee, who was paying off said loan (in teeny, tiny payroll deductions that were only a token gesture and everyone knew it). And Daisy owed it to herself. Unlike her mother, Daisy shouldn't wait until getting a degree became an ordeal.

And unlike Daisy, her mother shouldn't put off her own homework any longer. Admonishing herself for her wandering mind, she reopened *Pride and Prejudice*. At least lit class wasn't a trial. Certainly it could keep her occupied until Jon and Zeke arrived.

"Hi, Mom." Hank wandered into the room, bringing with him the scent of outdoors.

She closed the book, glad Hank's interruption had given her an excuse to keep her delusions intact. Besides, who could concentrate with the din upstairs? Their black Lab, Sugar, pranced up to the sofa, gave her a fast lap before she could turn her head, then flopped in front of the fireplace, panting happily.

She looked at the muddy prints Sugar had left and decided not to sweat them. They matched the animal fur that chased itself around under the furniture. She tried to keep things clean, but there was always too much to do.

"Could you give those logs a stir?" Competing with the music, she spoke louder than normal, then strained to hear his answer.

"Mmm." Not much of an answer. Hank held his hands out to the fire, lost in his thoughts as usual. His bony wrists stuck out a few inches from his jacket. She needed to get him a new one, but it would have to wait till spring since he'd need a winter coat more by the time she was able to shop again. Tiny lines split his brows, creases that had become part of his habitual expression. In the firelight, his nondescript brown hair turned to honey.

"Hank? The fire?"

He looked over, eyes finally focusing on her.

She sighed. Forget the fire. "Did you get the donkeys put to bed?"

He nodded.

"And did you check on Lily-Too?"

He didn't respond.

"Hank." This time her voice was sharper.

"I *will.*" His shoulders hunched. "Let me get my hands warm first. It's freezing out."

Sometimes frost waited until November and her morning glories bloomed through October, but not this year. This year winter was coming early.

"It's a good thing you got the garden picked yesterday."

Again Hank was silent.

"Oh, Hank. You did, didn't you?"

"I picked the tomatoes, and I put them in the pantry where it's dark so they'd ripen like Gran told me, but Daisy was in a hurry, so I didn't get to the rest."

Which meant he'd forgotten and the beans had died on their vines last night.

Frustrated, she stared at the back of his head. He needed a haircut. Something else she wouldn't be able to attend to. Without warning her eyes filled. She mopped them up with the back of her hand and scolded herself for her silliness. Jackets. Beans. Haircuts. They weren't important and she'd better not start thinking they were, because Zeke Townley was likely very limited in what he'd do around here. After making himself a serious fortune, he probably didn't remember his way around a sink of dirty dishes. If he ever had.

She sighed. Must be nice.

Mirroring her thoughts, Hank asked, "When's that guy going to get here?"

"You know his name. Mr. Townley." Her stomach turned over every time she thought of him. Living in her house, that is. "Soon. Now, about Lily-Too . . ."

"Lily-Too's *fine,* Mom. She was getting a heating coil to put in the chickens' water trough. Where's he going to sleep? I don't have to give up my room, do I?"

"No, he'll use mine."

Tears pricked her eyes again. She'd miss the glassed-in sleeping porch she used as her bedroom. Running along the back of the upper floor, it was an awkward shape, long and narrow, but it offered windows on a private world where she watched lightning dance in a summer sky, snowflakes float past in a winter one. Sometimes she pretended she was in a high-rise, far away from the maddening crowd below. But giving it to Zeke only made sense, since she couldn't risk the stairs yet. (Jon was right about the crutches, dang him.) She'd use the spare room down here; it was perfectly fine and near the downstairs bath. Zinnia and Pop had already made up the fold-out sofa and fetched her clothing.

"Good," Hank said, the relief in his voice audible.

Hank's room was his refuge, too. When he wasn't playing nomad, he could usually be found there, surrounded by his books, his astronomy charts, his fish tank, his hamsters, and his turtle. In a house filled with women, she didn't blame her sixteen-year-old for his habit of hiding out, but she was concerned because he didn't seem to have many friends.

Correction. *Any* friends. Nor did he date. And although she'd convinced him to get a driving-instruction permit when he'd turned fifteen, the lessons he'd started with Pop had dwindled, as he just wasn't interested in getting his license. She'd told herself he was a late bloomer, but she'd begun to wonder if he'd ever flower. This year, she'd insisted he join a club at school, but she'd lost hope that her insistence would help jump-start a friendship. The astronomy club had only three other members, and from what she'd seen, they were all equally reclusive. Recently, he'd added some bouts of truancy to her list of concerns.

Remembering, she held out her hand. "Do you have your card?"

Looking disgruntled, he pulled a rumpled index card from his pocket and walked it over. She studied it. Next to a list of his classes were the initials of each teacher, indicating he hadn't missed any classes last week. She nodded and handed it back. "Good for you."

He snatched back the card. "You're making too big a deal out of a couple of times."

"Three times."

"So? It's not that much, but ever since Michael got in trouble, you make a big deal out of everything."

"Three times in one month," she added. But privately, she thought he could be right. Ever since their cousin Michael's difficulties last year, her worries for her own children had intensified. "I just worry about you, okay?"

He turned back to the fire. "Worry about someone else," he mumbled. "Like Daisy."

"Should I be worrying about Daisy?"

He shot her a look, hesitated. Then, "Did you get a load of her last grade card?"

She didn't think that was what he'd been about to say, but she went with it. "She'll do okay. It's a brand new year. She started school younger than others at her level, so she just hasn't matured yet, that's all."

"It's her third semester in college. How long does it take to *mature*?"

"Maybe we should quit discussing your oldest sister and you should stoke that fire, then go check on your youngest like I asked."

"All *right*."

"And tell Daisy to turn down her music." Before we all lose our hearing.

Hank gave his hands a final warming, then, like usual, forgot the fire, forgot Daisy, and headed through the doorway into the dining room that lay between the parlor and the kitchen before she could remind him again. Thinking that checking on Lily-Too was more important than the rest, she didn't try to call him back, although it was likely that by the time he reached the back door, he'd forget why he was there. Like Henry, Hank was absentminded, but for the last year or so, he'd gotten increasingly worse. Or maybe he was developing a masterful skill with passive resistance.

Sugar realized her master had debunked and got up to follow, tail wagging at what she might find in the kitchen.

At the thought of food, Patsy Lee's stomach

growled. A chill had crept over the parlor and she looked longingly at the last flickers of fire. Hoping Rose was in the sitting room across the hall that bisected the lower floor of the house—the only place Patsy Lee would have a prayer of being heard—she rose on her elbows. Her book fell on the floor and bounced aside.

"Rose!" She stretched out an arm, but couldn't reach it. Tears sprang to her eyes yet again. Impatiently, she winked them away. If she gave in to self-pity after only one day, she'd be committed before the week was out. *"Rose!"*

Two more tries finally produced her fourteen-year-old. From the way Rose's pale hair had flattened in back, she'd been lying on the loveseat in the sitting room, indulging in her favorite pastime, reading.

"Sorry, Mom, but Daisy—" Rose pointed at the ceiling. "I couldn't hear. What's up?"

"Can you put supper together for everyone? I was thinking just grilled cheese and soup."

"Am I going to have to do this every night?" A crease appeared between Rose's dark eyes. "I don't think I can handle drill team practice, homework, chores, *and* fixing supper every night, not if I want to make the Honor Society when I'm a sophomore."

Patsy Lee didn't know why not. *She* managed to handle more than that. And Rose didn't need to worry about academics; the girl could sleep through her classes and still get straight A's.

Patsy Lee bit her tongue, knowing her situation was just making her waspish. Rose was simply as conscientious as Daisy wasn't. "I'm sure Mr. Townley will—" She stopped; he'd said he would, but everyone agreed with Zinnia, whether they intended to or not. "Pretty soon, I'll be up and around. The doctor said I should keep my foot up as much as possible for the first two weeks, but after that . . ."

After that, the doctor had said they'd have to see. Apparently everyone healed differently. He'd made no promises.

"Okay, fine." Rose flipped her hair behind a shoulder. "Do we have tomato? I don't want vegetable. It's gross."

No kidding. She'd made a vat of the stuff two nights ago, but she planned to never look vegetable soup in the eye again. She'd rather have canned. "I think there's some in the pantry."

Rose started off.

"Oh, hon? The fire—my book—"

But Rose disappeared into the kitchen. As the music paused, Patsy Lee heard her snap at Hank, then sibling bickering began in earnest. Great. Hank had forgotten Lily-Too. Opening her mouth to call him in, she closed it as the din upstairs resumed. She looked forlornly from the kitchen to the hearth to *Pride and Prejudice* and felt tears rise *again*. "Oh, for Pete's sake. Suck it up," she muttered.

Determinedly, she swallowed the lump that had worked into her throat. Maybe she couldn't build a fire, but she could get her danged book. Levering herself as close to the edge of the sofa as she dared, she strained to reach it. She wasn't totally helpless; she could . . .

Her rear end slid off and hit the floor. Pain sliced through her leg. She choked back a sob, then called for help, but her voice was lost in the cacophony. Squeezing her eyes shut, she mentally checked her ankle, still propped on the sofa. She didn't think the fall had caused further harm. But trying to rise unaided just might.

So she settled on the only other course of action she could think of. She dropped her head back and let the tears flow.

Chapter 4

"Turn around. I think I left my stomach eighteen miles back."

Riding along in Jon's SUV on his way to Patsy L—no, *Patricia* O'Malley's, his Hofner bass and luggage in the rear, Zeke feared his early supper might yet end up on his lap, much like Patricia's had ended up last night on his Bruno Magli's.

He grasped the armrest as Jon took yet another curve that topped yet another rise on County Road HH, and thought of said shoes, now in the trash can beside the O'Malleys' back porch. No big loss. Doubtful he'd need them out here. Besides, his surprise had paled next to Patricia's humiliation. He'd never thought to see anyone actually die of embarrassment, but for a few moments there, he'd worried for her life.

"Just a little further." Jon glanced over and grinned. "The locals call this the Hilly Highway."

"Admirable insight. Please, eyes back on the road."

Jon obliged. They dipped down again, then back up again. At each rise in the narrow highway, a vista splashed with purple sunset spread out around them. Steep hills folded over themselves, crowned with thick woods, their leaves on the turn. Occasionally, a cleared field flashed past. Dried cornstalks stood stiffly in some; cows stood equally stiffly in others.

"Tell me Patricia doesn't own cows."

Jon's eyebrows went up. "Patricia?"

"It *is* her preference."

Jon considered. "True, but not my mother-in-law's. Believe I'll stick with Patsy Lee. They're not cows. Steers."

Zeke sighed. "So she does."

"No. I meant, cows are female." Jon pointed. "That's a steer."

"Your knowledge is remarkable."

"I grew up around here, remember?"

"And just as I was coming to my senses and prepared to duck out, you egged me on last night so I could share the experience?"

"I believe you suggested it first."

That brought Zeke up short. "I did, didn't I?"

How ironic. He'd spent the first half of his adult life glad to have escaped hands-on obligation to family (sending checks didn't count), and the last years wanting a taste of what Lil and Jon had. But he'd stunned himself by swallowing *this* responsibility.

"You did," Jon agreed.

"I was moved by her plight."

"You were hammered."

"That, too. But you're supposed to watch my back."

Jon paused. "Believe it or not, I was."

Zeke narrowed his eyes at his friend, but didn't comment.

"Besides, quit bellyaching. You like it here. Admit it."

Zeke only grunted, but when Jon shot him a look, he finally said, "Perhaps I do," but only so Jon would turn his attention back to driving before they ran off the road. Jon did. Zeke relaxed and then examined that statement for truth, surprised when he found some.

Last night, he'd passed a peaceful night at the Cordelia Sleep Inn with nary a cockroach in sight. He'd slept late for what could be the last time in a long while, then, having been assured that his new responsibility and her family were being settled back into her home by Zinnia and Pop O'Malley, he'd joined Jon for brunch at his sister-in-law Alcea's diner, Peg O' My Heart Café and Bakery, on the Main Street of Cordelia's town square.

After breakfast—eggs, country sausage, a truckload of home fries, and, as if that weren't enough to harden his arteries, not one, but two, Tropical Blend Banana Muffins made from one of the owner's recipes—they'd lingered two hours over coffee, jawing with the locals before Jon had recalled his duty as host (helped by a cell phone call from Lil) to the wedding guests populating his guesthouse, and had dragged Zeke back home.

There they'd found Lil presiding over a late-afternoon supper buffet and a bevy of Zinnia's extended family from Arkansas. Their questioning had elicited the information that there may be one or two shared kin on Zeke's mother's side (the O'Malleys were related to the majority of the world's population), and they'd embraced his presence as though he'd grown up among them.

Despite his cynicism—which grated on him more and more with each passing day—he realized he'd enjoyed the companionship and the food more today than he had either one at last week's black-tie event preceding the San Francisco Symphony's performance of Mahler's Fifth. While the concert had been astounding, the food had been bland, the company predictable. While he loved music of any stripe, he vastly preferred the crush rocking at Fort Mason's Great Meadow at San Francisco's annual blues concert to attending the soirees offered to the membership of the Maestro's Circle, something he'd joined at

Christine's request. So why hadn't he unjoined now that she was gone? Habit, he guessed. His whole life was a habit.

A clearing occupied by a trailer, a clothesline, and a tumble of sun-bleached plastic toys came into view. He watched the mobile home slide by and a thought struck him. "Does she—"

Jon's mouth twitched. "She lives in a house. And not a small one, either."

"It's not that I'm a snob—"

Jon snorted.

"Okay, maybe part snob." On his father's side.

The residences he'd seen at odd intervals ran the gamut from mobile homes to modest brick ranches to tumbledown farmhouses. Occasionally, a dwelling with yards of glass, yards of raw timber, and presumably built with yards of money, rose in contemporary splendor above the trees. But his gut—which, after forty-six years of practice, had a habit of accuracy—told him Patricia O'Malley and family didn't occupy a home like Lil and Jon's. He could work with less. (Snootiness was absent from his mother's gene pool.). Still, it was good to know her abode was larger than twelve-by-sixty-five feet.

Long stretches came and went with no signs of habitation at all. Accustomed to the urban bustle and niceties just a few steps from his home on Russian Hill, Zeke wondered again why he'd lost his mind somewhere in the bottom of a champagne bottle last night. Restless longing aside, he thought that the look of appeal on Lil's face and Jon's goading, as well as sympathy for that flush he'd seen on the curve of Patricia's cheek while he'd sat behind her, had something to do with it. He thought back to last night. Patricia did have a very nice complexion.

Discomfited by the thought that her complexion had

registered somewhere in his brain, he looked around for distraction. "Nice. But lonely."

"Not if you have someone to share it with." Jon grinned.

"Which is, if I caught the general drift, what everyone's hoping I'll find. But not with Patricia." She was nice enough, pleasant-looking, but not his *type.* If one woman in fourteen years could be said to form a *type.* "I'm certain she has no designs on my virtue."

"How could she? You don't have any."

"Doesn't matter. I'm destined to end my days as a bachelor."

"You're not that old."

"I feel that old." The words slipped out along with a sour note Zeke didn't like.

Jon glanced over again, but didn't pursue the topic. That was one of the things Zeke liked about him. Jon didn't dig where Zeke didn't want him to. They were close. Closer than he was with his own siblings. The years when he'd helped shoulder family responsibility had elevated him above his younger sisters in a way that had invited their confidences, but put an end to his own.

But if he didn't feel like confiding, Jon wouldn't push. And if Zeke hadn't been indulging in a bout of the self-pity that sometimes overtook him since he'd reached middle age, he wouldn't have uttered anything that would have made Jon even give him one of those sideways, exasperatingly knowing looks in the first place. In fact, if he'd been thinking straight last night, right at this very minute, he'd be getting on a flight back to San Francisco. Not on a . . .

Oh, good God. He'd forgotten. "Donkeys. She owns donkeys."

Jon didn't smile. "You don't have to do this. If you backed out, nobody would be surprised."

Jon slowed the SUV and turned. RED HOLLOW ROAD. Woods lined either side; prairie grasses and sumac blushing with autumn crowded up to the crumbling asphalt.

Zeke stared out the window, surprised by the hollow in his chest where Jon's words now echoed. "No," he finally said as Jon turned into a graveled drive, crossed a culvert, and headed up toward a farmhouse framed by maples still bright against the darkening sky. "And that's the hell of it, you know. Nobody would be surprised."

After Jon pulled to a stop some feet in front of a railed front porch framed by gingerbread trim and needing a coat of paint, Zeke got out and paused to stare up at the two-story structure. Despite a few peeling boards and one shutter hanging slightly askew, the pale light spilling from windows into a scrubby yard made soft by sunset gave the whole place the aura of a Thomas Kincade.

Except he didn't think Thomas Kincade was likely a fan of Nickelback.

He moved up a few sagging steps to join Jon at the front door. Jon pounded and they waited, but apparently nobody could hear them over the rock band's music.

Giving up, Jon opened the door and they stepped into an entry. A stairway climbed along the left wall to a landing; a hallway opened up straight ahead. Jon ignored both and moved to a wide doorway on the right. "Patsy Lee? We knocked, but with the music . . . hell."

Moving up behind Jon, Zeke caught sight of the cause of Jon's curse and let out his own. Next to the sofa, Patricia lay on her back, feet still up on the cushions, tears running in rivulets into her hair. Jon hurried toward her.

"It's okay. I'm okay." Patricia waved a vague hand.

"Yeah, I can see that," Jon's voice was dry. He helped her back onto the sofa.

Dragging her forearm across her face, Patricia snuffled, then her gaze fell on Zeke, still standing in the doorway. She reddened. "Really. I am. I—I foolishly tried to reach my book. And when I couldn't . . . well, I'm just feeling sorry for myself, that's all."

Zeke's gaze moved from her face to the book on the floor to the crutches leaning against the hearth to the pile of dying embers. Then back to her. Pinched with pain, her expression was a mix of misery and embarrassment. Suddenly, he knew exactly why he'd leaped into the fray last night. It had been a knee-jerk reaction to his past, even though Patricia's situation was a pale shadow of what his family had experienced.

"Where is everyone?" Jon asked.

"Lily-Too is outside at the coop. Rose is fixing supper. Hank is . . . helping her."

"And Daisy?"

Patricia swallowed. "Studying."

For a moment, they all looked at the ceiling. Then Jon strode up the stairs and they heard him bellow loud enough to be heard over a train wreck. "Daisy! Open up! Downstairs, now!" The music stopped. Jon came back downstairs and hollered again, this time toward the back of the house. "Rose! Hank!"

"Jon . . ." Patricia's voice held appeal.

Jon grinned. "Oh, don't worry. I won't knock their heads together too hard. The little darlings just need a reminder that the sun doesn't revolve around them."

Zeke leaned against the doorjamb, thinking that while the self-absorption Patricia's kids had displayed made him want to shake them till their teeth rattled, their behavior was really no different than anyone else's in children-dom. It reminded him of his sisters long ago. Actually, it reminded him of himself long ago.

At least up until a day not too far past his sixteenth birthday. The day his mother had explained to him how the verdict rendered against his dad's estate had delivered their financial ruin. She'd tried to keep her voice hearty, her recital matter-of-fact, her tone optimistic, but he'd seen the despair in her eyes, the exhaustion in new lines that had etched themselves on her face. Coming on top of losing her husband, the judgment had sapped all her strength.

And in the days that had followed, as he'd watched her move heavy-hearted through the sale of their house and most of their belongings, their move to a dingy apartment miles away from the Bay, her foray into an unfamiliar world of employment where she earned a paltry wage and was left with paltry energy, he'd finally understood that, with his sisters all still in grade school, he'd needed to step into the breach. And he had. Not that his siblings had always appreciated their bossy older brother.

Any more than he supposed Patricia's kids would appreciate him now.

"Fast as oaks growing," Jon muttered. Grumbling, he left the room to search out Patricia's progeny, leaving Zeke and Patricia sharing an awkward silence. Zeke's gaze wandered around the parlor.

Patricia suddenly spoke up. "I'm sorry about—"

"*Very* nice," he commented simultaneously.

She flushed. "It's not like I *meant* to throw up on your shoes."

Amusement tugged on the corner of his mouth. "I wasn't being sarcastic. I was talking about the room. *It's* very nice."

"Oh." Her color deepened. "Thanks."

It was. The room was a tasteful mix of rich red

walls, polished walnut, and an artful use of old and new—a stately piano, overstuffed furniture, and an elaborate contemporary fabric sculpture over the fireplace. The lamps were faux Tiffany; the tables, Prairie School reproductions. Through another doorway, he glimpsed a dining room furnished in the same style—with fur balls dancing under the table. It wasn't that he was fastidious—well, all right, he *was* fastidious—but with four children in the house, surely one of them could run a vacuum?

Above him, footsteps clattered down the hall, then hit the stairs. Zeke turned, expecting a child, then straightened abruptly as a big lug of black fur hit the bottom step and launched herself forward.

"Sugar!" Patricia cried.

Too late. Zeke caught two muddy paws against his white shirt and looked down into the hopeful gaze of a big black Lab. She panted up at him.

Hands reached out to haul off the dog by the collar. "Sorry," Hank said, not sounding that sorry at all. He dragged Sugar toward the back of the house. His sisters filed into the room as he left, Daisy—a vision in bright orange khakis and lime green sweater that matched her eye shadow—whispering to Rose and giving Zeke curious looks, Lily-Too shielding herself behind them. The little girl wore a sweater as achingly blue as her eyes.

"Have a seat." Jon pointed his nieces to the now-cold hearth. "We need to discuss a little matter of selfish behavior when your brother returns."

None of the girls looked overly worried. Having seen Jon with his own two children, Zeke knew his friend never could bring himself to be too heavy-handed. Apparently, his nieces knew it, too.

After Hank had returned and edged in next to his sisters, Jon revved up, delivering himself of a sermon on thankless children and serpent's teeth, tangling up

Shakespeare's words into so many knots, the kids initially stared at him in bewilderment, then lapsed into barely repressed giggles.

Zeke couldn't help a smile. Not only was Jon ridiculous, but Patricia's children were an attractive foursome: all tall, all slim, all fresh faced and bright eyed. They were good kids. He shouldn't have any more problem getting them into some kind of routine than he had with his sisters.

Jon finally gave up. "You want to add anything?" he asked Zeke.

"Why?" Zeke raised a brow. "You've been quite clear."

Someone snickered, and Jon frowned. "You guys just remember that your mom needs your help now."

"I'm sorry, Mama," Lily-Too said, then the rest clamored apologies, rising to gather around their mother, stooping to give her hugs, before they started to move off as one toward the stairway.

"Hold on there." Zeke straightened. "That was all quite heartwarming, but may I point out that supper remains to be served? Dishes done? Donkeys . . . whatever one does with donkeys?"

"But I thought you'd be the one doing . . ." Hank's voice trailed off at the bland look Zeke bestowed on him.

"Well." Jon stood up. Zeke saw a glint of amusement in his eyes. "Think I'll be going. Zeke, my man, you've got the reins."

Seeing Hank's jaw harden, Zeke knew the teen wanted to argue the point. But Hank only gave Zeke a black look—and a measure of satisfaction when he followed his sisters off to the kitchen without saying a word. But Zeke's satisfaction faded when he looked back at Patricia. Her glance, before she ducked her head, wasn't much kinder.

Wow, this was shaping up to be a whole lot of fun.

Chapter 5

The fun started the next morning when the sounds of squabbling drifted up from the kitchen through the floorboards where he slept, intruding on his dreams.

"I did it yesterday!"

He stirred, picturing himself and his sisters hurrying to and from the huge maple table in the dining alcove that overlooked the San Francisco Bay, hustled along by his mom while his dad flipped pancakes, his smile flashing brighter than the sun.

"Didn't I, Daisy?" The voice continued. "I did it yesterday, so it's your turn, Hank."

Daisy? Hank? Zeke opened his eyes. Instead of the country and western posters he remembered curling on the walls of his childhood bedroom, his eyes met a ceiling mural of blue on blue, sponge-brushed with clouds. Darker lines suggested bridges, birds, bows of ships. But instead of the tang of sea breezes, a hint of rosemary hung in the air.

"Bite me," Hank answered. "Lily-Too can do it."

Frowning, Zeke rose on his elbows and focused on overstuffed bookshelves and solid pine furniture. A row of windows circled three walls, their light filtering through cotton curtains. Not San Francisco thirty years ago . . . Cordelia, Missouri, in the present—he glanced at the clock on the bedside table—at just after seven in the morning. Apparently, even an alarm set for seven thirty on a Sunday wasn't an alarm set early enough. It sounded like everyone had risen before him.

Sitting up, he rubbed his hands over his face until the cobwebs cleared. Scenes from the past hadn't haunted him for some while. Listening to the skirmish downstairs, it didn't take Freud to explain why they would now.

After tugging on a pair of silk pajama bottoms, he slid his feet into leather mules against the chill of the planked floor, then snatched up the robe he'd left on a chair near the windows. He'd rather face the fracas downstairs in real pants, but until he'd seen whether or not that four-legged bundle of mud that had greeted him with excessive enthusiasm last evening had been cleaned up, he'd leave them to the sanctuary of Patricia's closet. He pushed the curtains apart and looked out as he pulled the robe over his bare torso.

Last night, he'd examined the shelves of books (a surprisingly good collection) and admired the mural (which displayed unexpected artistry), but dark had flattened itself against the windowpanes by the time Daisy had shown him upstairs. Now the growing light revealed the property snuggled in the wooded arms of the Ozark hillside, smudged now with autumn mist. Sloping upward in a blanket of pastureland, it draped a rise about two acres beyond the house. Fence posts and the roofs of two outbuildings, neither of them large enough to aspire to barn-dom, were silhouetted against the rising sun. It was a lovely setting, he'd admit. A setting that would stir the blood of any—

A faint donkey bray and the squawk of chickens reached his ears. His thoughts shifted. He dropped the curtain, hoping Zinnia had been right about Lily-Too's expertise with feathered creatures, considering animal husbandry lay outside—far outside—his field of expertise.

"That's not fair." A small voice piped up. "I have to collect the eggs."

"Well, *I* have a lot of homework." Rose's voice. "So, Hank, you bring in more logs."

Zeke rolled his eyes. It appeared Jon's lecture on responsibility hadn't found fertile ground. Nor was he proving himself much of an example. He grabbed his toiletry kit and headed into the hall.

Out in the corridor, he was faced with the choice of multiple doors and not much memory of which one led to the bathroom. Underneath the noise from the kitchen, he could hear the tinny sounds of an old blues recording that he recognized as Robert Johnson. His eyebrows rose. Artistry, good books, the King of the Delta Blues . . . scratching his head, he opened the first door he came to and flipped on the light.

And blinked in the sudden explosion of color. Three walls were lined with transparent plastic bins filled with—he peered closer—yarn, in every hue known to man. Pinks and reds, blues and purples, greens and yellows. It was like standing in a box of crayons. A sagging armchair nestled in a multicolored afghan squatted in one corner. And dominating the center of the room was a loom, as big as a piano and as deep as Patricia was tall. The bench in front of it was worn with use.

He sneezed. All of it was covered with dust.

Bemused, he backed out and closed the door behind him, just as the phone rang, causing a momentary lull downstairs.

"Mom! It's for you!"

Damn. He'd hoped Patricia's ankle had kept her in bed. Zeke picked up his pace. No matter what, he'd be up first tomorrow. The bickering resumed as he turned into the next room—the right one this time—and was still rolling along by the time he exited twenty minutes later.

"Pipe down!" A voice yelled from the front of the house.

He stopped, as startled as the sudden silence downstairs. If he wasn't mistaken, that voice had come from mousy, gentle, *quiet* Patricia.

When he reached the kitchen, taking a route from the back stairs outside his bedroom and through a mudroom (aptly named, considering the paw prints), the kids were still shooting jibes at each other, but the energy had gone out of the argument.

Lily-Too spotted him first. Reddening, she closed her mouth and dropped her gaze to the floor, a none-too-clean checkerboard of black-and-white linoleum.

Skirting a suitcase strapped with a red nylon belt that rested by the doorway, he followed the scent of coffee to a pot on the counter, an attractive white tile intermixed with squares of bright color. It was spotless; the backsplash was not. He reached for a mug stacked with a rainbow of Fiestaware dancing behind smudged glass-front cabinets. The crockery vied for attention with the canary yellow walls. Despite signs that cleanliness was relegated only to what was necessary, the decor and a woodstove in the corner enveloped him in warmth.

"Good morning." He turned and rested his hips against the counter. An impressive and large fabric sculpture—skeins of woven cloth tugged and twisted and accented with beads and copper and wood—similar to the one hanging over the fireplace and another he'd seen in the upstairs hall, graced the wall over a long whitewashed table.

On a chair beneath it, watching him with serious

eyes, Rose murmured a greeting. Hank said nothing. A shank of hair hanging over his forehead, he squatted next to his dog, scratching its ears. The dog, an overfed—and clean, Zeke noted—Labrador, eyed him wistfully. Zeke frowned. Even though one of his white shirts was ruined, he'd done no violence last night and didn't warrant a stare *that* pathetic. His gaze shifted to Hank. Or one that frosty.

Standing at the stove, wielding a spatula, Daisy looked over her shoulder. She was dressed in tight jeans, a tight sweater that reveled an inch of flesh at its hem, and a rainbow of eye shadow. Remembering how he'd ribbed his oldest sisters about their liberal use of makeup, nostalgia brushed him again.

Daisy's chin rose. "Oh, you're up." Apparently, she'd mistaken his expression for disapproval.

Sighing to himself, he tried to soothe her feathers. "Eggs and home fries. Smells great." Cholesterol must have been invented in this part of the country. "Thanks for taking on breakfast"—he studied the other faces over the rim of his mug—"without argument."

She gave him a cautious grin and returned to her pan. "I have to leave pretty soon, so I thought I'd do my share first. You know, like you said."

"Good girl."

"I made the coffee," Hank muttered.

Zeke sipped. "You, uh, certainly did. Where's your mom?"

"In the parlor." Rose flicked back her hair. "She's on the phone with Bebe."

He remembered Lil's voice during the family meeting. *She's like a mother to you.* "A professor. Textiles, right?"

Rose exchanged an odd look with Hank.

"At the University of Missouri," Daisy said with a

frown at her siblings. "In Columbia. That's where Mom grew up. Where I go to school. She taught Mom how to weave."

"And helped her do those." Lily-Too pointed at a fabric wall sculpture over the table.

He wondered at the looks, but didn't pursue the subject. "I trust you took your mom some coffee?"

"She doesn't like coffee," Hank said.

"Tea, then. Or juice."

Gazes dropped.

"You know, I was hoping after last night that you'd understand—"

"I'll get my own tea, thank you."

Looking none too steady on her crutches, Patricia appeared in the doorway. She wore a white sweatshirt that draped to the knees of her white sweatpants, split up a seam to accommodate her splint, and a strained expression. He wondered if it was pain or if the phone call had brought bad news.

He was about to ask if she needed her Tylenol 3 when she dropped a protective hand on Rose's head and smiled down at her daughter. His tongue stilled. It was just a smile, a gentle smile, but with the maternal gesture and all that white, she looked like Madonna. The Bible one. At least, she no longer looked mousy. In fact, he couldn't figure out where he'd ever gotten that impression.

Studying her, he hadn't realized the kids had fallen silent. Four pairs of eyes had turned from their mother to him. Puzzled, he looked from them to Patricia. She was gazing at him now, and once again he didn't like that expression in her eyes. Maybe the Holy Mother hadn't been an apt comparison.

"I'll get the tea, Mama."

Lily-Too busied herself with a mug and a teapot. Rose got up to offer her mother her chair, then helped her sit, propping her crutches within easy reach. Hank closed the dog in the mudroom. Daisy turned back to the stove and in moments had handed off laden plates, which the youngest three carried off to far reaches of the house.

Taking a seat at the table across from Patricia, Zeke frowned. His family had always dined together. At least they had until the last few years he'd lived at home, after everything had changed.

Daisy set a plate in front of Patricia, then brushed her hands on her jeans. "All set? Do you need anything else?"

"No, this is plenty." Ignoring Zeke, who was increasingly feeling invisible, she watched Daisy bustle about, putting the pans in the sink to soak. "Aren't you having anything?" Patricia's voice was hopeful. She couldn't make it more obvious she didn't want his sole company.

"Nope. My ride'll be here in a few minutes." Daisy nodded at the suitcase.

"I thought your cousins weren't leaving for Columbia until late this afternoon."

"I'm not going back with Melanie and Kathleen." Daisy ducked into the mudroom. "Danny's picking me up." Her voice was muffled.

"Danny." Patricia's voice had gone flat. "You told me you weren't seeing him anymore."

"I know." Daisy returned, winding the kaleidoscope scarf around her neck. She gave a lighthearted shrug. "But now I am again. You like Danny. You know you do." She leaned over and bussed her mother's cheek.

"It's not Danny. I just wish you wouldn't—" Patricia threw a glance at him and pinked as if she'd just remembered he was there. "Maybe we could discuss this in the other room."

A horn honked from the drive that circled to the back of the house.

"Nothing to discuss," Daisy said airily. "Everything's cool."

But the way Daisy's smile faded as she turned to pick up her suitcase, Zeke didn't think it was. He glanced at Patricia to see if that brief bleakness had registered with her, but Patricia wasn't looking at her daughter anymore. Lips pinched, she was staring at him. When their eyes met, hers slid away. He put down his fork. For God's sake, he was here to help. He hadn't meant to intrude.

When Daisy turned back around, she was smiling again. He suddenly realized the imp had timed her departure to her advantage. Soften her mom with breakfast; avoid her by using his presence. And here he'd thought she wasn't the brightest bulb in the pack. He gave her a look of admiration; she'd make her way in the world just fine.

She dropped a kiss on Patricia's cheek. "Love you, Mom. See you at Thanksgiving."

She headed outside. Leaving Zeke alone with Patricia, who was looking at him as though it was all his fault Daisy had left. When his gaze met hers, she lowered her eyes. And long minutes after they'd heard the car pull off, she still hadn't murmured a word. Her full attention was on her plate.

As was his. The only sounds were cutlery scraping crockery and the continued whine of old blues from the parlor. This was childish. After breakfast, he'd figure out some other way to help her, since he was the one now holding the ball—but he was getting the hell out of Dodge.

He stabbed at a potato. He'd rather have a bagel and fruit. "Did you sleep well?"

She hesitated. "Yes."

Dumb question. The woman had just broken her ankle. "I did, too."

"Good." She didn't look up.

"Very comfortable." He felt a dogged determination to get a whole sentence out of her. He nodded toward the fabric sculpture. "I saw your loom. Lily-Too said you made that. And the mural upstairs?"

"Yes."

He waited, but there was nothing else. "You're talented." He wasn't sure he'd succeeded in keeping the surprise out of his voice.

There was a hitch in her chewing, but she just raised her eyes and regarded him steadily.

He nodded toward the parlor. "You like Robert Johnson?"

"Mmm."

"Most people don't know him."

This time she spoke. "Unless they love blues."

Finally. "Yes, unless they—" He narrowed his eyes at her—had that been sarcasm? Her gaze had dropped back to her plate.

He set down his fork. "Nice library upstairs. Hemingway. le Carré. Morrison. And I notice you're a fan of Jane Austen."

There was a long pause. She chewed, swallowed, then picked up her napkin to blot her mouth. "I'm not sure, actually. I'm reading that for an English lit class and, well"—she looked straight at him—"Mr. Darcy's conceit is hard to swallow. Don't you think so?"

Touché. He laughed. "Sorry. I don't know what I expected to find here, but—"

"—We *can* read and write. Imagine." Her complexion, normally a shade of peach, took on the hue of an apple. Picking up a tea bag, she dunked it up and down in her mug. Water slopped over the rim. "I'm sorry. I mean, I'm grateful you offered to help, but this is completely ridiculous, isn't it? I don't think it'll work, so you need to leave. Not right *now,* but soon. Later. Today."

Intrigued, he picked a toothpick out of a holder on the table, propped it between his teeth, and leaned back. "Are you firing me?"

The tea bag moved faster. Up and down, up and down. "Don't be silly."

"Silly?" He pulled out the toothpick. He didn't remember the last time anyone had called him silly. In fact, he couldn't remember *any* time.

"You shouldn't have said you'd do this, and I shouldn't have let you. You know that."

She'd just offered him an escape from this, well, silly arrangement. And now he didn't want to take it. Go figure. "Now who's being silly?"

Annoyance streaked across her features. Entertained, he popped the toothpick back in his mouth and gave her a bland look.

"I-I'll figure out something else."

"I believe the alternatives were studied, um, ad . . . nauseum."

Her color deepened.

"Although Zinnia O'Malley probably wouldn't mind talking it over again."

A muscle spasmed in her cheek, but the tea bag went still. He felt disappointed.

"I can't believe I'm in this fix," she murmured, dropping her hands in her lap. "But there's no need for you to be in it with me. She can't force you."

Nor can she force you. He sighed, leaving the words unspoken. Taking the toothpick out again, he settled his elbows on the table. "Look, Patricia." She looked startled at the use of her preferred name. Hell, he liked Patsy Lee, too, but if Patricia is what she wanted, she should have insisted everyone use it years ago. "I might have been addled Friday—"

"You were drunk."

Thatta girl. "Yes, I was. And you weren't much better."

Her color deepened, but she stayed silent. He felt another flicker of disappointment.

"I may not be the best resort, but it seems I'm your last resort: the only person in good health who is both available and lacks a life." Despite his upbeat tone, he realized the end of his sentence had slipped into bitterness. He smiled to lighten the words.

But her gaze had already sharpened. She was no fool. Considering him, she hooked her hair behind her ear. A small gold hoop winked from her lobe, matching the flecks in her eyes. Perceptive eyes. He resisted the urge to look away.

She finally spoke. "But you don't need to stay until my ankle heals completely. Not seven or eight weeks."

"Probably not," he agreed.

"Just . . . one."

A devil nudged him. "Four."

She frowned. "Maybe two."

"Three. I'll do a good job."

"You mean like this morning?" The words spilled out, and her face pinked.

He laughed. "Much better than this morning. I promise."

She looked dubious. "Okay, then . . . three weeks."

That devil prodded him again. "We'll have to see."

"But you said—"

He raised his brows.

She made a low sound in her throat. His hopes rose, but then she clamped her mouth shut and they fell again. Shoving away her plate, she pushed herself up and fumbled for her crutches. Feeling guilty for baiting her, he reached out to help, but she shrugged off his hand, seated the crutches under her arms, and headed toward the parlor, her swing unsteady.

Watching her back, straightened by dignity, he thought that getting to know Patricia O'Malley wasn't too unlike peeling an onion. He pitched the toothpick onto his plate and rose to clear the table.

The next few weeks might be interesting.

Chapter 6

But by that evening, he was wondering if he'd last even a few more days. Or if he'd ever know Patricia O'Malley any better than he did.

Since his household skill had been called into question, by that dubious look of hers, throughout the afternoon, he'd found himself determined to show his patient how useful he could be. After she'd hobbled from the kitchen, he'd trailed her into the parlor with Tylenol 3 and tea, settling her on the sofa with an intimidating tome titled *Basic Principles of Small Business Accounting, 7th Edition,* an afghan, and two of her cats, one a ball of white fluff named Nod, and another black with white boots, named Blinken. (He hadn't seen the third cat, but assumed it would be Winken, the final of the three fabled fisherman of the wooden shoe.)

Then he'd cajoled Rose from homework (and the occasional sneak peek she was taking at *Teen Beat*), Lily-Too from cartoons, and Hank off the Internet (with Lily-Too's help). Hank had scrambled to hide what he'd been surfing, bringing to Zeke's mind a long-ago image of his oldest sister fumbling to hide her backpack (and the cigarettes she'd secreted inside). Zeke had smiled at the memory—and made a note to look up Hank's Internet history later.

After they cleaned up the kitchen, he sat them down at the table, where they hammered out a household routine. Rose entered into organizing with enthusiasm and Lily-Too followed her lead, giving him shy, curious glances. Hank sat back with his arms crossed, refusing to participate despite Zeke's gentle prodding. No matter. Participate in the planning or not, Hank would do his part. Zeke had learned from watching his own sisters that sibling pressure would work where his own exhortations wouldn't.

After they made a schedule and divided up chores, Zeke handed off a mop, a dust cloth, and a toilet brush, and grabbed up a broom for himself. Everyone hustled to work, including Hank. As Zeke hoped, the girls cut short any mutiny their brother intended, Rose berating, Lily-Too coaxing. In short order, the house started to shine.

While he was on his way through the parlor to sweep the front porch, Patricia looked up from her book. "They aren't servants," she murmured.

"Nor are they helpless," he replied, stung into curtness.

And then on the way back in, wanting to smooth over that exchange, he stooped to pick up a piece of paper that had fallen from her book. It was her last semester's report card: all A's.

"Nice grades," he commented, impressed anew.

Unimpressed, she frowned. "Astonishing, I know." Looking startled by her own words, she dipped her reddened face back to her text.

Obviously, she'd decided he was a snob. Which wasn't fair. Even if he was beginning to wonder if he was.

After that, bringing her food only elicited a grunt. Asking if she was in pain, just a shake of the head. Unwilling to concede, he redoubled his efforts to impress—sweeping ashes from the fireplace, reloading the log holder, carrying out the trash, making sure he was always right under her nose. But no matter how much clamor he made or how busily he worked, not only wouldn't she talk; she wouldn't even look his direction.

By six o'clock, he wasn't just exhausted, he was again ready to bail. It was only sheer pride . . . maybe mixed in with a man's honor . . . and nothing to do with aimlessness, dammit . . . that was making him stay.

In the kitchen, he shrugged into his white leather jacket. It had grown dark shortly after five. Glancing at the clock for the eighth time since Hank and Lily-Too had left the house to do their chores an hour ago, he'd just announced his plans to check on Lily-Too to his audience of one. Patricia still kept to her sofa.

"You don't have to help Lily-Too." Rose informed him. "She knows what she's doing, and, besides, Hank's out there, too."

Slim and straight, Patricia's middle daughter stood with her back to him in front of the stove, waiting for a pot to boil. When he'd threatened to pull out the vegetable soup he'd seen when he'd inspected the contents of the freezer, pantry, and refrigerator earlier today, Rose had suddenly discovered an interest in their supper menu. She'd ordered Hank to work peeling potatoes, and had found Zeke two roasting chickens when he'd volunteered the information he was a passable cook, looking pleased that she could find *him* something to do.

He'd slathered them with butter and herbs like his dad had taught him, trying not to wonder if the fowl had been among the flock that had scurried away when he and Jon pulled up the drive yesterday. Now the scent of rosemary, thyme, and browning chicken filled the kitchen. Fiestaware formed a pretty pattern on the table.

"I'm sure you're right and Hank has matters in hand." Doubtful, considering the kid's short attention span, but he was learning to agree with Rose no matter what he thought.

Rose *hmphed.* "Hank is probably standing starstruck in the middle of the pasture. But at least Lily-Too can call him if something comes up." She glanced over her shoulder and caught him zipping up his jacket. She sighed. "If you're going, anyway, take a flashlight. There should be some in that basket by the door. And wear something else besides white."

He moved into the mudroom, picked up a flashlight.

Rose's voice followed him. "If you don't have anything else, we still have some of my dad's stuff that Mom saved for Hank. I can run upstairs and—"

"If my jacket gets dirty, I'll probably survive."

"That's not what I'm wor—"

Zeke stepped onto the back stoop and closed the door on her words. Rose had a streak of Zinnia O'Malley in her. Blowing out a breath, he watched the vapor vanish against a velvet sky liberally sprinkled with stars so sharp it almost hurt to look at them. He wouldn't blame Hank if he was rooted in place with his face tilted to the sky. Rarely had Zeke seen one so clear. San Francisco had vistas a man would sell his soul for, but this countryside was a heady rival.

And much more quiet. So quiet, it was unnerving. Although Jon and Lil's home was also stationed on rural acreage, it was positioned on a hillside overlooking town. The sounds of Cordelia and the traffic on the highways, while muted, were still a constant presence. Here not even a breeze stirred the leaves of the woods that formed darker shadows on either side of the house. Early frost had silenced the crickets that scraped through warmer evenings.

He looked across the expanse of land that sloped uphill ahead of him. The fence posts and a couple of benches, pale in the starlight, marked a ragged transition from yard to pasture. Light gleamed from a lone window in the smaller of the outbuildings, the one he assumed was the chicken coop. Switching on his flashlight, he started toward it, flinching when a blur of pale orange streaked past his feet, then nearly jumping out of his skin when Hank's voice sounded nearby, not loud, but carrying easily in the quiet.

"It's just Winken, probably after a field mouse."

Willing his heartbeat to normal, Zeke turned. Hank walked toward him, hands stuffed into his jacket pockets.

"Where've you been?" Zeke asked. "I thought you were up to donkey business."

"A walk, if you need to know. I like to walk."

He fell in beside Zeke. They walked in silence, then Hank glanced over at him. "You're from San Francisco, right? Must be cool."

Every kid seemed to think California was Nirvana. Actually, they were right. "It is. Skyline, bridges, bay . . . even in the fog that rolls in most evenings, I'd say it's spectacular. And if you like to walk, it's a good way to see it."

More silence, then Hank spoke up again, voice casual. "Lots of gay people, aren't there?"

Zeke wondered if he was dealing with a homophobe. "Diversity is a trademark of the city, yes." To forestall a possible bigoted comment, he added, "I have good friends that are gay."

"Really?" They'd reached the fence, crisscrossed wire strung between posts. "There aren't many queers around here. No guys I know, anyway. I was just wondering." About every fourth step, Hank tugged on the wire.

"What are you doing?" Zeke asked, hoping to change subjects before he was called on to defend those good friends.

"I'm checking the tension. Too loose and the donkeys could get out or tangled up and hurt." Hank's gaze dropped to Zeke's jacket. When he looked back up, Zeke thought mischief glinted in his eyes, but it was so dark he wasn't sure. "You want to meet them before I put them in for the night?"

"Sure," he said. Meeting donkeys was about the last thing he wanted to do.

They'd reached the side of the larger of the two buildings. Hank flipped a switch. Light fell through the upper half of a stable door. At the same time, a floodlight attached above it beamed across the yard. Enthusiastic braying echoed just beyond the rise. "All the wiring and switches have to be where they can't chew on 'em. They chew on everything."

"Including people?"

"They've never bit any of us." Hank opened the gate.

Not exactly total reassurance. Zeke hesitated, then squared his shoulders and followed Hank, shutting the gate behind him. Two donkeys, black shadows against the night, topped the rise, still calling.

Hank stopped just outside the pool cast by the floodlight. "They come when they hear the gate or see the light. They do the same thing when they hear the school bus in the afternoons."

The donkeys jogged toward them.

"The shorter one is seven; that's Dowdy. The other one's Dharma. She's nine. They're both jennets, because jacks aren't as good for pets. We adopted them from a donkey rescue place, or, rather, Uncle Jon did a few years ago."

"*Jon* did? I wouldn't have thought he knew his jennets from his jacks." Like *he* did?

Hank knew he didn't. His glance was filled with amusement. "Jennets are girls. Mom couldn't have afforded to take them on without Uncle Jon's help.

They eat lots. There's the vet. Plus, we had to get electricity out here so we could have some heat in their stable for winter."

"Still . . . why did Jon think your mom would want two donkeys?"

"She didn't. I wanted them after I saw one of the rescue sites on the Internet."

Not spoiled or anything, was he? The donkeys had reached the pool of light. Throwing an odd look of anticipation at Zeke, Hank stepped forward to meet them. Both animals were gray with white muzzles, their backs not much higher than his waist. The smaller one, Dowdy, brayed again and nuzzled a pocket. Hank pulled out a carrot just as Zeke, thinking they weren't quite the menace he'd thought they'd be, stepped into the ring of light. The taller one, Dharma, still a few steps behind her playmate, stopped abruptly. She did not look pleased.

Definitely not pleased. She shifted her weight forward, stretched her neck, and flattened her ears. Zeke looked at Hank. The boy wasn't looking back, but he was smiling. Then Dharma stomped a hoof. Hard. Hank's smile vanished. Feeling his neck hair rise, Zeke backed away, feeling like a complete idiot at being bullied by a little girl donkey, but not so idiotic he wanted to risk a bite from those teeth. He cursed under his breath. And not so addled he didn't realize where his foot had just landed.

"Hank, what are you doing?" A high voice sounded behind him. Lily-Too slowly moved past, extending her hand, holding it low. "Shh. Shh. I have a granola bar for you, Dharma."

When Lily-Too stepped between him and Dharma, and Dharma looked unimpressed, Zeke decided enough was enough. Death by donkey bite probably wasn't likely. He stepped forward. "Lily-Too—"

Behind her back, she waved a hand to halt him. "It's okay. She won't hurt me."

Before he could protest further, she'd moved directly in front of the donkey. Finally distracted from Zeke, Dharma raised her head. Her ears swiveled forward as she nipped the treat from Lily-Too's hand.

Coming to life, Hank hustled Zeke toward the gate.

"She have something against strangers?"

"No." Hank hesitated. "She just doesn't like white. We don't know why—she's just quirky that way."

"You call that *quirky*." Zeke felt his temper flare.

"She wouldn't have hurt you. Not really."

Hank shut the gate behind them and would have walked past Zeke, except Zeke grabbed his jacket, pulling him to a stop near one of the benches.

"So you wanted to spook me. Why?"

Hank jerked his arm away, but still didn't meet his eyes. "I don't like the way you've been ordering us around."

"And just telling me is too civilized for you?"

"I'm telling you now."

Zeke wanted to clock him. But then he caught something else in Hank's expression and his anger faded. Something wasn't right here. "Has your revenge been exacted? Or should I spend the rest of my stay looking over my shoulder?"

"Exacted? Oh. Yeah. I'm cool."

"You don't sound cool."

"Okay. I'm still mad. Maybe you're some kind of big shot, but you don't even belong to the family, so why do you get to tell us what to do?"

Zeke studied him. Patricia's stiffness began to make sense. "You have a point." He motioned to the bench. "Sit."

Hank hesitated.

"Please."

Reluctantly, Hank sat.

Zeke settled beside him. "When I was around your age—sixteen, right?—my dad died."

"Mine died, too," Hank's voice was grudging. "I was seven, though. I don't remember him that well."

"Helluva a thing to live through, no matter how old you are."

Hank made a noise that might have been agreement.

"After he died, there was a lot to take care of. I had four sisters, and my mom wasn't up to handling everything that needed to be handled, so I took over. When I landed here, old reflexes kicked in. My sisters always said I was bossy."

Hank snorted. "No sh—I mean, no kidding."

"I think I could be excused. I have a mother who can be somewhat overbearing."

"Like Gran."

"Like Gran," Zeke agreed. "And while my three oldest sisters and I have gone our separate ways without any problems, I have a little sister who tends to think I need her guidance."

"Kind of like Rose always telling me what to do." Hank's sigh was gusty. "Sometimes it's hard having only sisters."

"And a man needs to develop a forceful character under those conditions."

"No duh. But . . . guidance? Rose doesn't need guidance. Daisy does. Daisy needs a keeper. She—" Apparently recalling he'd decided Zeke was his enemy and nobody confides in an enemy, Hank stopped. "But I don't need one." Abruptly, he stood up. "I'm going inside."

Zeke watched him walk back to the house, thinking of the whisper of distress behind Hank's eyes. Maybe the boy didn't need a keeper, but he needed something.

Behind him, Lily-Too had led the donkeys into the stable. She let herself out of the gate and stretched to turn out the light. The switch was just beyond her fingertips.

"Lily-Too?" He got up to help her. "I need a friend."

She frowned and looked after her brother, her loyalties obviously divided.

"An advisor, then."

She switched her gaze to him again, frown deepening.

Zeke smiled. "In other words, would you let me know when I'm about to put my foot in it and do something wrong?"

Lily-Too looked at his shoes, then glanced up, smiling shyly. "You already did."

He laughed and reached to flip the switch. Just before everything went dark, he looked down at Lily-Too. Her expression was so achingly vulnerable, so reminiscent of his sisters in their youth, his breath caught in his throat. Damn. Seemed the whole family was sliding straight into his heart.

But considering the way Patricia had looked as he'd marched through the parlor with his broom earlier today, she wouldn't hesitate to jerk them back out.

Chapter 7

Late Monday morning, Patsy Lee rode toward Sedalia, an hour beyond Cordelia and home of her orthopedic doctor's offices, wondering how to get rid of her unwelcome guest. A blunt request hadn't done it, so what would?

Much to her annoyance—unreasonable, childish annoyance, which only made it more annoying—Zeke had taken the wheel after tucking her into the passenger's seat of her Cadillac. She'd picked up the old honker for a song from Rusty Peterson. It had belonged to his recently deceased wife. That transaction had been the start of a singularly short (dreadful) dating experience—at least on her side; he still called now and then—but she was glad for the Caddy. It ran well and felt wonderfully decadent, even if the upholstery was slightly moth-eaten.

Picking at a tiny hole, she stared out the window, wishing she could make the car move faster. After observing some niceties, conversation had sputtered out around the time that they'd left the Ozark hills behind and had entered the gentle countryside of middle Missouri. Swaths of farmland checkered in blunted hues spread out on either side of the highway, the only trees huddling in a brisk wind around creeks and ponds. Grasses waved from the ditches, exclamation points against dark earth. It was a gray day, the kind of day where . . .

"The scenery out here is surreal. The horizon has no edge, but seeps into the sky," Zeke said. "Lonesome."

No wonder he'd become a songwriter. "But a nice kind of lonesome." She started, belatedly realizing she'd spoken out loud.

But he just pointed up through the windshield at a hawk wheeling overhead. "Yes, like that." His mouth quirked. "Although I'm sure it's something you rarely experience."

She felt nettled. "Don't do that."

"Do what?"

"Don't you ever just have a conversation without . . . joking, mocking, throwing in a word nobody understands . . . whatever that is you do that keeps you at an arm's length from the rest of us?"

His laugh was without humor. "Not recently. No. Maybe not for a long time."

At his honesty, her bluster winked out. Smoothing the tunic vest she'd belted at her waist over a calf-length skirt that she knew was overkill for a doctor's office visit, she concentrated on the landscape, wishing she'd kept her mouth shut. Zeke turned his attention back to the road. Despite his comments that he'd never driven a car as big as a freighter, and despite his unfamiliarity with the area, he handled the Cadillac capably.

Of course, she was learning there wasn't much he couldn't do or wouldn't attempt. Helping with four sisters must have instilled a certain fearlessness. Early this morning, he'd even helped Hank clean out the donkeys' water trough before escorting Lily-Too up the road to the bus stop after the older children had left. From her place on the sofa, Patsy Lee had watched them walk down the drive under a sky flushed pearl gray by dawn, one dark, one fair, both straight backed and tall. The tilt of Lily-Too's head as she looked up at Zeke gave Patsy Lee a funny feeling that she'd attributed to jealousy—she wanted to be the one walking with Lily-Too.

A gust of wind hit the car, but Zeke held it steady. She snuck a glance. His white button-down shirt was open at the collar; a black unstructured jacket draped his square shoulders, and he drove with one wrist draped on top of the steering wheel, looking completely relaxed.

Well, she'd be relaxed, too, if she could walk. Only three days since she'd broken her ankle, but already she longed for mobility. Longed, craved, hungered, would sell her soul for mobility. Especially if it came with a few minutes alone. Zeke was right; she rarely found a solitary minute, but since her fall, time by herself had grown even scarcer. With Zeke's admonishments, someone constantly danced attendance on her except when she slept. And even then, she'd heard the door open and close at least once every night. She knew her children slept like the dead, so it must be . . .

Zeke. Who brought her pain pills, blankets, textbooks, tea, snacks, and meals in a never-ending parade, anticipating her needs before she knew them herself.

Zeke. Who organized her children and ordered her to rest and tidied things to his own satisfaction.

I swear, the man would try the patience of a saint. "You should—"

"What?"

Leave died on her lips at a glance from his dark eyes. "You should, uh, please consult me about supper plans from now on."

"I thought I did."

"No." She set her chin, wanting the record straight. "You *told* me."

"You don't want chicken-and-oyster gumbo? God knows you've got plenty of the former. And Jon's bringing the latter. He was in Kansas City yesterday and bought fresh."

"That's not the point."

Another glance, amused this time. "Oh, I know it's not."

Unable to think of a suitable retort, she fumed. They rode in silence for quite a few miles and she fumed some more, nudging a food wrapper on the floor with her foot until it was under the seat. He hadn't even cringed when he'd seen the trash-strewn state of her car. Probably because it wasn't as impressive as her kitchen floor, at least before he'd had Hank mop it.

"I don't have time to do everything."

"And that *is* the point."

She squeezed her eyes shut, opened them again. Horrible habit, blurting. "No, it's not the point. I was just thinking that between work and school and everything else, the house doesn't stay as clean as *some* people might like it. But it's not important. We're used to it." She was speaking too much and too fast and too loud.

He slowed the vehicle as they reached Sedalia's outskirts. Traffic increased as the roadway became crowded with gas stations, motels, and fast food joints. Dixie Doo Bar-B-Q slid by on the left. The state fairgrounds were just up ahead.

She cleared her throat, tried to slow down. "You don't have to clean while you're here. And if you bring the laundry downstairs, I can do it."

For heaven's sake, she didn't want him washing her *underwear*. The thought of her plain white cottons slipping through his long fingers—musician's fingers—made her squirm. And didn't improve her temper.

"Nothing much else to do." Despite a light voice,

she could tell the fact rankled. But when she glanced over, he smiled. "Besides, I really don't mind."

But I do. The words were on the tip of her tongue, but Zeke spoke first.

"I remember that arena." Zeke was looking at the fairground's main gates. There was a bittersweet look in his eyes.

"You must miss performing. The excitement." She thought of the traveling he'd done, the places he'd seen. At his glance, she realized she'd sounded wistful. She hadn't meant to. "I mean, if you like that kind of thing."

"As a matter of fact, touring got tiresome. I'm not ungrateful, but *ungodly* doesn't begin to describe the rigors—the crowds, the press, the schedule, and what passes for food."

"But when it ended . . . well, it must have been . . . quiet."

"Still is." The words were light, but she didn't miss a lonely undernote. He shifted. "But the gig here is a good memory."

Not for her. They drove past the grandstand, a hollow bowl now. But in her mind's eye, she saw hot concert lights against a pitch-black sky, the night exploding into music, and Van Castle holding the crowd spellbound. They'd performed there not long after Lil and Jon had married. The entire family had attended, her children so excited they could hardly stand it. Their aunt's marriage to a country superstar had been the stuff of fairy tales. And she hadn't exactly been immune from envy. Or from guilt.

"I was pregnant with Lily-Too when you played there." Henry hadn't been gone long.

"That's right. I remember you were the main reason—" He broke off, looking irritated at his lapse. "I'm sorry, that's none of my business."

Silently, she agreed. If you traced Lil and Jon's history all the way back, Lil had primarily agreed to marriage with Jon because of Patsy Lee's boatload of debt. No, Henry's debt—let's not take on blame she didn't deserve. It was dumb luck that Lil and Jon had ended up happy.

"I'm not ashamed I had to depend on Lil for help."

He shot her a look that told her he knew she was lying. "No shame in it," he said mildly.

Wasn't there? She didn't know. She'd been prepared to take two jobs, but . . . over the years, every one of Zinnia O'Malley's daughters had faced disaster and met its challenge. Faced with the family's approaching penury, Lil had leapt boldly into an unwanted life of celebrity, then profitably resurrected the bookstore business that Henry had brought to ruin. Left to fend for herself and her daughter after a bitter divorce, former socialite Alcea battled her way into self-sufficiency using her skills in the kitchen. And dragged back to her hometown by her sisters on the heels of a failed business and romance, Mari traded big-city ambition to share her new husband's dreams. All three had shown courage and imagination and determination.

But not their sister-in-law. Like good ol' Blanche DuBois, she'd relied on the kindness of strangers. Or, rather, in-laws.

Until now, she reminded herself. She was changing course, too—she'd finish college, take over the bookstores in a few years like Lil and she had planned, and she'd make sure they rose to even greater success. She sighed, not understanding why her ambitions didn't fill her with the same zeal she'd seen in their faces.

"None of them had a bevy of kids, Patricia."

She started. Great. Now he wasn't just gauging her mood; he was reading her mind.

"And your days are still as full as mine once were."

He was comparing her life to his? "With kids and animals and work and chores."

"With *life*. Look at all you have."

"Me? How could *you* think—?" She reddened. "I mean, you're the one with everything. You were even born rich." She bit her tongue. If he'd had any doubt she'd once read the gossip articles about him, he didn't now.

His glance was amused. *See?* "Well-off enough, yes, but we didn't rank with the Hiltons and Trumps. Nice home. One housekeeper. And we all still learned the business end of a broom."

She wondered if he'd had a socialite mother who couldn't be bothered. "Admit it, though. You had a lot."

"I did," he agreed. "Until my dad died."

Intent on making him see that painting himself as a poor little rich boy was ludicrous, she'd forgotten how his circumstances had changed. Figured. Just like her to put her foot in it. "I'm sorry."

"I still had family. Lots of family." He didn't sound sure if that was good or bad.

"I, uh, lost my mother," she offered. "Cancer. But I still had—"

"Your father?"

Anger stirred. Unintentionally, he'd poked a sore spot.

"No, Bebe." Great. She'd just landed on yet another topic she didn't want to discuss.

"The woman who taught you to weave?" He looked confused.

"Mmm." Bebe was much more than that, but she didn't want to elaborate. She never did. She'd had to stomach too many veiled, curious, or downright disgusted looks (or worse) over the years whenever she'd been backed into a corner and forced to admit she had two mothers. Gay mothers. Bebe had joined their household when Patsy Lee was ten. By the time she was eleven, she'd well understood what prejudice was. Undoubtedly, Zeke wasn't like that, but the subject had been at rest—most people around here had forgotten or they no longer cared—for far too long for her to want to exhume it again.

She moved the subject a different direction. "But I haven't sat at my loom in years. Once upon a time, I could weave when the children napped, but—" Remembering the silken strands sliding through her fingers, her anger eased. "You see, you need uninterrupted hours—you count yards when you measure the warp, and strands when you're threading. The possibility of error is huge. You also don't want to stop in the middle of each step because the tension can change, not to mention . . ." *God.* Couldn't she find a happy medium among tongue-tied, awkward, and boring him to death? "Sorry."

"I'm interested."

Sure he was. "Anyway, it's impossible with little children around."

Thinking of the loom Bebe had given her after she'd married Henry, her mood dipped into sadness, yo-yoing like it had been all weekend. She was a mess.

"They're no longer little," he pointed out. "And you miss it. Why don't you—"

Had she *said* she missed it? Annoyed all of out proportion and knowing it, she spouted. "When? This is the first time in years that I've sat down for more than a half an hour at a time."

She halted, appalled at how rude she sounded. Where was the person who stammered and blushed and made excuses? After the conversation she'd had with Bebe yesterday, something inside her had shifted. Maybe it had been shifting for a long while. But that didn't mean she needed to act like a shrew. "I'm sorry."

"For what?"

"For snapping." Her voice was tight and didn't sound sorry at all. "It's just that I remember what growing up without a dad is like. A little spoiling won't hurt them."

"I remember, too," he retorted. "And more chores won't, either."

Enough. She pointed ahead. "The medical offices are there on the right."

"What happened to your dad?"

"What?" Anger simmered again. "I never knew my father, okay? I—I just never knew him is all." And she never would. She was the result of a hare-brained, irresponsible *experiment*. Damn it!

"Okay, okay. Sorry." He gave her a curious look, but wisely let the subject drop.

Feeling like a bundle of neuroses, she plunked her chin on her fist and stared out the window.

All her life she'd thought her dad—that conspicuously blank line on her birth certificate—was a man her mother had once loved before she'd faced the reality of her homosexuality. Maybe because that had been what she'd told Patsy Lee. As a child—no, even now—Patsy Lee had, of course, always wished he'd never run off, had even, at times, hated him for doing so. But the knowledge that he'd been there somewhere in her past, that she'd been conceived in love, had made her feel . . . *normal*. More than that, she'd thought that one day he might just drop back into her life.

Now she knew he never would because he'd never known she existed. Nor could she tell him, because nobody had ever even known his friggin' *name*.

Forgetting Zeke, she sighed. Gustily. Oh, honestly. Nothing had changed since that phone call. She was the same person she'd been. As was Bebe. As for her mother . . . her mother was way beyond reach of recriminations. There was no point in stewing or blaming—or lashing out at anyone else.

She realized Zeke was tossing more curious glances her direction. She could give him credit, though, for respecting her silence.

"Sorry," she muttered.

"Apology accepted." He pulled the car into the lot. "While you're with the doctor, where could I pick up some new duds?"

Him? Here? A childish impulse seized her. "There." She nodded to the Wal-Mart across the street. "They'd have everything you need."

"You're kidding."

"And you're a snob." She wanted to sound teasing, but she sounded rude. Again. "I'm sorry. That's not the only choice, and someone is always making a trip to Kansas City or St. Louis, so if you want you can—"

"Stop apologizing." His mouth quirked. "Especially when you're right."

"Well, a lot of people around here do shop at Wal-Mart."

He eyed her vest. "But not you. Did you make that?"

"Yes." And she realized she'd put it on hoping he'd notice. She was such a sad case.

"Fashion design. Another talent." He put the car in park and opened his door. But before he stepped out, he looked back. "You know what, Patricia O'Malley? You're one very surprising woman."

He accompanied the words with a smile. He had a wonderful smile. She'd always noticed that about him, even when she'd only known him through the pages of *Country Dreaming* and his appearances with Van Castle on the Country Music Awards.

And that was all it took for her to sink back into

dithering. She suddenly wasn't sure she wanted him to leave at all. A bundle of neuroses didn't begin to describe it.

And not just neuroses, but murderous tendencies. By that afternoon, when they turned up Red Hollow Road, Zeke's departure had taken on more urgency. He needed to leave before she killed him.

It figured that now, *now,* when she would *lo-oove* to have him read every little piece of her mind, he was so distracted with his day's experiences that his intuition had deserted him. He'd become a complete chatterbox. For the first half of the trip back, he'd extolled the wonders of discount stores. For the second half, all the fun he was having chez O'Malley. It had been impossible to get a word in. And now, they were too close to home for her to let loose. Too close to Lily-Too's return from school. Her youngest got upset whenever anyone else got upset.

"And the day started before dawn. With a trip to the barnyard. Yet I've still enjoyed myself." He smiled. "Plus I've got new work boots. That's not far removed from hip boots. How poetic."

Hip boots? What in blue blazes was he talking about?

He finally realized she was still in the car. He looked over for the first time since he'd started yapping. "Leg hurt?"

Did her leg *hurt*? What did he think after manipulations on the X-ray table, followed by getting it wrapped toe to knee in glowing purple fiberglass (oh, the sacrifices a mother will make)? But that wasn't the worst of it. Not trusting herself enough to unpaste her lips, she just grunted.

He glanced at her again, apparently taking what she assumed was her resemblance to a prune for pain and not anger. "We'll get you some Tylenol."

Tylenol wouldn't help. The pain in her leg paled in

comparison to the beating her self-esteem had taken at the hands of the doctor's receptionist. No pill would help that.

The receptionist, a thin blonde brandishing fingernails polished to a sheen that would do the Hope diamond proud, was a country music fan, notably of the former Van Castle Band, as she'd oh-so-subtly displayed by drooling all over Zeke. Patsy Lee could have cared less who she—or he, for that matter—chose to flirt with, but when the receptionist had smirked at her with an unmistakable what-is-he-doing-with-*you* look, she'd been tempted to violence.

But that had been nothing . . . *nothing* . . . compared to the outrage she'd felt when Zeke—after bundling her up the elevator and into the waiting room and hanging around until she was summoned (looking *cool* while the receptionist salivated)—had asked the nurse to suggest that the doctor prescribe Patsy Lee a mild antidepressant.

She seemed, Zeke had explained, rather moody.

The receptionist and nurse had clucked. Oh, not over her. Over Zeke, sympathetic over the *moodiness* he had to put up with. And she . . . she'd been struck so completely dumb, she'd only been able to gape. Yet for all his psychic capabilities, he'd remained clueless to her feelings (you'd think the heaving bosom might have given him a hint). Instead, he'd given her an odd, expectant look, then looked disappointed when she said nothing. Disappointed? He should be glad that she hadn't lunged at him. But soon . . . soon . . .

She'd show him *moody*.

They pulled up her drive. Chickens scattered in front of the car; Sugar ran alongside, tongue lolling. As they reached the top, the school bus stopped to discharge Lily-Too, setting Dharma and Dowdy braying.

He braked near the front door. "We're home."

How astute. "Not here. Pull around back."

"It's a shorter walk from here."

"We always park in back."

"Not today," he said cheerfully.

She opened her mouth.

"Definitely not today. You've been the color of old paste since you got in the car." He rolled down his window, pulled a couple of biscuits out of his pocket and tossed them into tall grass. Sugar snuffled after them.

Old paste? "Clever way to keep your pants clean," she muttered, knowing the biscuits had nothing to do with protecting his clothes and everything to do with getting her into the house without Sugar's "help."

As he opened her door, his look said his cheer might be wearing thin. Grudgingly, she opened her mouth to apologize—although she'd demand a bigger one from him later—but the words died as she watched him watch Lily-Too. Lugging a backpack, her daughter meandered up the drive, stopping every few seconds to pluck a piece of grass or study a cloud. Finally looking up and spotting Zeke, she waved and started to run.

When he waved back, his heart was in his eyes.

She closed her mouth. He should have had children. When he looked back at her, his expression was tinged with regret, his smile strained. Why hadn't he? Her lips started to part on the question, but she pinched them shut.

He shook his head, mistaking discretion for more sourness. "C'mon . . . Alley-oop."

Instead of pulling her up by the hands, he used the technique the nurse had suggested to save wear on her arms. Leaning over, he cupped the backs of her elbows. Her hair brushed the side of his face; she smelled the crisp scent of lime. His touch was warm through her wool coat. The moment she was upright, he let go, leaving her to catch herself against the car while he rummaged behind the seat for her crutches. She sighed. Such an erotic moment.

Lily-Too ran up, more strands of hair out of, rather than in, the neat ponytail she'd started off with this morning.

Patsy Lee smoothed one back. "How was school today, Sunshine?"

"Okay," she said absentmindedly, gaze glued on the cast. "It's beautiful," she breathed.

"Really okay?"

Zeke's glance back was curious. She knew she sounded overly anxious. And if she got overly anxious, Lily-Too would get overly worried. But she couldn't help herself; she was a mom, for Pete's sake. He finally laid hands on her crutches and straightened.

"Kind of okay." Lily-Too bent to touch the fiberglass, then gave Patricia a worried look. "Do you like it?"

"Of course I do. Purple will keep me cheerful, just like you said."

"Ah, now I understand. Bright purple to keep your mom from feeling blue." Zeke winked at Lily-Too. "Good idea. Here, will you take this package while I help your mom?"

Pinking, her daughter smiled back, picked up the bags, and started toward the house.

"You're lucky." Zeke murmured, gaze following Lily-Too.

"I am."

He turned, as though just remembering her existence, and caught her staring. Hastily, she lowered her eyes.

"Do you know," he said, "how disconcerting it is when you see straight through my bullshit?" The words were light, but they had an edge.

She licked her lips. "If you'll just hand me my crutches, I can manage by myself."

His sigh was audible. "Don't be stupid. You'll fall and break your neck."

The screen door slapped as Lily-Too went inside.

"Don't be *stupid*?" The words burst out, propelled by all the day's frustrations.

"Yes, stupid." He gripped both crutches in one hand and with the other looped her arm around his neck. Grasping her around the waist, he steered her toward the porch.

Her tongue tangled with indignation. Her body grew more rigid with every step and her breath came in short puffs. He was so . . . so *alpha*. "Let me tell you something, Zeke Townley—"

The door squealed open again and she snapped her jaws shut, expecting Lily-Too. But it was Lil. As her sister-in-law stepped onto the porch, Zeke looked up and halted midstride. Patsy Lee lurched against him and pain shot up her leg. So what if his embodiment of everything female had just manifested itself—what was *she*? Dog meat?

"Sorry if I startled you," Lil said. "We parked in back."

"Told you," Patsy Lee muttered to Zeke.

"We brought the oysters." Lil's smile was mischievous.

Jon stepped out behind her. He was grinning, too.

Oysters . . . smirks . . . oh, no. Patsy Lee wanted to crawl under the porch with embarrassment. Were they nuts? She knew beyond the shadow of any doubt that an aphrodisiac was the farthest thing from Zeke's mind. But obviously it had lodged itself in theirs.

"Much obliged," Zeke said. "Chicken-and-oyster gumbo without oysters doesn't cut it."

"Sounds good." Jon jiggled Lil with his elbow. "Doesn't it sound good, hon?"

* * *

"Jon," she objected, but mildly, only mildly.

They exchanged a look and she felt Zeke stiffen. Oh, for God's sake, it wasn't one of those loving looks the two tossed around all the time; Zeke had no need—and no right—to be jealous. It was a wink-wink, nudge-nudge look. Anyone could see it. It was also the last humiliation she could stomach in what had been a very long day. She tried to push away, but Zeke's arm tightened.

He frowned at Lil and Jon. "What is this, high school? The woman needs a chair, a meal, and medicine, not lame jokes."

She was surprised, but his words didn't mollify her. She was tired of having him do her talking. Pushing again, she freed herself. "What *the woman needs* is to be left alone." She grabbed her crutches out of his hand and excused herself through gritted teeth.

Waving away Lil and Jon's apologies, she struggled up the steps, feeling Zeke's eyes on her back. She knew her gait was awkward, her hair mussed, and the only visible part of her face as red as if she'd been smacked with a paintball. She was also miserably aware that Lil looked perfect.

Reaching the door, she yanked it open, stepped inside, and let it slam behind her.

Chapter 8

By the next evening, as he steered the Cadillac in the direction of Cordelia to pick up Hank from astronomy club and Rose from drill team, Zeke felt as aggravated as Patricia had looked yesterday.

Surprisingly, he'd enjoyed yesterday. Barnyard. Pastoral drive. Prickly woman. And Wal-Mart. Go figure. But even before Lil and Jon appeared, the symbol of all the things he'd allowed to pass him by, he'd soured as much as Patricia. (Forget apples and peaches. She'd looked like a prune.)

One . . . watching Lily-Too had all too forcibly reminded him that the final straw that had broken Christine's back was his tentative suggestion that they think about children. And thinking of children, Christine, and lost opportunities had a way of wiping cheer out of his system. Two . . . he was tired of Patricia acting as though he'd come here with the sole purpose of making her life miserable. Three . . . when her hair, smelling of rosemary, had brushed his cheek, he'd grown all too aware of her flesh, warm and firm beneath her wool coat. . . . Beneath his hands. Hell. He'd dropped her like a hot potato. And four . . .

The last time he'd wanted anyone to lean on him,

he'd been fifteen. And by the time he was eighteen, he couldn't escape the responsibility fast enough.

He turned onto HH. He'd made this same trip late yesterday after Lil and Jon had left. When he'd returned with the teens, Patricia had already closeted herself in her makeshift bedroom. Lily-Too told him she'd asked for a sandwich, said she was tired, and had gone to bed. Even though a light had continued to shine under her door.

Resolving not to notice her absence, he'd shelved his plans for gumbo and whipped up a passable soufflé while the children did chores. The one thing he could count on from the pantry (besides chicken) was eggs. And more eggs. Feeling grouchy, he'd grated cheese. If it weren't for Patricia, they'd be dining out tonight at Lil and Jon's invitation and he could have avoided eggs all together.

Before they'd left, the Van Castles had urged Zeke and Patricia to accompany them to Philippe's, pronouncing it Phillip-*ees,* for supper. Correcting their French accent, he'd perked up at the possibility, however remote, of intercontinental cuisine. Until Jon, grinning, had informed him that it was not *Philippe's,* but *Phillip E's* (Phillip Esterharvey having earned a name for himself in the Tri-State Barbeque Competition, which had led to the opening of an all-the-ribs-you-can-eat diner on HH, not too far past the turnoff for Red Hollow Road).

At Jon's chortle over what was, after all, an understandable mistake, Zeke had become so cranky that Lil, after casting a look at Patricia's face, had suggested that perhaps they should wait for an evening out until her sister-in-law was better.

That was Lil all over, always smoothing things over, her feelings hidden under her carefully folded hands. Zeke knew he was being more cross than fair, but he didn't feel like giving Lil credit for short-circuiting plans that had needed short-circuiting. And he especially didn't wish to acknowledge that his ill temper wasn't Lil's fault.

Better to think that it was Lil who was bugging him rather than her sister-in-law, who wore her thoughts on her sleeve. Not that there was anything wrong with a few direct, maybe even some pointed, maybe even a dollop of far-too-insightful pronouncements, because at least a man didn't have to guess what was going on in her head. Unless he didn't want to know.

Or unless she wouldn't let him. Today she hadn't let him.

He turned off HH and onto the two-lane highway that led into town. Behind him, the sun dipped behind Ozark hills, leaving a sky bruised pink and purple.

Today Patricia hadn't even ventured into the parlor. She'd stayed in her room, claiming her ankle still hurt after yesterday's casting. She accepted the snacks he brought, the schoolwork he collected, and the prescription he picked up before collecting Rose and Hank last evening, but would only offer a thank-you before fixing her eyes firmly back on her books.

Beyond a ripple across her face that said she'd noticed, she didn't even comment on his new duds. He'd picked up shirts (realizing now that in an excess of zeal, he'd chosen wild plaids that even Daisy would approve of) and jeans at Wal-Mart, but his pièce de résistance had been a pair of overalls he'd thought would make her smile. They didn't. Although this morning the kitchen had rocked with the girls' hilarity (and Hank's smirk) when his overalls had made their debut.

After Patricia made it obvious she planned to play sphinx all day, he made himself useful again—making as much noise as he could. He banged the mop around the kitchen floor (with Sugar, daily mopping wasn't excessive), ran the old canister vacuum he found in a closet, and threw a load of clothes in the laundry, setting the dryer buzzer to high.

Feeling a tad sheepish over his childish behavior, he took Patricia lunch at midday, but when he returned with his own tray, suggesting they decide on an organized division of chores for the kids, she just stared at him with an expression as animated as concrete. "I have a headache. The noise, I think. I'd like to eat alone."

At that point, he'd almost stormed from the house forever. But the thought of Patricia's unsteady progress on those damnable crutches had stopped him. The image of Lily-Too's face . . . and Rose's . . . and Hank's . . . had stopped him. It wasn't fair for the kids to be saddled with her care. Even if the circumstances were far removed from the ones he'd faced as a youth, he hadn't been able to do it. Helping out was one thing; shouldering the whole load quite another.

He'd still stormed out—but only to stride along Red Hollow Road. Clouds the substance of cotton gauze had drifted across a blue sky checkmarked with geese pointing south, their honking a wistful echo in the woodland below. The sound had filled him with an odd yearning that had done nothing to improve his mood. Still, he'd been careful not to be gone too long. . . .

Just long enough to make her worry that he'd left for good. Not that she'd ever tell him if he'd succeeded.

Now, steering the Caddy around a curve, he entered Cordelia's town limits, marked by a Texaco Star Mart followed by the Sleep Inn, McDonald's, the post office, and a Dairy Cup, its neon ice cream cone glowing yellow and white against the gathering dusk. He continued to indulge his temper, starting with berating himself for allowing champagne and Jon's jibes to put him in this situation in the first place.

The highway narrowed as he approached the heart of town. He braked at a stoplight that was new since his last visit to Cordelia. Condos rose in Tudor splendor to his right; a strip mall spread out on his left, its new pavement black obsidian under the parking lot lamps. Unlike most small towns, Cordelia was growing as city folks welcoming retirement swelled the population, latching onto the town for its picturesque setting. Their presence had caused a boom in insurance companies, banks, and medical facilities, which had, in their turn, drawn new families here.

By the time he'd moved on, now watching the signs for the turn to the high school, he'd progressed to more recent grievances, images flickering through his head of Dharma's laid-back ears, Patricia's stubborn chin, the man-eating receptionist, and Hank's insolent gaze.

He barely paid homage to the charisma of the town. Normally, he appreciated the efforts to preserve the old square and its mellowed brick buildings that boasted storefronts with polished windows, freshly swept sidewalks, and flower boxes, currently stuffed with fading chrysanthemums. Cordelia had grown up around the square until it was a size where residents still found all the faces familiar, but the names now too numerous to remember. In the center of the square, St. Andrew's Church piously watched the comings and goings of the townsfolk, its gardens meticulously tended.

(At the wedding, Zinnia O'Malley had informed him that credit for the gardens belonged to the Ladies' Auxiliary, who had apparently spent last week's meeting discussing the fall bulb plantings. . . . As well as a certain pharmacist and the church's former choir director. The latter had seemed to occupy the most time on their agenda.)

He spotted the street and turned left. Traffic was light, but he remembered his first trip here during the summer almost a decade ago. The cars had been a never-ending ribbon unwinding between metro areas and the numerous lakes to the south.

He could leave. His departure wouldn't cause a stir beyond another hurried meeting in Zinnia O'Malley's kitchen. Certainly nobody, not even Patricia, would blame him. In fact, she'd jump (only metaphorically, of course) at the chance to help him pack. So what was stopping him? Pride. The ribbing that Jon would subject him to. Losing a bet. Breaking a promise. The children. And disappointing everyone, including himself.

Hell, any or all. He pulled up in front of the high school and resigned himself to finishing what he'd started.

When he returned with Hank and Rose in tow, total darkness wrapped the countryside. And his temper, which hadn't been improved by the squabble that had broken out after he mentioned a need for milk and Rose had suggested they stop at the Piggly Wiggly and Hank had objected.

"C'mon, Hank. I've got a huge test in American government tomorrow. It's on the way. Mom never has to know."

"It's not Mom. How can you ask me to—when you know I—" Hank had sputtered, cutting off his sentences every time he met Zeke's glance in the rearview mirror.

"I know, I know," Rose had soothed. "And I feel bad. But just this once? It's only milk."

Concentrating on navigating unfamiliar streets, Zeke had wondered what their shorthand meant—and what cause Patricia supported that was anti–Piggly Wiggly, but he'd left the kids to settle matters between themselves, only belatedly tuning in when he heard that the family usually withheld their custom due to a certain manager—one Ernie Beecham or Bertrand or Burcham or something.

By that time, they'd reached the store and Hank had given in, muttering something about bossy sisters. Thumping crossed arms on his chest, he'd said he'd wait in the car. After Rose and Zeke had finished shopping, it had taken them twenty minutes to locate the miscreant who had stomped off to watch the stars emerge.

When they finally reached the farmhouse and stepped inside, laden with groceries and backpacks, wonder of wonders, they found Patricia had deigned to leave her room. She was seated at the kitchen table, her foot up on another chair, watching Lily-Too, who was busy at the counter. Her bulky red sweater clashed obscenely with her cast, but did nicely complement the highlights in her hair and the blush on her cheeks. He thought she looked, well . . . cute.

Until she spotted the logo on the bags, that is.

"Why that store?" Her voice could freeze oil.

Apparently unwilling to rat out his sister, Hank frowned and said nothing.

Rose hesitated, then dropped her head. "I knew we shouldn't. I just—"

But Zeke slid in first. "They told me you'd object, but it was on the way. What do you have against, the, uh, Pig in a Poke, exactly?"

Lily-Too giggled. Hank looked at him with grudging approval, although the face he turned on Rose was one of continued disgust.

"It's Piggly Wiggly. The manager's a bigot," Patsy Lee muttered.

"Yeah?" Zeke glanced at Hank and wondered if

Hank's mutiny had any connection to the Internet site he'd visited two days ago, a site Zeke had looked up yesterday. Stayclose.org was a nonprofit devoted to helping homosexuals and their families maintain ties once the closet door was opened. He thought back to Hank's curiosity about gays in San Francisco. "I promise I'll avoid the place from now on." Shame stained Rose's cheeks, and he added, "Although it *is* convenient."

Rose gave him a small smile. Hank was shelving groceries and didn't look over, but now certainly wasn't the time to ask questions, anyway. Even if Zeke knew how to ask.

Apparently not wanting to pursue the topic further, Patsy Lee had pressed her lips together. He wondered if she knew something definite about her son, or if she just hated Beecham-Burcham-Whatever on principle. He couldn't ask that, either.

Lily-Too opened and closed a cabinet and Zeke looked over, only now registering a pan of water heating on the stove. Setting down his bags, he realized Lily-Too was opening a box. Of Kraft Macaroni & Cheese. The family size.

Over his dead body.

"Would you mind saving this for another night, Lily-Too?" Like after he was back in California.

She considered his words seriously. "I guess not. Not if I can help."

"Of course you can." With a cheerful demeanor designed not to hurt her feelings, he scooped the cheese sauce packet back into the box, hustled the box back into the cupboard, and dumped the pot. "We'll make gumbo before my oysters give up the ghost. They won't last much longer."

"Oysters? *Bleech.*" Continuing to groan—loudly—Rose deposited her bags next to his.

"And Rose, you can help Hank with donkey duty."

Rose stopped mid-*bleech*. "But I want to help, too. I'm a good cook, and I like hearing about San Francisco."

He glanced at Patricia; her face had gone even more sour. In just a couple of days, Rose had developed a curiosity about his hometown that seemed to grate on her mother. Or perhaps it wasn't Rose's interest in San Francisco that annoyed her; maybe it was just Rose's growing acceptance of him.

"It's your turn to help with the donkeys."

"But—"

"And Lily-Too didn't make those revolting noises when she heard the planned menu. Sounded like you needed an exorcism."

Rose grinned.

"Hank, when you come back, make sure Sugar isn't dripping mud. *And* make sure she understands that her bed lies at the foot of yours and not on my spare pillow. Today is the last time I want to open my eyes to a female with fur on her face."

Apparently recalling Zeke's outrage this morning, which included a sermon on the immorality of females who occupy men's' beds without an invitation, Rose's grin widened and Hank sniggered. They buttoned their jackets back up and headed outside, Rose tucking her hair under her collar.

He watched them go. "I don't think they took me seriously."

Lily-Too looked up at him. "Maybe that's because all the time you were talking about how mad you were at Sugar this morning, you were feeding her bread crusts."

He stopped as though struck by her wisdom. "Why, perhaps you're right."

She smiled shyly. "You're goofy."

Throughout the exchange, Patricia was silent as outer space.

After they'd unpacked the groceries (and he had rearranged some things in the pantry to make everything fit) and he'd helped Lily-Too pull down the Fiestaware for the dining room table (which he'd just decided would hold them all more comfortably than the one in the kitchen), he tied a towel around his waist and set to work.

Conscious of Lily-Too wandering in and out of the kitchen while he chopped chicken for the gumbo, he tried to ignore Patricia sitting behind him. Hard to do with her eyes boring two holes in his back. Finally, he couldn't stand it anymore.

He looked over his shoulder. *"What?"*

She nodded at the counter where he'd torn apart the chicken carcasses. "They won't eat that. I like oysters, but they don't. Most children don't."

"They can't always have their way. I like it. You like it. They'll get over it."

Out in the mudroom, Hank and Rose returned. Pulling off a stocking cap, Rose stuck her head in. Strands of her hair stood straight up in a fit of static electricity. "We're going up to start homework. Okay, Zeke?"

Patricia made a sound in her throat.

Thinking Rose could have chosen a better moment to ask him permission instead of her mom, he nodded, then ducked back to his task, hoping the tension mounting behind him would find an outlet somewhere else. The teens headed upstairs and a second later he heard Patricia fumble with her crutches. Thinking she was leaving, he blew out a breath he didn't realize he'd been holding. Then, smelling rosemary, he turned to see her just a few feet away.

She opened a cupboard. She reached in. Out came the box of macaroni and cheese.

"No," he said.

"Yes," she said.

Her face was mottled, that infernal chin hard as nails. Balancing on one foot, she scooped her hair behind her ear and ignored him.

Entering from the dining room, Lily-Too wandered up beside him. "Would you please get the salt and pepper?" She pointed up at a cupboard in front of him. "And the napkins."

Patricia had stopped to watch. Her disgruntlement was tangible.

He opened the door. On the top shelf—a very top shelf, considering the height of the ceilings in the house—were salt, pepper, napkins, sweetener packets, vitamin bottles, and a sugar bowl. "Why are all these things out of reach of everyone except Paul Bunyan?"

"Mom says when I was little, I used to like to empty everything out and play in it. So she took them off the table and put them up there."

"Hmm. And are you through indulging this weakness of yours?"

Forehead puckering, Lily-Too turned his words over, then her face cleared. She grinned. "No, I don't do it anymore."

"Then what do you say we put them down here?" On the bottom shelf, he pushed back some dishes to make room. After handing her the salt and pepper and some napkins, he started moving down the rest. Lily-Too headed back to the dining room.

"Stop it."

Zeke put the last item on the shelf, closed the door, then turned to face Patricia. "Oh, come on. It makes more sense to have things where everyone can reach them, and you know it."

Patricia's eyes narrowed. "I don't care how much sense it makes. Or doesn't make. I want them on the top shelf." She pointed with a crutch. "And I want everything you moved around in the pantry back the way it was."

He crossed his arms. "I'm not changing a thing."

He'd never seen anyone turn such an alarming shade of red. She wasn't one of those women whose looks were enhanced by emotion, although he found the flash in her eyes amazing. They were practically spitting gold ingots. For the second time that day, he witnessed a heaving bosom. Unfortunately, she caught his gaze making the brief dip to her chest.

"I have had enough!" Each word sliced the air. "You think you can waltz in here and take over without asking me about anything. Telling me what to do, ordering my children around, deciding what we eat, where we eat, when we eat, and where we buy our food. And now you want to reorganize my kitchen?"

"It is wanting organization."

"We liked everything the way it was. Now put those things back."

"I think you're forgetting that I'm doing you a service by being here at all."

"You can take your service and shove it."

Highly entertained, he stifled a smile. "Maybe I'm cynical, but it seems to me that—"

"You're not cynical," Patricia broke in. "You're bitter."

Zeke's good humor faded. "And you aren't reserved by nature. You're scared by life."

Silence fell.

They stared at each other. Lily-Too's frightened face peeked in through the doorway, then disappeared.

Patricia recovered first. "Lily-Too!"

They heard the front door open and slam shut.

"I need to find her. She gets upset when people get mad."

Before he could react, Patricia had wrestled her crutches into place and started toward the doorway, hurry outpacing skill. She swung wildly, then fell backward. Pushing off the counter, Zeke caught her under her arms just before she hit the floor.

"Easy."

"Hellfire." Patricia was near tears.

He helped her up, his head filling with rosemary, her hair silk soft under his chin. Concerned that she might have injured herself, it took a moment before he grew conscious that he could feel the seam of her bra and the soft flesh beneath. Under his fingertips, her ribs ended and her flesh swelled into the firm rounds of her breasts.

Good God, it was unbelievably erotic.

He practically dropped her onto a chair. "You're fine. Aren't you fine?"

When she nodded, he ducked into the mudroom, collected his jacket and Lily-Too's, then tucked a flashlight into his belt. Reentering the kitchen, he dropped Lily-Too's jacket over a chair, scrambled into his own, picked up hers again, and headed for the door. Patricia watched his frenzy as if he'd suddenly lost his mind.

"Don't you worry. I'll find her."

Reaching the main door, he thanked God Patricia's mind-reading skills had seemed to desert her. Better she think him insane rather than getting a peek at what had just gone through his head. Which *was* insane, come to think of it. He opened the door. The cold air hit him with a slap. Just what he needed.

Pausing on the front porch until his pulse was normal, he called for Lily-Too. Unlike the other night, the stars were hidden behind a web of clouds backlit by the moon. Flicking on his flashlight, he swept it over the slope to the road. The maples stood in dark silhouettes, rocking gently under a halfhearted north wind.

Halfhearted or not, it was still cold. He thought a

moment and decided a little girl without a coat would probably find refuge in the chicken coop, kept lit and above freezing through the winter. Not from compassion: something to do with hens' reluctance to lay when days grew short.

Turning up his collar, he trudged around back, chewing on Patricia's comment. He'd known when Christine had left that his usual cynicism had become tinged with a certain bitterness, so it wasn't a huge surprise that Patricia had pegged him correctly. But the swiftness of her insight bothered him. And hurt. Enough that he'd retaliated, something he now regretted.

Avoiding the darkened outbuilding where the donkeys were stabled (he and Dharma now tolerated each other, but they'd never be close), he headed toward the light spilling from the one small window of the coop. Left to roam where they would during the day to peck the earth for anything edible—and it seemed chickens thought anything was edible—the chickens were shut in at night to keep them from becoming fox fodder.

Reaching the coop, he peeked through the window. The grime on the glass smudged the scene, but he could see Lily-Too. Under a lone lightbulb, she sat on top of an upended wood box, leaning forward, chin on her knees, drawing in the dirt with a stick. He could hear her humming. The chickens' usual squabble was notably absent. Several wood contraptions, looking like short, broad ladders, leaned against (or maybe they were bolted to) the walls. Claws hooked around the ladders' rungs, more than a dozen hens had their heads tucked under their wings.

He moved to the door and tapped. "Lily-Too? It's Zeke."

Inside, the humming stopped. After a pause, the door opened.

He held out her jacket. "You must be cold." He kept his voice soft, but stirred up some disgruntled clucking, anyway.

Lily-Too took her jacket and stepped back. Expecting a foul odor to waft out, he was surprised to find only an odd, musty smell. He edged in, moving at slow speed to keep the disturbance down, and pulled the door closed. Beneath his new work boots, the earth was soft, a mix of wood shavings, sawdust, and other things he likely didn't want to know about. Across from the ladder-things, about two feet off the ground, were a series of cubicles, each fronted by a perch and holding a layer of hay.

"Hey . . . your mom and me got a little mad at each other. But it wasn't a big deal and everything's okay now." He'd make sure of it, when he returned.

Lily-Too didn't move. Holding her jacket, she watched him from big eyes.

He cast around for a topic to put her at ease. "This is quite an operation. Why don't they sleep in there?" He pointed to the cubes. "Looks a lot more comfortable to me."

A few hens grew louder.

"Shhh. Chick, chick, chick." She crooned, soothing them, not calling them. They subsided. Lily-Too studied him and, apparently satisfied his interest was genuine, her shoulders relaxed. Moving slowly, she shrugged into her jacket. "Those are nesting boxes, where they lay eggs. They use the perches for when they sleep, but they don't fall off because their claws lock, kind of like they're paralyzed."

One hen squawked. Reaching over, Lily-Too grasped the protester by the legs and cradled it in her arm. She stroked its neck and it settled.

Zeke seated himself on the box. "We weren't angry with you, sweetheart. Is that what you thought?"

She nodded.

"How come?"

She looked down at the hen. "People get mad at me a lot."

He snorted. "You're feeding me a line."

A wisp of a grin came and went. "Not everybody. But . . . I don't always pay attention. I try, but I just get, well, bored, I guess." She looked up, face suddenly fierce. "But I'm not dumb."

"Of course you're not." He was incensed. From what he'd seen, she was quite shy—and quite bright. "Who thinks you are?"

"Mrs. Sherlock."

"Your teacher?"

Tears filling her eyes, her gaze dropped again.

"Tell her to go to hell."

Lily-Too's head popped up and she giggled. "I can't do that."

Her giggle was wonderful, but the chickens took exception. Wings flapped as they stoked themselves to near panic.

"No, you can't." Zeke raised his voice over the increasing noise. "But teachers are people and they make mistakes. Mrs. Sherlock's opinion is only Mrs. Sherlock's. And . . . don't tell *anyone* I said this, promise?"

Solemnly, Lily-Too nodded.

". . . I think Mrs. Sherlock is the one who's dumb." When Lily-Too smiled again, he stood up. "I'm sorry. Seems I've incited a full-scale insurrection."

"A . . . ? Oh, a *riot*. That's okay. I can calm them down."

With that angel face, he wasn't surprised. "I'll wait for you outside."

He let himself out. Stuffing his hands in his pockets, he moved around to the window, curious what she'd do. Still stroking the hen, Lily-Too stood in the center of the coop, her hair a nimbus around her face. He shook his head. Idiot teacher.

Lily-Too's chest expanded as she took a deep breath. Turning in a slow circle, she let it out. In song. Her clear voice shimmered sweetly through the walls and rose into the night. Goose bumps formed on his arms. He'd heard plenty of singers in his day, and he could tell she was exercising restraint. He wondered what she sounded like when she let herself go. Something spectacular, he'd wager.

He forgot Mrs. Shylock, Sherlock, whatever . . . and his ill humor . . . as Patricia's daughter worked her enchantment.

After they'd returned indoors, the enchantment stayed with him all through a supper of chicken-and-oyster gumbo *and* Kraft Macaroni and Cheese. His acceptance of the latter and Patricia's urging the children to at least try the former established a truce between them, and the air was noticeably lighter.

After they ate, Patricia suggested Hank join her in the parlor since it was the girls' turn to clean up the kitchen on the schedule Zeke had set, but Hank remembered a math test on the morrow, or said he did, and headed upstairs to closet himself in his room as he did every night. Patricia watched him go with a worried look on her face before hobbling into the parlor.

Zeke sent Rose in after her to build a fire. The house held its usual chill except for the kitchen, which was toasty from the woodstove the kids had told him they'd use for real in coming months when they'd have the occasional downstairs camp-out. Apparently, during winter storms, the electricity failed with the same predictability as someone skidding into the ditch that ran alongside Red Hollow Road when it snowed. Lovely, living in the country.

Turning to the dishes, he squirted some soap into the sink.

Lily-Too sidled up. "Girls are s'posed to do dishes tonight."

"Since Rose is busy, how 'bout I help?"

"Okay." She watched the suds fill the sink.

"I heard you singing," he said, keeping his voice casual.

Her face turned pink. "The chickens like it."

"I'd think a lot more than chickens would like it." He handed her a dishrag. "You wash, I'll dry?"

She nodded.

"Have you ever sang before, like in a choir?"

"No." Her answer was quick and emphatic.

"Why not? Don't you like to sing?"

"Yes." Her hair had fallen forward, hiding all but the curve of her cheek. It was bright red. "But I'd be—it'd be—I just don't want to. Mom said I should try out for the Christmas pageant. There's a part at the end where somebody sings 'Silent Night' while everyone else freezes like they're praying over baby Jesus. She thought I could do that."

"You'd get the part, hands down."

She sneaked a look at him. "I would?"

"Definitely."

"You have to sing alone." She fell silent. Only the swish of dishwater broke the quiet. "Well, there won't be a pageant this year, anyway." She sounded relieved.

"Ah, that's right. Because of the illicit doings of a certain choir director."

Again those blue eyes looked up at him. "The ill what?"

Feeling a surge of protectiveness, he scolded himself. Nothing should ever be allowed to touch her innocence. Oh, he knew it would happen sooner or later, but on his watch, it wouldn't be sooner. "Nothing.

I mean there won't be a pageant, because the choir director left."

When they were finished, Lily-Too left to join Rose in the sitting room, where they flipped on the TV. The sound of a laugh track drifted down the hallway. He fixed two mugs of tea and carried one to Patricia. She was on the sofa, afghan over her legs, her accounting text in her hand. Putting down the book, she accepted the mug and, sipping, watched him over its rim. He settled into the winged chair and put his feet up. When their eyes met, she switched her gaze to the fire.

Okay, he'd go first. "I want to apologize. You're right—I've been about as subtle as a steamroller. As for my comment on your outlook, I ask you to put that down to a rude remark made by a"—he smiled slightly—"bitter old man."

"You're not old."

He laughed. "But I *am* bitter?"

"Well . . . sometimes it seems . . . And yet you've done so much. I mean, your music; you're leaving a legacy. You should be proud."

"I am. I was. But now I don't know what—" He stopped, annoyed with himself.

"—What to do with yourself," she finished, then looked annoyed with *her*self. "But that's none of my business, and I'm sorry I said that." She hesitated then reached out a hand. "Friends?"

"Friends." He half rose, leaned forward, and took her fingers. The memory of his hands on her flesh rose in his head. Trying not to appear hasty, he let go and settled back in his chair. "You're right, you know. That's not what upset me. You figured me out way too fast. I didn't think I was so transparent."

"Me, either. I'm scared of a lot of things, I guess." Her gaze returned to the fire. "It seems like whenever I drum up enough courage to do something, it doesn't turn out right."

"Like what?"

She started. "Oh. Well, there's school, for one thing."

"I know you had to miss classes this week, but with your grades, no problem."

"Except I hate them. Oh, I like English lit, but . . . Accounting Principles, Effective Human Resource Management . . ." She shuddered. "Last semester was even worse."

He paused, his mug halfway to his lips. "Then why take them?"

"For the business degree. For Lil. It's the least I can do after all she's done for me. Lil wants to retire in a few years after Michael is out of school, so that she and Jon can travel. She wants me to take over Merry-Go-Read, all three stores."

"She'll just sign them over?"

"Oh, I'll pay her from a percentage of the profits. A token gesture, that's all it is, but that's the way she wants it. She'd like to keep the stores in the family—maybe someday one of my children or hers, or our niece, Kathleen, will want them. There's so much about business I don't know, though. I think a business degree will help. I mean, it can't hurt. It would be awful if I took over and the stores failed because I didn't know enough."

"Surely you're already learning everything you need from experience."

"Maybe, except, well, it's something I wanted to do for myself, too. For my confidence, I guess. I've got credits from my first trip to college so—"

"What's your degree?"

She looked wistful. "I don't have one. I was in fine arts, but had to drop out after sophomore year when my mother got sick again. But the point is, I only have to go another couple of years to have enough credits to graduate. That's not so long."

He rubbed the rim of his mug with his thumb. "Unless I'm forgetting something, Lil doesn't have a degree. Yet she's been successful."

"But she has . . . well, *you* know."

"Uno?"

"You. *Know.*" She gave him a knowing look of a stripe he couldn't interpret. "She has grace. Style. Beauty. Intelligence. Warmth. Person—"

"I get it. And which of those things are you lacking?"

Patricia's snort almost blew out the fire.

He frowned. Her thinking was skewed, but given his earlier pledge to avoid high-handedness, he decided to let the matter drop.

She sipped at her tea again. "This is really good. I taste chamomile, maybe a hint of peppermint, lemon? Is it something Rose got at the store?"

"No. I got it in Sedalia yesterday. Wait—" Setting down his mug, he went to the kitchen.

When he returned, he held out the box of Celestial Seasonings tea bags to her. She took it from him, studied the label, and started to laugh.

She had a lovely laugh. Deep and rich, like her smile.

"Perfect," she said, looking up at him, eyes brimming.

"I thought so." He smiled back.

Before he'd visited Wal-Mart, he'd spotted a natural foods store and had stopped in. Knowing she was a tea drinker, he'd studied the various boxes, then had chosen one especially for her: Tension Tamer Tea.

"By the way," she said, looking at him over the rim of her mug, eyes still smiling. "I like your overalls."

And, damn, if the stuff didn't work.

Chapter 9

Patsy Lee didn't know whether it was Tension Tamer Tea, frank talk, or a busy schedule (at least for Zeke), but the tension in the household eased over the next ten days as the family found a new rhythm and Zeke embraced country life, in love with the novelty, Patsy Lee surmised, more than anything else.

Clad in jeans and one of the variety of loud flannel shirts he'd bought at Wal-Mart, he jumped new-boots-first into each day, letting Sugar out, ladling oatmeal, and filling cat bowls before the rest of them had even poked a toe out of bed into the chill of the mornings.

Then, after chores were done and the buses had collected the children for school (Hank not dashing back for something he'd forgotten more than twice a week now that Zeke had suggested he organize himself at night), he settled Patsy Lee on a lawn chair under a blue china sky, where she directed him at the tasks she couldn't do.

In the garden, while October wind chased leaves across the yard, he stripped dead vines off stakes, turned soil, and added compost. Donning a dust mask, but sneezing anyway, he broke up litter on the chicken coop floor and added new. He even mucked out the stable, his nose screwed up in protest, and chopped wood for the inevitable winter electrical outages, wielding an axe with more eagerness than skill while she covered her eyes. It wasn't long before his muddy boots were as common a sight on her welcome mat as his tall figure was at the stove in her kitchen, although she suspected his homesteading zeal would eventually fade.

But not his love of cooking. That seemed as genetic as his dark hair and eyes. One afternoon before the children returned home from school, she kept him company while he made supper. Outside, mist had painted the landscape in shades of gray. Inside, the kitchen was aglow with color, warmth, and the scent of meatballs browning for the Italian wedding soup he was making.

At the table, she peeled carrots for him. "Did your mom teach you to cook?"

"No, she reigned over the rest of the home, but not the kitchen." From what she'd heard, his mother still wielded a scepter. If Zeke left his cell phone on, he received a barrage of phone calls that he handled with a fond exasperation. "When it came to the kitchen, my dad was king. He cooked weekends; involved us all in the process." Chopping spinach, he chuckled. "When we were through, the kitchen didn't need cleaning, it needed demolition. Mom would scold us within an inch of our lives until we'd polished every last teaspoon."

"It sounds wonderful." It did; her childhood had been quiet and without siblings.

"It was until Dad died." He dropped the spinach in a pot of chicken broth. "After that, Mom did her best, but her heart wasn't in it. No grief counseling or Paxil, of course. Back then, you just soldiered on."

With five children. She thought back to when Henry had died. She'd grieved, certainly—Henry's death had left an emptiness that his laugh, quick hugs, and lazy charm had once filled—but she hadn't felt like throwing the covers over her head. Of course, she'd also been pregnant with Lily-Too and, with Daisy only nine at the time, she hadn't had any older children to lean on. Covers hadn't been an option.

"And then there were the money worries. The lawsuit wiped us out."

The lawsuit. "What happened exactly?" As soon as the question was out, she realized how intrusive it was. "I'm sorry—you don't need to tell me."

"It's okay. The sting's gone. He had wine with dinner. Not a lot, but enough. Enough to put the other driver in the hospital for a couple months. Enough for the other driver to sue his estate." Zeke shook his head. "Senseless. It was all just . . . stupid."

Senseless, stupid . . . and had stolen the rest of his youth. "I read . . . well, didn't you drop out to go to work and help with your sisters?"

He nodded.

"Then you saved your family . . . like Lil saved mine."

"Don't canonize me. For one thing, I hated school. For another, we all pitched in." He glanced over his shoulder. "Like with Lil . . . I'll bet you didn't sit around with your thumb up your nose."

Nice image. "Pitched in? You gave up high school, college . . ." She'd given up nothing, but she wondered at a mother who would ask her son for that kind of sacrifice.

He diced an onion, deftly, efficiently, just like he did everything. "But just like it did for Lil, everything turned out fine. Better than fine. I got my GED. I met Jon. I've read as many books as a PhD. I've traveled the world. And there is absolutely no doubt that I will end my days with a pot of gold and a sharp crease in my trousers. Money is what I was after when

I left home, and I found it. But as my mother now reminds me with tedious regularity, there's more to life than that."

"Except—" She bit her lip.

"Except what?"

"Well, it doesn't take Freud to figure out why you never wanted a family. You'd already had your fill."

There was silence while he scraped the onion off the cutting board into the pot. "For a long time, that's what I thought, too. I'm no longer so sure."

For some reason she couldn't identify, she felt flustered after that comment, but a phone call from Rosemary Butz had put an end to her awkwardness. The president of the Ladies' Auxiliary was calling to check to see if Patsy Lee would still be able to provide the dozen jars of spaghetti sauce she'd promised for the fund-raising booth at the approaching Oktoberfest.

Catching the gist, Zeke protested under his breath that nobody should expect her to cook in her current condition. Unable to clearly hear what either one of them were saying, she finally held the phone out, said, "Of course, you're right," and asked him to extend her apologies.

Putting the phone to his ear, he started out strong. "Listen, Ms. Butz . . ." but as minutes passed, his sentences became limited to *uh-huhs* and *mmms*. Adopting a look of polite interest, Patsy Lee propped her chin on her hands and watched him.

After a half an hour, he hung up. He looked dazed. "The number of jars is now two. . . ." His voice faded into a mumble.

"I'm impressed. Just two," she said, pretending she hadn't made out the rest.

He glared. "Two . . . *dozen*. And I'm afraid I'll have to break your neck if I hear even the tiniest hint of another chortle out of you."

But despite his grumbling, he not only ensured the

jars of sauce were made, boxed, and delivered early Saturday to the event's staging ground at St. Andrew's Church, but he returned to escort her and the children there later.

At the Oktoberfest, Zeke's former renown caused some stir. Although she could tell he wasn't thrilled with the fuss, he honored requests for autographs and the occasional gushing fan with a graciousness that successfully hid his distaste, although he did demur at taking a turn on the Gospel Pickin' Stage. Watching him, it struck her that it hadn't been flirtation she'd seen at the doctor's office last week when she'd been caught up in her own trials; he'd simply displayed the same cordiality with the nurse and receptionist that he was now according his fans, like them or not. While on that day she'd seen his celebrity as only one more misery she had to deal with, and now had grown accustomed to seeing him with muck on his boots, she'd do well to remember he was completely at ease with fame. Just as he was with wealth. His normal world was far removed from her small planet.

Which is why, when he brought her cider and kettle corn at her place on a bench just a little removed from the Ladies' Auxiliary booth (to their chagrin, set up next to the Budweiser Beer Garden), before shepherding Lily-Too to the Ferris wheel spinning in Memorial Park down the block, Patsy Lee wasn't surprised when the few appraising looks cast her direction faded as the day wore on. Of course they'd fade. Even soused, nobody could possibly believe he'd look twice at her, especially if they noted the way he stared at Lil whenever she chanced by with Jon.

Idiot man.

Knowing her rancor was overblown, she put her bad mood down to tiredness and then forgot it completely after they returned home and Lily-Too threw up her lunch, an unbalanced meal of Sno-Kones, funnel cakes, and cotton candy. Zeke looked so worried, she didn't scold him for his overindulgence.

Besides, he normally took good care of their diets. Under his command, their menu was heavy on vegetables, light on calories. She'd thought she'd gain weight with her lack of activity, but instead she'd actually lost a few pounds. She was also getting more rest than she had in years.

Along with lying in bed later than she had since Daisy was born, Zeke insisted she rest every day after lunch—as though watching him work in the mornings was taxing—her tea and books nearby, blues soft on the stereo.

She'd loved the blues as long as she could remember—the music didn't whitewash with false cheer, but neither was it dismal. It was real, that's all, and she preferred things unvarnished. Over the years, she'd picked up recordings that ranged from Robert Johnson and Muddy Waters to B.B. King and Eric Clapton.

Zeke knew them all, of course. While she attended to homework and Zeke to housework, he sang. And when the chores (more than she ever did in a day) were complete, he often grabbed up his Hofner to jam with the music. She'd continue to work, peeking to watch him, wondering if the passion he felt for music would ever anchor his life again the way it had when he'd played with Van Castle.

As absorbed as he was during those interludes, she was always surprised when he remembered to sheathe the Hofner in time to meet Lily-Too as she stepped off her bus. Watching them from the window, Patsy Lee finally identified the odd wrench she'd felt the first time she'd seen them walking together. It wasn't jealousy. It was regret. Lily-Too looked at Zeke the same way she would have looked at her father had Henry lived to know her.

How Lily-Too would handle Zeke's inevitable departure concerned Patsy Lee, but the way her daughter was blossoming under his attention outweighed her worries. Late each afternoon, Lily-Too joined Zeke at the upright, where he strummed accompaniment to her keyboard, adjusting his baritone to provide the harmony he'd once given Jon's tenor, offering her unobtrusive instruction and heaping her with praise.

Not once since they'd started playing together had Lily-Too returned from school with red eyes. Up until Mrs. Sherlock sent home a note requesting another conference, Patsy Lee hoped Lily-Too's problems in school had evaporated. But nobody could ever accuse Lily-Too's teacher of ducking an issue. Lily-Too's mother, though, was not nearly as unskilled: She stuck the latest note under a paperweight in the sitting room, and within a day it had been papered over by bills, ignored if not entirely forgotten.

Patsy Lee just didn't have the heart to jostle Lily-Too's world right now. Thanks to Zeke, her daughter glowed.

And she wasn't the only one. Occasionally when Patsy Lee looked up during Lily-Too's lessons, she was captured by the joy on Zeke's face. Feeling like she was intruding, she ducked her head back to her work, wondering who was benefiting most from these lessons, her daughter or Zeke. Or . . .

Or, thinking of the peace that stole across her heart at those moments, wondering if it was herself.

In the evenings, Zeke charged Hank (if he was sans an astronomy club meeting) with the start of supper and Lily-Too with evening egg collection while he headed off to collect Rose from drill team practice, now scheduled daily as the girls prepared for the homecoming game. When they returned, Zeke reclaimed the kitchen, directed after-supper cleanup, and then, despite Hank's protests that he didn't need help, accompanied her son on donkey duty.

One evening, she hobbled into the kitchen, intending to ask Hank for his attendance card just as they were shrugging on coats.

Stuffing a granola bar in his pocket, Zeke was giving Hank a wry look. "Thanks to you, Dharma now takes me for an easy mark. Bullies me into a treat every time I see her."

She'd noticed that Dharma had watched Zeke muck out the stable with a wariness unlike the normally friendly donkey. She'd wondered why. "What do you mean, thanks to Hank?"

At the sound of her voice, both of them started.

Hank's gaze darted between them. "When Zeke first got here—"

"Did I say, *thanks to you*? I meant *just like you*."

He had not.

"I noticed parallels between your son and that donkey from the moment I arrived." Zeke's smile was easy. "Stubborn, of course. And they both take a while to warm up."

Hank looked relieved, and her frown deepened, but once Hank handed over his card and she saw he hadn't skipped a single hour, she let the matter drop. Whatever Hank might have done, it seemed the two had settled things between them. More than that, she saw friendship developing, Zeke's tinged with a protective edge. Which was fine. Her son seemed fragile sometimes and in need of protecting.

Not only was her son present and accounted for and her youngest flourishing, but Rose was also benefiting from a household that ran with nary a tangle in its skein. Rose loved the new organization. Her normally great grades became stellar, although her complaints of boredom with her academics increased.

Noting Zeke's puzzlement while Rose bemoaned the simplicity of Algebra II over supper one evening,

Patsy Lee explained, "You see, Rose is in the AP classes that are offered, but she's outstripped their scope."

"I'll graduate after my junior year." Rose flipped back her hair. "Because I'll have already aced everything they offer."

"Except Humility 101," Hank said, rolling his eyes.

Rose tried to poke Hank with her fork. He ducked out of the way.

"Play nice." Zeke deftly plucked the fork out of Rose's hand and winged it toward a bulletin board next to the mudroom doorway. It stuck there, quivering. The children giggled.

"Zeke!" Patsy Lee protested.

"What? Oh." Zeke turned to the children. "Don't try this at home."

Rose got up to get another fork. "I wanted to go to private school, but Cordelia's so lame; the closest one is in Sedalia. I'd have to board and Mom won't let Aunt Lil and Uncle Jon pay for it." She plunked back on her chair.

Not this can of worms again. "Rose, please." Patsy Lee's voice held a warning, although she could understand her daughter's disgruntlement. Rose didn't understand her objections, especially since her mother didn't want to tell her they had less to do with increasing her debt to Lil and Jon and everything to do with Rose living away from home.

Zeke looked at Hank. "Is Humility 101 a prerequisite for Appreciation 102?" He turned to Rose. "Be thankful for what you've got."

Hank grinned. Rose ducked her head. "Sorry."

"No problem. We both put our foot in it." He turned a stern gaze on Lily-Too. "Something you're supposed to prevent."

She smiled at him.

"Besides, Cordelia is . . . quaint and charming. And

friendly," he added. Everyone stopped chewing to stare at him in disbelief. Apparently, he'd forgotten that following the hubbub he'd raised at the Oktoberfest, he'd privately grumbled that Cordelia was too small for safe human habitation. He looked around the table, "Okay. So it's also a little insular for a city boy."

"In-soo-what?" Lily-too asked.

He leaned toward her. "There aren't enough ethnic restaurants."

"Not like in San Francisco," Rose and Hank said in unison, grinning at each other.

Both had been captivated by his vivid descriptions of the city by the bay, and even Patsy Lee could admit the images he painted of Russian Hill, with its crooked streets and steep walkways, left her with a momentary yearning for bougainvillea and glimpses of white fog threading through the Golden Gate Bridge.

Later that evening, as they'd settled with books in the parlor, she'd resumed the conversation.

"I know Cordelia can feel stifling—it is insular."

And some of the people could be worse than narrow-minded. Remembering the feelings of ostracism she'd grown up with in Columbia, an isolation that had intensified once she'd moved here, where homosexuality was even less accepted, a familiar rash of loneliness mixed with resentment itched under her skin.

She realized Zeke was watching her, eyes sharp, and smoothed her expression. "I mean, anyone who doesn't grow up here is treated like a newcomer. But it's home." She sighed and opened her book. "I do wish Rose liked her school more, though. I'd hoped joining the drill team would keep her from being bored, but even though she loves it, it just seems like it's only made her more busy. Sometimes I worry she's not getting the challenge she needs."

"I wouldn't worry. There are far worse problems she could have."

The exchange warmed her far more than its brevity warranted. Unlike the other O'Malley women, she often felt the lack of anyone close to share her worries. She carefully chose what she imparted to the family, knowing her confidences would inevitably become fodder over O'Malley supper tables.

And she had nobody else but family to tell. Moving to Cordelia so late in her childhood, marrying Henry, and having children so rapidly, not to mention her rural isolation, and a reserved (dull) personality, she'd not made many friends. Not close ones, anyway.

So having Zeke here was nice. It wasn't, she hastened to tell herself, that Zeke was particularly close, but right now he was . . . handy.

Not just as a sometime confidante, either. Since her accident, Lil regularly called, as did Zinnia, but Lil rarely dropped by and Zinnia not at all. Lil because work and home left her little time; Zinnia because Zeke was adroit in discouraging her efforts, something Patsy Lee found surprising until he explained his own mother had given him years of practice.

Zeke did see Jon, though. On evenings when Zeke's chauffeur services weren't needed, he'd meet Jon at the Rooster Bar & Grill in town. After his second such outing, Zeke told her he'd be helping Jon some weekends with the Van Castles' charitable efforts at Vreeley Home in Kansas City. Jon, Zeke said, had deemed it a mission of mercy.

"Although I think I've done my share of *merciful* already."

Despite his grumbling, Patsy Lee saw a spark, a version of the one that lit his face when he worked with Lily-Too. It was a glow she thought he should fan. But she didn't say anything, afraid to disturb the camaraderie growing between them as they talked.

And talked. Over chores, over supper, over their books.

Listening quietly and privately thinking it seemed he'd been a long time without real companionship (*et tu*?), she learned not only about his years with Van Castle, his love of San Francisco, and his parents, but also about his sister, Teresa. In her midthirties, Teresa had divorced several years before.

"For the third time, to our mother's disgust," Zeke said one afternoon over the tea he'd brought her. "Her husbands are still stunned at the speed with which they found themselves married, divorced, and divested of a good chunk of change."

"Is she married now?"

"No. She's devoted herself to becoming a Paris Hilton clone. She parties. She shops. She travels. Everywhere. In fact, in her last phone call—I was too slow with the off button—Mom mentioned that even though she just got back from the Costa del Sol, Terri's off right now on a trip to Vegas with—" He stopped.

She frowned. "With?"

"Her best friend. Christine." He lapsed into silence.

"Emerald eyes, magnolia skin."

"What?"

"Nothing." Feeling her face fire up, Patsy Lee bent her head to her tea cup. She remembered Christine. Hair the gold and red of sunset. Willowy figure. She'd accompanied Zeke on his last visit to Cordelia seven, maybe eight, months earlier. Jon had mentioned a breakup.

Did Zeke still mourn? She looked at him through her eyelashes. Or was that look on his face because he was thinking that his sister's hollow lifestyle wasn't that far removed from his own?

She decided not to pry. Not only was it none of her business, but she didn't want to talk about regrets.

Her enforced idleness had given her too much time to think of the past and wonder about the future. She felt like life was suspended. Watching Zeke's maniacal attention to everything in her household, guessing that his activity was a sop to boredom and too many deep thoughts, she wondered if the productive bustle of her own life before she'd broken her ankle might have been masking a similar discontent.

A discontent that had followed her into her present inactivity. She wished she could relax and enjoy this interlude, but too many things disturbed her peace: an e-mail from Daisy that had mentioned Danny too many times and her classes not at all; there was that note from Mrs. Sherlock, and Hank's continued isolation; and what she'd learned about her father. . . . Still agitated whenever she thought of her mother's lies and Bebe's subterfuge, she still couldn't manage more than shallow chitchat during Bebe's near-daily calls to check on her.

She felt shadows lurking in the corners, too elusive to define, but waiting to pounce.

By the time Zeke's second week with them ended, the pain in her broken ankle had subsided a great deal, but, tired of its solo act, her good foot now ached come nightfall. She'd done as instructed and kept both feet elevated as much as she could, which was fine with her, as she hated her crutches. But hate them or not, she practiced with them each morning and evening, Zeke hovering nearby.

In a compromise they'd reached between her insistence on limiting his stay to two weeks, his concerns she might need him for four, and Zinnia's meddling to keep him there for the rest of his natural life, they'd decided he'd leave in another dozen days. Patsy Lee wanted no reason for him to stay longer.

Because among all her concerns, one had started to overshadow all of the rest: her realization that she'd become partial to the scent of lime soap served up with her breakfast and the sound of a baritone wishing her good night

Zeke shivered. "Cold out here. You warm enough?"

Just shy of halftime at the Cordelia High School homecoming game, exactly two Fridays after she'd broken her ankle, Zeke caught her shoulders in a hug that couldn't be called anything other than brotherly. He'd scooted up close when Lily-Too had abandoned her seat between them for the concession stand.

"I'm fine." Wishing she'd remembered gloves, she untucked her hands from between her thighs and tugged down her cap. She appreciated the warmth of his arm, but death from exposure was less important right now than getting his arm out from around her. His touch reminded her of the moment when he'd caught her from falling, his fingers innocently pressing against the sides of her breasts. A woman could only take so much.

In front of them, the Cordelia Bulldogs in their green-and-gold glory fought back against the Versailles Tigers. For the last two quarters, the two teams had chased each other on the scoreboard, leaving little distance between them from when they'd started. First one team was up a few points, then the other. Right now it was the Bulldogs' turn.

Under rows of lights that struck the field like high noon, and with only forty seconds left on the scoreboard till half, quarterback Brody Peterbury fired off a pass and the crowd roared to its feet. Since all she could see was the back of the brown wool coat in front of her, Patsy Lee was clueless until arms pumped and sound swelled. Touchdown. The band keyed up the school song. Her hands clapped, but her eyes stayed pinned on the brown coat now swaying with the music.

Every time she thought of Zeke's fingers splayed along her breasts—and she thought of it way, way too often—she felt an ache so deep she could hardly stand it. She didn't know what it was exactly. Of *course* it was sexual. . . . She wasn't a moron. But that wasn't it entirely. It felt similar to the feeling she got whenever she thought about the Wal-Mart pharmacist and the choir director he'd run away with.

Maisie Ann Phelps.

Patsy Lee thought back. She'd spent her senior year in high school with the preacher's future wife, long before Maisie Ann had become choir director, but at a time when her reputation as a scarlet woman was already getting a foothold. Dark curls a riot around her face and blue eyes sparking with mischief, Maisie Ann had been what Zinnia would call a wild 'un. Patsy Lee had been alternately appalled by her behavior and envious of her devil-take-all attitude.

Maybe, she thought suddenly, *I still am.*

Silly idea. When everyone sat back down, she turned her attention back to the game. Flushed with success, the Bulldogs' offense ran off and the defense ran on. With only a few seconds to halftime and the crowning of the king and queen (scuttlebutt had it that Brody Peterbury and his girlfriend, Pauletta, would win hands down), the band and drill team, their uniform tassels gleaming as bright as the brass section, shuffled onto the field's apron.

Patsy Lee craned to see Rose. Zeke nudged her and pointed. There she was. Straight hair nearly white in the lights, chin up, and cheeks rosy, Rose stood tall and straight, pom-poms tucked at her narrow waist, her hips a gentle flare under her green-and-gold skirt.

She nudged him back. "Driving her to practice means you get to take some credit."

He shook his head. "The credit's hers. And yours. She's something else."

Yes, Rose was something else. Practical, confident, intelligent, capable . . . and almost all grown up. Patsy Lee slumped, her sudden melancholy surprising her.

Zeke poked her again. "Who is that?"

Patsy Lee followed his gaze. An Ichabod Crane figure with nondescript brown hair and bowed shoulders stood apart at the fringes of the crowd, grasping a Bible. "That's Preacher Phelps. He still offers a prayer at halftime to keep the players safe. Nobody's filed a lawsuit yet."

"So. The cuckolded Phinnaeus Phelps."

"How did you know about that?"

"How could I not know? Around here, gossip blows across the countryside like so much wheat chaff."

Patsy Lee smiled. "That's what Pop O'Malley says."

"That he does. I should be more careful when appropriating someone else's metaphors."

"Finn—Preacher Phelps—is a sweet man. Actually, so is Maisie Ann. I wish people would just leave them alone."

"Maisie Ann is—was—the wife?"

Patsy Lee nodded. "I don't know her very well since I didn't move here until just before my senior year, but she's always been nice to me."

"Why *did* you move to—?" He stopped. "Sorry. What I was about to say would sound rude. Possibly because it is."

A corner of her mouth lifted. "Cordelia strikes you as someplace people move away from, not to. But people move here all the time. There are those retirement communities. And Alcea's husband settled here."

"Retirement doesn't count. And Dak's a writer. All writers are crazy."

"And Jon."

"Jon doesn't count, either. He grew up near here. Plus he's always been strange," Zeke said with the confidence of the man's best friend. "And he had a powerful reason to stay because—"

"Because of Lil." Patsy Lee wanted to suck back the words. Her flat tone had shouted out what she thought about his feelings for her sister-in-law.

Zeke's glance was puzzled. . . . Or was that worried? "Yes, but I was actually thinking of his mother-in-law. Zinnia O'Malley would have hunted him down and dragged him back if he'd bucked Lil on settling down here."

She thought it was worried. Well, despite her lapse, she wouldn't let him know that she'd guessed his emotions. She turned the subject back to his question.

"My mother moved"—ran away—"to Columbia when she was pregnant with me, but she'd grown up here. After she found out she had cancer, she wanted to come back. She'd loved it here, still had friends here, like Zinnia, even though—" She broke off. Stomach clenching with the anxiety she always felt when she needed to discuss her family, she let her explanation drift off, not wanting to explore *even though*. "Even though she hadn't lived here for almost eighteen years," she finished lamely.

"It must have been hard on you. Moving in high school. Mother with cancer."

She knew he could relate, but at the sympathy in his voice, she blinked back tears, surprised to find her feelings so near the surface after so many years. But maybe that wasn't so odd. She'd loved her mother. Finding out she'd lied had left her emotions raw.

She swallowed. "Moving wasn't that bad." Because she didn't known anyone that well in Columbia, either. "And then the cancer went into remission, so I went on to college. When Mom got sick again, I moved back and worked the night shift at the poultry plant so I could be home days to take care of her."

"Who watched her nights?"

"Zinnia sometimes. Bebe . . ."

"Bebe moved here with you? Must have been a good friend."

"Uh, yes. Yes, she was . . . *is*."

"By the way, she called again this afternoon when you were napping."

There was speculation in Zeke's tone. Probably because he wondered why she sometimes made up excuses not to talk to Bebe. They watched as the band fanned out around the edges of the football field while the clock counted down the final seconds.

"So," Zeke asked, when she didn't comment further, "tell me more about Maisie Ann."

"Oh. Well. She got pregnant in high school. Nobody was surprised."

"And the good preacher stepped into the breach to marry her."

"He wasn't a preacher yet—he was a classmate. And the father of her baby."

"Whoa."

"That *did* surprise everyone." She motioned toward the bottom row of the next bank of bleachers. A thin woman, her back hunched with age under a fur coat, followed the proceedings with quick movements, her chin darting in and out of the ruff of her collar like a ferret. "Especially his mother. She was—is—very religious, so Finn went to Bible classes and Sunday school, sang in the choir, went to church camp. He was so quiet. Kept to himself. Chess club type, you know?"

"Actually, I do. I was the chess club type myself."

"You?"

She looked up at him; he smiled down at her.

"I enjoyed reading, my music, time alone, and hated high school; I never fit. Like your preacher. And like—" He broke off.

"And like Hank," she said slowly. "That's what you were about to say, isn't it?"

"Hank's specialty is stars, not music." It wasn't a yes or a no. "So go on."

She tucked her concerns away. She'd learned that when Zeke wanted to avoid a subject, was as adept as she was herself.

"When Mrs. Phelps found out, she had a royal fit. For as long as anyone could remember, she'd told people that Finn would one day serve the Lord. She wasn't about to let something like a baby stop him from seminary. People said she tried to bribe Maisie Ann's family into moving somewhere else or giving up the baby for adoption. But Maisie Ann stood up to her."

Patsy Lee remembered that day in May, a day when the pear blossoms blew past her like driving snow as she waited at the bus stop after school. Her gaze following the blizzard they'd made, she'd almost missed seeing Mrs. Phelps and Maisie Ann standing toe-to-toe outside the school entrance. Patsy Lee had been too far away to hear the words that were exchanged, but she remembered how Mrs. Phelps had bent like a wire reed against the wind.

But not Maisie Ann. The wind had whipped back her jacket, revealing the bulge of her belly, and sent her hair slashing across her face, but she didn't even sway. She didn't even blink. Maisie Ann simply held her hair out of her eyes and gave Mrs. Phelps stare for stare.

And then, when Mrs. Phelps drew back her arm, apparently ready to slap the toughness off Maisie Ann's face, Finn was suddenly there. He'd grabbed his mother's wrist. The bus had arrived at that moment, and Patsy Lee had been forced to turn away. She'd boarded the bus, picking pear blossoms out of her hair.

"Finn finally stood up to her, too. Anyway, Maisie Ann and Finn got married right after graduation. For a while it seemed like things might work out—Finn went to seminary, Mrs. Phelps even bought them a little house. But Maisie Ann miscarried, and, the following year, she miscarried again. After that, nobody saw her for quite a while. We just knew that Mrs. Phelps moved both of them in with her and the little house got sold." And Mrs. Phelps had worn a smug look, while Finn had looked beaten.

"Depression?"

She nodded. After two miscarriages and living with Mrs. Phelps, it was easy to see why. "After Maisie Ann was up and around again, she started working with the ladies' auxiliary and became the church's choir director. She didn't talk about that time—she wouldn't let anyone get close." After all the gossip Maisie Ann's life had generated, Patsy Lee could understand her wariness. "Maybe it would have helped if she had. But it probably would have helped more if she'd moved out of her mother-in-law's house."

After Maisie Ann had surfaced from her self-imposed exile, Patsy Lee had never again seen a snap in her eyes or heard her voice ring with laughter. She'd attended to her business with lowered eyes, deferring to her husband, who deferred to his mother (and, one hoped, God).

"She finally did. With the pharmacist," Zeke pointed out.

"Simon Stigmeier. He's the pharmacist. Or was. I heard he quit."

She wondered if Simon had made Maisie Ann laugh again. And if he had, then . . .

Even if Maisie Ann had hurt Finn and had sent her mother-in-law into near heart failure, was what Maisie Ann had done so terribly, terribly wrong?

The half ended. People blocked her view again as the team ran off the field. When Brown Coat sat down, she saw Finn Phelps making his way to the drum-major podium "He's a good man. I shouldn't talk about them. Gossip is cruel." She might be uncertain about a lot of things, but that wasn't one of them.

"I don't think I'd ever call you cruel." Zeke was still watching her face. "But you're glad she left him, aren't you?"

"Of course not! I mean, Simon isn't married, but Maisie Ann—" She broke off, realizing he wasn't fooled. "Maybe I am. A little. I don't know; I shouldn't be, but . . ."

She tilted up her head and tried to fasten her gaze on the stars. She couldn't. They were blurred by the banks of lights. ". . . But I've been mixed up lately."

"Not surprising, homebound as you've become. I know I'd go bonkers with mostly myself and Jane Austen for company. Although I hope my being there has helped." He paused. "Has it?"

"Yes, I—I've liked having you around. Sometimes."

He laughed. "Good enough."

She hesitated, then decided for whatever reason to confide, "It's not my ankle that's made everything seem confusing. Last year when Daisy left for college, I just started thinking about things. Like my future, I guess. I mean, I know what I'm going to do—I have for a long time. I'll finish school. I'll own Lil's stores."

"You don't sound enthusiastic. In fact, you sounded more enthusiastic when you told me last week you were dropping a class."

She looked down at her hands. They were red with cold. She'd dropped just one of her classes, deciding that with her ankle she couldn't cope with more than two right now. "No, that's what I want. But I wonder what it will be like. And if it will be . . . enough."

"The question we all face: Is that all there is?" Zeke's hand went over hers. He gave it a gentle squeeze. "Do you remember what you said on Monday when we were driving to Sedalia? About the hawk?"

She thought back, then nodded.

"I've never known a nice kind of lonesome, but I can imagine it. Maybe that's what you're looking for."

"But I don't want to be alone. At least, I don't think I do."

"Who does? No, I meant that maybe you want to chart your own flight path. Follow your instincts. Not care about what anyone else thinks. Like the hawk. Like Maisie Ann Phelps."

She looked up at him. His eyes were black like the sky and deep like the heavens. Inside them, something shifted and he released her hand, stripped his gloves off. "Your hands are cold. Take these and pay attention to the weather next time."

She objected, but he insisted. As she pulled them on, her fingers not even approaching the tips but luxuriating in the warmth he'd left behind, she thought about his words. The thought of being alone that had first surfaced when Daisy left, the idea that someday she'd be able to make decisions just for herself and only for herself, after so many years, had filled her with fear, yes, but also with an odd kind of elation. That emotion, she could understand. What she didn't understand was how the idea that she'd already mapped out her future and could see it spread out in front of her didn't bring her contentment. Instead, it filled her with panic.

And she wondered if that was how Maisie Ann Phelps had felt.

And she wondered how Zeke had so easily sensed it.

"Mama?" Just as the drums started rat-a-tatting for the players to march onto the field, Lily-Too slid onto the bench. Her chin was trembling, her mittened hands empty of food.

"Sunshine, what's wrong? Where's your hot dog?"

"Mrs. Sh-Sherlock was at the stand, and she said to tell you—tell you—"

Zeke leaned forward to hear.

"—That you've got to answer her notes because I need some kind of testing." Lily-Too chewed her lip. "I asked her what kind and she said not the kind I'd have to study for. Just tests to make sure everything is okay. Mama, is there something *wrong* with me?"

"Oh, pet, of course not. Of course there isn't." Insensitive witch. "Mrs. Sherlock is just concerned because you aren't doing as well as you did last year in school, that's all. We'll get everything straightened out. I'll call her and arrange to see her Monday, I promise."

Lips tightening, Zeke sat back, apparently deciding not to ask questions in Lily-Too's presence. Good. Because now wasn't a time when she wanted to answer any. Along with anger at Lily-Too's teacher, guilt swept her. She should have addressed this problem when it first raised its head, and she was pretty sure Zeke would have no hesitation in pointing that out.

Her gaze flicked along his strong profile, then down to his lap, where he'd dug his hands into his coat pockets. Once again, that odd ache rose in her chest and she turned her eyes away.

Preacher Phelps had finished with his prayer for the second half. Up on the podium, the drum major raised his arms as if in benediction, then snapped them down. Music bounced to life.

Patsy Lee pulled Lily-Too against her, and they watched Rose perform. Part of her brain silently reviled Mrs. Sherlock for her big mouth. She wished she had the guts to do it out loud. But wouldn't that just make things worse for her daughter? And what if Mrs. Sherlock was right? With another part of her brain, she registered Rose's high kicks and gleaming smile.

And with another, she thought about Zeke Townley's hands.

Chapter 10

On Saturday morning, the bells tinkled over the door of Merry-Go-Read: A Children's Bookstore. Zeke looked up from his pint-sized seat at a pint-sized table in front of the bow window that overlooked Cordelia's town square. Across the road, clouds kneaded into ropes over St. Andrew's steeple. A bevy of maples sidestepped the walkways that twisted through the church green.

Behind him, a dozen customers, most with children in tow, lingered amid the bookshelves. The floor, its wood dark with age where it wasn't painted with colorful renditions of Dr. Seuss and Winnie-the-Pooh characters, creaked under their footsteps.

Jon's daughter, Melanie, recruited to help on a weekend trip home from college, stooped to help a towheaded child inspect a pop-up book, her dark bangs falling into her eyes. Glancing up, she waved at her dad. Near her, Patricia had been cornered by a member of the staff, a small man with a shiny dome surrounded by white fringe like an egg nestled in shredded paper. Patricia had introduced him as Mr. Stuart.

Jon closed the door against the chilled air and hailed Zeke. "Quite a game last night, eh?"

"Yep."

Actually, caught up in conversation with Patsy Lee, he'd hardly watched the game, but he wouldn't tell Jon that. Jon would undoubtedly—and gleefully—misconstrue that little piece of information. The thought irritated him. Mostly because he'd spent some long moments last night misconstruing it himself. He'd finally realized he was just more lonely than he thought.

"We saw you, but we were working concessions. By the time we'd cleaned up, you'd left. Michael hasn't made varsity yet, but we do our bit. Lily-Too all right? Lil said she ran off before she got her popcorn."

"Nothing a swift kick to her teacher's rear wouldn't cure."

Patsy Lee had murmured that she'd meet with Mrs. Whatzitlock on Monday. He'd dearly love to do the honors himself, but it wasn't his place. Nor was it his place to spill any secret of Hank's. Which he'd nearly done last night with that "didn't fit in" remark. He felt uncomfortable keeping anything from Patricia, but consoled himself with the thought that the sites Hank chose to surf on the Internet proved nothing. Or at least, nothing much. He sighed. Sometimes this family was a frustration.

Jon accurately heard the sigh as aggravation, but guessed the wrong source. "Ah, Mrs. Sherlock . . . Michael had her for sixth grade. Pain in the butt, until Lil set her straight."

Lil had grown more assertive than she'd been in her more malleable youth. Zeke liked a strong woman, but—he thought of Christine—maybe there was something to be said for the more pliant type. His gaze wandered to Patricia.

"So," Jon said. "Admit it. The Bulldogs could hold their own against the 49ers. Especially the way they've played this year. Cordelia has at least one thing that tops that city where you left your heart."

"What?" Jon's words had barely registered. He looked up at him.

His friend's eyes danced. "Or maybe more than one." He nodded toward Patricia.

Zeke frowned. "What are you babbling about?"

"Never mind. Say, where's Lil? I need to talk to her before we leave for K.C."

Today was the first day of the charitable work at Vreeley Home that he'd promised Jon. He wasn't exactly sure what would be expected, but he wasn't pushing for information. Whatever it was would be worth a day spent somewhere with four-lane streets and buildings higher than his eyeballs. Plus, Jon had promised him an early dinner at a restaurant where the fish was fresh, not frozen in little rectangles, and where there wasn't even a hint of a vinyl booth. Small towns were all well and good—and he'd even admit to a very soft spot for Cordelia—but every once in a while, he wanted an infusion of noise, crowds, and, especially, fine dining. They'd return tonight.

They'd met here, as Patricia had wanted to stop in before joining her mother-in-law for lunch at Peg O' My Heart. The diner was only a few doors up the street, anchoring one corner of Main. Sin-Sational Ice Cream sat on the opposite end. O'Neill's Emporium and Merry-Go-Read lay between.

Zeke tipped his head toward the rear of the store. "Lil's in the back room doing whatever one does in a back room. She said she'd be right back, so take a load off." He nudged a small chair forward with the sole of his boot. "And we'll both be able to chew on our knees."

Jon lowered his voice to a conspiratorial whisper. "I happen to know there are Big People chairs in the back."

"Except Patricia told me Lil doesn't want those chairs out front where a customer with a wallet might sit down instead of browsing through the merchandise." He'd thought exceptions should be made and had told Patricia so, but she hadn't budged. He found her occasional obstinacy attractive. . . . occasionally . . . but he'd rather she bucked Lil, not him. He sighed.

"Aw, is that why we're so cranky? Not comfortable?"

Zeke shoved the chair smack up against Jon's shins.

"Yow. All right." Grinning, Jon sat. "Lil's working late. How will Patsy Lee get home?"

"Zinnia. After Patricia receives a progress report here"—he wasn't sure which she'd wanted most: information from Lil on the store or from Melanie on the subject of her eldest daughter—"they're having lunch. Patricia mentioned a salad I made for supper—included crab, quite good—and now Zinnia is certain that I'm starving her to death."

Both men's gazes went to Patricia. She was leaning on her crutches at a counter, still listening as Mr. Stuart gestured with his thin, freckled hands. From what Zeke had overheard, Mr. Stuart was incensed at Lil's recent insistence (following a computer meltdown at another store) on daily printouts, backup discs, *and* e-mailed copies to her home of their bookkeeping reports. Mr. Stuart felt the tasks redundant. He'd apparently been hesitant to empty his frustrations into Lil's ears, but had no such reserve about filling Patricia's.

With reason. Patricia's softness was simply more approachable than the efficiency Lil had developed during her years of owning the bookstores. While Zeke watched, Patricia tilted her head. The lights hanging from the high stamped-tin ceiling shot copper through her hair. With an orange scarf draped around her neck, she looked as warmly autumn as the scene outside.

"Zinnia's wrong. Not skin and bones; a woman in her prime," Jon remarked.

Zeke bristled. "She's not a 4-H exhibit."

Jon's eyebrows went up, but he was smart enough to keep his mouth shut.

Jon switched his gaze from Patricia to Mr. Stuart. "Wonder what's up with the Stumeister. Lil says he's a good employee, but a worrywart. Of course, so is my wife, so maybe that's why they butt heads."

Zeke watched Mr. Stuart. Actually, his hands were now making only an occasional leap into the air and he no longer looked like he was in danger of heart failure. When she wanted to, Patricia could soothe a situation. Over their days together, he'd watched her adroitly calm the usual flare-ups between her children. Occasionally, that gentleness lent itself to timidity. And that bugged him. But he had to admit he liked her soft voice and the way her brown eyes went quiet. And her mouth . . .

Zeke frowned, suddenly noticing the whiteness around her mouth. "Surely the fool can see he needs to stop yapping so she can sit down?"

Patricia's legs would ache tonight and he knew she'd refuse his offers of a massage, just like she had the night before. His annoyance increased as he realized that *that* annoyed him, too. He glanced at Jon. His friend was watching him. His eyes had a catlike tilt and a catlike color. . . . And right now they looked particularly catlike sly.

Zeke rolled his eyes. "Oh, stow it."

"What?" Jon said, cat eyes going round with innocence. "I didn't say a word."

Zeke didn't respond. He rose and strode toward the rear of the store, bypassing customers and displays of educational toys, DVDs, and sing-along CDs. Ignoring Patricia's puzzled look, he ducked into the back room. Lil had the rear door open and was directing a UPS man stacking boxes. He pointed toward a folding chair and mouthed Patricia's name. She nodded, her smile going as sly as her husband's. Shaking his head, he picked up the chair and strode back out. He didn't bother to excuse himself when he interrupted Mr. Stuart, whom he'd decided was a self-centered fool.

"Sit." He flipped the chair open and pushed it up behind Patricia.

She glanced back. "I told you—"

"Miz Patsy Lee, you *must* sit down." Mr. Stuart shot a timid look at Zeke. "I am so sorry. I should not have kept you standing."

Zeke gave Mr. Stuart a look of approval. Maybe the man wasn't a *complete* self-centered fool. "Listen to Mr. Stuart. He's proving he's a man of unique perspicacity."

Mr. Stuart frowned at him, pride evidently overriding fear. "I beg your pardon."

"Acuity."

"Sir." Mr. Stuart puffed up his chest.

Patricia sucked in her bottom lip. "He means you're making a lot of sense."

Zeke sighed. "Right. Just . . . sit," he repeated to Patricia, hoping she wouldn't snort and insult Mr. Stuart any further. Catching eyes filled with laughter before she lowered them, she sat. No snorting. Good girl. Zeke went back to the table at the front of the store.

"Yep, football isn't the only thing in Cordelia that's floating your boat," Jon said.

"Don't get ideas. I enjoy her company, that's all."

"Uh-huh," Jon said. With a smirk, he leaned back, toppled his chair, and landed with a sprawl of arms and legs, giving Zeke the warm feeling that everything in the universe was in divine order.

As Jon righted himself, Zeke determined to keep his gaze totally off Patricia. Fortunately, Lil entered from the back room, giving him a new focal point. Her pale yellow suit and light hair were like buttercups on a winter day. She headed toward Patricia and Mr. Stuart, but before she could reach them, was waylaid by a plump woman who would have done well to avoid horizontal stripes and bubble hairdos. The woman held the hand of a boy with a tuft of yellow hair. Zeke heard, "Did you hear the latest about the Phelpses?" before the woman lowered her voice. Lil's eyes lit with interest.

The whole scene was so entertaining, it took a few moments before he realized Patricia's gaze was resting on him. He caught a thoughtful expression before she lowered her head back to the ledger. He glanced over at Jon. Hands locked behind his head, Jon looked highly entertained himself.

Zeke growled in his throat.

Jon held up his hands like he was warding Zeke off. "Okay, okay. Let's get going."

He waved to Lil, who smiled at Horizontal Stripes and excused herself. But before she'd made it to their table, another customer had stopped her.

Now Jon growled in his throat. "Business may be good, but I'll be glad when these stores are off her hands."

"And onto Patricia's?"

"So she's told you their plans? It's rather fitting—what goes around, comes around. Patricia's husband owned this store first. Lil told me Henry used up the rest of a small inheritance Patsy Lee had from her mother; the first bit paid the down payment on the farmhouse. Fancied himself a truck farmer. Then a proprietor. Neither one took off."

"Not a good businessman?"

Jon glanced at Lil, apparently to make sure she was still involved with her customer. "Not good for much of anything. From what Lil's said, he sounds like he was a likeable enough, but"—Jon shook his head—"a big talker, heavy on the blueprints, not much on the hammer and nails. You know the type."

He knew the type. Zeke watched Patricia and wondered why she'd chosen him.

Jon continued, "He left Patsy—I mean, Patricia, heavy on debt and children. Remember? Lil rescued her by marrying me."

"I remember." He thought back to the whole scenario when he and Jon had first encountered the O'Malley family: A pregnant Patricia had taken two jobs. Lil was losing hers at the soon-to-be-bankrupt bookstore. The parents were about to bail everyone out and ruin themselves instead, and then Jon came along. "You were Cowboy Savior of the Poor. As long as the poor had long legs, bright blue eyes, and a dazzling smile."

Jon smiled. "It helps."

"Then Lil bought this bookstore from Patricia?"

"No. Lil's sister Alcea's husband—not Dak, her first husband, Stan, who owns the one big bank in town, or at least did, before he got competition in the form of—"

"Jon."

"What?"

"You have picked up a disconcerting tendency to talk like a member of the Ladies' Auxiliary. Long story short?"

Jon's mouth quirked. "Long story short. Patsy L—I mean, Patricia, had a mortgage on this building. A big one. Plus two on her house. She'd worked out a deal with the bank, put this up for sale, then I stepped in and bought it and gave the property to Lil. We settled her home mortgages through Lil's parents."

"Nobody said anything to Patricia first?"

"Why? Patricia was burdened, not to mention pregnant and with three already at home, so between us, Lil and I removed the burden."

"Good of you." Zeke sat back.

Good, understandable, and also high-handed. Lil

had probably viewed her sister-in-law's situation as desperate, so she'd acted swiftly without considering Patricia's feelings. Undoubtedly, Patricia had been grateful. Still, it must have rankled to watch Lil do what she'd been unable to. He wondered how much of Patricia's feelings from back then were tied up in her quest to own the place now, plus the other two stores Lil had opened.

While she was gossiping, the striped woman had released her boy's hand and he'd wandered to a bookcase near Patricia that was filled with everything Harry Potter. Out of sight of his mother, he reached up, tugged, and a stack of books tumbled to the floor. He burst into tears.

Zeke got to his feet, but Patricia beat him to it, rising and swinging the few feet to the boy. As she stopped in front of the youngster, Zeke sat back down. Jon was looking at him, eyebrows up in his hairline again.

Zeke shrugged. "Old habits die hard. Reminded me of my little sister at that age."

Patricia untucked a tissue from her pocket and dried his tears. The mother peeked around the corner, smiled, turned back to her talk. Within seconds Patricia had the little boy settled on her good knee, a book open in her hands. Her voice drifted toward him, a melody.

Zeke felt a pang. "Poetry in the ordinary," he murmured.

"Sounds like the title of a love song."

Zeke started. While he'd been gawking, Lil had walked up. She gave him a slight smile he couldn't construe as anything other than an *atta boy*. He glowered and her smile just grew bigger. She was as bad as Jon.

For a few minutes, she and Jon discussed the family schedule, then Lil lowered her voice. "Penny Mason just told me Maisie Ann Phelps and Simon Stigmeier are back in town, staying over at Simon's house."

Behind Lil, Zeke saw Patricia leading the little boy back to his mother. She turned to swing their way. Zeke excused himself to fetch her chair.

When he returned, Lil was still explaining. "Paddy O'Neill says after Maisie Ann and Simon settle matters here, they'll head for Minnesota. Maisie Ann's family moved there in the early nineties. But Penny just told me Betty Bruell heard Simon had accepted a job at a Walgreen's in Omaha. Either way, I can't believe they'd just leave the town where both of them were raised. I wouldn't want to."

Helping Patricia seat herself, Zeke met Patricia's eyes and knew they were sharing the same feeling. Poor Maisie Ann and Simon. He thought of gangly, sad-eyed Preacher Phelps. Poor everyone.

Lil continued. Mrs. Phelps had sent Lawyer Murphy to tell Maisie Ann she wouldn't get *one thin dime* from the Phelps estate. Incensed that anyone would think she even wanted *one thin dime* of their money, Maisie Ann had grabbed an umbrella from the stand near the door.

"At least everyone thinks there was a stand near the door, since the umbrella had to be close at hand, although it's possible it was a broom handle, as only old Mrs. Brambauer saw it and you know she's blind as a bat."

Wielding the umbrella—or broom handle—Maisie Ann had forced the poor barrister into an undignified gallop up the street.

Lil's eyes widened. "Isn't that awful?"

A few weeks ago, the picture of a lawyer being chased by a wild woman waving a weapon would have amused him. But thinking of the story Patricia had told him of the Phelpses' past, Zeke didn't find it amusing at all.

"It's not awful. Good for Maisie Ann." Patricia was abrupt.

"Patsy Lee, she's *married.*" Lil blinked at her sister-in-law. "To our preacher. I know Finn was hurt a great deal. Surely you don't think what she and Simon did is okay?"

Patricia's color had heightened. She looked down at her hands, apparently trying to keep her composure, then straight up at Lil. "I don't know whether it is or isn't. But it's not . . . it's not our place to say."

For whatever reason, Zeke felt a measure of pride. Whether because Patricia had stood up for the hapless pair or because she'd just stood up, period. Though why it would happen over a woman she hardly knew with her sister-in-law instead of over her daughter with the teacher she hardly knew, he couldn't fathom.

The horizontally striped Penny Mason stuck her head into the conversation. She was sans son again. There was a sudden crash and wail from the other side of the store. Ms. Mason didn't react, but Melanie did. Jon and Lil's daughter darted down an aisle in the direction of the noise.

"Lil, how much are these darling feathered things? I can't find a price." Ms. Mason held up a dream-catcher, but didn't look at Lil. Her gaze darted back and forth between Jon and Zeke instead. He recognized the signs of the starstruck looking for an indirect intro into their oh-so-stellar orbit. She'd know Jon, of course, but she didn't know him.

"Let me get Mr. Stuart to check." Lil performed introductions, then went to find him.

Penny Mason lingered behind, still looking between him and Jon. Getting no acknowledgment—Jon was clueless, Zeke was unimpressed—she turned to Patricia. "Did I hear you talking about Maisie Ann Phelps? Can you believe the latest? As I told Lil—"

"You heard right." Zeke rose. "Interesting, but *made tedious by morality.*"

Walking back up, Lil exchanged a puzzled look with her husband. Jon shrugged. Patricia was looking at him with gratitude. He liked the feeling.

"Excuse us . . . Mrs. Mason, was it? We're on our way out." Turning away, Zeke held out a hand to Patricia. "Do you want Jon and me to drop you at the O'Malleys'?"

"Please."

Lil gave Jon a peck on the cheek. "See you later at home."

Zeke helped Patricia to her feet, then the three of them headed for the door. Penny Mason watched them go, expression puzzled. "I—it was nice meeting you."

Zeke saluted.

As they stepped outside, Jon leaned in close. "What in the hell did that thing about morality mean?"

" 'Scandal is gossip made tedious by morality,' " Patricia said. "Oscar Wilde."

Her recognition of the line might have amazed Zeke at one time, but it didn't now.

"To interpret, my man, Wilde was commenting on how there's nothing more irritating than self-righteous busybodies." Zeke paused. "Except, maybe, horizontal stripes."

Patricia laughed.

Zeke met her eyes and thought for the umpteenth time how her smile always transformed her face into something wonderful. He liked being able to make her laugh. He just wished he didn't like it quite so much.

Chapter 11

Despite the way Zeke's gaze had stuck on Lil from the moment she walked out of the back room at the store Saturday, Patsy Lee's shared amusement with him had given her a glow that had lasted all through lunch with her mother-in-law. But far from warming her, it scared her. Because she recognized it for exactly what it was.

She'd felt it before. In fifth grade, when Petey Granberry slipped her one of his Hostess Cupcakes at lunch.

As a junior in high school, when she watched star player Warren Simpson shoot hoops, even though he only had eyes for head cheerleader Beth Banowski.

As a newly hired worker, brushing fingers with Henry in PicNic Poultry processing plant's break room as they both reached for the same Snickers bar.

She'd even felt it as recently as last year when she'd dated Rusty Peterson, although, with him, that feeling hadn't lasted longer than one brief tumble into his bed before she'd realized that not only couldn't he uphold his end of an intelligent conversation, he was only looking for a replacement to mother his four children. Just the thought had exhausted her.

She recognized the feeling, all right. . . . It was the

harbinger of romance. Girlish romance. Fun, loopy, giggly romance.

But, thing was, she was no longer a girl. She didn't want the way Zeke's dark gaze could fasten on hers to have an impact, particularly since she knew without a doubt that her gaze had no such effect on him. It wasn't that her optimism had faded over the years. But there was *optimism*. . . . And then there was *simplemindedness*.

Like it or not, though, she had to admit the glow had lent strength to her backbone when, over chicken salad and lime Jell-O at Peg O' My Heart, Zinnia had introduced schemes to keep Zeke dancing attendance on her past this upcoming Wednesday when he was scheduled to return to Lil and Jon's. Patsy Lee had argued that three-and-a-half weeks was the most they should stretch Zeke's generosity. (Maybe she owed Lil, but enough was enough.) Zinnia had looked puzzled at her uncharacteristic stubbornness but had finally subsided with a "You might be right, honeybunch." She'd been relieved.

But even if Zinnia had grown angry, she'd been prepared to stand her ground. More than her mother-in-law's disappointment, she feared her own emotions. More than her desire to shield Lil from the feelings Patsy Lee suspected Zeke had for her sister-in-law, she wanted to shield herself.

But by that evening when Zeke had returned home, hailed like any other member of the family by a fanfare of donkey brays and dog barks, that blasted glow had fanned right back to life.

In the sitting room, where she and Rose had whiled away the day on homework, Patsy Lee giving an occasional wistful thought to how she'd prefer to spend her time, he'd hardly had his jacket off before he was regaling them with an account of his day, an effort to organize about twenty of the Vreeley boys into a band in preparation for the facility's holiday concert. To his surprise, the activity had outshone even a meal of honest-to-God fresh seafood at a restaurant with actual linen draping its tables.

Charmed by the light in his eyes, and by the unusual way he'd left his jacket in a heap in his enthusiasm, she'd been content just to listen. After he'd left to start supper, Rose following after him to help, she'd taken herself to task, trying to douse that glow forever.

Zeke was handsome. Zeke was magnetic. Zeke was droll and talented and intelligent and helpful and thoughtful and a thousand other things. And she wasn't the first one to notice. All those traits had helped win the Van Castle Band a shelf of CMA Awards and propelled them onto the charts.

Of *course,* her heart would feel an occasional zing in his presence. He could captivate with the effortless, unconscious ability of the sun rising in the morning. It wasn't a studied endeavor, it was simply inevitable, and had happened with thousands of women before her. If he couldn't zing a heart with ease, he'd never have reached the pinnacles he had.

Her self-scold had helped put things into perspective. On Sunday she'd kept that glow tamped down. And by today it was entirely gone. Not, unfortunately, because she'd discovered a previously unknown well of determination, but because her mind had been overtaken by a new anxiety. Mrs. Sherlock. Nothing like juggling a bunch of neuroses.

Nearing noon on Monday, the students at recess, Patsy Lee sat at a children's desk in Lily-Too's empty third-grade classroom waiting to meet with her youngest's teacher. She knew the miniature seat put her at a disadvantage, but she couldn't stay on her feet nor bring herself to sit on Mrs. Sherlock's chair (throne). Despite her advantages—she was older (about twenty years) and taller (half a head, believe it or not)—dread had overwhelmed her original anger. Maybe it was petite Mrs. Sherlock's tiny waist or the way no gold hair ever escaped the maze of French braids on her head or possibly a gaze that seemed capable of punching holes in cement.

She studied the cursive alphabet over the chalkboard, hoping that the vegetable-soup-and-textbook-glue odor particular to grade schools didn't make her sick all over her good wool skirt. She'd worn black, hoping the hint of sophistication (and the fact that she'd woven the matching jacket) would bolster her confidence. Her bright purple cast rather spoiled the effect, but Zeke's pressure on the car horn had driven her out of the house before she could change clothes a fifth time. Next week, she'd get a fresh cast. And it wouldn't be purple, no matter what Lily-Too wanted.

Through the slatted shades, she could see no break in the gray skies that had accompanied them to Merry-Go-Read on Saturday and then had persisted through Sunday and into this morning. A few flakes of snow drifted aimlessly, melting on contact with ground still too warm for true winter weather. Real snow usually didn't arrive till January, although a stray storm wasn't unlikely in November or December.

Which is about how long she felt she'd sat here. When she'd arrived, Mrs. Sherlock had, with brittle cheer and no apology, informed her the recess monitor was ill, so her supervision was required on the playground. Patsy Lee had been tempted to use the delay as an excuse to leave, but decided it would be too cowardly, even for her. Not getting an argument (and undoubtedly not expecting one), Lily-Too's teacher had promised to return in twenty minutes.

Patsy Lee glanced at the clock and sighed. It had been twenty-five. Trying to occupy herself until Mrs. Sherlock returned without having to resort to thinking of Mrs. Sherlock, she let her thoughts wander to Saturday again, pushing away images of Zeke and concentrating on the store. She'd return to work in a week.

Where she hoped there would be no more feathers to soothe. Knowing Lil's policies stemmed only from a desire to keep the stores successful (and her employees employed), Patsy Lee had done her best to placate Mr. Stuart, reminding him that once she was back, she'd take over the (what she also privately thought was senseless) bookkeeping job that was driving him batty. Lil would once more divide her concerns among three stores, so her focus on the Cordelia outlet would lessen.

She smoothed her skirt, fervently hoping that a business degree could substitute for Lil's organization gene, since Patsy Lee knew systematic thinking didn't hold sway in her own DNA.

She sighed again. Well, this line of thought had certainly cheered her. She didn't know if it was the thought of more bookkeeping that weighed her down. Or simply the idea of assuming control of the stores. Running a business and making it thrive took a lot of resolution. It was no wonder Lil had already planned her retirement. But it *was* a wonder why Patsy Lee was so hell-bent on jumping into her place.

Possibly, she thought dryly, *it has something to do with a small thing called income.*

Given that fact, she'd do well to develop some of Lil's dogged determination. Maybe that thread of steel wasn't always as attractive as Lil's milder personality of yesteryear, but back then some people considered Lil gutless.

As gutless as Patsy Lee often was. Especially around people like Mrs. Sherlock.

The door opened. Patsy Lee straightened. But Mrs. Sherlock didn't enter; Zeke did.

"You were supposed to wait in the car," she hissed.

"This isn't a church," he mimicked her whisper. He entered, closed the door behind him, and spoke in a normal tone. "You said twenty minutes and it's been thirty. I'm cold and bored."

"What are you, six?"

"Sometimes." He stuck his hands in his pockets and wandered to the back of the room where the latest projects were displayed. He paused in front of a tempera painting marked with Lily-Too's name. "She's creative. Artistically, musically." He sounded like a proud father.

"How did you get in here?"

He turned around, gaze innocent. "I walked."

"Visitors have to check in and get a badge. You need a reason for the badge. And you have a badge. So what did you tell them in the office?"

She was amazed when the tips of his ears went pink. She'd never seen him embarrassed.

"I told them I was your husband."

"My *what*?"

"Your husband."

"Nobody would believe that. I mean, this town isn't as small as it used to be, but, remember Lil and Jon? If a celebrity married a local, believe me—"

"I told them we eloped."

Patsy Lee closed her eyes and prayed. When she opened them, her prayers hadn't been answered. He was still there. "And what difference does that make? They know me, most of them know you, and they know the idea that we would get married is patently ridiculous."

"Why is that?"

"Because I am—and you are—oh, never mind."

"Are you trying to tell me that you don't think you're good enough for me?"

Patsy Lee raised her chin. "No. I'm telling you that *you're* not good enough for *me*."

Zeke laughed. Patsy Lee couldn't help it: A snort slipped out.

And on that note, Mrs. Sherlock stepped into the room.

"She walked all over you."

An hour later, Zeke and Patsy Lee sat in a booth in Peg O' My Heart, having a late lunch of chicken noodle soup and apple-walnut salad. Past the noon rush and nearing its midafternoon closing time, the diner was empty except for old Paddy O'Neill, wizened owner of O'Neill's Emporium (not that he spent much time there), and his cohorts, Erik Olausson, a Swede with hair fuzzed like dandelions at seed, and the Steeplemier twins, Eddie and Freddie, both in coveralls that stretched across their broad bellies. Every day, the quartet took up residence in the first booth, the one that commanded a view of the entire square and possessed the best proximity to the coffeepot.

When she and Zeke had entered, Paddy had called out, "You two get yerselves hitched?" The tuft of hair on top of his head stood up like an antenna.

Oh, for God's sake.

Zeke snickered.

She glared at him, then smiled wanly at Paddy. "That was just a bad joke."

"Figured it was." Losing interest, he'd gone back to his Bottomless Cup for a Buck.

See? Ridiculous idea. Still, she was glad Paddy had asked. What the old man knew would be communicated faster than a billboard on Main.

Behind the counter, Tansy Eppelwaite scraped the grill. The fry cook's shoulder blades moved like pruning shears, her energy undiminished by seventy-odd years. Waitress Lisa Bartlesby ran a mop over black-and-white tiles. Not long out of high school, she was doing her best to spoil her youthful looks with a star-burst hairdo and a yard of black eyeliner. Light from the wall of windows next to them bounced off the puddles of water she left behind.

"I didn't think Mrs. Sherlock walked all over me." Patsy Lee spooned her soup, knowing full well she had.

"Yes she did. Except for saying *yes, uh-huh, I understand,* and turning a shade of magenta that told me you disagreed with everything she said, you didn't utter a peep." Despite the teasing note in Zeke's voice, Patsy Lee heard exasperation.

"I didn't disagree. I was embarrassed."

And that was the truth. At least the last part. Mrs. Sherlock had walked into the room, raised her plucked eyebrows, said, "I understand felicitations are in order?" and that was all it had taken for Patsy Lee's bones to turn to jelly.

She'd stammered some kind of pitiful excuse for Zeke's lie, ha-ha, and then withered under the look the teacher used on wayward children.

"Besides, all she wants is for Lily-Too to be tested. As she said, third grade is a pivotal year; we don't want Lily-Too to fall behind."

"Tested for ADD." The exasperation had become disgust. Zeke put down his spoon. "If you would have let me say—"

"I couldn't let you act like you—you . . . it just wasn't right." Mrs. Sherlock might intimidate her, but Zeke didn't anymore. She'd squashed any interference he might have intended by glaring so hard it was lucky he hadn't flattened under the strength of her stare. The charade he'd tried . . . she refused to become a laughingstock. "I can handle things myself."

"I know. But it occasionally crosses my mind that

you don't think so. Why not let me take some of the punches?"

"I do, too, think so and—" She stopped. "Why should you take on any of my burdens?"

Zeke looked mildly puzzled, too. "I just meant—I mean—it's that Lily-Too has absolutely nothing wrong with her. She's shy, that's all."

"Maybe." Patsy Lee hated the doubt she could hear in her voice, but it had crept in while she was distracted by Zeke's uncharacteristic stammering.

"That's all." His voice was once again firm. "From what she said, ADD is marked by an obvious lack of concentration. The only time Lily-Too's mind wanders is when she isn't challenged. And I don't doubt it wanders all the time with that, that Shylock—"

"Sherlock."

"—In charge of the classroom. She needs someone more encouraging, more flexible. And that woman is about as flexible as bedrock."

"I didn't know you were an expert."

"Teaching Lily-Too piano and voice made me an expert. She is *completely* focused when she's working on her music."

Patsy Lee abandoned her soup and stared. His voice had actually risen. Behind him, the men's coffee klatch had fallen silent. Paddy O'Neill's head turned, ears perked.

Zeke glanced at them, then leaned forward, lowering his voice. "In other words, Mrs. Shylock is dead wrong."

"Mrs. Sherlock."

"What*ev*-er," he replied with the same inflections Daisy would have used.

"Look, you have some kind of gift with Lily-Too. You're a natural with kids. You're patient. You make her lessons fun and interesting, but Mrs. Sherlock doesn't have time to—"

His stare grew more pointed.

"Okay. Even if it makes her job harder, I'll admit she could probably adjust her approach for someone like Lily-Too if she wanted. And I've put off the testing because, well, because . . ."

"Yes?"

She frowned at him. "Lily-Too does have *some* traits of ADD. It's not like people think; she doesn't need to be hyperactive. That'd be ADHD. But she is forgetful and isn't doing well in school. She's not organized and she has—"

"You could be describing half the population."

"I've researched it; I've worried about it. Don't look at me like I'm a bad mother. Some kids need the drugs."

"But not her. And I don't think you're a bad mother."

She glared at him a few seconds more, then deflated. He was right. Lily-Too may be forgetful, easily distracted, and sometimes painfully shy, but her schoolwork hadn't been affected until she'd hit a teacher who motivated through shame rather than praise and put classroom control and organization at the top of her priority list.

"Okay, not her," she finally said, unable to find a way to concede that he couldn't gloat over. "I think it's like a spectrum of behavior, with some kids normal and others tending toward one end or the other. I don't think Lily-Too's so far to one side she needs drugs. Her problems are probably because she doesn't have a lot of confidence—maybe because she's felt overshadowed by her sisters or because she grew up without a father, I don't know." But she had some knowledge of the latter, so she thought she was right. "So there. Are you satisfied?"

"Yes. No testing."

"But testing won't hurt. In fact, it would prove Mrs. Sherlock wrong."

"Patricia . . . you don't need proof to stand up to that woman."

She was silent.

"The point isn't proving Shylock wrong, it's helping Lily-Too. This could *hurt* her confidence. You heard her. Even the idea of testing makes her think something's wrong with her."

He was right again. She should have just dug in her heels and refused Lily-Too's teacher. She'd *planned* to. She really had. And maybe she would have. Except Zeke's presence—especially under false pretenses—had rattled her even more than Mrs. Sherlock normally did.

"I did manage to get the whole thing put off until after the holidays."

"Big whoop."

"By then, though, maybe . . ."

Glancing outside, she caught sight of Preacher Phelps mounting the steps to St. Andrew's, coattails blowing in the wind. The gears in her head suddenly kicked in. Of *course*.

As Preacher Phelps disappeared inside, she looked back at Zeke. "By *then*," she repeated, "maybe something will happen that will give Lily-Too more confidence. I've thought of at least one thing that might help."

"Hopefully that *thing* involves transferring her into a class with a teacher who has at least one patient bone in her body."

"No, I already checked and Mrs. Carswell's class is full. Plus the principal discourages changing classes midschool year. Strongly discourages it. I guess I could homeschool her. . . ."

Zeke's look was incredulous.

"But that would add to a pretty full schedule."

"No duh," seemed to be all he was capable of.

Whatever? No duh? Big whoop? The children's influence was showing.

She smiled, thinking of all the slang he could pick up by the New Year. "Don't you think Lily-Too would be a shoo-in for the solo at the end of the Christmas pageant?"

"That's what I've told her, but I don't see . . ." He looked out the window, thinking. "Yes, I do see. Not a bad idea. I can work with her to ease her stage fright. If she managed even one moment in the spotlight, it could help her shyness." He looked back at Patsy Lee. "So the pageant is back on? Who is filling the daring Maisie Ann's shoes?"

"It sounds like you had a wonderful time working with the kids at Vreeley Home."

"I did, but what's that—" Zeke sat back. His eyes lit with both amusement and disbelief. "Hold your horses. I have no intention of—"

"Put your money where your mouth is." Her smile widened. "We need a director who will make sure Lily-Too gets the solo spot. I can't do it. Not only am I crippled; I'm tone deaf."

"But that doesn't mean—"

"I'll cancel the tests."

"Now?" A sly look crossed his face.

She wasn't a fool. "*After* the pageant."

His face fell. "But I don't know the first thing—"

"Lily-Too needs you."

"That's hitting below the belt."

She shrugged.

Zeke gave a mournful sigh. "All right. I'll do it."

Chapter 12

So two evenings later, Zeke found himself with Preacher Phelps, plowing through the detritus in St. Andrew's basement storage room in search of the plywood flats that formed the traditional backdrops for the annual St. Andrew's Christmas Pageant.

He'd stopped by the church on his way to pick up Hank from astronomy club and Rose from drill team practice, intending only to schedule pageant rehearsals. Patricia had told him they normally began after try-outs the week following Halloween.

Up close, Phinnaeus Phelps was even more gangly than Zeke's first impression at the game. His hands sported knuckles like marbles, his elbows threatened to poke holes in his sleeves, his shoulders were a pair of mallets. All that hardness belied a soft voice, an eager gaze, and a nervous habit of smoothing his hair and talking with barely a breath between sentences.

After the preacher had asked "my right hand, Lynette Schroeder," a round-bodied, pleasant-faced woman who beamed as he'd introduced her, to look through a calendar to assure Harmony Hall was available on Tuesday and Sunday evenings for rehearsals, he insisted on showing Zeke the sanctuary. On their way out of the office, Zeke noted how Lynette's gaze followed Phelps with a wistful air that was at odds with her no-nonsense demeanor.

In the sanctuary, washed with the blue light of early evening filtering through stained-glass windows set deep into stone walls, Phelps had paused long enough for Zeke to agree the altar would make an adequate stage. But before he could also make his excuses, an explanation of how sheets would be used to protect the new rose carpeting led to how the backdrops also acted as a fence of sorts to keep small fingers out of the chalice and off the cross hanging behind the altar. Which in turn led to a trip to the basement to search for said backdrops.

They'd found the pageant's costumes easily enough, packed away in boxes shoved just inside the storage room door. (Some were stained, some moth-eaten, and others would do.) But the backdrops eluded them.

Still chattering, Phelps pushed into the room, moving boxes aside, waving away Zeke's attempts to help. Even without the odor of mildew, the blotches on the concrete were testament to a history of leaks.

"As I recall," Phelps said, smoothing back his hair, "the backdrops were damaged during that downpour we had in September, but possibly not beyond repair? I just don't remember their exact condition because that was when—" Phelps smoothed his hair again, twice, and Zeke ascertained that was when Maisie Ann had likely left home. "It was, I mean, a very busy time. I do remember I asked the high school art teacher—Mr. Caruthers, a nice man, but keeps to himself—if he could restore them to their former state. They have, after all, been the traditional pageant backdrops since I started serving here. But he avoided commitment and I hesitated to ask again. Mari O'Malley might have helped, since she has an art degree and her mother is one of the fine leaders of our Ladies' Auxiliary, but she was busy with wedding preparations. I couldn't blame her for refusing. The only other person of any artistic ability that I know . . . well, it wouldn't have been appropriate for me to ask her." Smooth. Smooth. Smooth. "Normally we are much more organized, but Maisie Ann used to take care of the pageant details. And she kept the storage room in order. Maisie Ann—"

His hand dropped from his head. "I miss Maisie Ann."

The simple words held a world of heartbreak.

For one of the only times Zeke could remember, he couldn't think of anything to say, so he said nothing. He imagined the preacher had been unable to open his soul to any of his congregants, and Mrs. Phelps certainly hadn't looked like a bundle of compassion. Only a stranger could offer the preacher any comfort, and Zeke had none he could think of to give.

Ears reddening, Phelps glanced at him. "I'm sure you heard my wife left me. With the way people talk here, you'd have to live on Mars not to know my wife left me." He didn't seem to expect a response. "I can't blame her, either. I wish with all my heart I could."

"Uh, yes, I heard. I'm sorry." Zeke felt inadequate. He never felt inadequate.

"Me, too." Phelps turned his gaze directly on Zeke. "Duty's a funny thing. I've been preaching it to my congregation my entire adult life: duty to God, duty to community, duty to family, duty to self. Like I know what I'm talking about. But God hasn't seen fit to show me how to choose one duty over the other with any assurance my choice is correct."

Zeke understood the preacher was thinking of his wife and mother—and maybe himself—but he still couldn't think of anything to say.

Phelps looked briefly disappointed, then turned back to the boxes with a shrug. "Maybe someday I'll get it sorted out. But God bless duty, anyway. It provides purpose, and purpose breathes passion into life. Where would we be without it?"

"We would be living my life." The words slipped out, startling Zeke.

Pushing aside a rusting coat stand, Phelps looked over his shoulder, a small smile playing over his mouth. "Not now, we wouldn't. Right now you have more duty than you can handle under Patsy Lee O'Malley's roof. And now the pageant." Phelps smile broadened. "For which I thank you more than you'll ever know for reasons you'll more than find out. Children of God are more than capable of acting like the devil's spawn, you know."

Zeke was breathless with anticipation.

"Or maybe," Phelps said, "you've done this sort of thing before, and they no longer hold the ability to terrify you? I'll admit I've never had a touch with children. Not like Maisie Ann."

"And I'll admit my charitable efforts have been limited to writing checks."

Upstairs the phone rang. Phelps glanced at the ceiling and grimaced. "My mother. If I'm not home promptly at five thirty for supper, she feels honor bound to check on me. But Lynette will take care of things. She's been with me so long, she's learned to handle even Mother."

Zeke wondered if Finn Phelps realized Mother wasn't the only thing the church secretary wanted to handle.

"Ah, here they are. No wonder we didn't see them."

The backdrops had ended up flat on their backs, piled over with music stands, chairs, and more boxes. Phelps pulled some things off them, then knelt, his knees punching against the fabric of his slacks like big fists. Using a handkerchief, he polished a spot in the midnight blue of a desert sky. Traces of mildew stayed stubbornly put.

"What a shame. After Maisie Ann left, I should have sorted through this room. Surely they can be salvaged—I'd hate to lose them." He looked up at Zeke. "I don't suppose you have any talent for art?"

"None."

The preacher looked disappointed. With the tenderness of a lover, he touched the painting. Zeke studied what he could see. Vibrant colors, stylistic rendering. Whoever had created these had a talent for mimicking Renaissance art. It *would* be a shame if they couldn't be saved.

"I take it the artist is no longer in Cordelia?"

"Oh yes. She is. At least for the time being. Except . . ." Phelps's Adam's apple rolled in his throat. "Except the artist was my wife."

His words fell into a gentle silence, and something responded in Zeke. He knew the emotions Finn Phelps was experiencing, only it wasn't over the loss of someone he'd loved.

Instead, Zeke mourned at the sudden realization that he'd never loved anyone like that. He hesitated. "Maybe I know someone who can help."

Darkness had settled over the countryside by the time they were on their way home. While Hank and Rose talked over their day, Zeke made noncommittal replies and hoped, in that fleeting moment of connection he'd felt with Finn Phelps, he hadn't given the preacher false hope.

Because he knew she was artistic, Patricia had been his first thought, but not his last. She'd take the task on, of course, just like she shouldered any other thing anyone asked of her. Which was exactly what she shouldn't do. She already had plenty on her hands with school, work, and a broken ankle. He mulled things over and by the time they turned onto HH, he thought he'd found a solution. Maybe.

And only maybe. Bebe was only known to him by hearsay as a friend of Patricia's mother's. He didn't know her himself. He didn't know if Patricia would ask her to help. He didn't even know if a professor of textiles could do what they required. Altogether he was, he decided as he turned into the drive, suffering from a sad lack of knowledge.

When they got out of the car, Dharma and Dowdy set up their usual welcome-home braying, Winken and Blinken (Nod was undoubtedly in his usual place by the fire, smart cat) wound figure eights around their feet until distracted by a noise in the underbrush that might mean a snack, and Sugar, with much leaping, reassured Zeke she'd managed to (just barely) survive the heartbreak of his absence. For some reason, Sugar had transferred her allegiance to Zeke and, God help him, he'd grown accustomed to seeing her whiskered mug on the pillow beside him each morning.

"Stupid mutt," he muttered.

She sighed and looked at him with adoration. Stripping off a glove, he scratched her ears.

Looking on, Hank grinned. "I warn you, dude. She's fickle. A few Milkbones from me and she'll be putty in my hands."

"Then by all means, bribe her."

Knowing he didn't mean it, Sugar panted happily. Behind them, the donkeys' requests for their own supper grew more strident.

"I've got a ton of reading to do. Hank, can you do the donkeys tonight?" Rose grabbed her backpack and headed toward the house. Zeke sighed. It was her turn.

"If you'll do the dishes, I will!" Hank called after her. Waving a hand in assent, she didn't turn around. " 'Why, thanks, Hank. You're the best brother anyone ever had.' Sisters." Glancing up at the sky, Hank pointed. "Look at that. Taurus."

Zeke looked but only saw the night, a brilliant display of diamonds scattered on black crepe, but nothing unusual. "Where?"

"See that really bright star? That's Aldebaran, one of the brightest stars in the sky. And that tight cluster—looks like about six of them? That's Pleiades. It's really hundreds of stars located close to each other. They're part of the Taurus constellation."

"You sound like one of the Sidewalk Astronomers."

"Sidewalk—what's that?"

"A group in San Francisco that hauls telescopes out into the streets and waylays pedestrians to show them the wonders of the sky. Not that San Francisco always offers up a clear one, but when it does, it's pretty stunning."

"Sweet. There's not many people around here who know much about astronomy."

Zeke was still squinting upward. "I'm not sure I'm making it out."

Hank moved up beside him and extended his arm, so Zeke could sight along it. "Aldebaran is the bull's-eye. And there are the horns. They're a sign of, well, you know, fertility." There was a blush in the his voice.

To put him at ease, Zeke made his voice matter-of-fact. "A bull? Not exactly feminine. Demeter—one of the earth goddesses—is a better definition of fertility, don't you think?"

"Well, mom's birthday's in May." Hank was still gazing upward. "Taurus is her sign. Fertility. Practicality. Creativity." Hank grinned. "And stubbornness. So it fits."

"Gee . . . ya think?"

Hank's grin widened. He shouldered his backpack and turned toward the house.

"Donkeys?" Zeke reminded him in a mild voice.

"Oh yeah. Right." Hank stopped and held out the backpack. "Could you take this in for me, dude?"

"Sure . . . dude." The word almost stuck on his tongue. He glanced at the chicken coop, where lights were glowing. "Check on Lily-Too, too, would you? And, hey!" he added as Hank started off. "Are we still on for driving lessons tomorrow?"

Hank nodded, but the grin that had widened at Zeke's slang faded.

Pulling his glove back on, Zeke watched him go. The nights of sharing donkey duty had paid off. Hank had lost his aloofness, but not that continual undernote of disquiet or his aversion to obtaining a license. He'd agreed to driving lessons only because Zeke had pointed out his family could really use another driver, especially after Zeke returned to Lil and Jon's next week. Although Patricia had driven a little already, using two feet on the brake, Zeke worried daily use would hurt her recovery. Fortunately, like a lot of rural kids, Hank had acquired some rudimentary skills over the years as well as some lessons from his grandfather after he'd gotten his instruction permit. It wouldn't take long to complete the process.

Zeke shouldered Hank's pack and turned toward the house, wondering if Hank's reluctance to drive stemmed from a greater unwillingness to grow up. Growing up meant learning to deal with adult issues. Including sexuality. Zeke didn't know if the slight evidence he'd seen meant Hank was just curious about homosexuality or struggling with the issue himself. But he suspected the latter. He'd hoped that during their lessons, Hank would open up, but so far he hadn't.

In the mudroom, Zeke abandoned both backpack and Sugar, who suddenly showed more enthusiasm for the fat scraps someone had left in her bowl than she had for Zeke.

"Fair-weather friend," Zeke muttered and entered the kitchen.

Home assailed his senses: warmth from the woodstove, cheer from Patricia's decorating palette, and sustenance in the form of something simmering in a pot. Stomach rumbling, he peered in, then frowned. While she'd grown more adept with crutches and her ankle ached less often, Patricia shouldn't have stood for as long as it must have taken to chop all these vegetables and trim beef.

Wondering if she'd listen to a reprimand (and pretty much figuring she wouldn't, but deciding to try, anyway), Zeke made his way through the dining room, table already set, and stopped on the threshold to the parlor. The urge to scold his patient abruptly faded.

Studying a paper in her hands, Patricia was in her usual spot on the sofa, her legs stretched out and covered by Nod, an open book, and the afghan. Lending her complexion a soft bloom and highlighting the red in her hair, a fire crackled on the hearth. A whisper of rosemary hung in the air. It was a normal scene, a mundane scene. But suddenly a thought snuck up and struck him hard. *She* was home.

She looked up. "Oh, hi. Where are the kids? And before you say anything, I chopped up everything while sitting at the table. Lily-Too helped."

"Good." Tightness gripped his chest, weakening his voice. Swallowing against the sensation, he took his usual chair, hooking an ankle over his knee. "Rose is reading something so dense I'm not even sure it's English. Hank is with the donkeys; Lily-Too, the chickens."

She shook her head. "What a marvel. I don't even have to badger them anymore."

"They're good kids. They just needed a reminder that they aren't the center of the universe."

Earlier in their acquaintance, them would have been

fightin' words, but Patricia just smiled. God, what a smile.

"So." He nodded to the book. "What now?" She'd completed *Pride and Prejudice*.

She grimaced. "*Babbitt.* It's tough going."

"Yes, but Sinclair is one hell of a writer."

"Yes, but the character is so . . . shallow. I can't like him."

"No, the fellow isn't likeable," he agreed. But he wondered if it wasn't the character's inner restlessness that had, by brushing too close to home, actually sparked her distaste.

"But easier to swallow than this." She looked back down at the paper and sighed. "Daisy's quarter report. She sent it with a note telling me not to worry, she'd bring up the grades before the end of semester."

He'd like to smooth away those lines on her forehead, shoulder some of her load. A natural reaction, though, wasn't it? He'd always rooted for the underdog. The tendency had led him to hook up with Jon all those years ago, believing in Jon's talent before Jon had fully believed it himself. He studied Patricia's face. And just like Jon, he knew Patricia was graced with more competence than she thought.

If she wasn't, he thought wryly, *I wouldn't be directing the pageant.*

"I wish I could believe what she says, except from what Melanie said on Saturday, the only thing Daisy is studying is Danny. I wish Daisy could live here while she went to school."

"Eliminate the distraction?"

"Not really. I mean, it would be strange if she didn't want to date, and Danny is a nice enough boy; she grew up with him and I know his family. But Daisy's letting herself get sidetracked, just like she did with him in high school. If she was here, I could still, well, you know. Help her with homework."

He blinked. A college coed would still need a mother sitting at her elbow? "I, uh, take it she needed help all through school."

"Yes. Some kids do."

Although he'd think by now . . . "Um, maybe if she still needs help, school isn't for her."

"Surely you don't think she should quit?"

He shrugged. "Just something to consider."

"You can't mean that. Those three young women—Daisy and her cousins—will be the first college graduates in this family."

"If you don't beat them to it."

"Yes, if I don't beat . . ." She looked at him suspiciously. "What do you mean by that?"

"Nothing."

"Daisy has an opportunity the rest of us didn't have at her age. She needs to get that degree before she's loaded down with responsibilities. I mean, look at me."

"No problem."

The color in her face deepened. "I *meant,* look at how hard it is for me to go to college now."

"Maybe that's something else you need to reconsider."

"You think you know everything, don't you?"

"Darn tootin'."

"Well, you—" She stopped and peered at him. "Darn tootin'?"

"I'm learning the local lingo. You may thank Tansy Eppelwaite for that one." He steepled his fingers, knowing the pedantic gesture would drive her nuts. "I hate to point this out—"

"Then don't."

He really did love these exchanges. "—But you are truant from class tonight."

"I told you earlier I just—that I was tired. That my ankle hurt. That—" She pursed her lips. "This discussion isn't *about* me. It's about Daisy. And Daisy doesn't need to give up. What she needs is a tutor, someone to keep her on task."

"And that someone is you?"

"Of course. Maybe. I'll talk to her when she comes back for the fall birthday party." It was tradition for the O'Malleys to hold a seasonal birthday celebration. "I can insist she return home each weekend; I do still hold the purse strings."

"You can," he agreed. He thought back to their conversation concerning Lily-Too's problems in school. "And you can also convert the weaving room upstairs into class space so you can work there with Daisy on the weekends when you aren't homeschooling Lily-Too."

Patricia sat up straighter, bouncing Nod off her lap. The cat scrambled to land on his feet, then gave her a look of mild disdain before turning his large blue orbs on Zeke with an expression that dared Zeke to refute that he'd *meant* that to happen.

"What, *exactly,* are you trying to tell me?"

"Just that I find it disturbing how ready you are to bend your life around your children instead of insisting they stand on their own. If I weren't here, you'd also be adding pageant directing onto your to-do List, I suppose fitting it into the five minutes of spare time you might have each week between running this household, mucking out stables, working, attending to your studies—which you hate, by the way—chauffeuring the unruly mob, tutoring Daisy, and homeschooling Lily-Too. When what you'd rather be doing is working at your loom." He was no longer feeling so amused.

"This really isn't any of your business. And I didn't say I was definitely going to—"

Exasperated, he held up a hand. "You're right. This *isn't* any of my business."

They subsided into silence, Patricia looking grumpy.

She finally spoke up. "At least I have a purpose to my life."

"I do, too, thanks to you."

"I appreciate your help with the pageant and what you're doing for Lily-Too." Patricia's voice was sulky. "I talked to her, and she's willing to work with you on 'Silent Night.' She'll try out next Tuesday, if you can manage something private. But she won't promise she'll do it."

"I'll find her an understudy, if it helps, although she *will* perform. Once she knows she's better than the others, she won't be able to stand anyone else stealing her limelight."

Patricia's eyebrows rose. "You're speaking from personal experience?"

"Yes, as a matter of fact. I was the best." He had been.

"I so hate displays of false modesty."

Entertained again, his mouth quirked. "But while I know music and figure I can manage this show, I've hit a problem. Preacher Phelps and I were hoping you could help."

"You know I'll do whatever I can."

"I do. As long as it's for one of your children." He shook his head when she puffed up. "No, don't get started again. That was a cheap shot and I take it back."

"You'd better. Now, what can I do?"

Briefly Zeke described the indignities the backdrops had suffered. "We need an artist."

She opened her mouth.

"No, not *you*."

"But—"

"Good God, woman. Weren't we just talking about your lack of spare time?"

"Okay, okay. But if not me, who?"

By her disgruntled expression, he figured she

wanted to argue, but since they'd just finished bickering, he guessed she'd decided to hold off. "Maybe your mother's friend Bebe?"

"Bebe? I can't ask her to—she doesn't even live here."

"Not a problem. Once she's seen the backdrops, if she thinks she can repair them, I'll get them up to Columbia and she can work on them when she has time."

"But—"

Zeke leaned forward. He felt . . . gads . . . silly, but he knew she'd understand. "Patricia, maybe this is sentimental nonsense, but tonight Finn Phelps said Maisie Ann was the original artist. It would mean a great deal to him if he had at least that much left of her."

Patricia studied him. "It also means something to you."

"The man is in pain." Zeke sat back and looked at the fire. "I don't doubt Maisie Ann had more than enough reason to leave—or at least one big reason in the form of Mrs. Phelps. But there's usually fault on both sides for the ruin of a marriage. Maisie Ann has her pharmacist for consolation, so I think Finn Phelps should be allowed his backdrops. At least until he recognizes that the good Lynette is more than ready to take Maisie Ann's place."

"I always thought Lynette was sweet on Finn."

"She most definitely is." He looked back at Patricia and let his gaze wander around the smile that had finally softened her lips. "And she also seems more skilled at handling Mrs. Phelps than Maisie Ann apparently was. So . . . will you ask Bebe to help?"

Her smile disappeared. "I'm not sure I can."

He frowned; he'd thought that smile had meant success. "But why—"

"I should say, I'm not sure that I *want* to."

Chapter 13

She left it like that. And perhaps because he realized he'd skated on thin ice with all those comments about her management of her family, Zeke had let her drop the subject.

Not that he could have inserted a word edgewise at supper, anyway. Rose angsted over her first tests of the quarter while her siblings rolled their eyes, knowing she'd ace them all, Hank waxed poetic over not one, but two, shooting stars that had streaked across the sky while he was corralling Dharma and Dowdy, and even Lily-Too babbled, filled with nervous excitement over her tryout next week.

After they'd cleaned up the kitchen, while the children did homework, Patsy Lee and Zeke shared the parlor, Ray Charles on the CD player, and the warmth of the fire. There was plenty of opportunity to talk, but both were engrossed in their books.

Or that's how it seemed. Patsy Lee felt Zeke's gaze resting on her more than once. And she was rereading the same page over and over while she wrestled with what he'd said about Daisy and with whether she wanted to tell him about Bebe.

Eventually, but not without a struggle, considering she'd skipped class tonight not because she was tired, but just because she just didn't want to go—dang his,

his *perspicacity*—she was able to dismiss his comments about Daisy. Of *course* Daisy should get her degree. Was he nuts? No matter what else Daisy wanted to do, she could do it just as well a few years from now with a diploma hanging on her wall. What to tell him about Bebe wasn't so easily settled, though.

When Lily-Too came in to wish them good night, Patsy Lee took the opportunity to escape to her room, dragging her quandary with her. Not that it was such a big deal, really. She was astute enough herself (thank you very much) to understand that her reluctance to discuss Bebe stemmed from the hurts she'd suffered on her parents' behalf in the past, not from how she expected Zeke to react now. . . . Right?

So once morning had dawned and the children had left for school, she joined him in the kitchen to explain. He'd flipped off the overhead fixture and worked by the diffused light of early dawn that was teasing the colors in the room to life. Days were growing even shorter as the end of October neared.

"Here, I can do that." Patsy Lee leaned her crutches next to the sink and reached for the skillet he'd used to make whole-grain pancakes.

Humming, he relinquished it and moved around the room, putting away syrup and butter and carting dishes to the counter. She darted a look at him, suspecting his nonchalance was an act while he waited for her to apologize or at least explain why she'd refused Bebe's help.

Hating that he usually guessed her intentions, she washed the pan, then pulled out the canola oil that had replaced the Crisco she'd once used. Since Zeke had moved in, they'd all learned more than they really wanted to about good and bad fats. While she rubbed it into the pan to season it for the next use, he plugged the drain and turned on the taps. The billow of steam, the clatter of dishes, and the warmth of his arm as it brushed hers helped settle the tapping feet in her stomach.

"Zeke, I, um, thought maybe you deserved an explanation for why I didn't want to call Bebe. I roped you into the pageant. The least I can do is tell you why at the first opportunity, I'm refusing to help."

He glanced down at her. "Patricia, you don't owe me. I volunteered to do the pageant. I *want* to do the pageant. For Lily-Too. And the pageant can make do with something other than the traditional backdrops."

"But I want to explain."

Placing a stack of Fiestaware into the sink, he smiled. "Yeah, I can tell."

"I do, it's just . . ."

She set the skillet aside and picked up a towel. It was just that no matter how sophisticated, cosmopolitan, and tolerant she knew Zeke to be, she preferred keeping this quiet, not dredging it up. Every time she brought it up, she was forced to relive memories of more than two decades ago. She could hear the taunts from her high school classmates as she hurried through the hallways, see the smirks of townsfolk when she walked down Main, suffer the pitying looks from members of the Ladies' Auxiliary. Not everyone had jeered, of course, but even a few bigots wielded the power to hurt. And the uncomfortable silence from others had been almost as bad. Over the years—with the exception of people like Ernie Burcham—most people had either forgotten or no longer cared, and she was happy to just leave things that way.

But this was silly. This was *Zeke*. She took a deep breath. "Bebe moved in with us when I was ten. My mom wasn't married; my father nonexistent." Just how nonexistent, Bebe had only recently told her. "She helped raise me, and after Mom died and I got married, she became like a grandmother to my kids."

"It sounds like she's a very close friend."

"More than a friend. She was my mother's lover. Her life partner."

She kept her head down, watching his hands. He didn't drop a plate. The circular motion of the dishrag didn't falter. She didn't hear even a tiny gasp of dismay. She glanced up.

A shocked expression on his face, he was staring out the window. "Good *God.*"

Alarmed, she peered out, too, and saw nothing. *"What?"*

"The world didn't end."

Anxiety shedding off her like rain, she laughed and poked him with an elbow. "This isn't a joking matter."

"Nor is it a world crisis." He set a plate in the drainer. "Did you really think that would make any difference to me?"

"To you . . . no. But you've lived too long in San Francisco. Bigotry is alive and well off the beaten path. And that's why I don't like to ask Bebe to come here. She already sacrificed enough *living* here when this is where Mom wanted to spend her last years. Bebe would have done anything for her. Maybe moving wasn't a picnic for me, but it was harder for her. For them. It was always harder for them. Especially here."

"It probably wasn't easy for them anywhere." He turned and cupped her chin. A single rivulet of water traveled down her neck and under her shirt. The sensation was unbelievably erotic. "Bigotry exists all over the place, Patricia, not just here." Something in the back of his gaze shifted. He released her chin.

His touch lingered, soap bubbles tingling where his fingers had lain. "I know. But here . . . so many people know each other and they whisper. And there are others, like Ernie Burcham, who do more than whisper."

"Ernie who?"

"Burcham. He owns the Piggly Wiggly. He thinks anyone who's not white, Protestant, and a member of the NRA isn't worth as much as the dirt on his shoes. Maybe that wouldn't matter so much, except he's important in this town, so people listen to him."

"Maybe they listen. But that doesn't mean they share his beliefs." Zeke handed her a juice glass. "So that's why Hank objected so strongly to stopping at the Piggly Wiggly."

"I've told them I don't want Burcham to get even a dime out of us."

"Your children know about Bebe?"

"Yes! I knew about my mom and Bebe all my life and it didn't corrupt me. I loved them."

"Whoa. I don't believe I said you shouldn't have told them. Why so defensive?"

She slapped the juice glass onto a shelf. "Because you always have an opinion—and not a good one—on how I manage my children."

"I imagine you told them because, one, you'd like them to grow into tolerant human beings, and, two, you want them prepared to deal with any dirt that's flung her way when they're with her. Good reasons." Done washing, Zeke dried off his hands. "That's assuming they ever *are* with her."

"Of course they're with her. Why would you think they aren't?"

He shrugged. "Her absence since you broke your ankle. Columbia is less than two hours from Cordelia, but even though she calls repeatedly, she hasn't made the trip. Nor have you invited her. In fact," he continued, "she wasn't seriously considered as a possible caretaker, nor was she present at Mari O'Malley's wedding."

He didn't have to be so observant. "I told you why I don't like to ask her to come here. And she couldn't have, anyway. She works in Columbia."

"From what I've gathered, she would have pitched in."

"And she wasn't at the wedding because . . . because she doesn't know the O'Malleys that well. My mom was friends with Zinnia, but Bebe didn't meet her until we moved here."

"Zinnia O'Malley is far from reserved about welcoming stray chickens into her flock. Witness myself." He set the towel aside.

"All right! I take the children to Columbia to visit at least four times a year, but I don't invite her to come here very often. Satisfied?"

"Because of the Ernie Burchams in Cordelia."

"Yes." She folded her arms.

"So because of Ernie Burcham, I will not receive any help on the backdrops from the only artist I'm aware of in this vicinity."

"Not the only one. I can—"

"The only one who has two intact ankles *and* the time *and* would like to do something to help." Giving a mournful sigh, he opened a cabinet door and pulled out two mugs. "Maybe if I shot Ernie Burcham . . . ?"

In spite of herself, she gurgled." It's *not* just him. It's . . . the last time Bebe and I talked, we had an argument." Actually, Bebe hadn't said anything sharp; only Patsy Lee had. She sobered. What had happened wasn't Bebe's fault, but she wasn't ready to let go of her anger. Not yet. "So I don't think now is the right time to ask her for anything."

"The right time for her . . . or for you?"

In the waxing light, the colored tiles gleamed like costume jewelry.

"Would you stop with the insinuations? You don't understand!"

Dropping her towel on the counter, Patsy Lee grabbed her crutches and hobbled to the table. She lowered herself into a chair and ran a hand through her hair. Zeke poured coffee into his mug; steeped tea in hers. When it was done, he slid it onto the table, then took a chair beside her, angling it so he faced her.

"Do you want to talk about it? Note, I'm not insisting. And I promise not to say a word."

"Give yourself a minute. You'll come up with something."

Eyes lighting, he toasted her with his mug. "Not bad. Now, tell me about this argument."

She eyed him.

"You'll feel better."

"And you might get an artist to help with your pageant."

"There *is* that, of course."

She laughed and he gave a satisfied smile that grew soft as he looked at her. "You really will feel better if you tell me, though. I promise."

Under the caress of his gaze, she thought maybe she really would. She toyed with the handle on her mug. "It's hard to explain, exactly, but it started when Daisy left for college. . . ."

That morning had bristled with activity and laughter. They'd flown around the house to get Daisy—perpetually late—ready to go by the time her cousins arrived. The three cousins' excited voices as they'd loaded Daisy's gear into Melanie's Blazer had rung sharp against the quiet woodland. Long after the Blazer had topped the farthest hill, long after the dust had settled back onto the grasses that lined the ditches, Patsy Lee had stared down Red Hollow Road, knowing her first child would never come home again, not in quite the same way. Then she'd wandered up to Daisy's room and sprawled across her daughter's bed, clutching Daisy's blanket, smelling Daisy's shampoo on the pillows, feeling the passage of time unlike she'd ever felt it before. For a while, she'd cried.

"When Daisy left, I felt—"

"You said *it started*. What started? The argument?"

"No. You see, when Daisy left for college, I felt like part of myself had come undone. Like she'd left a gap. Then the gap started filling with new thoughts. And I was thinking—"

"Bad thoughts?"

"Not really. I just started questioning some things, considering things I hadn't considered before. And one—"

"What kinds of *things*?"

She glared at him. "Cripes. You told me you wouldn't say a word."

"That's better. You were sounding like Eeyore. *Woe is me.*"

"Fat lot of good it would do me. You don't have the compassion of Winnie-the-Pooh."

He smiled. "Go on."

She settled for one last glare, then continued. "I thought about my father. I'd never known him. I never even asked Mom much about him—I thought it might hurt her and Bebe. That they'd think I wasn't happy with them—you know. Mom told me only that he'd been the last boyfriend she'd had before she'd accepted she was wired differently than most women. She was only nineteen when she got pregnant and still confused about her identity. Anyway, she said after my dad found out she was pregnant, he joined the service and she never heard from him again. 'Good riddance,' she'd always say. 'Who needs him?' "

"If that's all she said, she had admirable self-control. Sorry, but he sounds like an ass."

"That's what I thought. Maybe not *that* exactly. But from what she said, he wasn't anyone I wanted to know. I put him out of my mind. Except for, well, you know—childish thoughts that maybe he'd one day swoop into my life and love me. But mostly I didn't think about him. And after Mom died, I was wrapped up in grieving. And then I married Henry. And then I started having babies before the ink was hardly dry on our wedding certificate. So who had time to think about him much?

"But after Daisy left, I started asking myself if I really wanted to end my life not knowing anything about him, even if he was a . . . well, an ass. And I thought maybe he might feel differently now. I mean, they were young."

"That sounds reasonable."

"But it still took me a while to work up my courage. Not long ago, I asked Bebe about him, but she discouraged me from trying to find him, said she didn't want me to get hurt, said she couldn't help me, that she didn't know any more than I did. I could tell she wasn't telling me everything; I was certain she knew who he was. The weekend I broke my ankle, I'd planned to go to Columbia and give it one last try. When I couldn't go, she called me—that first day you were here, remember?—and told me she really *didn't* know who my father was."

"So she'd been telling the truth."

"Not entirely. The reason *she* didn't know is because neither did Mom."

"I'm not following."

"It was all a lie. A big fat story. Mom never had a boyfriend. Ever. I'm a seed that was planted during an experiment to see if her pendulum really swung the way she thought it did. I'm the result of—of one night's drunken *rutting*. The night she graduated from high school, she traipsed into a bar with a fake ID, got loosened up on liquor, picked out a fella and *voilà*, here I am."

Her voice wavered. She wasn't sure if it was a lump of sadness in her throat or a kernel of anger. "I'm mad. At her for lying. At Bebe for keeping quiet. I trusted them. I don't understand why Mom lied.

And . . . it hurts, that's all. Maybe it shouldn't matter, maybe I'm silly to be so sensitive about it, but I thought I had a history and—this sounds so corny, but it's the way I feel—a beginning that had at least started in love. And now I just feel like—like a piece of trivia."

Setting down his mug, Zeke moved his chair until their knees were interlocked, then pulled her forward so her head rested against his chest. The flannel of his shirt was soft beneath her cheek, his chest hard, his heart the sound of forever.

"There's another way to look at this, you know." His chin rested on her head. "Instead of one of life's ciphers, I could argue that your conception was a wonder of synchronicity. Meant to happen—isn't every child meant to happen?" Holding her by the shoulders, he pushed them apart until he could look into her eyes. "Quit selling yourself short, Patricia."

He hesitated. Then, before she grasped what was happening, he pulled her toward him and his lips found hers. It was a tiny kiss at first, one that landed at the corner of her mouth. Her breath hitched. His, too. Then his tongue did a gentle glide along her upper lip and he gathered her closer, folding her into his arms, pressing her full against his chest, his mouth urging hers open. For long moments, their tongues danced. Her senses swam. And then he pulled away.

They gazed at each other in disbelief, their breathing rapid.

Zeke shook his head. "Well, wasn't that a helluva note?"

"Um. Um, yes." Patsy Lee let her breath out slowly, wondering what in the blazes had come over her. Okay, not really wondering that—what had come over her was a hormonal surge that had left her wanting to strip him naked and have him on the kitchen table. And wouldn't he have lived to rue that adventure?

She gave a short laugh. “Let’s call it, uh, too-close quarters and a lapse in judgment brought on by emotion.”

He was silent a moment. “I guess we could do that.”

“Darn tootin’.” Knowing her face was flaming, Patsy Lee pulled her crutches over and rose. “I guess it’s a good thing you’ll be moving out next week.”

She felt his eyes on her back as she swung herself through the doorway.

“Darn tootin’.” His voice was quiet.

Chapter 14

Midafternoon on Halloween, three days after that kiss and three days before Zeke moved back to Lil and Jon's—time that wouldn't pass quickly enough—Patsy Lee let herself out onto her in-law's screened-in porch, juggling her crutches and a bag of chips she held with her teeth. Laughter echoed from the backyard.

Since sunrise had fired a day of brilliant blue, Zinnia had set up the party outside. They were still calling it the O'Malley Fall Birthday Celebration, but since Pop was the only family member who was both in town and had a birth date that qualified, Zinnia had expanded the event into a Halloween gala. The picnic table on the porch held a plump jack-o'-lantern and a punch bowl of Sherbet Shiver Punch that smoked with dry ice. Other tables, draped with orange-and-black crepe paper and costumed children, dotted the carpet of leaves in the backyard.

Depositing her chips between the fruit ambrosia and five-bean salad, Patsy Lee picked out various members of her family. Helped by Jon, Lil wielded a brush at the face-painting table. Rose and her cousin Michael manned apple-bobbing at another. And looking like he might be enjoying the festivities more than the kids, Zeke, with Lily-Too acting as assistant, helped decorate pumpkins at a third. Her gaze lingered there before moving on.

At the barbeque pit near the detached garage, wearing a brand-new fishing hat that would probably be lucky to see three minutes' use before he plopped the old one back on his head, Pop poked at hot dogs with a long-handled fork. Around him, a number of people had gathered, paper plates in hand. Most she recognized, but a lot she didn't.

Nostalgia plucked at her heart. Once upon a time, only O'Malleys and a very few favored guests had populated these celebrations, but as the family had grown and scattered, these seasonal celebrations had faltered. Unwilling to concede anything to time, Zinnia had started to bolster attendance by inviting her neighbors, mostly young families who had moved into the coveted homes near the town square as the older generation had passed on.

Helped by its proximity to the lake region to the south and by an astute city council led by a shrewd mayor (Evelyn Noflinger wielded tax incentives with the same skill that the Pied Piper had brandished a flute), Cordelia was fortunate to be growing, not dying, like many of the surrounding small towns. Still, Patsy Lee found some changes bittersweet.

Bittersweet. Her gaze returned to Zeke.

Laugh lines crinkling, his eyes snapped with pleasure as he helped a toddler pour a mountain of glitter over a mountain of glue, both of them oblivious to the mess they were making. She smiled. He had a knack with youngsters. His cynicism and fastidiousness—both affectations, if you asked her—completely dissolved in their company. It was one of the things she'd learned to lo—*like* about him.

Smile fading, she turned away. They'd dismissed that kiss with a few (stiff) jokes since it so obviously had only been a moment when opportunity had overridden common sense, and they hadn't mentioned it since. But a reserve had grown between them, new and different from the one they'd experienced during their first days together.

That was a helluva note, wasn't it?

Remembering his words, her face heated. If he hadn't stomped on the brakes at that precise point, if his reaction hadn't been wide-eyed surprise, if he'd pulled her back into his arms instead . . . "I'd probably have jumped his bones."

She started at the sound of her voice, then closed her eyes in mute thankfulness she was alone. When she opened them again, Zeke was still in her sights. Today he was dressed all in black, suitable for the occasion, he'd said. Black denim hugged his thighs and black flannel molded his shoulders. But he didn't look scary at all. What was scary was how often now that she noticed those thighs, those shoulders. . . . Those hands and eyes and mouth and . . .

God. She wiped her brow. Who *was* she? Sometimes she didn't know anymore.

Behind her, Zinnia elbowed open the screen door, arms laden with a bowl of potato salad, damp curls stuck to her forehead. "I sure do wish the girls would've come home this weekend."

"Me, too." She'd wanted to talk with Daisy about her grades. Zeke's words had stuck, but she still thought there was something she could do to help her. "But you can't really blame them. MU had a big game against Nebraska yesterday. Today they've got homework." At least she hoped that was really why Daisy had seemed reluctant to come home.

"I suppose." Zinnia set down the bowl and scanned the backyard. "So Zeke moves back to Lil's on Wednesday."

"Yes."

"Too bad. Don't suppose you've noticed the way he's lookin' at you today? All he'd need is a little encourage—"

She couldn't stand it. "Stop." Believe you me, she'd studied Zeke's expressions with the same concentration Winken gave a mouse, and she would have known if he'd felt anything more than vast relief. Whatever Zinnia was seeing was a hopeful figment of her imagination.

Momentarily silenced by Patsy Lee's unusual protest, Zinnia recovered fast. "I'm only telling you what's plain as the nose on your—"

Thank God, Hank stepped out on the porch before she had to resort to violence. He held a tray of cupcakes Zeke and Lily-Too had baked yesterday while Patsy Lee stayed (hid out) in her room, pretending to study. "I just saw Bebe pull up. I didn't know she was coming."

His glance at his grandmother was anxious. Patsy Lee didn't blame him; Zinnia's reactions to anything she hadn't planned herself were unpredictable.

"Good. She made it." Patsy Lee made her voice casual, like Bebe attending an O'Malley party was a common event. In reality, it had been years since they'd all been together. She'd told Zeke the truth—she did invite Bebe here on occasion, but just not, well, *here*. Bebe came to the farmhouse, and any trips they made into Cordelia were brief.

Zinnia took the tray. "You invited Bebe? Well, I'll be. I haven't seen her in ages."

"I was just thinking about her the other day, and decided this might be fun."

Right. What she'd done was react out of guilt to Zeke's insinuations that she was ashamed of Bebe. He was wrong. She didn't invite Bebe to these things simply because not inviting Bebe had become habit. And she was still uncertain if she should have done it this time. She didn't want Bebe to suffer any unpleasantness.

Her stomach squirmed, and she glanced at Zinnia. Her mother-in-law looked bemused but not dismayed. And most of the rest of the party didn't even know Bebe (or, more specifically, Bebe's orientation). Everything would be fine.

Outside, there was a crash, then a child squalled.

Zinnia shook her head. "Looks like Penny Mason's son has gotten into the garbage. Why that woman can't keep track of that boy . . ." She pushed through the screen door and trundled down the walk to rescue the tot.

Zeke pushed his way in. "Hank? Would you—"

"Yoo-hoo!"

The back door banged open and Bebe shouldered her way onto the porch, her crest of silver hair styled straight up, a Dumpster of a handbag over one shoulder, a plastic grocery bag in her hand, and a dazzling smile stretching across her elfin face.

Hank was nearest. "Bebe!"

He hugged Bebe with more enthusiasm than Patsy Lee had seen from him in months, crushing the bag between them. Guilt nudged her again—she should make a point to see Bebe more often. Apparently forgetting whatever he'd been about to say, Zeke leaned against the door frame, face alive with interest. Bebe had that effect on people.

"Wmfph!" Bebe replied, her face buried in Hank's jacket. A petite woman, she barely reached his armpit.

"Oh, sorry." Hank let her go.

Shaking her head, she looked up at the boy she considered her grandson. Beaded earrings, multicolored like her poncho, bounced. "Whoa, you've shot up. And it's only been a couple months since I saw you. Isn't it a couple months? I can't keep things straight anymore; I don't know where the damn time goes." She turned to Patsy Lee. Her smile stayed bright, but wariness muted her sharp blue eyes. "Dear, c'mere." The plastic bag slapped Patsy Lee's rear as Bebe's arms went around her.

"I'm so glad you came," Patsy Lee said, meaning it, all her ire and anxiety slipping away in the comfort of a refuge she'd known as a child.

"And I'm so glad you asked me." She looked at Zeke. "I know you. Van Castle, right? Zeke Townsend. No, sorry, brain's going. Townley. That's it." She held out her hand.

While they shook hands and exchanged some small talk, Bebe glanced at Patsy Lee, who gave her a slight nod back, communicating to Bebe that Zeke knew their relationship. It was a coded exchange they'd used through much of her life.

"Here, take this." Bebe handed off the bag to Patsy Lee.

Patsy Lee peeked inside at a clutch of celery sticks and a block of creamed cheese. "Still a regular Martha Stewart."

"Hey, be thankful for getting even that. I didn't remember until a few blocks from here that I was supposed to bring something. The only place on the way was the Piggly Wiggly."

Patsy Lee tensed.

"So, hoping against hope that That Man—what was his name?" Bebe poked Hank. "Bernie Urchel? Hurlin' Burgers?"

Hank snickered. "Ernie Burcham."

"Yep, him." Bebe combed her hair with her fingers. "I'd hoped he'd died a horrible death a long time ago, but there he was. Still haunting the place. Made some comment about muff—"

"Bebe!" Patsy Lee glanced at Hank, then Zeke. She could tell Zeke was biting the inside of his cheek.

"Oh, pooh. Hank's almost a man. Zeke's a man-about-town. They've heard it all before." Bebe ruffled Hank's hair. "Anyway, he told me that me and my lack of family values weren't welcome in his store. Which was too bad. Because I was so shocked and insulted, I'm afraid two jars of pickled beets slipped right out of my hands and smashed on his shiny white linoleum."

Hank's snicker became mirth; Patsy Lee couldn't resist a snort. Zeke laughed.

And a hoot sounded from the outside stoop as Zinnia pulled open the screen door. "Lord love a duck, it never does cease to amaze me why Ernie Burcham doesn't see the mortifying lack of IQ he displays every time he opens his mouth. Nobody with sense listens to the man, he just thinks they do, so don't you pay him no never-mind." She made her way toward Bebe, eyes dancing behind her glasses. "Family values, indeed! Up to his eyeballs in divorce court a couple years back for cheating on his wife, he was. The man wouldn't know a family value if it walked up and bit him."

Zeke's raised brows practically shouted *I told you so*; she ignored him.

"How lovely to see you again, Zinnia." They released each other and Bebe wiped her eyes. "Oh, my. Sorry for the waterworks—you were just such a godsend when Ruth was dying."

Patsy Lee stared. It wasn't that Zinnia hadn't been a help; she just didn't remember Bebe and Zinnia becoming close enough for warm embraces. Nor had she thought Zinnia had been motivated by sheer altruism back then.

It was during those dark days before her mother died that she'd attracted Henry O'Malley's notice. He'd asked her out, she'd refused, unwilling to overburden Bebe while she did something so frivolous as dating. Charmingly—oh, Henry could be so charming—he'd persisted. Around that time, Zinnia had volunteered to help. She'd always assumed Zinnia had lent a hand less out of friendship than from a desire to further her son's cause. She bit her lip. What had Zeke said about her *kids* feeling they were center of the universe?

Bebe apparently noticed her surprise. "When you were at work and the nights would get long, sometimes Zinnia would come over and we'd just sit and drink tea and talk into the wee hours. And there she was, with kids at home, needing to get up and going in the morning. . . ." Bebe smiled at Zinnia. "But you always had time for me and Ruth."

Zinnia shook a finger at Bebe. "Now, why haven't you taken me up on one of those invitations I've sent along over the years?"

"Oh, you know how it is. Things are just always so busy; time just slips away."

Inside, an oven timer dinged. "Brownies." Zinnia bustled to the door. "Back in a mo'."

"Ze-*eke*!" Out at the pumpkin-decorating table, Lily-Too clambered up on the bench, holding glitter and glue out of reach of smaller hands. Hair sticking straight out like sunrays, she glowered at the porch. "You said you'd get Hank and come *back*!"

"My, my." Bebe smiled. "That child just said more words in one chunk than I've heard out of her in years. And raising her voice . . . ?"

"Zeke's giving Lily-Too vocal and piano lessons. It's helped her shyness some."

"Is he, now?" Bebe looked between them. Patsy Lee sighed at the speculation in her expression. If Bebe joined Lil and Zinnia in a matchmaking triumvirate, they'd have more power than the Axis of Evil.

"Dude." Zeke poked Hank. Hank didn't bother to

hide his grin. The word always sounded silly in Zeke's mouth. "The pumpkin patch is more popular than the two of us can handle. I'm begging for help."

"But Bebe just got here."

Patsy Lee marveled. Despite Hank's words, the grin stayed on his face. Gone was the usual fretful expression. Zeke had noticed, too. His eyes as they rested on Hank were thoughtful.

Bebe shooed him away. "Go help your sister. I promise I won't evaporate. Your mother doesn't know it, but I've invited myself to stay for supper." They high-fived, and Hank followed Zeke out. Bebe rearranged a platter of veggies to make room for the celery. "I really am tickled you invited me, dear."

"I would have . . . I mean, I had no idea you and Zinnia . . . why didn't you tell me?"

"What's to tell? We formed a bond while Ruth was dying. But after she died, I didn't stick around long, remember? You had Henry, you didn't need me as much, and I needed to get away from the memories and back to Columbia. Cowardly, maybe, but that's the way it goes." She deposited the last of the celery and wiped her fingers. "I didn't make an effort to keep that friendship going. At first, I didn't want to. Zinnia was too strong a reminder of a horrible time. Later . . . well, life moves on."

"But I had no clue she'd invited you here. Why didn't you say anything?"

Bebe's eyes met hers. "To be frank, I wasn't sure you wanted me."

Patsy Lee flushed. "But . . . I didn't think *you'd* want . . . I mean, with Ernie Burcham and the treatment you and Mom got in this town, and the way you left so fast after Mom died, I just assumed the less time you spent in Cordelia, the better you'd like it."

"Dear, I encounter Ernie Burchams everywhere. Big city. Small town. In between. Doesn't matter.

Over the years, I've developed a tough hide. It was either that or let small-minded people like him control my life. Plus, every once in a while, I get in a shot of my own. Or a pickled beet, as the case may be. You don't need to protect me. If, indeed, that's—" She stopped, looking annoyed at herself. "Never mind."

"What?"

She hesitated. "Truth is, I've thought the person you've really been protecting is yourself." She held up a hand as Patsy Lee started to object. "If so, I don't blame you. I know you love me. I know you loved your mom. Having us as parents didn't make your childhood easy. I know, and I've wished things could have been different for you. Say, shouldn't you be off that foot?"

Patsy Lee was silent while Bebe shook out a couple of folding chairs that had been leaning in the corner.

Still turning over what Bebe had said, Patsy Lee sat down. Bebe settled beside her, and they watched the backyard activity. They'd never really talked about any of this. Not too surprising, really. Not only were the topics uncomfortable, but after her mother died and Bebe moved back to Columbia, Patsy Lee's mind had been occupied by marriage and babies and work and making ends meet. Introspection hadn't been high on her priority list and had only snuck up on her after Daisy left home and she realized how fast time was passing.

She finally stirred. "Okay, sometimes it was hard—very hard—having you and Mom as parents, but you made me a wonderful home. I know that. I don't regret anything. It's just sometimes I was confused. And now . . . now I'm even more confused."

"About your father."

"I know that one-night stands happen all the time. And one night-stands sometimes result in babies. I'm not unique. But I always trusted Mom. . . . And all that time she was lying to me. About something important. About my history. It hurts. I'm angry."

"Take it out on me. I knew. I lied, too."

"Oh, I'm mad at you, too, but you know it's not the same. I wouldn't expect you to tell me something she didn't want me to know, not even after she was gone. You loved her; you were—are—loyal. That's the way it should be, I guess. It's just that all those years, I carried around the idea it was her and me against the man who didn't want us. It was a bond between us, even after you came along. Or at least, that's what I thought."

Anger snuck up and tightened her throat. "But she never even tried to find out who he was. She never gave him a chance. He didn't reject *us*; she rejected *him,* along with any chance I had for a father. It's too late for me to find him now. How could I? Take out ads? Even if he remembered some night that long ago, it's not like he'd want to step right up and admit to being a woman's last—and only—lover before she turned to a life as a lesbian."

"You make her sound cheap. Stop it."

Out in the backyard, Hank got up from the pumpkin-decorating table.

"I'm sorry." Patsy Lee bowed her head. "I'm sorry."

"Your mother—"

Hank reached the porch, cutting the conversation short.

Patsy Lee was glad. Because she wasn't sure she was sorry at all.

Pumpkins all gone, Zeke watched Lily-Too run off to put her own creation into the car, then follow Hank. Jon and Lil were still consumed with their patrons at the face-painting table, Pop with the barbecue pit. Before he reached the house, the screen door bumped open and Bebe helped Patricia down the steps, Hank behind them.

Zeke automatically smoothed his face into the noncommittal lines he'd worn around Patricia ever since that kiss. Knowing how she could read his mind, it had been a relief to be with Jon at Vreeley Home yesterday and free of the need to pretend he wasn't affected by what had happened.

Because he was. But he couldn't sort out his feelings. Had she just looked lovely in the morning light? Had an urge to comfort gone too far? Or had it all been just been a matter of opportunity? A pair of sweet lips. A pair of warm arms. And far too long since Christine.

No. That last rang false. He'd never allowed his dick to rule his head, and he doubted he'd picked up the inclination now. But the alternatives . . . he wasn't sure he wanted to examine the alternatives. That was the bad thing about being a grown-up. He could see all the potential pitfalls. And there were a lot.

He sidestepped as a boy he recognized as Penny Mason's son darted past, chased by another kid.

That was a helluva note, wasn't it?

Remembering his words, he winced. *Way to go.* Although if he'd wanted to root out any possibility of anything more between him and Patricia—and that was exactly what he should do—it *had* been the way to go. Like she'd said, it was a good thing he'd be moving out soon.

Hearing a crash, he glanced back in time to see Penny Mason's son tip headfirst into the wash tub, splashing the apple bobbers. Habit had him changing course before he realized it. He reached the drenched and yowling child just as Lil did. By the time they hauled him out and hustled him to his mother, Patricia and Bebe had seated themselves in lawn chairs on the patio.

He approached, admiring the way the sunshine shot silver through the mahogany of Patricia's hair, the way it traced the tiny lines that usually faded into her glowing complexion, revealing the character in her face. She was one of the few people he knew who could stand the scrutiny of bright light. Watching her as she began to realize her strengths was more alluring than unfaded hair and smooth skin and, if he wanted to admit it, had more to do with that kiss than anything else. He suddenly realized she was watching him, her face as inscrutable as he hoped his still was.

In case it wasn't, after a perfunctory greeting Patricia answered with a grunt, he switched his attention to Bebe's poncho. "I can see where Patricia inherited her love of color."

"Thank you. Patricia, is it?"

"I, um, I've always liked that name better, remember?" Patricia said.

"You have?" When Patricia frowned, Bebe shrugged. "Whatever."

Zeke glanced at Patricia. Where he once might have met her eyes, all he could glimpse of her averted face was a pink cheek.

"Well." Bebe cleared her throat. "Pats-*Patricia* wove this fabric in class before she aborted college to come back here to help with Ruth. I've always wished she'd gone back after her mother died. Granted, I'm not the most objective judge, but she has quite a flair for textiles. When I passed that loom on, I knew she could give it a better workout than me. But instead of weaving, she upped and started popping out babies."

"If I hadn't," Patricia murmured. "You wouldn't have four doting grandchildren."

"Doting, my ass. I've hardly seen Daisy a whit since she started at MU."

Patricia sighed. "Nor, I'm afraid, have her professors."

"Quarter report wasn't a cause for celebration, hmm? Well, you know I love that child, but we can't claim she's ever been the greenest leaf on the tree. Perhaps college is not her forte."

Patricia met Zeke's eyes, looked away. "She needs the degree."

"Just like you need yours in business, I suppose." Bebe's voice was mild. "I wish you'd pursue art instead."

"We've been over this before. I can't uproot all of us to move to Columbia—"

"I don't see why not."

"And it wouldn't be practical even if I could. What would I do with an art degree? I can't earn a living weaving."

Zeke frowned. "Why not?"

"She's right, much is the pity. Skill and artistry aren't the problems. It's the market. Even a few sets of placemats—and they're relatively easy to do—are a full week's work. In this part of the country, not enough people are aware of the value of handwoven fabrics or, if they are, they don't have the money for them or don't want to spend it on such stuff, God bless their hard-working frugality. And fabric sculptures? I'm afraid Elvis on velvet would do better. She can't charge enough to make it worth her while."

Carrying a paper plate mounded with enough food to anchor a ship, Zinnia settled next to Bebe. Following her, Lil and Jon paused to collect more chairs. As Jon worked to untangle his, Zeke got up to help Lil unfold hers.

"So." Zinnia nodded at Bebe. "Has Zeke recruited you yet?"

"Recruited me?"

Sitting down again, Zeke glanced at Patricia. He wouldn't ask if she didn't want him to.

Patricia hesitated. "There's a problem with the

backdrops for the Christmas pageant. Zeke needs your help, if you have time." Her words were rushed. She pushed to her feet. "Excuse me while I get something to eat."

He rose, but she waved him down. "I have to learn to fend for myself again once you're gone."

"Gone?" Jon frowned. "Oh, that's right. You planned to move to the guesthouse come Wednesday, didn't you?"

"Mmm." Patricia's abrupt departure telling him that she wasn't reconciled to his request for Bebe's help, Zeke watched her swing off, admitting to himself she had grown skilled enough with the crutches that she no longer needed him, startled to realize how much he wished that she still did. Suddenly, it registered that Jon had used the past tense. "Is there a problem?"

"Oh, Zeke, we're sorry." Pretty concern bloomed on Lil's face. "But I'm afraid you can't move into our guesthouse."

Chapter 15

Wednesday around noon, as Zeke took the turnoff east toward Cordelia, Patsy Lee stared out the car window at the countryside, bleak under clouds tumbling in the early November wind. Turned down low, Aretha Franklin wailed for respect on the radio. At the orthopedic offices in Sedalia this morning, she'd been uncasted, x-rayed, and sonogrammed. No blood clots, bones healing, new cast (a dull gray this time), and the news that, even though she still shouldn't bear weight on her foot, in a few weeks she'd have the relief of a removable cast.

The good report had done little to lift her spirits, which had fallen after that kiss, dipped lower when she'd learned Zeke would continue under her roof, and then had completely bottomed out after she'd returned to work two mornings ago. She wasn't finding it easy to fit back into her groove. Merry-Go-Read felt flat.

In fact, "*Everything* feels flat."

"Why's that?"

She realized she'd spoken aloud. "Because . . ." She clamped her mouth shut. *Because I'd hoped by today to have you out of my house—and out of my head.* "I just don't understand why Lil and Jon can't take you in."

Actually, she did understand—or at least, she understood the reasons they'd given—but she was feeling a cranky need to poke at her sore spots.

Zeke gave her a knowing look before reciting what he knew she already knew. "The pump for the guesthouse well broke. The new pump won't be in for a month. They're blowing out the pipes so they won't freeze. There won't be water."

When Patsy Lee had returned to the circle sitting outside on Sunday, Lil had still been in the thick of apologies, blaming her husband for his lack of forethought. Jon hadn't delayed in calling Wamego Water Well Service once he'd realized the pump had broken, but when he found out Wamego was stretched thin with problems that had surfaced after that first freeze, he told them there wasn't any rush.

He'd forgotten all about Zeke, Lil said. Expression bland, Jon replied that it wasn't that big of a deal; Zeke could just stay right where he was.

Patsy Lee had eyed them both, sensing conspiracy. Jon would do anything if it pleased Lil, and Lil's face had been wearing a too-innocent look. They were still playing matchmaker. Or at least Lil was. Jon . . . she'd worried that maybe Jon had guessed Zeke's feelings toward his wife and was attempting to keep him at arm's length. With that thought, Patsy Lee had decided it wouldn't be wise to press Jon harder for the truth. Or at least, that's what she was telling herself.

"But what about Melanie's room? You could use that."

Zeke rattled off Lil's excuses. "Let's see . . . there's my anticipated distaste of ruffled bed skirts, the sanctity of a young woman's room, and where would Mel sleep over the Thanksgiving holiday?"

Bunch of hokum. Lil had always been a rotten liar.

"And, not wanting to put you out any longer—"

"It's not that, really. I—"

"—I asked about staying at the O'Malleys.' But from what I was told, Zinnia's angina is recurring and she's teetering on the edge of her grave."

Patsy Lee rolled her eyes. "She is not." But she didn't expect help from that quarter. "And the Sleep Inn?"

"With its roach population?"

"They don't have roaches."

"Nor do they have a room to rent long term. I checked." He sighed. "I feel like Joseph, wandering the streets of Bethlehem."

"Then why don't you just go back to Nazareth?"

He paused. "That's rather blunt, even for you." The jocularity was gone.

"Sorry. I'm . . . sorry." God, she was back to apologizing for everything again. She leaned her head back and closed her eyes. "Actually, I don't want you to go."

"You don't?"

At the odd note in his voice, she rolled her head to look at him, but he didn't look back. Her eyes traced his profile, grown so familiar in the last few weeks. "No, I don't. After all, where would we get another pageant director?"

He didn't smile.

She straightened, alarmed. She really hadn't meant to offend him. And she *really* didn't want him to bow out. "You looked tired when you came in last night, but tryouts weren't really all that bad, were they?"

He continued to stare straight ahead.

"Zeke?"

Now Zeke closed *his* eyes.

"Hey!" She grabbed for the wheel as the car drifted.

He opened them again. "My apologies. Thinking of tryouts, I felt faint."

Some of her bad humor fled. She laughed. "They *were* that bad, huh?"

They entered Cordelia; the Texaco Star Mart slid by.

"Not if you like complete chaos. But all the parts are cast. Josephine McGraw is Mary. She's the only one who can project to the back of the room."

Patsy Lee looked skeptical.

"Okay, okay. They all can project their way clear to Omaha; but only Josephine does so on command. And only on command. She also has Madonna-like eyes to recommend her. Although a very small bladder, given how often she visited the little girls' room." He pondered. "Now that I think of it, they all share that affliction."

She laughed again. "Who's playing the other parts?"

"Damn."

"What?"

"Just realized I have to remember *all* their names. The Innkeeper is a hand-twister with a stammer, but bribed me with four hay bales for props from his uncle's farm. The part of Joseph went to a chronic arm swinger, despite my certainty he'll inadvertently clock the Angel of the Lord—" When Patsy Lee choked, he looked over at her. "Exactly what I think."

"Lily-Too was excited, though. I thought she'd never fall asleep last night."

"It was the promise of makeup. And an elaborate headdress with a veil."

"You're kidding?"

"Nope. Once she realized the rest could barely carry a tune, she wanted the 'Silent Night' solo. But now she wants to disguise herself while she performs."

Patsy Lee shook her head. "I guess I'll just have to be grateful she's doing it at all." Next to the McDonald's, the post office appeared up ahead, its flag whipping in the stiff breeze. She glanced at her watch. She had a few minutes before Mr. Stuart would expect her back. "Could you pull in? I want to copy these registration forms for next semester."

Zeke obliged. Patsy Lee gathered her purse.

"Wait." He put the car in park.

"I can do it. You're more likely to throw them in the trash."

"It's not that. Patricia . . ."

She sighed, bracing herself for another dose of Townley wisdom on her future. "What?"

"Do you want to know the real reason I don't just go home?"

"Oh, Zeke, I was being a crab. You can stay as long as you—"

"Let me finish. Home for me is big, sterile town house. Don't get me wrong; I'm not playing a violin for the lonely boy in the indifferent city. San Francisco suits me. But I was bored. Since I've been here . . . I'm not bored. Should be obvious, but I've only just realized the monotony stemmed from—" He glanced over, caught her checking her watch again, and stopped. "Am *I* boring *you*?"

"No, it's just, well—yes. I'm sorry, but I need to be back at the store in a few minutes or Mr. Stuart will yammer all afternoon about how his late lunch hurt his delicate stomach." She opened her door. "But I *was* listening. You were going to say that since you've been here, taking care of us, working with Vreeley Home, and probably even with the pageant, you've discovered your boredom stemmed from a lack of anything to do. Anything meaningful, that is."

"True, but—"

"And you were about to tell me that unless I want to find myself in the same boat, I should think again about whether I find school all that meaningful."

"I do think you should, but that's not what—"

She gathered her crutches, eased out.

"Would you get your rear back in the car so I can ex—"

"Bebe already told you I can't support us on the few dollars I'd get from craft shows." She leaned back in for her purse. "You've made it plain what you think about my decision to pursue a degree, so let's agree to disagree and consider this subject closed—"

She stopped. He wasn't looking at her anymore. He was staring at McDonald's.

She followed his gaze to the restaurant, but didn't see anything. "What?"

"What?"

She sighed. Who was boring who? "I said you've made how you feel quite clear."

She backed out and closed the door, hardly registering his, "No, I haven't."

Obviously, he'd made himself as clear to Patricia as . . . as a mud hole full of wallerin' hogs. (Thank you, Paddy O'Neill.) But Zeke decided that he couldn't compete with Mr. Stuart's stomach and dropped Patsy Lee off without again broaching the subject he'd wanted to discuss.

Pulling away, he shook his head. For once, she'd put the wrong words in his mouth Yes, he thought college a waste of her time Yes, he realized his boredom had sprung from a lack of purpose (only a moron couldn't see *that*). But something that had clouded the edges of his brain for quite some time had just recently become crystal clear: His restlessness hadn't just been a dearth of any*thing* to do, it had been an absence of any*one* to do it for.

He pulled away from the curb. For years, the Van Castle Band had been more family than family—more family, even, than Christine. It was a tiresome cliché, but past celebrity and current wealth had made him suspect everyone's motives, an attitude that hadn't lent itself to making new friends. Since Van Castle's disbanding, and particularly since Christine had absconded, his primary connections were with his mother and youngest sister. And Jon and Lil. And none of them had needed him for a thing.

Not that Christine ever had, either. That had been a paramount attraction. When had it become a liability?

Zeke steered the car around the square, then pointed it back toward McDonald's.

Years ago, he decided. He'd felt the first nips of discontent when Jonathan Van Castle had been knocked for a loop by Lil O'Malley. As Jon had made the decision to retire, as Zeke had watched his former bandmate happily wrap himself in the ties that bind, that discontent had continued to gnaw at his unconscious. But he hadn't realized where his unconscious was headed until he'd heard himself suggest *family* to Christine. He hadn't known which of them had been more surprised. And when she responded by leaving, he hadn't known whether he'd been dismayed—or relieved.

At least, he hadn't known until he'd spent this time in Cordelia.

But they'd taught him. All of them: Jon and Lil. Hank and Rose and Lily-Too. Pop and Zinnia O'Malley. Even the townspeople like Preacher Finn Phelps, Paddy O'Neill, and Rosemary Butz (who never failed to sing his praises over the jars of spaghetti sauce he'd heaped on her Oktoberfest booth), the children at Vreeley Home, even the kids at the pageant.

And, of course, Patricia.

Unwittingly, by sharing her life and family with him for the last four weeks, she'd pointed him in new directions. Maybe what Lil and Jon had was a pipe dream for him at this stage of life, but he now had commitments. He had new ideas. He wanted to see those obligations through. He wanted his ideas to flourish. And he didn't want any uneasiness between him and Patricia during the rest of his stay, whether it was under her roof or someone else's.

He turned into an alley that ran behind McDonald's.

Earlier, when Patricia said she didn't want him to go, he'd felt a momentary burst of alarm. The emotion had puzzled him until he realized it stemmed from a fear that she'd read something more than he'd intended into that foolish kiss. Then they'd slid into their old footing and he'd decided she already knew that their embrace had sprung from his loneliness and her vulnerability. There was no need to discuss it. Still, he wanted to tell her how much he owed her for what she'd given him. He'd try again later. . . .

He parked the car where it couldn't be seen from inside.

. . . But right now, he had something else he needed to do.

He replayed what he'd seen while he and Patricia had been busy miscommunicating in the post office lot. It was midday. A school day. Yet Hank darted into McDonald's. . . . Holding a tissue to one very bloodied nose. Zeke hoped he was still here. And okay.

Inside, past the lunch hour, the restaurant was empty except for a mother with three small children she fought to keep corralled, a couple of matrons engrossed in their conversation across a pile of food wrappers, and Hank.

Collar turned up, he sat in a corner booth, back to the door, slouched so far down only the top of his head was visible.

At the counter, Zeke ordered a large coffee, a large Coke, and a Quarter Pounder from a twentysomething redhead with ASSISTANT MANAGER pinned to her chest.

She handed off a tray and he made his way to Hank's booth. As he slid in, Hank straightened, body banging the table. A bruise, new and still purpling, blushed one cheekbone. Bloodied tissues littered the table before him, but his nose looked to be in one piece. Hank scooped up the tissues and stuffed them in his pocket.

"So whazzup?" Zeke set the coffee in front of himself, the rest in front of Hank, and the tray aside. Resting his forearms on the table, he cradled the Styrofoam cup. "Thought you'd given up hooky."

Biting his lip, Hank reached for the burger. Zeke noted the red knuckles. That Hank had been in a fight surprised him; he didn't think Hank knew anyone well enough to punch him.

"I'm not truant. Not exactly." Hank took a large bite. "How'd you know I was hungry?"

"If the world is turning as it should, you're empty-handed because you forgot your wallet this morning."

"I did." A ghost of a grin crossed Hank's face.

"And you've been here through lunch. Ergo . . . hungry." When Hank looked puzzled, Zeke explained. "I saw you walk in when I was at the post office. With your mother."

"Did she see me?"

"If she had, would I be here alone?"

Hank's shoulders sagged. "She'll know soon enough. Vice Principal Shanks has probably already called her. I kind of took off when he suspended me. I'm dead."

"Somehow I doubt murder is in your mother's heart. But right now you need to let her know you're okay."

"Will you call her?"

Zeke smiled, but only pulled his cell phone from his pocket and slid it over.

Looking resigned, Hank punched in Patricia's number. When he said, "Mom?" Zeke heard a burst of speech before Hank explained where he was and who he was with. There was another burst, Hank mumbled "Okay," turned off the phone, and handed it back.

"She told me to stay put and she'll come get me as soon as Mr. Stuart gets back from lunch. Pop'll bring her. She wants you to wait so I don't skip out and then you can take us home." Hank pushed his burger aside. "Pop. The whole family will know."

"I don't think they'll hold it against you forever."

"You don't understand. I don't care if they know about the fight. Skeeter Burcham deserved to get pounded. It's just—" Hank dropped his head back to stare at the ceiling. "Crap."

Skeeter Burcham. Undoubtedly, Son of Hurlin' Burgers Burcham, victim of Bebe's pickled-beet assault in the Piggly Wiggly. Zeke studied Hank. Except for the purple cheek, Hank's face was pale and drawn. This was about more than a schoolyard brawl.

He took a sip of coffee and sat back. "Something he said about Bebe?"

"Yes. He said—"

Zeke held up a hand. "I'm sure it was succinct. And so you threw a punch. Looks like he threw one back. I don't think anyone in your family will raise hell, especially your mother."

Hank straightened. "But you saw how everyone was excited to see Bebe Sunday—especially Gran. Now that'll all be ruined. They won't want her to come back—Mom won't want her to come back—because they'll think having her around just causes trouble. And now I can't—" He broke off. "This'll just mess everything up again."

"You can't what?"

Throat working, Hank looked at the table.

"Hank?"

"I can't tell Mom I'm gay."

Zeke knew the disclosure had taken every ounce of

the boy's courage. It was there in the quiver that shook his chin before it hardened resolutely. In the way his body had tensed, poised to flee. In the pleading behind the determination in his eyes. Zeke wanted to do nothing more than pull Hank into a gruff embrace, but right now, less was more.

"Why not?"

Hank frowned. "You aren't shocked or anything?"

Zeke shrugged. "I don't judge people by their religion, race, sexual orientation, or length of their earlobes." He stopped and considered. "Although I'll admit prejudice against horizontal stripes. Regrettable, but I have to draw a line somewhere."

A corner of Hank's mouth went up.

"That's better." Zeke hooked his eyes. "Hank . . . this is rough. It will continue to be rough, but you'll find your footing. I'm proud of you. Proud you have the strength and courage to be who you are."

"Thanks." The word was said with quiet dignity. "But will my mom feel the same way?"

"Why wouldn't she?"

"It's just, she's never included Bebe in stuff, not like she has Gran. I know she loves her, but it's like she hides her. She'll want to hide me." That quiver was back. "I . . . she'll be ashamed."

At the kernel of truth in the boy's words, Zeke hesitated. He couldn't guess Patricia's reaction. But he did know her love for her son was rock solid. And now was the time for reassurance, not doubt. "Maybe she does hide Bebe. Not out of shame, though. Out of love. She tries to protect her from the stupidity of people like our friend Hurlin' Burgers."

"Then she'll hide me."

"Hank, I know it will be hard to tell her. She'll want to protect you. She'll worry for you; she'll be sad because she knows your life will hold more bumps than it would have if you were straight. You can't stop those reactions—they're part of the territory that comes with motherhood. But you can trust that she won't be ashamed." God help them if he was wrong. He nodded toward the window. "There she is now."

They watched as Pop's car negotiated the parking lot. Patricia got out, shoved her crutches under her arms and made her way to the door, an Angry Mother expression firmly on her face. Pop pulled away.

"Promise me you won't tell her now." Hank looked panicked. "I'm not ready; I want to think about everything."

Patricia shouldered her way through the door and looked around. Zeke lifted a hand and she hobbled forward as fast as she could carry herself.

He looked back at Hank. "It's not my place to tell her. It's not my place to tell anyone. It's yours."

Patricia stopped next to the table. "Tell anyone what?"

Chapter 16

They hadn't told her everything, not by a long shot.

Oh, she didn't doubt Skeeter Burcham had made some ugly comments about Bebe, or that her son had been quick to Bebe's defense, but Hank had never before solved his problems with his fists. She found it hard to fathom that he'd start now, no matter how much he loved Bebe or how nasty the insults had been. Although—considering Skeeter Burcham's gene pool—perhaps Hank had accurately guessed that Skeeter would understand muscle better than reason.

Still, given the odd way Hank had kept glancing at Zeke while they'd sat in McDonald's, there was something more to this quarrel. . . . She suspected—no, she *knew*—that Zeke Townley understood exactly what it was. But over the next three weeks, no matter how she approached the subject, he deftly sidestepped her prodding until, hurt, she quit prodding at all.

A new constraint grew on top of the ones already existing between them. Conversations turned awkward; silences uncomfortable. The ease they'd shared that had started collapsing under the pressure of a kiss couldn't withstand the weight of a secret. They avoided being alone.

Not at all difficult, considering her Monday-and Wednesday-night classes, his Tuesday-and Sunday-night pageant rehearsals, her Saturdays in the circle of her brood or Merry-Go-Read, his at Vreeley Home with Jon or practicing with Lily-Too or giving Hank a driving lesson, and her school and work demands, growing as the peak shopping season of the year approached.

Not long after Halloween, Lil extended the store hours as they swung toward the holidays. (Unable to capture the holiday spirit, Patsy Lee had grumbled to Mr. Stuart that someday they'd be hanging mistletoe right after they lowered the Fourth of July flags.) Midterms came and went and due dates for final projects loomed. She didn't need to feign spending time on homework; she was buried beneath it. But she wouldn't give up the time she'd grown accustomed to having for her children since Zeke had moved in.

In spare minutes she didn't really have, she baked pumpkin pies with Rose to help fill the St. Andrew's Christmas Care baskets, and fashioned foil snowflakes and stars with Lily-Too, which they hung from doorways all through the house. She tried not to worry overmuch about Daisy, whose voice sounded too bright on the two occasions she called, and she let Hank drive her all over kingdom come, first on his permit, then, close to Thanksgiving, on his newly acquired intermediate license. While his newfound desire to drive encouraged her, it hadn't alleviated her concerns. The anxiety that had briefly disappeared from his face with Bebe's visit had returned.

Since Hank was rebuffing her questions, their car trips together were strained, but she was still grateful he was driving. It provided another way to dodge Zeke. That she was doing so became more than obvious when her six-week checkup arrived, scheduled while Hank was at school, and she asked Pop to drive her to Sedalia. Experiencing the hurt that flickered across Zeke's face was far better than the discomfort of time trapped together in the car.

After X-rays of her ankle showed the formation of a bridging callus, the fiberglass cast got ousted in favor of a removable walking cast. The doctor warned her to continue use of the crutches, although she could partially bear weight beginning the following week. It would hurt, he said, but get better each day.

He was right. While it was a joy to loosen the cast or dispense with it completely when she bathed or slept, her leg throbbed by day's end. It joined the fatigue in the rest of her body and the ache in her heart that she barely acknowledged under the onslaught of her schedule.

By the time she reached Thanksgiving, a blur of food and faces in Zinnia O'Malley's lace-trimmed dining room, she found herself wishing she'd break her other foot. Maybe then someone would shoot her and put her out of her misery.

Nobody thought to bring a shotgun to the family feast, but fate—and her own machinations—helped her, anyway. Twice. And not in a manner that caused personal injury.

Near noon, more than a dozen people crowded around Zinnia's dining room table with barely enough space between them to lift a fork. Patsy Lee had found her table card next to Zeke's, but she'd exchanged it for Lil's when nobody was looking. Now Lil sat at Zeke's elbow while she sat at Jon's, ignoring Zinnia's glower, and grateful for a flat-bottomed vase stuffed with scarlet mums, orange lilies, and butterscotch cushion pompons. The flowers provided a screen from Zeke's gaze across the table.

Alcea and her husband had sent the bouquet. Still traveling, the eldest O'Malley daughter and Dak were the only missing members of the clan. Newlywed Mari, vibrant as the red in her hair, and her husband, as easy-going as Mari was animated, had joined them, journeying from their new home in Kansas. And the eldest trio of cousins—Kathleen, Melanie, and Daisy—had returned from college (along with Danny, who had stayed glued to Daisy since their arrival last night).

While they piled mounds of food on Zinnia's good Haviland china amid a hail of conversations pinging every which way, Patsy Lee heard Lil, sounding morose, inform Zeke that Wamego had finally installed a new pump at the guesthouse, so he was now free to move in. Unless, Lil added on a wistful note, he was quite comfortable where he was . . . ?

Zeke glanced between fronds at Patsy Lee. She pretended she hadn't heard and dodged his eyes. After a tiny beat of hesitation, he thanked Lil and told her he'd move tomorrow.

Initially, relief bathed her, but as the meal progressed, sadness gained a contrary upper hand. Just as she forked a last bit of pumpkin pie, wondering how she'd keep Zeke from seeing her perverse disappointment at his departure, Jon tapped his glass and fate smiled on her again.

Instead of a Christmas present this year, Jon announced, he and Lil and had arranged an all-expenses-paid, two-night stay in Kansas City for the entire O'Malley clan, plus Zeke, of course, and even Danny.

Babble erupted around the table. On Thanksgiving night, a switch was thrown on Kansas City's Country Club Plaza and more than a quarter-million bulbs outlining every window, doorway, and turret of the district's Spanish architecture blazed to life. The youngest of the group had never seen it. The oldest enjoyed it, not the least because they'd devote tomorrow to ransacking the area's high-end shops. With Lil and Jon playing host, they knew none of them would return empty-handed. The plan was to leave after Zinnia's table was cleared, and return on Saturday following Jon and Zeke's weekly rehearsal of the boys' band at Vreeley Home.

Patsy Lee glanced at Daisy, expecting her face to be lit with excitement—shopping and Danny all in one weekend—but only a thin-lipped smile carved her face. Patsy Lee filed away the look, wondering if her daughter's usual sparkle was tarnished by the dismal state of her GPA (which they had yet to discuss). Now wasn't the time to probe.

Her attention on Daisy, she thought she'd only imagined a triumphant expression on Lil's face. But when she caught Zinnia's sly gaze hurrying away from hers, she nudged Jon. "What, exactly, are the sleeping arrangements?"

Grinning broadly, basking in the thanks ringing around the table, Jon's answer was distracted. "Lil made reservations at The Raphael. All I know is she booked suites."

Patsy Lee looked over at Lil. Lil wouldn't be so bold as to put them in the same bed together, but she'd bet she and Zeke would share one of those suites with only a child or two as chaperones. If that.

"And will we take a carriage ride?" Romantic rides through the warren of streets in the glow of The Plaza's Christmas lights was a holiday institution.

"I think she mentioned something along that line."

Of course. And she and Zeke would find themselves thrust into a carriage for two.

"And dinner tomorrow night?"

"She couldn't get all of us into the same restaurant, so everyone's scattered around."

With her and Zeke cloistered in a private booth at the dimly lit Plaza III, no doubt.

Jon frowned, finally looking at her. "Why all the questions?"

"Just curious," she assured him, then raised her voice. "I'm not going."

There was a sudden lull. Then Lil and Zinnia protested. Loud and long.

Her face went hot. "I mean, it sounds lovely, but with all the holiday furor . . . well, I just think I'd like a couple of days to myself. It's been a long time since I've had time to myself."

They renewed their assault, and she felt herself wavering.

Then Zeke's voice knifed through the hubbub. "You shouldn't be left alone."

Incensed, she peered at him over the mums. "I'm not a child."

"Child or not, you have a broken ankle and the farmhouse is too isolated," he said.

"Exactly." Zinnia bobbed her head in agreement.

"Absolutely." Lil chimed in.

She felt herself grow calm. Enough was *enough*. She carefully folded her napkin and laid it beside her plate. "I stayed by myself all the time when I was pregnant and Henry worked nights." When he worked.

Zeke threw down his napkin. "Just because some men—" He stopped, apparently realizing he was about to alienate his allies.

"Now, Zeke, she was perfectly fine out there when—" Zinnia stopped, apparently realizing she wasn't helping her cause .

"Exactly," Patsy Lee echoed her mother-in-law. "I was perfectly fine then, and I'll be perfectly fine now."

Zeke glared. She glared back.

And her heart started thumping irregularly, never mind that his expression was a far piece removed from anything even approaching loverlike. Giving her attention to her plate, she schooled her pulse back into order.

So she was attracted to him. So what.

That fact just added more strength to her determination to remain behind.

A little more than an hour later, her obstinacy had been rewarded by Zinnia and Lil's grudging capitulation. But Zeke was still pouting.

His mouth pinched as an old man's, he'd driven her and her brood home as soon as the Haviland had been washed, dried, and put away, followed by Zinnia's van, Jon's SUV, and Melanie's Blazer, all packed to the gills. After he'd helped tend to the animals, packed an overnight bag (and from the time it took him, probably the rest of his things), and joined Jon in adding her family's luggage to the back of the van, he'd climbed into the SUV behind Lil without having found any necessity to utter a word. In the whirl of activity, nobody else seemed to notice he'd gone mute.

Lingering in the driveway, propped up by a crutch on one side and a mournful-looking Sugar on the other, Patsy Lee called out good-byes as the vehicles started down the drive. Her farewells were echoed by everyone except Zeke. The child.

Shaking her head, she'd started to turn away when the SUV crunched to a halt. She stopped and waited, expecting Daisy or Hank to come running after something forgotten. But instead, Jon's window slid down.

"Almost forgot. On the way out here, Lil called up some friend of Rose and Michael's to do the animal chores tomorrow and Saturday for you."

"Thanks . . . who?"

Lil leaned forward. "Lonnie Peterson."

"Oh. Uh, yeah, thanks." Kind of. On the one hand, she was grateful she wouldn't have to manage alone. On the other, Lonnie was Rusty Peterson's son. She hoped her onetime beau wouldn't use his sixteen-year-old as an excuse to drive out here.

"You're welcome. But it wasn't my idea." Lil beamed. "Zeke knew you'd need help."

Patsy Lee glanced in back. Head back and eyes closed, Zeke looked for all the world like he'd fallen asleep. But she knew better. And she knew he thought that by leaving a proxy of sorts, he'd won even if she'd triumphed in being left behind. Disgruntlement itched, but she just folded her arms, knowing that objecting would make her look as immature as he did.

As Jon put the SUV back in drive, Zeke's eyes opened, his gaze falling squarely on her. He gave her—she saw it distinctly—a slow, lazy wink before Jon turned the SUV and showed her the back of his head. She would have stomped her foot if her foot had been willing, but as she watched the caravan of cars disappear, her aggravation gave way to a chuckle.

Shaking her head at his audacity, she looked around and her mirth faded. The woods ringing the sweep of her yard stood in stark silhouette under a sky cushioned with clouds. No birds chirped; even the donkeys and chickens were silent. As the noise from the engines faded in the distance, only the sound of the wind sloughing through the boughs penetrated the sudden quiet. The weather report had called for rain, and there was a new bite to the air. Impatient with herself, she shook off a shiver of loneliness. Well, she'd just hope rain didn't spoil the event on the Plaza; she certainly didn't plan to let it spoil *her* evening.

She glanced down at Sugar. The dog's tail thumped. "I guess it's just you and me and our furry friends, kiddo. How about some leftover turkey?" They went inside, Patsy Lee trying not to notice how the slap of the screen door echoed through the house.

After feeding Sugar, she ignored her pile of homework and gimped from room to room, taking in the novelty of solitude. After a halting climb upstairs, she opened the door revealing her loom, thinking she might fuss a few minutes with her weaving, but the sight of the warp that she'd so carefully threaded through the heddles such a long time ago was lowering.

Closing the door on the sight, she moved on to her own bedroom. As she'd suspected, Zeke's packed bags were neatly aligned at the foot of her bed, ready for transport to Lil's; she noted he'd actually changed the linens, too. Her spirits fell further. As she carefully descended the back stairs to the kitchen, a patter of rain sounded on the rooftop. Its lonely dance didn't help matters any.

Chastising herself for letting her loom, Zeke, and the rain spoil some hard-earned hours alone (and the triumph she still felt over foiling Lil and Zinnia's schemes), she built a fire, fixed popcorn, and finally settled on the sofa with her afghan, a fat Anya Seton historical novel (*Basic Principles of Small Business Accounting* could wait till tomorrow), and a snack bowl. Blinken and Nod curled in the hollows by her legs and Sugar flopped on the floor nearby, alert for stray kernels. The rain became a steady tattoo.

After only thirty minutes, she started to squirm. The fire's crackle made her jump. The downpour outside smacked of Chinese water torture. What was wrong with her? Once upon a time—granted, a very long time—she'd *loved* being alone.

Lowering her book, she dropped her head back and let her gaze wander over the room.

Everything is the same; everything is familiar. But it all looks strange.

She sighed, knowing the problem was in the beholder. She'd started October with the growing conviction she didn't really know her spot in the universe as well as she thought she had, and she was ending November with her mind in more of a tangle than it had ever been.

Everything is the same; everything is familiar. But it all looks strange.

She pushed the thought out of her head. Having only herself for company was certainly not the big treat she'd thought it would be. She missed her kids.

Her sigh became gusty. And, dang it all, anyway, she missed Zeke.

Shivering as a burst of wind tunneled down the chimney before sucking smoke back up the flue, she hauled herself up, much to the cats' disgust, switched on the TV for company—a dismal litany of the day's news—then headed to the kitchen for Tension Tamer Tea.

While she was steeping the bag, the weatherman's excited tones penetrated her thoughts, which were rapidly gathering themselves into one big fat pity party. Glad for a distraction, she carried her mug back to the parlor and lowered herself to the footstool to study the weather map displayed on the screen. After whipping through a flurry of explanations on colliding fronts and jet streams and barometric pressure and moisture from the gulf, the weatherman finally got to the point. Arctic air from the north was pushing in much farther and much stronger than expected, and it's collision with the warm wet rain from the south meant, "Folks, looks like we're in the path for one of those November surprises."

A winter storm was expected to dump a good eight inches of snow and, for the next few hours, high winds would rattle her rafters. Wonderful. She watched a bit longer, reassured that the storm was developing east of Kansas City, although her family should have already arrived in the metro. She needn't worry about them.

She glanced at the log rack. Although she did need to spare a few thoughts for herself. If the electricity did its usual light's-out act and she was forced to rely on the wood-burning stove and the fireplace for heat, she'd need wood. But although she'd heard Zeke tell Hank to fill the rack yesterday, not a big surprise to find the chore only half-done. Whatever trouble her son was hiding, it had made him even more absent-minded than usual.

She pushed herself back up. At least she knew Hank and Zeke had split logs this week. There were plenty. She'd just need to haul them inside.

In the mudroom, she pulled on a slicker and Hank's leather gloves and replanted a crutch under her arm. Opening the back door, she peered out. The rain was a steady sheet, but at least the tarp-covered pile wasn't too far away—less than ten feet from the house. She took a breath and plunged forward. The rain hitting her hood was deafening.

Before she'd lugged three logs inside, a slow endeavor with only one arm to use as a caddy, the rain had turned to sleet, the TV had turned to fuzz—the satellite dish had surrendered to the elements—and she was shivering against a steady wind.

When she'd reached nine logs, the storm had thrown a thin sheet of snow over a layer of ice, a dart of pain arrowed sporadically up her leg, and her shivers had become full-blown shudders.

And by the time she headed out the door on a final trip, early nightfall had whirled in on the storm's shoulders, the lights had flickered twice, and the pain was no longer sporadic.

Just as she stepped down from the back stoop, the cordless rang inside.

Starting at the sudden noise, her balance wavered. The lights blinked out and the walkway went dark Her cast skidded. Frantically, she poked at the crust with her crutch but failed to find purchase. Her last thought before she fell was that she wished to hell she'd bought a house in town.

Anxiety setting up shop in his stomach, Zeke watched as Zinnia punched in a number on the cell phone she'd shanghaied from him after he'd fumbled dialing Patricia's number himself. She listened, then turned a worried face to the group of adults gathered in a tight circle on a sidewalk of the Country Club Plaza. "It rings, but she's not answering and the machine's not on. Her electricity may already be out."

Nearby, the O'Malley progeny, from Lily-Too up to the college-aged coeds, had their noses pressed to the windows at Saks, entranced by the mechanical elves, oblivious to the tension that had invaded their elders ever since they'd passed The Sharper Image and had seen the winter-storm-warning banner scrolling across the bottom of the flat-panel Toshiba TV on display.

A short while ago, at the flip of a switch, the more than seventy-five miles of lights that outlined the Plaza had flashed the start of the holiday season, accompanied by an eruption of *oohs* and applause from the quarter-million-strong crowd. Fireworks had lit the sky, and a choir had burst into the hallelujah chorus. Spellbound during the ceremony, people now ebbed and flowed on the sidewalks. At the base of the clock tower, carolers yodeled.

Jostled by elbows, the adults all stared at each other, their breath forming icy vapor in the freeze that had dropped down from the north. Zeke tipped his head up and studied the sky. Unlike the storm raging to the south, here only a light mist drizzled from a pearly sky, guaranteeing a slippery walk back to the Raphael Hotel, a few blocks away, if they waited too long. But nothing more dangerous than that.

"We'll call someone. Paddy? He'd contact Fire and Rescue. He's still an honorary volunteer." Worry creased Zinnia's brow. "Or maybe the local police—Rusty Peterson?"

Paddy O'Neill? Not exactly Captain Marvel. Zeke opened his mouth, but Pop spoke first.

"Highway patrol might be a better bet than Rusty.

I like the man, but his attic's dusty. Or Ed Bauer—he's the sheriff and a friend"—Pop explained in an aside to Zeke—"Ed'd go check."

"If you can reach him." Tension clenching his jaw, Zeke wadded the cup he held and tossed it into a nearby trash can. "The police will have their hands full. It could be hours. I'll go."

"Don't be stupid. It would take you hours to reach her, too," Jon said.

"If you reached her at all." Lil said. "You can't go. You don't know how bad it will get."

The others added their objections.

Reason usually held some appeal, but right now Zeke didn't find waiting reasonable. He never should have left her by herself, and wouldn't have if he hadn't been sure he'd spill Hank's confidences if they were left alone. He knew his avoidance about discussing that day in McDonald's had hurt her. And he didn't like hurting her.

He cut through the babble. "The report said the storm is moving fast. It'll likely be gone by the time I'm south of Sedalia—and that's the earliest I'd hit it. From there, it's not that far."

"In this weather, it is." Zinnia frowned. "It'd be pure-all crazy for you to take to the roads. I'm sure Patsy Lee is fine; she's been through this before."

"They're right," Jon said. "You don't have a car. You don't know the way that well. And you, California dude, don't drive on snow."

"Christ. I can drive your SUV; you can pick up a rental tomorrow. I've made this trip with you a dozen times, I can follow directions, and I do drive on snow. In Aspen and Zermatt."

Actually, he hired a driver when he skied Colorado, and Zermatt didn't allow cars, but he chose not to share those tidbits.

"That still doesn't mean this makes sense."

"If you won't loan me the SUV, I'm certain the concierge will find one for the right fee."

Jon sighed, dug into his jacket pocket.

Lil gripped Zeke's sleeve. He looked down into her eyes.

Zinnia suddenly changed her tune. "Maybe it *would* be a good idea if you went on down there." There was an edge to her voice.

Puzzled, he glanced up, saw her dart a worried look at Jon. When her gaze landed back on him, her eyes were hard. He hadn't a clue why, but he wasn't going to stop now to find out.

He looked back at Lil. "I'll be fine, Lil. Let go."

In his worry, his voice was unintentionally harsh. He was about to apologize, but Lil smiled slightly. "That's okay."

Now Zinnia suddenly looked puzzled. While Jon abandoned his jacket pocket to mine the ones in his pants, she looked between her daughter and him and then her face suddenly cleared. "Lord love a duck, I was wrong."

"What?" He took the keys Jon finally held out.

"Never you mind." She caught his eyes. "You be careful, Zeke Townley."

Shaking his head over the strangeness of women, he headed for the hotel parking garage. As he let himself into Jon's car, the image of Lil's eyes faded, replaced by a pair of appealing brown ones, wide and soft as sable.

Patricia *had* to be all right. The engine roared to life. She *had* to.

Her leg was all right, Patsy Lee reassured herself.

For the tenth time since she'd bundled up on the sofa, she flipped back the comforter to see. At her movement, Sugar looked up, thumped her tail once, then laid her muzzle back on her paws with a sigh indicating that even though five hours had passed, she was still totally exhausted from watching Patsy Lee haul in wood. All three cats stirred—abandoning field mice to the elements, Winken had joined Blinken and Nod—but, long resigned to Patsy Lee's restlessness, none of them bothered now to even open an eye.

Wrapped in a wool sock, in the light of the lantern she'd set on the end table, her lower leg looked as scrawny as it had since they'd removed the fiberglass cast. The ache was a familiar feeling, no sharper than usual at the end of a day. There was no swelling.

She lay back again, relieved for only an instant before she thought of a different worry. She rose on her knees. Finally pushed beyond their endurance, the cats gave her looks of disgust and jumped down. Ignoring them, she tugged aside the draperies over the window behind the sofa and pressed her nose against the glass.

The night was chiaroscuro: light and shadow. According to Buck Preston of Fire and Rescue (who had plowed a path down Red Hollow Road and up her drive at Paddy's behest after Zinnia had given the old man a call), the storm had squeezed out snow almost up to Buck's knees, all across the Ozarks during the three hours after Patsy Lee had fallen, gotten up worried about her ankle, but otherwise no worse for the tumble, and lugged in the last log.

And as Sheriff Bauer had put it when he'd checked on her (at Pop's request, since he hadn't trusted Paddy to remember), it hadn't quite wrung itself out before it had moved on to give St. Louis a fine ol' time. The wind had died two hours ago, and now only a few lazy flakes drifted into a silence broken only by the *whoosh* of an imploding log and Sugar's soft snore.

White yard, black woods, white sky. Horizontal stripes . . .

Zeke. She dropped the drapes and looked at the telephone sitting fat and silent on the floor beside the sofa, its cord stretched from the jack on the far wall.

When the electricity had failed, so had the cordless. After she'd dragged the last log inside following her fall, she'd limped around the house to open spigots so a trickle of water would keep the pipes thawed, then had dug around the pantry for an older phone that needed no electricity. It had taken twenty minutes to locate it on the top shelf, another ten to hook it with her crutch, and another fifteen before she'd found the lantern she kept for these kinds of emergencies.

Normally, it was just inside the pantry door, *with* the phone, but Zeke, drat his organized little hide, had moved it on that long-ago day when he'd rearranged the contents of the pantry to his satisfaction.

Zeke. Pulling up the comforter, she shivered.

Drafts eddied around the room, despite the fires she'd stoked in both the fireplace and woodstove, but it wasn't the currents that made her blood run cold; it was the idea of Zeke somewhere out in the storm between here and Kansas City. Not ten minutes after she'd plugged in the old phone, it had rung, Zinnia's relieved voice sounding on the other end. After her mother-in-law had assured herself Patsy Lee was fine, she'd told her Zeke had galloped off to her rescue. She'd sounded pleased as punch.

Zeke was an idiot. They were all idiots. How could they have let him leave? After hanging up, Patsy Lee had tried to call to let him know she'd already been rescued twice. But dialing his cell had only returned her to her mother-in-law. Apparently, Zeke had loaned Zinnia the phone, then they'd all promptly forgot she had it.

Clutching the comforter, she tried to whip worry into aggravation. Of course, a gallant rescue would appeal to Zeke, but why would he think she'd need one? For Pete's sake, she'd lived out here more over two decades. Not only could she handle a little snow, but this was *Cordelia* country. The flipside of the Ernie Burchams and Penny Masons were the Paddy O'Neills and Ed Bauers, not without fault but certainly without fail, always coming through when the chips were down.

Ears pricked, Sugar's head suddenly came up. Patsy Lee listened intently and was rewarded by a low rumble, still a short ways off. She scrambled to her knees again. Sugar jumped up beside her and nosed the draperies apart. They both peered out. Headlights approached up Red Hollow Road; a vehicle crept into view. She held her breath as it started a cautious turn into her drive, carefully negotiating the hump over the drainage ditch. She made out a bulk. Jon's SUV.

"It's him!" Giddy, she ruffled Sugar's fur. The dog's hindquarters danced.

But before the SUV completed its turn, its tires lost their grip. Instead of steering into the skid as he should have, Zeke stomped on the brakes. In response, the SUV skated off the drive and thumped onto its side in the ditch, rear sliding to rest against the back of the gully, headlights glaring cockeyed up the hill to the house. The engine fell silent.

Patsy Lee held her breath. Sugar barked twice. Except for the snowflakes' slow waltz across the SUV's beams, she saw no movement. What if he was pinned? What if he'd cracked his skull? She bounced to a sitting position and fumbled for the still-damp clothes she'd left spread on the floor.

Zeke *had* to be all right. She grabbed her crutch. He *had* to.

Chapter 17

Clenching her teeth to keep them from chattering, Patsy Lee sat on the hearth in the parlor. She was stripped of her wet jeans and socks, embarrassed to be half-naked, although the long sweater she still wore despite the damp around its edges would provide modesty if the comforter wrapped around her waist slipped.

At least that's what she hoped. She'd poked her leg out of the folds, stretching it along the stones as close as she could come to the fire without scorching her flesh. As far as she could tell, her toes weren't the white that indicated frostbite, but she had probably come close. Sounds drifted down the hall: Zeke poking through her clothes, Sugar's nails tap-dancing on the floors.

She didn't know who had been more thankful to see Zeke in one piece, Sugar or her. After she'd scrambled into her clothes, she'd snatched a hammer out of a kitchen drawer (only tool that came readily to hand) and shoved a first-aid kit in the pocket of her parka before hobbling as fast as snow, night, and her ankle allowed down to the ditch. When she reached it, the muffled noises coming from inside—a lot of swearing and thumping—told her she wouldn't need the first-aid kit.

Lightheaded with relief, she pushed her way through a drift to the edge of the ditch until she stood in front of the SUV, its headlights arcing just over her head. She could see Zeke through the windshield, crouched in an awkward stance, swinging something upward at the passenger window.

She yelled. Sugar barked. Zeke looked up. In the dim glow from the dash, she saw his face slacken with relief—at seeing her or getting rescued?—before he yelled back. He couldn't fire the engine to lower a window, and apparently the impact had damaged the door lock. He'd managed to unlatch and partially open the gate window, but the vehicle's tilt toward the rear wouldn't let him widen it enough to crawl out. He was trying to break the window with a flashlight, but had succeeded only in making a few starbursts.

She held up the hammer. He smiled.

Sliding down into the ditch was easy, although keeping her feet dry was not. By the time she managed to pass the hammer through the narrow opening of the back gate window (at his insistence, although she could have busted it herself), her toes were numb. Pulling herself out of the ditch required more work. When, panting, she reached the driveway, snow had melted inside her parka. Ignoring Zeke's entreaties (demands) to return to the house, she'd instead waited for him to break free. He'd done so with only a few blows, but the SUV would never be the same.

He'd barely gotten himself out of the ditch before he'd scooped her up to wade through the snow, unheeding of her protests that they'd go faster if he'd put her down. When they'd reached the house, he'd first called Zinnia to report his triumphant arrival (and give Jon the bad news about his SUV), then he'd helped her to the couch, ignored her continued objections, and matter-of-factly pulled off her walking cast and boot, rolled off her socks, and ordered her out of her jeans. Taking her crutch so she wouldn't get back up, he'd headed off to fetch dry clothes.

But this time his high-handedness hadn't set her teeth on edge. She'd been more concerned at the thought of him fumbling through her underwear drawer—why had she always thought that Wal-Mart's Just My Size were good enough?—but she'd followed his instructions, dispensing with her denims and wrapping herself up until he could return.

Zeke's voice sounded from the hall. "Here you go. Now it's my turn."

She covered both legs as he came through the doorway, but she needn't have bothered. He paused only long enough to drop a bundle of white in her lap and a pile of blankets on the sofa before bounding up the stairs two at a time, Sugar at his heels.

When she heard a faint, "God*damn,* it's cold up here," and his footsteps striding into her room, she hurriedly shed the rest of her wet clothes. Shivering as the heat from the fire hit her bare backside, she picked up her sweatshirt from the small pile of clothing.

She frowned, then reached for her sweatpants. She gave both garments a shake. "No underwear?" Her voice rose.

"What?" He called down.

"Uh, nothing," she called back up.

Well. Maybe he'd assumed that what she had on was dry.

Hesitating, she looked at the cold and soggy bra and panties at her feet, but before she could make up her mind, his tread sounded again in the hallway, this time headed for the back stairwell. As his foot hit the first step, she threw the sweatshirt over her head, before the fourth, she'd yanked up the pants, and by the time he reached the mudroom, she'd kicked her underwear under the sofa, thrown the comforter over her shoulders, and had settled back down on the hearth. She clasped the comforter closed at her chest.

She'd nursed four children; no need for him to know what havoc that and time had wreaked.

Fortunately, since she didn't want to explain why her sides were heaving, he paused in the kitchen. The faucet went on and dishes clattered. Breathing slowing to normal, she stretched her leg back out across the hearth. Her toes still felt hot with returning circulation, but she thought they'd be fine.

Sugar still his shadow and a teapot and hot pads in his hands, Zeke entered through the dining room. He'd exchanged his own wet jeans for sweatpants and his boots for leather mules.

Not one to ever leave a button undone or a shoe untied, the frigid air upstairs had obviously hurried him along since the red flannel shirt he'd slipped on still hung open. It was the first time she'd seen his chest. She tried very hard not to notice that his Italian blood showed in the smooth expanse of dusky skin that slid over a still well-developed set of pecs and into a waistline that age had given just a hint of love handles. It wasn't warmth from the fire that suddenly had her flushing.

"I thought I'd see if we could heat some water for tea in the fireplace." He halted, staring at her bare leg.

And now she knew what a hot flash felt like. She covered up her leg.

Shaking his head, Zeke set the teapot near the fire, then dropped to one knee near the hearth, pushed aside the comforter, and pulled her injured foot onto his other knee. He cradled it in his hands. Thank God she'd used the seaweed scrub and mountains of moisturizer the doctor's assistant had recommended. Her skin was at least no longer reminiscent of a plucked hen's. She tried a gentle tug, afraid to yank harder, but he didn't release it.

"I wish you'd gone back to the house when I told you to."

Swallowing hard as sensation traveled clean up her leg, making things that shouldn't tingle, well, tingle, she kept her eyes trained on the flames. "May I remind you that it was you who required saving, not me?" She was pleased when her voice came out normal, light.

"True. I should have known you wouldn't need a white knight. You've reminded me often enough that you don't want any help carrying your burdens." He paused, his thumbs still gently stroking the bottom of her foot. "Would that you did."

He spoke the last phrase so low, she wasn't sure she'd heard him correctly. She swallowed hard again. Settling her heel in one of his palms, his other hand pushed up the elastic hem of her sweatpants to massage the back of her calf. She closed her eyes before she could moan.

"Patricia."

She opened her eyes and met his. They were darker than the night.

"Patricia," he repeated.

And in one fluid movement, he reached for her shoulders and pulled her down into his lap. She went, unresisting, her comforter pooling beside them, her hand skimming up the skin of his chest and curling around his neck. Gently, he tilted her head back, his eyes still holding her gaze, his breath soft on her face. Then he lowered his head.

His lips settled on hers, and every one of her nerve endings stood at attention. And when he deepened the kiss, they collapsed in quivering heaps just as fast. It had been so long . . .

So long that when his hand framed her face, then slid down her neck to push the fabric of her sweatshirt aside to bare a shoulder . . . so long that when his mouth left hers to run a trail of kisses in the wake of his hand until his tongue grazed the hollow of her throat . . . so long that . . .

. . . She panicked and pushed up to her knees.

He rose with her, murmuring, his lips finding hers again. Their tongues danced, their breathing quickened. She felt choked with need. Until his hands glided under the back of her sweatshirt. And suddenly, Christine was right there in the room with them with her perfect body and her perfect face. All Patsy Lee could think was *crap, crap,* crap. She wasn't twenty anymore. She wasn't even thirty, for God's sake. And when he grasped the hem of her sweatshirt and pulled it over her head, she totally froze.

Patricia was so still, Zeke hesitated. This was like trying to make love to a damn rabbit. He could feel her quiver under his touch, but he was beginning to suspect it was from nerves—maybe even fear—and not passion.

So now what? He looked at her for a clue, but she'd turned to rock. Her mouth, swollen from his kisses, lips slightly parted, didn't move. Her eyes, wide and deep with emotion, fixed on his but didn't blink.

He felt like an idiot, poised with her breasts filling his hands, but afraid to move. Afraid to offend, like a peasant supplicating a goddess. "Demeter," he murmured without thinking.

One of her eyebrows rose almost imperceptibly and a shadow of laughter crossed her face. "Now I'm an earth goddess?"

"You doubt it? Goddess of the harvest. Of fertility."

Now she did laugh. "An understatement. But I'm so very, *very* glad you didn't invoke the name of Hathor."

The cow goddess. He laughed. "I wouldn't dare." He sobered. "And it wouldn't be true. Patricia, your body is unbelievably erotic." It was, all curves and soft flesh and . . . *woman.*

Biting her lip, she looked away. He tilted her chin up with a finger, forcing her to meet his eyes. "It is." And he proceeded to show her.

Pulling the mound of blankets off the sofa, he fashioned a bed of sorts on the rug in front of the hearth, and laid her back upon it. His hands and mouth lingered on her breasts and then found that sweet, sensual roll of flesh that softly swelled below her belly button and above the elastic of her sweatpants. Breathing in a heady scent of rosemary, he teased and caressed until her tension had melted away and she returned his explorations with her own.

After stripping himself with her help, he took his time rolling down the waistband of her pants one fold at a time, his tongue tracing lines on newly uncovered flesh until she was writhing under his hands. And before his mouth had barely touched her, she cried out and shuddered.

His own body quivering with need, he steeled himself to patience until she was ready once again, and then he cradled himself between her thighs and found home.

Above the farmhouse, the stars twinkled.

Behind them, the teakettle blew a soft whistle.

Setting her drained teacup on the hearth, Zeke added another log to the fire.

Feeling suspended in time, Patsy Lee lay back on the cushions they'd pulled from the sofa and watched him. Shadows danced with the flames' reflection on the ceiling. It must be somewhere around two; they'd be exhausted tomorrow. Tomorrow? Two bouts of lovemaking, and she was already exhausted. By sunrise, she'd be half dead. And full of regrets.

She pushed the thought away, along with anything

else approaching common sense. She knew tonight was an aberration; time enough to admit to it in the morning. Now was the time for magic. She'd never allowed herself much magic.

Zeke joined her, burrowing back into the covers with an exaggerated shiver and pulling her close until her cheek rested on his chest. Lazily, one hand played with her hair. "Warm?"

"Mmm."

"I'm not." He snuggled her closer. "This is a grand old house, but energy-efficient, not."

She yawned. "Henry and I weren't thinking of practicalities. We were young."

"And blind with love."

She didn't respond. Along with all the other thoughts she'd had over the last year, she'd examined the reasons she'd married Henry. She wasn't sure love held a paramount place among them.

"Weren't you?"

"I . . . you know, I don't really know anymore. I met Henry when my mother was sick. He helped me through a tough time."

The hand in her hair paused. "So you married him because you thought you owed him?"

"Of course not. Not the way you're thinking, anyway." *Surely* not the way he was thinking. "Mom died. Bebe left. I could have gone with her, but I loved Henry. Or thought I did. Maybe, though, it was the O'Malley family I loved the most. After all that quiet and sadness, they were so . . . lively."

"And so normal."

"Yes, that, too." She'd never known normal before them.

"If you believe in normal."

"What do you mean?"

"Just that what's normal for one person isn't for the next." He was quiet a moment. "Christine and I never had a normal relationship, not in the true sense of the word. In fact, when we tried *normal* instead of the hit-and-miss rendezvousing we did through most of our time together while I was touring, things fell apart—slowly, but they fell apart. I probably knew at some level that we wouldn't survive that kind of closeness, or maybe that she wasn't a fan of *normal*. Van Castle, the glitz, the fame—it's not reality. But for me, if not her, knowing Christine was home in San Francisco helped me feel like I belonged to the human race."

She was silent, pondering his words. "You think I married Henry so I could feel I belonged?"

"Aren't you still here in Cordelia for that reason?" Touch tender, he hooked a curl of her hair behind her ear.

Irritably, she unhooked it. "Why would you say that? I'm here because I've made a home here. My family is here. My children belong here."

"*Henry's* family is here." He stifled a yawn. "And where your children belong will soon be up to them. But, yes, you've made a home here."

"And there's something wrong with *here*?"

"No, nothing wrong with Cordelia . . . if Cordelia is really what you want."

Maisie Ann Phelps flitted across her mind. She flopped over on her side.

Turning, he pulled her up against his body until they were nestled together. "You never know. . . . You might be happier somewhere else," he murmured into her hair.

Not knowing how to respond to that, she didn't. In a few moments, she felt his muscles go slack. In a few more, his breathing was slow and even.

Well, it was a good thing she already knew that this night had been only a brief enchantment. And that she hadn't been entertaining any idea that he'd stick around in Cordelia à la Jon Van Castle. Because it was quite obvious that he wouldn't.

A tear tried to form, but, resolutely, she shut her eyes, reproaching herself for self-indulgent emotion.

Chapter 18

Someone pounded on the front door.

Patsy Lee jolted awake, and Sugar shot to her feet with a bark. Zeke only grumbled and rolled onto his side. Scrambling up, Patsy Lee glanced at the windows. Full light showing in the chink between the draperies told her it was not far off noon. The pounding sounded again. Tail wagging, Sugar danced to the door.

Yanking on her sweats, she called, "Who is it?" more to give herself time than anything else. It was undoubtedly Lonnie Peterson, come to care for the livestock. No reason for her panicked heart to be going full-tilt boogie. She could get him underway without him suspecting a thing. "Just a minute!"

Zeke pulled a pillow over his head. She poked him in the back with her crutch, hissed, "Get up," and finger-combed her hair on the way to the door. As soon as she cracked it open, Sugar squeezed past, pausing for a mild leap and a brief sniff at the visitor's shoes before bounding into the yard to do her business. What a guard dog. Patsy Lee squinted at the silhouette outlined against the blaze of white snow.

Damn. She didn't open the door farther. Not Rusty Peterson's son. Rusty Peterson.

Narrow chest puffing against his police uniform,

Rusty doffed his hat, revealing a crop of fading red hair that matched his freckles. From the knobs on his joints to the acorn knuckles on his hands, he was the definition of raw. Even though at the time they'd dated, she'd been groping around trying to find what her life might look like postchildren, she was still amazed that she'd once thought they might suit each other. Especially this morning.

Especially after Zeke.

He turned the hat in his hands. "How-do, Patsy Lee. Your mama-in-law, she called up the station last night and asked us to get on out and check on you. Sorry, but we were tied up with accidents all night and Ed Bauer mentioned he'd gotten over here, so . . . quite a snowstorm we had, wasn't it, now?" His voice was polite, but, like magnets to steel, his eyes kept dropping to her breasts. "Saw Jon's SUV in the ditch down there. Just making sure everyone's okay."

"Everyone's fine. I'm fine and . . . everyone's . . . fine. Thanks for checking. You have a nice day, now." She started to close the door. Behind her, she heard Zeke moving around.

"I thought s'long as I'm out here, I'd take care of your livestock. I told Junior he needn't bother, since I was headed this way, anyways. But if Hank's already gotten home . . ." He craned, trying to see the source of the noise. He gave up and his gaze returned to her. "Sure is cold out here. Cup of coffee would be nice."

"It would, except it's hard to make without electricity."

A thud sounded, and Zeke cursed.

Rusty craned again. "Well, now, 'lectric is back on all up and down the road. Your lights should be working." He shouldered his way past her before she could object "Maybe I'd better take a look-see. . . ."

Rusty flipped the foyer switch and light spilled into the darkened parlor, fully illuminating Zeke, who sat on the sofa, clad only in his sweatpants and rubbing his foot. He must have stubbed a toe.

He glanced up, but didn't seem perturbed. "Whazzup."

Rusty frowned. "Nothin' much." His gaze traveled through the room, from Zeke's bare feet to ashes gone cold to the tumble of blankets on the floor then back to her, fully taking in her braless silhouette. Patsy Lee saw everything through his eyes and knew that even Rusty could add up this sum. From the disappointed expression in his eyes, it hadn't even taken him more than a few seconds.

She looked from Zeke to Rusty. One urbane and, well, *cool*. One rumpled and, she sighed, *not*. Not only did she feel she owed an explanation about Zeke to Rusty, she'd have to explain Rusty to Zeke.

Great.

"Nobody with half a brain—even his half of a brain—would believe those excuses you gave for the blankets on the floor. *Sugar was cold?*" Zeke rolled his eyes. Using the fireplace shovel, he dumped ashes into the paper bag she'd opened near the hearth.

As soon as Rusty had left, she'd closed herself in the bathroom and turned the water on to roar so Zeke couldn't hear her ranting to herself; then she'd dressed (thoroughly and completely) before throwing open the draperies—nothing to hide *here*. She'd insisted on tidying the room, which smacked more than a little of closing the barn door after the fact, but she did it, anyway. What was she thinking? That Rusty was just the beginning of a steady stream of sightseers? She guessed she did.

He continued. "I still don't understand why the local cop finding out is such a big deal."

"I told you. Erik Olausson is Rusty's uncle. Paddy O'Neill is Erik Olausson's best friend. And when

Rusty tells Erik and Erik tells Paddy, which you can bet he will, because gossip is the only thing those old men have to do, we might as well take out an ad in the *Cordelia Daily Sun* announcing that we . . . you know." Balancing on her good foot, Patsy Lee grabbed another blanket off the pile and snapped two corners together.

"But why would he tell Uncle Erik in the first place? In his line of work, this pales beside other tales he could tell."

Patsy Lee folded the blanket and dropped it on the sofa. She didn't look at Zeke. "Because his feelings are hurt."

"His—why would his feelings be hurt?"

"Because I dated him and he's still carrying a torch."

"You dated—?" Zeke bit off his sentence, which he'd probably planned to end with *that hayseed*. "No way."

"Way." Patsy Lee kept her voice matter-of-fact, but her cheeks were hot. Just like she compared herself to Christine, in short order, Zeke would weigh himself against Rusty Peterson. Even if there weren't fifteen dozen other reasons for him to marvel over his physical attraction to her after Christine, it was just human nature. And after he chewed on the idea of her former lover awhile, he'd certainly wonder what he was doing with a woman who had only previously attracted the Henrys and Rustys of the world.

She snatched up the comforter, knowing her thoughts were so *high school*. But it hadn't been her experience that men's egos changed that much between teendom and manhood, and while Zeke could be kind and compassionate and sensitive, he also had more than his fair share of self-worth.

"So Peterson tells Uncle Erik and Uncle Erik tells Paddy and the world is next to know. So what?"

Besides the embarrassment to both her *and* him? "So, just like you said, everyone knows."

"Not quite everyone. Cordelia's not that small."

"But most topics of gossip aren't as big as you. Believe me, everyone will know."

"Still—"

"The O'Malleys will know." Patsy Lee punched the air pockets out of the comforter.

"And Zinnia will undoubtedly fly into a fit of rapture."

She hadn't realized he'd seen through her mother-in-law's matchmaking efforts. Her embarrassment increased. "And Lil and Jon will know." She put a slight emphasis on *Lil.*

"They will," he agreed.

She glanced at him. She'd thought Lil knowing might bother him, but apparently if one carried an unquenchable torch, it didn't matter. "And my children." The thought made her stomach roll. "The oldest will take things in stride and handle whatever anyone says. But Lily-Too . . . Lily-Too already considers you a-a father substitute. Now she'll get her hopes up for no good reason."

"For no good reason," he repeated.

"Because one of these days you'll go back to San Francisco. Don't say you won't. You know you will."

"I didn't say I wouldn't. I will." He now sounded irritated. "And that means . . . ?"

God. Why was he acting so dense? They both knew the score, so why should she have to explain it point by point? "That means you'll leave. And I'll stay. And even though I knew going in that this was just a-a one-night *thing,* from now on, the people in this town will point at me and whisper."

She was overly agitated and knew it, but she'd hoped she'd put her days as a hot topic of gossip long behind her. She swallowed. "They'll say, 'There goes

Patsy Lee O'Malley, poor dear. . . . *Poor fool* . . . who was once so delusional she thought she'd end up just like Lil and Jon Van Castle.' Especially since you started that stupid rumor we eloped. Even if I say I never loved you, and that I knew you never loved me, they won't believe me. They'll still think I believed that, that this"—she gestured at the room—"was actually serious."

Zeke continued shoveling. For a while there was only the sound of the scrape of the fire iron along the hearthstones and the ashes hitting the bag.

She finished folding. "Now do you see? I think it's best if you move out right away so we can take some of the bite out of the gossip. I mean, we can't . . ." Knowing her face flamed, she waved a hand toward the blankets. ". . . You know, anyway. Not with the children here."

Not only that. She couldn't *you know* again without doing serious damage to her heart. There were limits to her ability to act the sophisticated adult.

When his gaze met hers, it was void of expression. "I understand." Tires crunched on the snow. Zeke glanced out the window. "Your family is home."

"They can't be. They weren't supposed to be here till tomorrow, and it's only three." Patsy Lee leaned over the sofa to look. Sure enough, Zinnia's van was pulling into the drive. She hobbled as fast as she could toward the door. "Something must be wrong."

"Yes, something's wrong." But Zeke's voice was impassive.

That something wrong was Daisy.

Late last night, Daisy had gotten sick. This morning, hoping it was only a mild bug, quickly over, the family had left her to sleep. But when they'd returned to check on her at noon, she'd been no better, unable to keep down even the broth and crackers Lil had ordered from room service. After a family consultation, they'd decided to cut their trip short and come home.

An hour after their return, Zeke sat on the sofa in Patricia's neatened parlor, thumbing through a magazine, waiting for Zinnia and Pop O'Malley to take him to the Van Castles'. Lil and Jon had gone ahead to arrange for Cowboy's Tow to haul Jon's SUV from the ditch. They'd meet him there.

Stretched near his feet, head on her paws and gaze on his suitcases, Sugar heaved doleful sighs every few minutes. Overhead, he heard Patricia's uneven footsteps and Zinnia's voice as they tended Daisy. Pop was outside helping her siblings complete the chores Rusty Peterson had left undone after he'd taken a gander at Zeke.

If his hide was tougher, he'd offer to help. But although they'd known he'd leave soon, the children were wearing longer faces than Sugar's. Especially Lily-Too. He'd already reminded her he'd see her at rehearsals and for her lessons, but her eyes had still welled when they'd landed on his bags. Avoiding her sad gaze now wasn't just a means to lessen the melodrama of his leaving. After Patricia's remarks, he didn't need the sight to further erode his spirits.

A one-night thing . . . I never loved you.

He threw the magazine aside and stared at the fire he'd just built. Patricia had been so intent on damage control that maybe she hadn't intended the words quite how they'd sounded.

But did he really want her to intend anything else? Could he say, in all honesty, that he loved Patricia, or that *he'd* intended more than a . . . *a one-night thing*? He'd never indulged in screwing just for the sake of screwing before. But until last night, he'd also never done anything without so little forethought.

So who was to say what he'd intended—or if he'd intended anything at all. Last night had just . . .

happened . . . undoubtedly growing out of his concern for Patricia, the tension of the drive here, the relief she was fine, not to mention that he himself had arrived in one piece.

But love? He explored his feelings and hit a wall. He enjoyed Patricia's company, he worried about her, their minds often met on the same plane, and he could play father with her children. But was that love?

And if it was, was it enough? They both dragged decades of baggage between them. While with Christine, he'd thought he might want a child, but his images had lent themselves more to a talcum-scented baby, singular, and . . . nannies, he supposed. Not the disordered world of the O'Malley clan, where personalities rubbed up against each other—sometimes like silk, sometimes like wool. And sometimes very reminiscent of his childhood. A time he both treasured . . . and had to escape.

While he'd grown more than fond of Patricia's children—his gaze dropped to Sugar—as well as certain four-legged creatures, he didn't know if he wanted full-time parental responsibility for the real thing. Also, given his gut reaction this morning to Officer Peterson, he suspected he was more of a snob than he'd thought (which made him a pretty big snob), even if he'd grown attached to jeans and flannel shirts.

But he was definitely certain he'd never develop a soft spot for chickens, except in a gumbo. Patricia was Cordelia—or thought she was—whether or not it made her happy. He was San Francisco, whether or not it made him lonely. If the adventure palled, he could no longer run off and join a rock 'n' roll band.

If he wanted to be honest, he had to admit he felt relief at Patricia's reaction mixed in with his confusion.

Making a sound of self-disgust, he turned away from the hearth just as Patricia and Zinnia came through the doorway from the foyer.

"I think she must have eaten something bad. She doesn't have a fever." Patricia's gaze glanced off his bags, then off him.

He couldn't tell if he saw relief or regret. Maybe some of both, like he felt. He took a seat on the footstool.

"She'll be all right after a day's rest." Zinnia eased herself down on the sofa, gaze falling on the suitcases. "Oof. That shopping wore me out this morning. Just as well we came back today. Since you're needing to tend to Daisy, maybe Zeke here should stay through the weekend. You'd lend a hand for a couple more days, now, wouldn't you, Zeke Townley? Especially considering I've heard the two of you up 'n eloped last month." She chuckled. But when neither of them smiled, her eyes narrowed. "Did you two have a falling-out of some—"

"I won't need Zeke. Daisy's headed back tomorrow, sick or well."

Zeke tamped down his irritation at being summarily dismissed.

Zinnia frowned. "She should stay and go on back with her cousins on Sunday."

"Danny's leaving tomorrow and she wants to ride with him."

The fact that Patricia had apparently not insisted Daisy stay here spoke volumes.

"Even if Daisy leaves, we can still go get our Christmas tree, can't we, Mama?" Tugging off her pom-pom hat, Lily-Too came in through the dining room, followed by Pop, Rose, and Hank. Their cheeks were ruddy from the cold. She smiled at Zeke. "It's really fun. We go out in the woods and cut it down. Hank trained Dharma to pull it back to the house, and sometimes she doesn't want to go and he gets mad and it's so-oo funny."

Despite the smile, Lily-Too's gaze was mournful.

Sweet little sunshine—trying to put a good face on things for his benefit. He patted the stool and she joined him.

Hank sat down on the hearth and rolled his eyes. "Yeah, real funny."

"I think it is, too." Grinning, Rose dropped cross-legged on the floor nearby. Pop joined Zinnia on the sofa.

"And then we make popcorn and string them and put them all over along with all our old ornaments. There are candy canes, and Mama makes hot chocolate and we sing Christmas carols, even though Mama sounds awful. But if you could be here . . . can you come back tomorrow?" Lily-Too looked at Patricia. "Can he come, too?" There was a tiny tremble in her voice.

Zinnia stared at Lily-Too. "Lord love a duck, I do believe that's more sentences than I've ever heard that child string together at one time."

Suddenly self-conscious, Lily-Too dipped her head. Maybe the change seemed abrupt to Zinnia, but over five weeks of lessons and three weeks of rehearsals, he'd watched Lily-Too bloom with confidence. Her grades had inched up, too, but shyness was still close to the surface.

Zeke caught up her hand. "I think that sounds like family time to me. We'll have other times just to ourselves."

"Okay, but . . . but you're family. At least, you're like family. Isn't he, Mama?"

All eyes landed on Patricia. Pinking up, she smiled weakly. "I guess if Zeke wants to—I mean, if you're not doing anything, you could—"

He put her out of her misery. "Lily-Too, there's nothing I'd like better than to hunt down a Christmas tree with you, but—"

"Is it Dharma? I'll make sure she behaves."

"No, it's not Dharma. Your Uncle Jon and I have rehearsals at the boys' home tomorrow. I told you about that, remember?" And even though he enjoyed the time he spent there, looking into Lily-Too's downcast face, he suddenly thought nothing sounded more enjoyable than a trip into the woods. In the snow. With a donkey. Good God.

Rose spoke up. "But we'll see you next week when you come give Lily-Too a lesson, right? If you come on Thursday when Mom doesn't have class, I'll make . . ." Twirling a chunk of hair between her fingers, she grinned. "I'll make chicken-and-oyster gumbo."

Hank groaned. "Gross."

"All for a good cause." Rose untangled her legs and stood up. "But now I need to study."

"That's all you ever do," Hank said. "You're boring."

"That's all there is *to* do," Rose retorted. She hesitated, then stooped to give Zeke a hug. "We'll miss you."

His heart clenched. "Me, too."

As Rose released him, Lily-Too tugged on his arm. "So you'll come on Thursday?"

He didn't even glance at Patricia. "I wouldn't miss it."

"Good." She hugged him, too. Hard. He breathed in the scent of her hair, peach shampoo and winter cold. She released him and turned to Hank. "Will you take me sledding?"

"Well, I . . ." Hank's gaze went to his mother, and he swallowed. "In a little while. There's something I want to talk to Mom about."

"She can come, too," Lily-Too said graciously.

"Privately," Hank said.

Zeke's antennae went up. From the way Hank's Adam's apple worked in his throat, it appeared he'd finally decided to tell his mother. Zeke felt relief. If he'd known Hank would take this long, he probably wouldn't have made a hasty promise to keep the truth from Patricia.

"And there's something I need to talk to all of *you* about after everyone leaves." Patricia's gaze bounced off Zeke and the color in her face deepened. "So don't disappear."

Zeke supposed they'd have to know something. If she was right, Rusty Peterson would waste no time spreading the news. But he wondered just how she would break the big bulletin to her children that she'd slept with their houseguest.

"It won't take long, will it?" Rose paused near the window. "I have an English paper."

Zinnia's eyes danced with curiosity. "Is there anything I can help with, Patsy Lee?"

"Dear." Pop patted Zinnia's knee.

"What?"

"I think we'd best get on the road. Lil will worry if we take much longer."

Zinnia pursed her lips. Zeke could see the wheels turning.

"No, she won't," Rose announced, looking out the window. "Because she's here."

Hank rose to see. "With Uncle Jon. And there's some other people, too."

Zeke joined everyone staring out the window. Watching her husband, Lil stood beside an SUV that had stopped in the drive, same make as the one in the ditch. Jon must have rented a replacement. Opening a rear door, he helped a woman out. Another followed. Both thirty somethings, one petite, one tall, one all curves, one a willow. Recognition dawning, Zeke's curiosity shifted to shock.

Apparently spotting them through the window, the smallest of the two gave a wave, setting her brown curls and ample chest bouncing. It was his little sister Teresa. Standing beside her, face serene, her hair a flame against the snow, was . . .

"Christine." Patricia's voice was flat.

Chapter 19

"Guess who Jon and I discovered at the car rental lot?" Lil came through the foyer into the parlor, a draft of cold air and her guests following behind. Despite her smile, she looked like she wasn't completely happy with her find.

Black eyes snapping, face merry, the shorter woman with the hourglass figure pushed past Lil. "Surprise, brother dear!" Rising on her tiptoes, she gave Zeke a peck, ignored his startled *"What are you doing here?"* and turned to Patsy Lee. Her movements were quick and set her dark curls bouncing. "You must be Zeke's patient. He's mentioned you to Mother. I'm Teresa Tommaso."

"Tommaso," Patsy Lee repeated dumbly.

As Teresa turned to meet everyone else, Patsy Lee looked past her to watch Christine glide—yes, she did indeed glide—into the room in Teresa's wake. She murmured greetings, briefly brushed Patricia's hand with cool fingers, then stopped in front of Zeke. There was a pause, then a light embrace, before she seated herself on the sofa at Zinnia's invitation. Her face was carefully blank.

And as flawless as Patsy Lee remembered. More so, since, until this minute, she'd convinced herself that her imagination had adorned Zeke's former lover with more perfection than was possible. It hadn't. Copper hair pulled back revealed an exquisite face: Intelligent emerald eyes. Pearl skin smoothed over delicate bones. Aquiline nose. Full lips. And of course, the package came with a slender figure, melodic voice, polish, and the confidence that came with knowing no other woman could ever look better than her.

Patsy Lee looked down at her feet. And no other woman should probably try.

"Yes, Tommaso. After the divorce I ditched my married name and reverted to my maiden one." Teresa dropped her coat next to Christine before Patsy Lee even thought to take it. She turned to the fireplace, holding her hands out, staring up at the fabric sculpture. "Wow. What a fabulous piece of artwork."

"I thought Townley . . . you did say your *maiden* name?" Zinnia was studying the newcomers as though aliens had dropped into their midst.

"*Maiden* is rather misleading," Zeke said, eyes still on Christine. He didn't explain that Patsy Lee was the artist who had created the fabric sculpture.

"She wasn't talking about *that*." Giving him a look of fond rebuke, Teresa turned away from the sculpture. "Zeke changed his name a long time ago. He didn't think Italian would sell country records."

"A name makes a difference." Zeke finally seemed to remember Patsy Lee. He gave her a small smile. "Right . . . Patricia?"

"Unh." What repartee. Not that he'd notice. His gaze had slid almost immediately back to Christine. Patsy Lee felt like she'd just drank one of Alice in Wonderland's potions. She felt herself grow smaller and smaller.

"So why are you here?"

Even though Zeke had addressed the words to Christine, Teresa was the one who launched into explanations that sounded lame even to Patsy Lee (who was afraid her powers of—of *perspicacity* had been temporarily disabled along with her powers of speech). If Teresa was to be believed, apparently Zeke's failure to return home for the Thanksgiving holiday, added to their mother's disclosure that he wouldn't be back in San Francisco until after Christmas, had resulted in a stopover in Cordelia "just so we can *see* you, you know." They'd stay here a week before continuing on to New York for the holidays—

"Don't tell me Mom came, too."

"No. She'd planned to. She's worried about your self-imposed banishment to the country. But we argued over"—looking stricken, she stopped. Her eyes darted to Christine, then away—"oh, just *stuff* like we always do, and she got huffy and decided to stay behind. Which is fine by me. I didn't want to listen to her cluck about your or my lifestyle. Boring, boring, boring." With an infectious laugh, Teresa turned to the rest of them. "Mother doesn't approve of me, you see, but why shouldn't I have fun, since my husbands have been so generous?" She sighed. "But I'll bet her concern over you, dear brother, has her joining us, anyway. Marta Tommaso doesn't let anything stop her for long." Again, a glance at Christine.

"She's not worried; she's nosy." Zeke looked thoughtful. "It might be that mention I made of donkeys and chickens."

Patsy Lee's smile was reflexive, but it melted when Christine spoke up.

"So that explains the Farmer Brown couture." Her green eyes invited him to share her amusement. "It's quite becoming in a strange way, but then I've never known clothes to wear the man where you're concerned."

"Husbands?" Zinnia was still watching Teresa.

"Ex number three is footing the bill for this trip. Not that he knows it." Teresa looked at Christine, fortunately missing the expression on Zinnia's face. "New York will be fabulous. Christmas with all the trimmings. And stores." She twinkled.

"What about your work?" Zeke asked Christine.

"I'm only practicing part-time now. I wanted to leave time for . . . other things." The look she gave Zeke was loaded with meaning. He looked surprised.

"Practicing?" Patsy Lee blushed when Christine's gaze shifted to her. "I mean, so you're a musician, too?" She couldn't remember what she'd been told.

"A lawyer." Christine's look was appraising before her gaze moved on. Feeling like an idiot, anger stirred under Patsy Lee's embarrassment. She knew that look; she'd just been dismissed as unworthy of any consideration as competition.

Teresa grinned. "But don't hold it against her. She's actually a lot of fun."

Oh yeah. A barrel of laughs.

"Anyway, we decided that if we stopped and spent some time with Zeke, we could tell Mother he was okay."

"You expect me to believe that?" Zeke said.

Teresa stuck out her tongue. "*And* she'd stay home. If you'd keep your cell phone on, she wouldn't worry all the time. She said she hasn't been able to get you since last week, even though she's tried a dozen times a day."

"I'm glad you warned me. I'll leave it off." Folding his arms, Zeke leaned back against the jamb and looked at her. "C'mon, Terri. Don't tell me you came out of concern for me, or even to keep Mom out of your hair. That's stretching credulity."

"Teresa," his sister corrected him. "And since I haven't the faintest idea what credu-whatever means, I don't owe you any more explanations."

Zeke raised his eyes to the ceiling.

Teresa looked at the others. "Anyway, we took a

puddle jumper from Kansas City, then ran into Jon at the car rental office. We'd booked a place called . . . what was that place, Chrissy?"

"The Sleep Inn." Again, that note of amusement.

"But the lady at the car place said it has roaches." Teresa shuddered. "So Lil invited us to stay with them. We'll be sharing the guesthouse with you, brother dear."

"Really?" Zeke said, his gaze settling back on Christine.

When Christine met his eyes, Patsy Lee felt something flare between the pair. Her spine went stiff. The guesthouse had multiple bedrooms, but she suddenly wondered if only Teresa's and one other would be put to thorough use. If that happened . . .

Well . . . so what? They'd made no promises and spoken no vows; nor had they ever intended any. They had no *real* relationship, and the one *he* had—past, present, *or* future—with Christine was none of her business.

Still, she felt herself shrink even more. Fastening a polite smile on her face, she refused to think of what had transpired in this very room the night before, and heartily wished every one of the people in it would disappear.

But an hour later—an hour that had felt like a millennium—after her visitors had left and Zeke's departure had been accomplished with a minimal amount of pathos (due to what she had to admit was his skilled, gentle handling of Lily-Too), she didn't feel any better.

Despite the cats twisting around her feet, Sugar's panting presence, and four children, the house seemed unusually empty. She read a little, ate a little, tended Daisy a little, and moped a whole lot, although she told herself that wasn't what she was doing.

Then Hank pulled her into his room and spilled

what was on his mind. It drove everything else completely out of her own.

On Sunday evening, shivering in dropping temperatures, Patsy Lee made her way toward the side door of St. Andrew's Church, wishing she'd worn her insulated parka instead of her good wool coat. In the last two days since Hank's disclosure, she'd thought of little else, but when she called Zeke to arrange this meeting, vanity had crept back in.

And left her overdressed in a split skirt, peach-colored blouse (the only silk one she owned), and a tunic vest that she'd woven years ago using hand-dyed brushed mohair that had taken her months to save for. Jeans and a sweatshirt would have done just as well for an appearance at the Christmas pageant rehearsal. Or would have if she wasn't thinking that Zeke, having now spent forty-eight hours in the company of his sister and Christine, would make comparisons.

Despising herself for caring, especially now, she maneuvered around a puddle that was forming a crust of ice. In the light from the lamps that lined the walkway, the maples and sycamores cast long shadows across the churchyard, now a quilt of melting snow and faded grass. No snow could hold up long under the capricious weather of this time of the year.

Which was fortunate. Now that she could put some weight on her foot, she'd waved away Hank's offer of a lift. Having him here would have been more than awkward, since he was the reason she was.

Her self-confidence might still be shaken from Christine's appearance on her doorstep—and, really, what woman in her right mind wouldn't feel a wobble in her ego?—but it was nothing compared to the quake in her spirits since Hank's revelation.

She had to talk to someone. And since Hank had

pledged her to secrecy, Zeke was it. Like she'd suspected, on that day in McDonald's, Hank had revealed far more to Zeke than he'd let on. She wanted to be upset Zeke hadn't shared the information, and at first she was. But after some reflection—and under the same restriction herself—she'd (grudgingly) had to admit he'd had no choice.

Since Friday evening, she'd attempted to be matter-of-fact about Hank's . . . situation . . . as matter-of-fact as Hank had indicated Zeke had been. But as she thought of her son, anxiety shot through her veins. Stumbling, she stopped, putting a hand on the rough stone of the building to steady herself.

Her son. Her *gay* son.

She took a deep breath, nostrils pinching on the chilled air. Her mind still wanted to hide in denial, despite Hank's earnestness, despite his conviction, despite her own deep-seated knowledge, drawn from some hidden spot of maternal intuition, that what he'd said was true.

Dear Hank. Dear, brave, *gay* Hank.

She wished she could get over thinking of his sexual orientation every time she looked at him, but right now she couldn't. She supposed (fervently hoped) her focus would blur with time. Along with the shock (well hidden, please God) that had reverberated up her spine and the apprehension for what he'd face (not an unfamiliar feeling to her) that had soured her stomach.

Still, even as her body had thrummed with distress as she'd listened, even as she'd had to clasp her hands tight to keep from betraying her agitation, she'd never loved Hank more than she had in that moment of revelation. His gaze had been steady, his voice roughened with the maturity of insight; his body free of normal teenage fidgets. And she'd seen the tremendous well of courage he'd called on to take the risk of making himself vulnerable. A vulnerability she could sense in the plea that lurked behind his eyes and in his voice.

But mature or not, brave or not, before their talk was over, he'd cried. And she'd held him and rocked him and assured him that, of *course* she still loved him. What she didn't tell him was that her heart wept, too.

Wanting to rail against a fate that had chosen this path for her son, she'd drawn instead on the stoicism she'd developed in her youth, feeling her way on a landscape that was all too familiar if not recently traveled, knowing that whatever devastation she felt was nothing compared to the emotions Hank had experienced—was still experiencing—while he struggled to come to terms with himself. Being a teenager was rough; adding sexual confusion and, ultimately, a realization he didn't fit society's—especially small-town society's—version of normal must have been hell.

She'd hurt for him far more than she'd hurt for herself, so she'd kept her emotions bottled inside until her calm demeanor had been rewarded. His arms had crept around her waist until he'd held her as tight as she had him, just like when he was little. Over supper later that night, she noted much of his former tension had melted.

At about the same rate that hers had increased. She'd kept a smile on her face since that evening, but her heart had grown heavier even as the knowledge grew more familiar. She knew, far better than him, the lifetime of discrimination he'd face. Every time she thought of it, her unease deepened.

Pushing off the rough wall, she moved into the light cast by a single bulb glowing over the arched side entrance to the church. The door opened as she reached for it, knocking her off balance. She did a little hop on her good leg and a hand grabbed her elbow. Steadied by the grip, Patsy Lee looked into a pair of concerned hazel eyes topped by a headful of brown fluff styled by the wind. Her mind still full of Hank, it took a moment for recognition to dawn.

"Maisie Ann! I wouldn't have expected—I mean, I've been thinking of you and—"

"Seems most people have." Maisie Ann's voice was dry. She stepped out and the door drifted shut behind her. "Finn and I just had some things to go over, but he's free now."

"Oh, I'm not here to see Finn. I'm here to . . . well, that doesn't matter. Um, how are you?"

"I'm fine. Well, I hope I didn't hurt you any. You take care, now." Tucking her hands into her pockets, Maisie Ann brushed past her and started down the walk.

This might be the last time she ever saw the woman who had been haunting her thoughts; Patsy Lee had heard Maisie Ann and Simon would be moving out of Cordelia around Christmas. Suddenly, she couldn't let her leave. Not without . . . something.

"Maisie Ann!"

Maisie Ann halted. Patsy Lee hobbled toward her, stopping when they were an arm's length apart. In the wariness at the bottom of the other woman's eyes, Patsy Lee saw how deeply she'd been wounded by the town's tongue. Whatever she'd intended to say—words she hadn't even formulated—dried up in a sudden feeling of connection. "I just—I hope you'll be happy. You and Simon, too."

"Thank you."

Maisie Ann's quiet response wasn't what Patsy Lee wanted. What exactly she did want, though, was beyond her understanding. And suddenly she realized it was beyond Maisie Ann's, too. Maisie Ann had no more answers than the rest of them did.

Feeling stupid, Patsy Lee turned back toward the church.

"Patsy Lee?"

"Yes?"

"This may not be any of my business. In fact, I know it's not. But I've heard some talk. . . . I mean, well, you know what I mean. And I wanted to tell you, don't you pay them no mind." Maisie Ann's expression grew fierce. "Don't pay any of them no mind, you hear?"

Slowly, she nodded.

Maisie Ann hesitated. Then she reached out and gave Patsy Lee's shoulder a quick squeeze before turning away. Patsy Lee watched her go. Whether Maisie Ann was right or wrong in what she'd done, the woman had courage. More courage than Patsy Lee.

Patsy Lee let herself into the church. The stairwell was warm. Grip tight on the handrail, Patsy Lee limped down to a wide basement hallway shiny with high-gloss enamel and fluorescent lights. It echoed with children's voices raised in the chorus of "O Little Town of Bethlehem."

I've heard some talk. Suddenly weary, Patsy Lee stopped at the bottom of the steps. She hadn't needed to ask Maisie Ann for an explanation. She'd already had one from Lil.

Knowing Zeke would be at Vreeley with Jon all day Saturday, Patsy Lee had waited until Saturday night to call him at Lil and Jon's guesthouse to ask him to meet her about Hank—not wanting to trust his confidences to the phone, in case someone else picked up. But the phone had rung through to the main house and Lil had picked up, explaining that the others had traveled to Kansas City: Zeke and Jon to their volunteer work, Christine and Teresa for shopping and lunch. Lil would be meeting the group in a while for supper.

Lil hesitated. "Do you want to join us? Or would you feel uncomfortable?"

"Uncomfortable?" Absolutely, but why would Lil would think so?

Lil's sigh whispered through the line. "I was in Peg's yesterday and, oh, dang, Patsy Lee. I don't know how to tell you this, but I guess you should know. There's a lot of talk going on. Apparently, Rusty Peterson told Erik Olausson that—"

"I know what he told him." Patsy Lee snorted. A halfhearted snort, but maybe Lil wouldn't notice. "When Rusty stopped by, he saw blankets on the floor and Zeke half dressed. I could see what he was thinking so . . . well, I'm afraid I made things worse by blurting out some stupid story about Sugar getting cold. Actually, things looked like . . . just what they looked like. We'd slept together—but in separate blankets in front of the fire. The other rooms were way too cold." It was the same whopper she'd told her children.

"Oh. Oh, I see. I thought maybe it was something like that."

"Cross my heart." Burning in hell was a better option than leaving herself wide open to gossip. She'd had enough, and after Hank's secret became common knowledge, they'd be in for a whole lot more. She plunged on. "Could you talk to Zinnia? I mean, between the two of you, you can probably put a halt to the rumors. They're silly, anyway. Me and Zeke Townley?"

"I don't think that's silly. In fact, I'd hoped—" Lil sighed again. "Never mind."

Never mind was right. Since she'd seen Christine again, Lil must have realized what a big, fat pipe dream *that* had been. They'd rung off, Patsy Lee hopeful that she'd just stopped rumors dead in their tracks. Or sicced the one person on them that could.

The strains of "O Little Town of Bethlehem" stopped. The closed doors of Harmony Hall burst open. Children flooded out, headed for bathrooms and drinking fountain. Patsy Lee moved against the flow, heart warming as she spotted Lily-Too in the thick of things, chattering madly with Josephine McGraw and looking like she'd never harbored a shy bone in her body.

Lily-Too caught sight of Patsy Lee and ran up, pulling Josephine by the hand. "Did you come to watch us?"

"To watch and to talk to Zeke. How's rehearsal going?"

"Okay, I guess."

"Something wrong?"

Josephine scrunched her nose. "Zeke's not much fun tonight. He's got some ladies with him."

Patsy Lee's stomach sank.

Lily-Too did a little dance.

Patsy Lee forced a smile, remembering Zeke's remarks on the size of children's bladders. "You go on to the little girls,' Sunshine. I'll be here when you get back." Even though she wanted to flee back to her car.

Instead, she stepped into Harmony Hall, a lofty name for a linoleum-floored space that was half the size of the high school gym and not much more elegant. A few children raced around a plywood "stage," jiggling the easels set up to simulate the backdrops Bebe would later deliver. Playing organist, Lynette Schroeder pounded out measures of "Silent Night" on an upright piano. Patsy Lee had heard the preacher's secretary had shared a booth and the country buffet with Phinnaeus Phelps over in Cole Camp the other day. From the way the chords were bouncing off the concrete block walls, Lynette was either invigorated by her date or annoyed by the gossip about it. Cole Camp lay close enough to tangle with the Cordelia grapevine.

Backs to her, exuding money and privilege (or at least, that's how it seemed), Christine, Teresa, and Zeke sat in folding chairs facing the stage. Several more chairs were scattered around the room, music stands crowded one corner, and fold-up cafeteria tables stood in another.

Feeling like a deer about to cross the interstate, Patsy Lee paused to finger-comb her hair. Both women undoubtedly smelled as expensive as they looked in wool ensembles that cost as much as her house. She thought of the Estee Lauder cologne she saved for only the most special occasions. She'd dabbed some on before she'd left. She sighed. She couldn't compete; she shouldn't try to.

Her gaze moved to Zeke. He was leaning back in his chair, ankle on his knee. Gone were the denim and flannel, replaced by a white shirt and the black unstructured jacket she hadn't seen since the day he'd visited Wal-Mart.

Teresa's enthusiastic voice sounded over the music. "This is all just so quaint. It's just so . . . so *Norman Rockwell.*"

Zeke's sister sounded charmed.

"On one of his bad days," Christine said.

Christine didn't.

"In fact," Christine continued, "since I've been here, I've decided *quaint* is overrated."

Because she wasn't.

Patsy Lee waited for Zeke to object. When he said nothing, her anger stirred. He'd lived here long enough to know that despite its warts, Cordelia was deserving of more than ridicule.

She forced herself to move toward them. Maybe she

didn't have designer clothes and expensive perfumes and an aquiline nose that spent all its time in the stratosphere, but she suddenly realized she had far more class than some people did.

Chapter 20

Hands locked behind his head as he waited for the children to return for the final minutes of rehearsal, Zeke thought he should spring to Cordelia's defense, but decided protest was a waste of time.

For two days, he'd suffered the women's comments on the town, thoughtless on Teresa's part—which made sense because she rarely had a thought—and slyly humorous on Christine's. Since they were made only to him and with what seemed to be an odd sense of desperation on Christine's part, he'd abandoned his efforts to staunch them. In fact, he'd gone a step further, adjusting his wardrobe rather than continuing to subject himself to their (oh-so-hilarious) repertoire of Farmer Brown, Old MacDonald, and American Gothic remarks. They were determined to find him, his efforts, and Cordelia amusing, so they could amuse away until he carted them off to the airport on Saturday. A day that sometimes felt like forever away.

He glanced at Christine. Or sometimes heartbreakingly close.

Her presence confused him. As did the jumble of emotions she'd provoked.

The efficient Lynette signaled the end of the break by sounding minor chords, putting real muscle into it when Finn Phelps followed the children in and took a chair near the stage to watch. He carefully smoothed back his hair. The secretary was so loud, her surreptitious looks at the preacher so unsurreptitious that Christine's eyebrows went up and Teresa stifled a giggle.

Since they wouldn't understand the real pleasure he took in watching the budding courtship of the preacher and his secretary, he decided to skip explanations. Whistling for the children's attention (not that it ever worked), he stood up and caught sight of Patricia heading toward him. The peach of her blouse did incredible things to her complexion. But not as incredible as what the glow of firelight had done to her skin during a certain winter snowstorm.

Smiling a neutral greeting, his heart softened even as he buried the image, as he'd done each of the thousand times it had surfaced in the last several days. His smile wasn't returned; the stillness in her face indicated she'd overheard Teresa and Christine. Not only overheard, but—judging from the way her gaze pinned him—had decided he was tainted with the same brush.

Right now he didn't have time to mount a defense even if he wanted, and he wasn't sure he wanted. She'd made it obvious she didn't think they belonged together. And he wondered if she just might be right. He waved her to his vacated chair. "We'll be done in less than twenty."

She barely acknowledged him. After an abrupt greeting to the other women, she sat down, her expression wooden.

As he walked toward the makeshift stage, he felt three pairs of eyes boring holes in his back. Tired of underlying emotions, he ignored them and gave his attention to the kids, who wouldn't know an undercurrent if one swept them away, bless their innocent little hearts.

Before Lynette launched into the opening chords of

"O Little Town of Bethlehem" for the sixteen thousandth time that evening, he reassured Josephine McGraw that the Virgin Mary's pipe cleaner halo would preclude the need for her to curtsy to identify her role every time she appeared on the stage, and instructed the Angel of the Lord, freckle-faced Annabeth Spangle, to sing as loud as she'd squealed when Eldon Noflinger, the chronic arm swinger he'd cast as Joseph, had yanked on her braids.

His remark earned him one of those delightful kid giggles that gave him the reason to put himself through this, but they didn't divert him for long. A good chunk of his thoughts returned to the women behind him. Especially Christine.

He didn't know what to make of her presence, and she hadn't said anything to enlighten him. In fact, she'd ducked his questions. After her one and only visit to Cordelia eight months ago—when Jon had decided to entertain them by taking them to the Tenth Annual Jaycees' Testicle Festival (no joke)—she'd vowed never to return. At the time, he'd felt her decision had been more than an aversion to mountain oysters (although that by itself probably would be enough). So what was she doing here now?

Simply accompanying Teresa on her self-avowed journey to reassure herself and their mother of his well-being? Yeah, right. He'd dismissed his sister's explanation as soon as it had left her lips. The youngest of the family, and babied to the hilt once their dad had died when she was five, Teresa was spoiled rotten. While not possessed of true spite—hard, considering that most of her thoughts were devoted to herself—she didn't give a hoot about Mom's concerns. And given those glances she'd thrown at Christine in Lil's parlor, it looked like she and Mom had exchanged words on her motives for the trip. Her ulterior motives. That Teresa would book accommodations that didn't include at least a day spa indicated she had some.

That Christine would let herself be led by his sister said she did, too.

Had Christine changed her mind about their breakup? Or was Teresa trying to change it for her? Either would account for an argument between his mother and his sister. His mother had always been lukewarm where Christine was concerned, hardly able to hide her relief when they'd parted ways. Just as Teresa couldn't hide her desire to have Christine as a sister-in-law. Her attempts to throw them together privately in the last two days had only been subverted by Christine's equal talent in sidestepping her efforts. And he . . . he'd just kept trying to puzzle everything out. He was no longer sure his heart had been mortally wounded by Christine's desertion, but he was just learning to fill the gap she'd left.

Still, if she'd changed her mind . . .

Maybe he'd need to reconsider his own.

He blew out a breath. *Confused* didn't begin to cover how he felt.

The children had just reached "everlasting *li-iight*" when Eldon Noflinger unintentionally socked their innkeeper in the gut. The innkeeper took exception. Zeke signaled Lynette to halt the music while he separated them.

When things had settled down, he glanced back toward the women. Teresa was chattering, but he couldn't claim either of her companions was still listening. Patricia watched him with the same stolid look she'd walked in with; Christine with a bored one. He recognized his former lover's expression all too well.

He turned back to the children. Because it mirrored the one he'd worn until not long ago.

* * *

Thirty minutes later, Harmony Hall had mostly emptied. Parents had swooped in to pick up their little thespians; Lynette had left at the same time as Preacher Phelps, both keeping a careful distance from each other. Zeke would bet one of the fine members of the Ladies' Auxiliary had (with arched brows) made a passing comment about the fine strudel at Der Essen Platz. Sometimes he wondered how Jon—or anyone—managed to swim this fishbowl.

But it wouldn't be politic to make a comment now, since he stood next to Eldon Noflinger's mother—who doubled as the town's mayor. Zeke reassured her yet again that there would only be a slight bruising on Eldon's arm from the innkeeper's bite. After the clucking politician had led her son off, he headed for the piano, where Lily-Too was doodling a carol.

He rested his hands on her shoulders. "Good rehearsal."

"Really?" She tilted her head way back to see him.

His chest tightened. Even upside down, her gaze was like a flower following the sun; adoration he hadn't earned. But, as with most kids, generously given.

"Darn tootin,' Sunshine. You're the best there ever was."

And she was. She had quite a future if she could put stage fright behind her. They'd made progress. He'd convinced her she didn't need to hide under a headdress, although she still wanted to cover that sweet face with stage makeup.

Winking at her, he told her he wouldn't let her mother jabber too long and left her to join the women, although his thoughts stayed behind. He'd leave in another month. By then, he'd have fulfilled his commitments to the pageant and Vreeley Home. And long worn out his welcome. He wasn't exactly dreading his departure—he missed the city and now had more reasons than culture and cuisine to be impatient to return. Enthusiastic over their work in Kansas City with the youth home, he and Jon had been tossing around ideas to expand their charitable endeavors; plans he'd further once he was back in San Francisco.

But whenever he thought of leaving Cordelia, fishbowl and all, he was disconcerted by a host of conflicting emotions. Among them, regret for Lily-Too.

Who would continue to nurture her talent? It sure as hell wouldn't come from Mrs. Shylock. Patricia was tone-deaf. And while he'd fished the local pond of music teachers, he hadn't caught anyone with vocal experience. Her Uncle Jon could fill the bill—except her Uncle Jon had commitments, his own family, and the attention span of a gnat unless his concentration was snagged. Well, Zeke would have to do whatever he could to snag it on Lily-Too.

He joined the women. Teresa and Christine had already collected their coats, apparently having forgotten—or choosing to ignore—that he'd said he needed to talk to Patricia before they left.

"And that sculpture above the fireplace?" He'd caught Teresa in midsentence, big surprise. "Yum. You really do have talent. And I haven't seen anything at Barty's—or at La Di Da, for that matter—that's even half as fabulous as that vest." As usual, his sister was focused on her reason for living: shopping, be it on Union Square or anywhere else. "Don't you agree, Zeke?"

"With what?"

"That Patricia's vest is fabulous. Look at it." Teresa reached down to pick up the hem of the material off Patricia's lap. She ran it through her fingers. "She could make a mint. You should send Barty some samples," she said to Patricia. "He'd take them on consignment. Wouldn't he, Christine?"

"I couldn't say. Perhaps with a word from you." Christine took a pair of leather gloves out of her DKNY clutch and snapped it closed.

"And those sculptures . . . they're easily as good as what we see in the Fowler Gallery." Teresa dropped the fabric and tapped a fingernail against her teeth. "With our family's patronage of the arts, I'd think . . . wow. Can't you see one of her sculptures there, Chrissy?"

"Fowler is more perspicacious than you," Christine replied.

Teresa hesitated. "Uh, exactly. They'd *love* her work."

Giving his sister's lack of *perspicacity* a mental head shake, Zeke frowned at his former lover. She wasn't normally so rude. Handing him her coat, Christine returned a bland look, and he suddenly realized she thought Patricia wouldn't understand the meaning of *perspicacious*. Reflexively, he held open her coat. What she didn't know was Patricia was far from an idiot; what she'd probably guessed correctly, though, was Patricia lacked claws.

As Christine slipped her arms into the sleeves, her perfume, a promise of Far Eastern eroticism, tickled his nose. He inhaled sharply to ward off a sneeze and sought a change of subject. "So," he addressed Patricia. "Did you get that Christmas tree trimmed?"

Patricia's eyes were black ice, but she only murmured, "Yes, we did. I—*we*—missed having you there." She rose, hooked her crutch under her arm, and gathered her things. "Shall we talk over there?" She limped toward two chairs near the stage.

Slaughter averted, he gave an inward sigh of relief. Settling Christine's coat on her shoulders, he let his hands linger just in case she got a sudden urge to follow. Patricia glanced back.

Teresa's face fell. "I thought we were leaving."

"I was under the same impression." Twisting, Christine looked up at him.

He studied her face. Even over emerald eyes, arched eyebrows really did look arrogant. He made a mental note to check his tendency toward eyebrow raising.

"You know what?" Patricia stopped. "This can wait."

"No, we can talk now."

"Oh, c'mon, brother dear." Teresa winked at Patricia. "You're just so sweet."

He winced. Teresa sounded patronizing. Maybe because she was.

Patricia's face wore that wooden look again. "We can talk tomorrow," she insisted. "I'll be at the store all day if you can spare the time to drop by."

"Store?" Teresa perked up. "Maybe we can all drop by. Clothing?"

"C'mon, Sunshine, we're leaving." Patricia called, then looked at Teresa. "No, Lil's bookstore, but you still might like it." Patricia shrugged into her coat, sidling sideways a step when he reached out to help. "Yes, I'm sure you'd like it," she continued, voice thoughtful. "You see, when it comes to what she carries, Lil is very perspicacious."

Christine went pink. Teresa looked confused. Lily-Too ran up, giving Zeke a bright smile. He managed a weak one in return.

Touching Lily-Too's shoulder to follow, Patricia started off, then hesitated and turned back. Her face had gone bright red, but her voice stayed conversational. "You know, my art history teacher in college—I'm not sure if you know I went—said there was a place in the world for all art, from the popular to the innovators. So while she taught us the Pollocks and the Picassos, she didn't neglect the Rockwells."

Gaze sharpening, Christine flushed.

As did Teresa. "When I said Cordelia was so Norman Rockwell, I didn't mean—well, I mean, I *did* mean—but I *never* meant—"

"It's okay, it's just that some people don't like Rockwell because they think he wasn't a real artist, just an idealist with technical talent who was out of touch with reality. But you know what he said? He said, 'Common places never become tiresome. It is we who become tired when we cease to be curious and appreciative.' "

Zeke could relate.

Patsy Lee looked from Teresa to Christine. She didn't look at him at all. "From what Zeke says, San Francisco sounds lovely, and I'd like to see it one day. But humdrum as it is, Cordelia has its own quiet merits." She sounded almost apologetic. "It's like comparing Pollock to Rockwell, you see. There's just really no point."

Openmouthed, Teresa and Christine watched her leave. As did Zeke, wondering exactly what he was allowing to walk out of his life.

Chapter 21

On Monday morning, sunshine streamed through the bay window at Merry-Go-Read, creating tiles of light on the hardwood floor and reflecting off Mr. Stuart's bald head. He had just turned the placard to OPEN, PLEASE COME IN! and was rearranging the window display. They changed it weekly during the holiday season to emphasize the new merchandise that arrived daily at this time of year.

Seated on a stool behind the counter, making a show of bookkeeping, Patsy Lee thought about all the boxes left to unpack. But it was only a passing thought before her mind snapped back to the scene she'd made last night.

All right, it really hadn't been a *scene*. Scenes were accompanied by screeching or cursing, and she'd conducted herself, she thought, with dignity. But while standing up for Cordelia (herself) had given her a sense of exhilaration, it had also brought a niggle of shame. At least for the way she'd lumped Teresa in with Christine. Zeke's sister wasn't intentionally cruel, and she'd said such nice things about her weaving, but as for Christine . . .

The woman was . . . *intolerable*. Although *some* people obviously didn't think so. Her mind played over the way Zeke's gaze had stayed pinned on Christine, how he'd caught his breath while holding her coat, the way he'd rested his hands on her shoulders and looked into her upturned face. . . .

She picked up some invoices and knocked them into line. Good thing she'd determined—long before they'd spent that night on her parlor floor—that she needed to hold firm to her heart. The man was . . . what did Daisy and her friends call it? . . . a player.

She slapped down the papers and picked up her pencil, knowing that *player* didn't fit. Maybe because he'd spent fourteen years with one woman and, according to the *National Tattler* (not known for its tendency to whitewash), he'd never strayed. But maybe Christine's desertion had muddled his brain. He wouldn't be the first man to hit a midlife crisis, and what other description fit? He loved Lil. He loved Christine. And he'd gone to bed with Patsy Lee.

"See," she muttered. "A player."

"What?" Mr. Stuart looked over.

"Nothing, I . . ." *I should be thinking about Hank, not wasting time on Zeke's love life.* ". . . I said I'll have to *pay her.*" She held up a bill. "The woman who makes the dreamcatchers."

The bells over the door tinkled. Seeing who it was, she ducked her head and wrote busily.

"Fine morning to you, Mr. Townley," Mr. Stuart said.

"That it is, Mr. Stuart." Zeke acknowledged.

She glanced up as though just noticing he was there and gave him a false smile. The one he returned was genuine and full of amusement. She *hated* that she could rarely fool him.

Looking like he'd found a compromise between city and country (and looking better than he had a right to) in a snowy white shirt and denims, Zeke walked up and leaned in close. "That was quite a performance last night. *Brava.*"

Before the scent of lime could work any magic, she started writing again. "That wasn't a performance. It was how I feel."

"Teresa was sorry."

"And I'm sorry if I offended her." She put only a slight emphasis on *her,* but glanced up to see a corner of his mouth quirk. It irritated her. "You'll apologize for me?"

"You can apologize yourself. Lil asked me to invite you to dinner Friday night. A bon voyage celebration—Christine and Teresa are leaving Saturday."

"I'm sorry. I can't."

"I understand. All those demands on your time. And then there's the matter of that broad yellow stripe right down the center of your back."

"I'm busy."

"Ba-*wock*-bok-bok-bok."

The clucking wasn't funny. But what did *she* have to hide from? She plunked down the pencil. "All *right*. I'll come." *But not for long,* she didn't add.

"Lil also asked me to take you to class tonight. She can't. She's driving to Sedalia—some problem with the store there—and doesn't know when she'll be back." He paused. "Why did you ask Lil, anyway? I'd take you; you know that."

Great. She'd let Hank have the car to drive to school and he had astronomy club tonight. Now no Hank. No car. No Lil. "You have company."

"Not a problem."

"It's not necessary. I'll ask P—"

"I'll take you. Now . . . you wanted to talk about Hank?"

Aggravated, she almost told him to forget it, but she *did* want to talk about Hank. Glancing toward Mr. Stuart, she saw that although he was still busy, his neck was craned so far in their direction it was a marvel he didn't topple over.

"Back here." Patsy Lee motioned to the back room. "Mr. Stuart, Zeke will help me receive some inventory. Yell if you need me."

"I will?" Zeke asked, following her.

"You will. If I don't make up an excuse, next thing you know everyone will be talking about our assignations in the back room at Merry-Go-Read."

She continued to keep her voice matter-of-fact. They were all adults here. They'd both enjoyed what had happened, but now it was over.

She flipped a switch and fluorescents hissed to life. The room was strictly utilitarian. Windowless, it held shelving, a counter where they boxed phone orders, a few stools, a table with unsteady legs, and an old refrigerator. At the rear was a garage door that opened to the alley. At the counter, she cleared a space, then indicated the boxes delivered earlier by UPS. Zeke hefted one and plunked it down. She tore an envelope off, opened the box with a swipe of a utility knife, then, perching on the stool, unsheathed the packing slip, fastened it to a clipboard, and picked up a pen. "As you take out the books, tell me how many of each title and I'll check them off."

"You're very efficient," Zeke commented, pulling out several books. "Three *Harry Potter and the Half-Blood Prince.*"

"I'm efficient in order to get it done. It's putting the merchandise out for display that's fun, but the part-timers do that."

Zeke set the books aside. "So besides playing with the goodies and being around children—which you can get your fill of at home—there's very little you like about this job. *Harry Potter and the Goblet of Fire.* Four."

"Don't start again." She kept her voice even.

Daydreaming over Teresa's suggestion had already wasted her time last night. Maybe she *could* get her weaving into a San Francisco boutique with Teresa's help—if Teresa even remembered her offer—and that would pave the way to other upper-crust shops that could charge what the garments were worth. She wasn't sure how the whole process worked. But she was sure of a few things. She didn't have anything to sell. She was out of practice. She didn't have time. Nor did she have the money to spare for supplies.

"Besides," she added, "I don't want to discuss my future. I want to discuss Hank's."

"Fine." Zeke stacked the received inventory on an empty shelf. He opened another box. "What about Hank's future?"

"You know *what* about Hank's future." She clipped another packing slip to the board.

"No. I really don't." He counted off some books and pulled out another few.

She made a checkmark. "Look, I'd talk with someone else except I promised I wouldn't. Hank said he might tell the family after Christmas, but that's too long to wait before I need to make some decisions. So can you be serious?"

"I am serious. What decisions?"

She'd been holding images of Hank at bay, but that barely veiled fear in his eyes when he'd told her he was gay flooded into her head. She let the clipboard clatter to the counter. "How come he told you first and not me?"

"My reaction wouldn't matter as much as yours."

"Reaction? My parents are gay women. And I love him. He *knows* that."

Zeke hesitated. "He was afraid you'd be ashamed." Accurately reading the disbelief on her face, he backpedaled. "Like you seem to be. Of Bebe. Hank thinks you hide her."

"I don't hide her. I protect her. Or try to. I just don't understand—why didn't I see?"

"Yes, you do try to hi—"

She pressed her lips together. What she did or didn't do with Bebe didn't matter right now. *Hank* mattered.

Zeke blew out a breath. "Okay. Maybe you're just too close to him."

"I guess that could be—" His words sunk in. "Wait a minute." *Maybe you're just too close to him. . . .* To see what's apparent to others? "You knew *before* he told you, didn't you? How? How could you know?"

Zeke held up his hands palm out. "I didn't know. I only wondered. The boy's sixteen, not interested in girls. No close friends. He's a great kid and he's not shy, so why so reclusive?"

"But why would you think he was gay? He could have been a . . . a . . . slow developer."

"Maybe. Except when I first came here, he asked me about gays in San Francisco. I saw him visit a Web site on the topic. His reaction to the Piggly Wiggly seemed pretty intense, even if he was supporting a family cause. Once I knew why you avoided the place . . ." Zeke shrugged. "Then there was his driver's license. It's a rite of passage for boys, a step into adulthood, but not with Hank. Hank—"

"Avoided it." Listening to Zeke enumerate the reasons, she felt like a maternal failure. She should have seen what he'd seen. *Before* he'd seen it.

He continued. "And that means—"

"*Hellfire.* I can figure it out! He didn't want to grow up. It meant he'd have to deal with who he was."

"Anything wrong back there, Miz Patsy?" Mr. Stuart called from the front, tone hopeful.

"No—no. Everything's fine." Patsy Lee called back, feeling ashamed of her outburst. Zeke was here because she'd asked him to be here. He was only trying to help.

"You didn't do anything wrong," Zeke said quietly. "He didn't want you to know."

Looking down, she fingered the corners of the papers clipped to the board. "Do you think . . . maybe he's mistaken. Maybe he's just confused. Going through a phase." Even as she spoke the words, she knew he wasn't. She sighed and looked back up. "Except he wouldn't say anything unless he felt certain, would he?"

"Probably not."

"So what do I do now?"

"Do? Well, ask Bebe what her experience was as a teen. See if he'll talk to her; they seem close. And there may be local chapters of some national groups that offer support to gay teens. Probably not right here, but Columbia probably—"

"That's not what I meant. If you saw through him, other people might, too. *Before* he's ready to tell them. And then—"

"And then he'll have to deal with it. Whether he decides to be open or not. It will be hard. And hard for you to watch, but—"

She frowned and looked away. "I need to help him."

"Patricia. What exactly can you do?" For the first time, Zeke sounded impatient. "Put *protect Hank* on your list along with *homeschool Lily-Too* and *do Daisy's homework*? You're making their problems yours. Maybe so you don't have to look at your own."

"They're *my children*. And I don't have problems."

Her only problems *were* their problems. She didn't know why he always implied her life was somehow out of whack. Maybe she felt unsettled these days, and maybe her discovery that her history wasn't what she thought it was had disoriented her, but she had things under control, she knew where she was headed (at least for the most part), and she—

"Go to San Francisco with me."

Her thoughts froze. "What?"

He hesitated. Looking back at him, she saw her surprise at his words mirrored in his face. Surprise he quickly veiled. "San Francisco. Come with me."

"Why?" she asked bluntly.

"I . . ." She'd never seen him look uncertain, but he did now.

"Never mind." She relieved him of the consequence of his uncharacteristic impulsiveness. "I can't."

I won't. Even though she'd been torn between relief and sharp disappointment at his . . . *nothing* . . . answer. Even though she'd wavered for just a flash, thinking of his descriptions of sunsets that turned the city gold, the jumble of tourist treats at Fisherman's Wharf, sails dotting the bay, the majesty of the ancient trees in Muir Wood . . . thinking, truth be told, of *him,* she knew if she went, it would lead right back to . . .

And she wouldn't become another member of his harem. Okay, *harem* was a slight exaggeration, but— She wouldn't take her place sandwiched somewhere between the paragon who still wanted to be part of his life and the one that never would. It would crush her.

". . . People will talk?"

"Huh?"

"I said, are you afraid people will talk?"

Her heart was still intact. She planned to keep it that way. But let him think gossip was her only reason. "Oh, don't look so annoyed, Zeke. You don't have to live here."

"Here's a news flash. Neither do you."

"What does my choice of where to live have to do with a-a . . . whatever it is you want from me? I'm tired of explaining myself. My home, my living, my *future* is here. As are my children's lives. And you . . . if you're thinking of—of another, well, fling with me . . ."

She took a breath. "Look, right now we can part without anyone getting hurt. Let's leave it that way.

Our feelings aren't involved." The sting of his silence perversely unleashed the blunt side of her tongue. "But in case you haven't noticed, Christine's still are."

That evening, dusk dimming the countryside, Zeke steered Jon's leased SUV toward the strip mall that housed the satellite campus where Patricia had class. Knowing Christine as well as he did, Patricia hadn't told him anything he hadn't already known. Just something that he wasn't sure he wanted to see.

Christine's pride was keeping her silent on the subject of reconciliation. That she regretted their separation had become increasingly apparent as departure day neared—in the longing that lurked in her gaze, the number of intentionally unintentional times she brushed up against him, and the fact that Teresa had taken to haranguing him about a reunion every chance she had. Undoubtedly, Christine was waiting for some sign from him. But he couldn't make one. Not while his own feelings were still proving a bitch to unravel.

In the passenger seat, Christine stirred but kept her head turned toward the window. The silence in the vehicle since Patricia had slid into the backseat was deafening, but, caught up examining his earlier behavior, he let it lay among them unbroken.

At the bookstore earlier, asking Patricia to travel home with him had arrived in his mouth unannounced. He hadn't known that's what he'd wanted, hadn't even known, for God's sake, what he'd *meant*. He still didn't. *Vacation* seemed inadequate; *lifetime* was overkill. But did his intentions matter, considering she'd rejected even the least of those two options? He felt the same stab of disappointment he'd felt earlier and tried to convince himself it was only his ego that had suffered. But he knew the wound went deeper than that.

He pulled into a slot in front of Flowerama Florists,

right next to the former commercial spaces that now served as classrooms. Knocking the gearshift into park, he twisted to see Patricia and caught her gaze on him, her eyes huge in the reflected light. She started and her backpack spilled to the floor.

He unlatched his door. "I'll help with that."

"I can manage." Her answer was clipped.

Fine. Slamming the door, he faced front again. As he'd explained to Patricia when he'd gone inside to fetch her at the farmhouse, Christine had practically thrown herself into the SUV as he was leaving Lil and Jon's. Had she really expected him to shove her back out?

While Patricia fumbled in the back with her things, he glanced at Christine. Not that he would have even if he'd dared. Her timing sucked, but they were long overdue for a private discussion, and here and now was as good a place as any. Probably better. At the guesthouse, they had little privacy from the ever-curious Teresa.

Shouldering her backpack, Patricia got out, her good-bye a slam of her door. As soon as she'd disappeared inside, he turned to Christine. Even in the half-light, her eyes gleamed emerald. They were mesmerizing; they always had been.

Before he could speak, she lay cool fingers on his lips. "Come with me. To New York for the holidays."

He pulled her hand down. "We need to talk."

"What we need is this."

She leaned over the console and kissed him. And damn, just like one of Pavlov's dogs, he responded to the familiar touch. His lips parted, her taste a balm after Patricia's rejection.

Flicking his upper lip with her tongue, Christine's hand slid into his hair.

Knowing this was selfish, knowing he'd have hell to pay for it later, he let her soothe his bruised ego, let a small, childish part of him exult in the knowledge that she regretted her decision to leave.

The back door handle rattled and the overhead light blinked on. "Oh," Patricia said.

He and Christine broke apart.

"Forget something?" Christine asked, voice irritable.

Face blank, Patricia didn't answer. She reached in and snatched a book from the floor.

"Patricia—" he started.

The door slammed. Clutching the text like a life preserver, her spine stiff, her shoulders back, Patricia bumped her way as fast as the crutch would carry her back to her classroom.

Zeke watched her, then dropped his head back against the seat. Headlights swept the interior of the SUV as another car pulled into the lot.

Christine's brows arched. "Seems someone has gotten her nose out of joint."

Closing his eyes, Zeke held up a hand. "Not now, Christine."

"I'm sorry." The archness had dropped out of Christine's voice. "Zeke, I—"

Someone tapped on the window. Zeke opened his eyes to see Lil looking in. Turning the ignition, he pushed the switch to open the window.

"I was on my way home and thought you were Jon." She motioned to the car. "His SUV and everything. What are you doing?" She eyed Christine.

Instead of thinking cross thoughts about interfering women, Zeke was glad for Lil's interruption. "Nothing. Patricia has a class so we—"

"You're waiting? Well, there's no need for both of you to stay." Lil motioned to Christine. "Come on home with me. You don't want to hang around here all night. How boring."

Christine cast a look his direction, obviously hoping

he'd object, but although he thought Lil's obvious ploy to separate the two of them was heavy-handed, he said nothing. He wanted—he needed—to talk to Patricia. Alone.

But after the two women had left, despite the hour he had to stew in his thoughts, when Patricia reappeared, he found he didn't know what to say. Christine's kiss had only served to heighten his confusion.

But Patricia seemed content with his silence. Beyond an "I'm tired," she said nothing, keeping her face resolutely turned toward the window all the way home.

Chapter 22

A few evenings later, night flattening itself against the windows even though it was still early, Patsy Lee reclined on her bed, back wedged against pillows, homework heavy on her lap. Her electric heater thrummed. The two cats at her side glared when she shifted, but didn't move from the warm hollows of the afghan over her legs. It was colder here than downstairs, but she'd wanted the room farthest from the parlor. Reaching for a calculator, she tried to focus on the balance sheet she was creating for her accounting class, but the image of Zeke and Christine locking lips kept getting in her way.

A perverse part of her didn't want it all to be over, even though she'd known before she saw that kiss that nothing had ever really gotten started. Because she hadn't let it. And given another choice now—she'd make the same one. Instead of moping, she should be counting the blessings—she swallowed hard; yes, *blessings*—that had resulted from Zeke's stay.

Lily-Too's sweet voice singing "Silent Night" drifted up the stairs, along with the aroma of Rose's chicken-and-oyster gumbo. Blessings like Rose's newfound fondness for the kitchen. And the bloom of Lily-Too's confidence.

A slam of the back door told her Hank had just

come in from taking care of the animals. Blessings like the routine the children still maintained. The boost in confidence Hank had found. The mentoring Lily-Too had received. *And,* she told herself firmly, *the companionship Zeke and I have shared.* There was no need to hide in her room.

Except that it made things easier.

Downstairs, Lily-Too paused. The chords of Zeke's Hofner resonated for several measures before their voices rose in harmony. She could picture them in the parlor, a fire crackling on the hearth, the scent of pine from the Christmas tree filling the air. Zeke's hands would skillfully dance over the frets of his guitar, his smiling eyes would rest on Lily-Too.

Easier—and harder.

She threw down the calculator and reached over to turn up the volume on the B. B. King recording she'd put in the player on her nightstand. Earlier in the day, when the second of December had ushered in clouds plump with snow, her hopes had risen that Zeke wouldn't be able to make the trip to the farmhouse for Lily-Too's Thursday-night lesson. But the snowfall had only amounted to a sift of powder, not enough to keep him away.

Hearing footsteps on the back stairs, she picked up her pencil again and pretended to study her assignment, relieved when only Rose appeared in the doorway.

"Supper's ready, Mom."

Only Rose. She thought that too often. "C'mere." She held out her arms. She hadn't been gracious when Rose had invited Zeke to stay for supper, and she'd seen hurt in her daughter's eyes. Rose leaned over and they exchanged a hug. "You're a good person—and a more considerate soul than I am."

Rose straightened, and she reached up to smooth the hair alongside her daughter's face. "It seems I've always got my attention on one of the others, but you're just so capable, I don't worry too much about you. But I do love you. You know that, don't you?"

"Yep." Rose grinned. "And if you fussed over me like you do the others, I'd go nuts."

"I *fuss*?"

"Totally. Oh, don't freak. Do you know any kid who wants *more* attention from parents? I mean, Lily-Too might like it, but the rest of us don't need you to worry about us so much." She paused, then added. "Not even Hank."

"You know, then?"

"He told me a few months ago. I couldn't tell you—he made me promise. But it's okay—I mean, with you, isn't it?"

Patsy Lee felt a stab that Hank had felt more comfortable telling his sister than he had his mother. "Of course it is."

Rose looked relieved. Why relieved? Hank, Zeke, Rose . . . had they really thought she'd reject him?

"Come down in a few minutes or it'll be cold." Rose started toward the door.

"Ask Hank to bring me a bowl up here, would you? I've just got so much to do."

Rose hesitated, then nodded and left.

Scratching Nod's ears, Patsy Lee lay back and closed her eyes. From the expression on her daughter's face, Patsy Lee didn't think Rose was fooled. She knew her mother was avoiding Zeke. Which meant Hank did, too. And probably even Lily-Too. God, all her children were growing up. She yawned. Maybe she was, too. Maybe all her odd feelings were just part of some—what had Zeke called it?—rite of passage. A *midlife* rite of passage. She snorted sleepily. Most people would call it perimenopause. . . .

"Rose said you were too busy to join us."

Patsy Lee started. Blinking, she focused on Zeke.

"But I decided you needed a break." He held out a bowl. Steam wafted up to disappear into the clouds painted on her ceiling.

She took it and murmured a dismissive thanks, hoping he'd take the hint.

He didn't. Pulling up a ladderback chair from next to her dresser, he sat down and cradled another bowl in his hand. "Besides, you can't avoid me forever."

Flustered, she made a business of fussing at the cats. They'd both gotten to their feet to sidle closer, their noses working like pistons. "Shoo." Helped by a gentle push, they landed on the floor and minced out, headed for greener pastures where children didn't like oysters. "I'm not avoiding you. I have a lot of work to do."

"I can see that." His voice was dry.

"I do. The semester's ending. And the store is open longer hours, so I'll be busy there most of the weekend. There's also Christmas shopping. And baking. And—"

"Okay, okay. Still no reason we can't share a meal."

She could think of a few, but she decided objecting would look immature. Instead, as they ate, she offered a steady stream of stiff small talk, trying to keep him away from broaching the topic she knew was uppermost in both their minds. She told him that Rose was on her way to top of her class at the end of semester, that she still worried Daisy wouldn't pass any classes at all, and that Lily-Too was showing improvement according to the progress report she'd just received. While Mrs. Sherlock hadn't gone so far as to suggest canceling the ADD tests, maybe she would before Patsy Lee had to.

She realized that sounded cowardly, although this time it was less nerves over facing the teacher and more a desire to avoid wasting time she didn't have on another conference. But Zeke didn't scold as he once would have. Nor did he repeat his feelings on the subject of Lily-Too's teacher although she knew they were adamant. She wondered if he was even listening. She moved on to detailing everyday life at Merry-Go-Read, boring him, she was sure, as much as she was boring herself.

"Patricia." Setting his bowl aside, he interrupted her narrative about the new hairpiece Mr. Stuart had sported today. "About the other night with Christine . . ."

"I don't need to know anything about the other night."

"It was something that . . . just happened."

"I know. Just like what happened with us."

"No. Not like that."

"Okay, more serious than that."

"No!" He dragged a hand through his hair, leaving it uncharacteristically messy. "Christine had just asked me to go to New York with her and Teresa for the holidays, then return home to San Francisco from there. They—"

"And you're *going*?"

"I don't know . . . you know I planned to go home right after Christmas anyway, but . . . you don't want me to?"

"I—" She bit off her words. For Pete's sake, she'd known he'd eventually leave. She'd even thought it might be with Christine. It was only the suddenness that had surprised her. "You'd miss the pageant."

"And the pageant is all that matters."

She looked down. "No. I mean, the children matter. Think how Lily-Too would feel."

"I have. Among a lot of things." When she looked back up, his gaze gave nothing away.

"Tell me something." She was embarrassed, but she needed to know. "For the last three days . . . three nights . . . have you . . . I mean, have you and Christine . . ."

"Is *that* what you think of me?"

Her temper flared, too. "You kissed her. You're thinking of leaving with her."

"Tell me why you care."

"I don't." She had no claim on him. "I hope you'll be happy."

He stood and picked up his bowl, then reached for hers. Their fingers brushed. "Patricia—" He stopped.

And she knew why. He didn't know what to say, didn't know what he could offer. Or even if he should. He was torn. Torn between, oh, her and Christine, or Cordelia and San Francisco, or one lifestyle and another. Who knew? Just torn. And if she asked him to choose right now—if she *wanted* him to—his eyes said he might just choose her. But tomorrow? What would he choose then?

He was in love with Lil. He was indecisive about Christine. He wouldn't be happy here. It was reflected in the frustrated gaze that ranged over her face. And it was quite simple. He didn't know what he wanted, and that was a novel experience for Zeke Townley.

But not unfamiliar to her. She looked away before his eyes could hook hers. It was so tempting to throw away prudence. So simple to let her heart go and grab whatever pieces of his life she could get—long-distance; on again, off again; casual; unbinding; whatever—and be damned with the future.

Yet she knew she couldn't live with a loose-weave relationship like Christine had. She had to think of her children. They belonged here. So did she. And he didn't.

Her anger deflated. Nobody's fault.

"You shouldn't come here anymore." Hurt flashed at the back of his eyes, but she kept calm. When he thought about it, he'd know she was right. "No matter when you leave, it will upset the children. Better if you distance yourself gradually. Better for them. For . . . all of us."

"The children are all you—"

"Don't." Her voice was sharp.

He blew out a breath. "Patricia, I'm sorry I—"

"And if you do decide to go to New York, would you let me know so I can explain to Lily-Too? I think it would be best coming from me. You can talk with her after."

She set her bowl on the nightstand, then looked up at him again, surprised at the chill that had crept into his gaze.

"After tomorrow night, I'll stay out of your orbit."

She frowned. "Tomorrow night?"

"Lil's supper party."

Oh . . . *damn*. She'd forgotten. "I—"

"Yes?" His eyes dared her to back out.

Anger sparking again, she poked up her chin. "I'll see you there."

Chapter 23

The next evening, she wished she hadn't let her aggravation overcome her urge to bow out of the supper Lil was hosting for Christine and Teresa. She even had a new excuse: Her leg had set up a steady throb following her first appointment with the physical therapist. But every time she'd reached for the phone to cancel, she'd pictured that dare in Zeke's eyes and had pulled back her hand.

With all three stores in full holiday swing, Lil had left the details to Jon and he'd arranged the party at Phillip E's, not stopping to consider (or maybe he had) that their San Francisco elite probably weren't partial to bibs, raw plank floors, and licking barbecue sauce off their fingers.

When Patsy Lee arrived a few minutes late—continuing to hem and haw with herself had taken an extra ten minutes before she'd finally departed—everyone was already seated at one of a couple dozen picnic tables covered with checkered oil cloths that ranged around the barn-sized room. She was surprised (dismayed) to see that the party was limited to Lil and Jon, the San Francisco trio, and herself. No Zinnia. No Pop. There'd be no hiding behind Zinnia's babble.

There'd be no hiding at all. Christine, Zeke, and Lil sat on one side of the table. Across from them, a space had been left for her between Teresa and Jon, putting her directly across from Zeke, oh, joy.

She tottered over, awkwardly using the cane she'd found at O'Neill's Emporium after the therapist had told her she could throw out her crutches. Jon helped her over the bench. All eyes on her, she flushed. She couldn't have gotten further away from Christine's *glide* if she'd been hobbled.

As conversation started up again, she whispered to Jon, "Where are Zinnia and Pop?"

Jon leaned in close. "Zinnia had a lucky bout of angina. Read: unimpressed with Christine and shocked over a thrice-divorced woman who shows no signs of remorse."

He turned back to the conversation between Lil and Zeke, leaving her to the mercy of Teresa and Christine, debating with each other across the table on the calorie count of smoked versus barbecued chicken. And they thought Cordelia dull?

Through drinks (hers just iced tea, no Long Island to it) she kept quiet. Not that she had much choice, anyway. Teresa bubbled with her usual energy, and tonight Christine was keeping pace. She was unusually animated, her talk nonstop, her laugh brittle. Noting the looks she threw at Zeke, Patsy Lee wondered if she'd caught on to Zeke's infatuation with Lil.

She glanced at Zeke and caught him glancing at her. He immediately averted his gaze, letting her know he was still . . . what? Angry? Hurt? . . . at her dismissal last night. She sighed and turned her attention back to the women. It was a fun time in the old town tonight.

Once smoked chicken had been declared the winner of the dietary debate and they'd placed their orders, Teresa excused herself to visit the little girls.' Christine didn't let her best friend's absence still her tongue. Instead, to Patsy Lee's unenthralled audience of one, she indulged in a soliloquy on her current diet, a carbohydrate-counting, fat-trimming regimen. . . .

". . . That sucks all the joy out of life," Patsy Lee murmured.

"What?" Christine paused.

"Nothing." Christine and Zeke made the perfect pair.

While Christine launched a new subject, Zeke steadfastly kept his head turned toward Lil and Jon—whether because he was besotted with Lil or because he didn't want to risk his gaze meeting Patsy Lee's again was anyone's guess. But the more focused he was on that end of the table, the more—and louder—Christine talked. Patsy Lee felt her eyes cross. Tuning everyone out, she nodded at appropriate intervals and wished for the evening to end.

Teresa finally, mercifully, returned, tucking her cell phone back in her handbag. "I just talked with Mother. She's coming to Cordelia early in the week before Christmas to see you." She sighed heavily. "Then joining Christine and me in New York a few days before the holiday. We'll then be able to, joy, travel back to San Francisco *together* before New Year's. When she's planning to host a soiree. She insists both of us attend."

Zeke stared. "Well, butter my butt."

Teresa looked morose. "My thoughts exactly. I wanted to see the ball drop in Times Square."

"I mean that Mom's coming here. What excuse did she give?"

"Something about mountains and Mohammed, although what they have to do with anything, I can't tell you. Oh, don't look so shocked, Zeke. You know Mom."

Christine didn't look pleased, either, but for once this evening, said nothing.

"She can stay with us while she's here," Lil said into the silence.

Christine appeared to recover. "And hopefully, if I can't convince you to join Teresa and me sooner, she can at least convince you to travel to New York with her so we can all be together for Christmas." Smile overly bright, Christine touched Zeke's arm and looked around the table. "Although I think I'm making some headway. Have I mentioned all the things Teresa and I have planned to do?"

Without waiting for an answer, she launched into a minute-by-minute account of their itinerary: Rockefeller Center . . . . Bloomingdale's . . . the Four Seasons . . . Broadway . . . blah, blah, blah. But it was impossible to ignore her beauty and vivacity, so, *butter my butt,* nobody did.

Through wedges of iceberg lettuce and Thousand Island dressing, Christine moved on to an explanation of her usual activities in San Francisco, activities that—when she wasn't litigating at her high-profile law firm—revolved around an array of charity balls, formal dinners, premieres, gallery openings, and black-tie events. She underlined the fact that Zeke had once shared her lifestyle, dropped enough names to fill a compost pile, and made her intentions as subtle as a sledgehammer on eggshells. She wanted to assure that . . . Lil? Patsy Lee? . . . understood Zeke felt most at home in rarefied circles, and Cordelia had none.

She needn't have bothered. Patsy Lee already knew it, and from Lil's glazed eyes, she'd stopped listening about two philharmonic galas ago. A slight frown between his brows, Zeke lazily turned a fork end over end in his hand. Jon had zoned out, coming alive only when the family-style supper arrived.

Even smoked chicken, ribs, and brisket didn't staunch Christine. While they passed platters, she inventoried the many charities Zeke supported, so absorbed in her own recitation, she absentmindedly ladled her plate with enough meat, slaw, Country Kickin' Beans (which did), and Three-Cheezy Potatoes to feed a continent. She didn't seem to notice the deepening lines on Zeke's face.

But when she named the sum it had taken for Zeke to earn a Shooting Star designation at one of the Bay's repertory theaters (an amount that would support Patsy Lee's family for a year), he finally spoke up. "C'mon, Christine . . . I've been driven by the bottom line on my income tax return, not by altruism."

"You're too modest. There are other ways you could protect your bottom line if you weren't also moved by generosity."

Zeke opened his mouth, but Lil interrupted. "She's just proud of you, Zeke. And considering what you've been doing recently—both you and Jon—I'm proud of you, too."

Christine wasn't about to be upstaged. "Yes, like Lil, I've admired your dedication to the boys' home."

"That's been wonderful of them, but I was talking about—"

"And then," Christine said. "There's Zeke's work with the Christmas pageant."

Lil frowned. "That's not it, either. I—"

"How about we drop this whole—" Zeke tried to interrupt.

"*And* how he's given your niece singing lessons." Christine's look dared Lil to come up with anything else.

Lil looked bewildered.

"Christine." Zeke's voice was sharp.

Christine turned a dull red. She busied herself with her plate, looking amazed at all she found there.

"St. Zeke," Jon said noncommittally. "Has a nice ring."

"Except before he's canonized, he has to be dead," Patsy Lee murmured.

Despite the edge to her words, Zeke laughed and the tension broke. Even Christine managed a tight smile.

Face lit with curiosity, Teresa addressed Lil. "Well, what *were* you talking about?"

"The nonprofit idea he's working on with Jon. They're starting an organization that will pair volunteer musicians with places like Vreeley."

Christine frowned at Zeke. "Why haven't you said anything?"

"Because there's nothing to say. All we've done so far is talk to a few lawyers, And it's not such a big—"

"Yeah, it is. I'm aiming for sainthood even if you're not," Jon interrupted. "We want to find musicians that have the time and money to sponsor kids, give fundraisers, teach kids. Like Lil said, for places like Vreeley, but maybe down the line, we'll expand into teen rehabs or children's hospice programs, things like that."

Teresa propped her chin on her hand. "Fabulous. Where would you start?"

"Here." Jon stabbed the table with his fork. "So I won't have to travel."

Zeke rolled his eyes. "We haven't decided. Music industry centers probably—Nashville, L.A., New York—then take it from there."

"I knew I'd have to travel." Jon looked gloomy.

"If it kills you," Zeke said. "You'll be one step closer to sainthood."

Jon grinned. As the men continued to outline their plans, Patsy Lee sat back and watched Zeke. His face was stripped of the cynicism it had worn during his early days in Cordelia. And he hadn't raised his eyebrows since the conversation about his new project had begun.

"I'm happy for you." The words spilled out and her face heated. "I mean, for all the people you'll help." Although that's *not* exactly what she'd meant. She lifted her chin. "It's exciting."

Zeke smiled. "I think so, too." Their eyes held.

Teresa clapped. "This could be *huge*. I want to do something, too. Who are you thinking about approaching? I could help with that; I mean, I'm good with people, you know. Especially men," she added. "Tim McGraw is *so* hot."

Jon's mouth quirked. "And so married."

"So what? Faith Hill isn't *that* big of a deal. If you're going to ask him, can I . . ."

Still warmed in spite of herself by the look in Zeke's eyes, Patsy Lee looked away from him and met Christine's gaze. The other woman was watching her, her expression appraising.

For the rest of the evening, even though Christine interjected all the right comments, she was quiet. She probably had an upset stomach after all that food. Either that, or the redhead was busy forming objections to Zeke's plans because it sounded like he'd have less time in the future to dance in ballrooms. Patsy Lee tried to tell herself she didn't care if that was the case.

After all, what Zeke and Christine did was none of her business. None at all.

Two gently sloped acres between them, the Van Castle's guesthouse shared a hilltop with the main residence, as well as a contemporary style heavy on glass and timber. Woods didn't push up to the dwellings' boundaries like at Patricia's farmhouse, but politely kept to the valleys that outlined the property's pastureland as it rolled toward Cordelia. From where Zeke stood, looking through doors that opened onto the balcony shared by the bedrooms, the town was an assortment of children's blocks and tiles, scattered in the forested Ozark hills. The scene took on magic at night, gold glowing at the windows, streetlamps a diamond chain, the sky strewn with pearls. Somewhere in the distance, a train whistle called and, for a moment, Zeke believed in Norman Rockwell.

But just for a moment. He turned away from the window and looked at Christine. She was emerging from the bathroom. Despite the pale face and disheveled hair, she looked elegant in a silk nightgown that shimmered in the light from a bedside lamp.

"Feel better?" He'd heard her retching through their adjoining wall. She'd admitted him from the balcony just minutes earlier when he'd grown concerned and knocked.

"Much." She slipped back under the covers, but only slid down partway, eyes shadowed.

It was the first time they'd been alone since Patricia had stumbled upon them sharing a kiss in Jon's SUV. He hadn't wanted to talk to her until he knew what to say.

And he still didn't know.

He reached for the door handle. "If you're all right now, I'll let you get some sleep."

"Zeke."

He paused.

"Don't go yet. Sit down and keep me company a minute." Christine patted the bed. There was no hint of seduction in her voice. "Please."

Hesitating a moment, he finally crossed the room and sat down beside her. Her forehead was beaded with perspiration "Are you sure you're okay?"

"Probably food poisoning."

"More like food overload. I've never seen you eat as much as you did tonight. Or talk that much."

She looked away. "You've never seen me that desperate."

"Desperate?"

"The other night when we kissed . . . if Lil hadn't come along, would you have slept with me?"

He weighed the question, tried to be honest. "Maybe. I don't know. I know I would have been tempted."

"You know what?" Christine asked.

"What?"

"You're an asshole." The words were uttered without heat.

"An opinion I sometimes share." Like right now. He didn't know what he wanted from Christine. Didn't know what he wanted from Patricia. Yet he'd gotten mad at Patricia last night when he'd taken the bowl of gumbo to her and she hadn't given him . . . whatever it was he didn't know that he wanted. He rubbed his hand over his face. See? An asshole. "But what makes you think so now?"

"Because you would have slept with me even if you don't love me anymore."

How could she know what he wasn't even certain about himself? He studied her. "Why are you here? Really."

She plucked at the covers, then sighed. "Teresa . . . she said you were lonely. You were aimless. You were pining for me . . . she can be damn persuasive."

Lonely, aimless. True. Pining for Christine? He was no longer sure. "But you're no pushover. Even for my sister."

"You're right. It's not fair to put it all on her." She fell quiet for a minute, then looked up at him. "You know, I thought I had us—had you—all figured out." She shrugged. "Turns out I was wrong. Your mother will be happy to hear it. I'm sure she's swooping into Cordelia primarily to stick a spoke in my wheel in case you decide to join us later in New York."

Undoubtedly. But his mother had never deterred

Christine before. "What did you think you'd figured out?"

"Ever since Jon and Lil married, I've known you thought their lives were perfection. For a long time, I even thought you loved Lil. I was jealous. But she was with Jon. Here. I was with you. There. So I didn't think it mattered."

He frowned. "But I wasn't in love with Lil. I love her, but . . . not that way."

"I know. Now. But then . . . well, you started mentioning marriage. Maybe a baby. We went to Europe. And stopped here on the way. And I got a long, hard look at you—with them. That was what you wanted. What Lil and Jon had. I realized it wasn't *Lil* you loved, it was *them* you idealized. And you and me . . . we'd had one relationship one minute and the next you wanted everything to change. I got scared. I didn't know if I was ready. But I knew I wasn't Lil. And you weren't Jon. So I left."

"But now?" He was torn between hope and fear at what she would say.

"They provided me with a convenient excuse not to wrestle with some tough issues. But it turns out that I wrestled with them anyway. And when I realized I'd rejected something I actually wanted, I came to tell you." She laughed. It was a sad sound. "And now . . . it's so stupid. So cliché . . ."

He was still torn between hope and fear. "What is?"

"Now I'm too late."

"Too late? Why?" He wasn't feeling any sudden surge of excitement, but they'd been good together once, and here she was, offering what he'd wanted from her. "Why not consider it? Let's—"

She put fingers to his lips, stopping his words. "That look you used to turn on Lil and Jon. It was still there tonight at the restaurant."

"Wait a minute. I know I'm not Jon Van Castle.

Maybe I've decided I want some of the same things, but living here isn't—"

"Not just an asshole." Christine rolled her eyes. "An idiot. I'm not talking about a lifestyle. I'm talking about a *person*. That look was there when you turned your gaze on Patricia O'Malley."

Chapter 24

Early evening chill biting her nose, Patsy Lee limped along the sidewalk of Cordelia's town square Tuesday night, eleven days after she'd last seen Zeke. She'd grown more certain that dismissing him from her life was the right thing to do, despite the way he'd looked at her across the table in Phillip E's. His eyes had been warm, true, but even if they had been *hot*—which they had not—the looks he'd turned on Christine, and Lil, for that matter, hadn't exactly been *cold*. So she'd pushed him out of her head. His adherence to his promise to avoid her had helped make it easy.

As had the season. Lights and garland and wreaths entwined with pinecones graced store windows; hints of cinnamon and bayberry wafted through doorways as shoppers hurried in and out. In front of St. Andrew's, luminaries outlined walkways and spots blazed on a nativity scene. From here she could see baby Jesus's hand raised toward Mary's bowed head.

It was all very pretty, very . . . Rockwell. Thinking of Christine's dissertation on New York and San Francisco, she wondered for a moment what it would feel like to be caught up in the bustle of the holidays in a big city. Maybe someday she'd find out. . . .

Like when she won the lottery and had fewer people on her Christmas list.

She stopped in front of the Stationery Stop, scanning the window for gifts. Leaving Rose in charge of Lily-Too and Mr. Stuart in charge of Merry-Go-Read, tonight she'd vowed to make a dent in her shopping. She could at least find something for Bebe—she'd see her in a few nights at the O'Malleys' annual open house and could mark at least one gift delivery off her endless list.

The holiday open house worried her. Zinnia had urged Bebe to come, and Patsy Lee had added her own entreaties. Not only did she want to prove that she didn't hide Bebe, she'd decided to break her promise to Hank and confide in her, although she hoped Hank would do it first. But since Zinnia didn't issue formal invitations—only telling a few people who told a few more until her house was filled with a crush—there was a small chance Ernie Burcham might poke his nose into the party. Just because he was the type that liked to make a stink. She devoutly hoped not.

Noting an attractive letter box filled with handmade paper that Bebe would love, Patsy Lee stepped inside to make the purchase, then moved on to the next person on her list, halting in front of Parson's Sound Arcade and Sandwich Shoppe (proprietor Stella Parsons believed in making money where money was to be made, never mind logic) as she stumbled over Zeke's name. She'd made out her gift list some time ago. . . . Should he still be on it?

Of course he should. (How Christian of her.) It would be odd if he wasn't, after all he'd done. She'd sign his present from the entire family and have the children hand it off at the holiday party; she could avoid him in this, just like she was in everything else.

Since that night at Phillip E's, she hadn't seen any need to see him at all, not even when Lily-Too had her lessons. Hank drove his youngest sister where she needed to go, including pageant rehearsals and Jon's private recording studio, where she now studied with Zeke.

Patsy Lee abandoned Parson's—she imagined Zeke had all the CDs he wanted and couldn't use a corned beef on rye—and continued around the corner, bypassing Peg O' My Heart Café and peeking in Merry-Go-Read's window. Mr. Stuart, new hairpiece askew, was ringing up customers four deep while seasonal part-time help scurried to help others. They were busy, but everything seemed in order. Reassured, she let her thoughts return to her youngest.

According to Lil, after really listening to his niece at Zeke's urging, Jon had become as enthusiastic about Lily-Too's talent as Zeke, even recording a few Christmas carols complete with professional mixing and added effects. Too excited to wait until Christmas morning, Lily-Too had given Patsy Lee the CD last week. They'd listened to it together, and as Patsy Lee watched her daughter's eyes, she understood why Lily-Too's confidence had grown by leaps in the past weeks. Her daughter had finally recognized her gift.

Lily-Too's gaze no longer dropped in a stranger's presence. A stubborn note now crept into her voice when she argued with her siblings (and even sometimes won). There was no more talk about heavy stage makeup on pageant night. Her grades (while still mediocre and less than Patsy Lee knew she could do) had improved. And while she still came home from school tight-lipped on occasion, it was no longer from frustration. It was from anger.

It hadn't been long before Patsy Lee received another note from Mrs. Sherlock.

I'm pleased to report a modicum of improvement in your daughter's schoolwork, she'd written, *but am unhappy to report that Lily has developed a discon-*

certing habit of verbalizing her displeasure with certain aspects of the classroom.

In plain English: Lily-Too had learned to talk back. Patsy Lee felt torn—proud of her daughter's growing ability to defend herself, but fearful her behavior would alienate her in the classroom.

Stopping at the display window of O'Neill's Emporium, she pondered again what to do. Since it was likely neither Mrs. Sherlock nor Lily-Too would do any shape changing, there was probably little point in trying to make square pegs fit into round holes. Attempting again to get Lily-Too switched to a different classroom was also likely to prove futile.

Her eyes grazed the merchandise in front of her, not really seeing it as she examined an idea that had been growing on her. Perhaps the best course of action was doing nothing at all. This wouldn't be the only situation Lily-Too would encounter that wasn't tailor-made for her quirks and talents. Public schools hadn't the resources for custom educations—at least not the ones around here. And some teachers hadn't the inventiveness to personalize their approach—certainly not Mrs. Sherlock.

She sighed. But was letting go of this situation an acknowledgment of her child's need to learn by experience—or an act of cowardice? It certainly didn't address the issue of the ADD testing, even though she was as certain as Zeke that it wasn't her daughter who was disordered. She'd felt ready to leap in. . . . But she wasn't sure where to leap.

Turning up her collar, she focused on the jumble in the window, which only served to remind her of the jumble in her head. Zeke. Mrs. Sherlock. Lily-Too. Hank. Merry-Go-Read. The holidays. At least she no longer needed to worry about her classes. *Babbitt* was mercifully behind her, her papers and tests concluded.

For a moment she was cheered, then her gaze fell on a sash in the far corner of the display and her mood dipped again. Wildly purple, paisley, and silk, the sash reminded her of Daisy. Who, if her silence in the past few weeks was a clue, hadn't experienced anything about her own final exams to write home about.

One more thing to pile onto the jumble. Patsy Lee pulled open the door to the Emporium and focused back on her shopping. Concern about Daisy could wait until tomorrow, when Daisy would return home with her cousins for winter break.

But Daisy didn't come home with her cousins. Instead of Melanie's Blazer, it was Danny's old Honda that scrunched over the gravel the next afternoon, a bunch of boxes roped into the trunk. Out back, the donkeys honked while Sugar leaped with delight. Laughing, Daisy pushed the Lab away before Sugar could smear her yellow sweater, bright as sunflowers against the drab day.

Waving away offers to help, Danny unstrapped the luggage. From the front porch, Daisy watched him, and Patsy Lee watched her daughter. Her heart fell at the softness she saw in Daisy's eyes. Things were more serious than she'd hoped. Not that Patsy Lee had anything against Danny himself. She'd known him since childhood, when his knees had been as scuffed and his clothes as mud packed as Daisy's had been. Daisy had recently announced he planned to become a lawyer. Tall, dark, handsome, and with good prospects . . . easy to see why he'd turned her daughter's head away from her studies.

Apparently sensing her disquiet, Daisy chattered nonstop about everything (except grades) as they moved into the foyer. Danny made multiple trips up the stairs with Daisy's baggage. It was the usual assortment—dirty laundry, cardboard box, suitcase strapped with red nylon belt, Christmas presents. . . . Patsy Lee frowned. Plus two duffel bags, the boom box Patsy Lee had bought Daisy before she'd left for college this fall, as well as the laptop computer Lil and Jon had given her for high school graduation. All for winter break? She turned questioning eyes on her daughter. Daisy was twirling a yellow earring with so much vigor, it was a miracle she still had an earlobe.

When Danny hauled out the last load, the Honda practically sighed with relief. As did Patsy Lee when Danny refused her polite invitation to stay.

"Thanks, but I told Mom and Dad I'd get in by three." Danny dropped a kiss on Daisy's upturned nose. It was a casual gesture, yet somehow so intimate, it made Patsy Lee feel like a voyeur. "Call me after—" He glanced at Patsy Lee. "Just call me later."

After Danny had pulled down the drive, Patsy Lee followed Daisy into the house and up the stairs, responding robotically to Daisy's chatter. Sugar raced ahead.

As they reached the landing, Daisy marveled at the progress her mother had made.

"My last therapy session was this morning."

Luckily, she'd been able to schedule them at the local hospital. She'd been unsure if she could make it to Sedalia on her own. Driving still hurt and she hadn't wanted to pester . . . anyone . . . into acting as her chauffeur.

"Oh," Daisy said brightly. Too brightly. "When can you get rid of the cast?"

"I don't really need it anymore, but I still feel more secure with it on." Story of her life.

Stomach heavy with dread, she trailed Daisy to her bedroom, a sixties explosion of flower-power graffiti over violet walls. Sugar sniffed around, then flopped on the puffy orange rug at the foot of the bed. When

Daisy was fourteen, she'd painted the faux French Provincial furniture that Patsy Lee had unearthed at O'Neill's Emporium in a dizzying array of colors. Daisy plopped her macramé handbag on her dresser top, scattering some hair clips and a few of the empty perfume bottles she'd once collected.

Patsy Lee perched on the corner of a tie-dyed bedspread. "Daisy . . . what's going on here?"

Daisy upended the little cologne bottles, her eyes fixed on her movements. "I'm not going back to school."

Patsy Lee's heart sank as her fears were confirmed. "You most certainly are."

"No, I'm not."

"Yes, you—"

"Mom, just listen."

Dropping an Evening in Paris vial, Daisy sat down next to her. Their thighs touched, warmed each other. A longing to have the years fade away swelled inside Patsy Lee, and her eyes teared. She wanted Daisy four years old again, crawling into her lap, wanting nothing more than to please her mother.

"You know I'm not cut out for school. I never was."

Patsy Lee willed her eyes dry. She needed reason, not sentiment. "Cut out or not, you can't give up this chance to get a degree, sweetheart. Even if it's a struggle, even if you don't always have good grades, that paper at the end will be worth it. Maybe it doesn't seem that way, but it will be. Drop out and you'll have limited your options far more than you realize now." She squeezed Daisy's knee. The bones felt so fragile, so vulnerable under her grip. "And you *will* realize it. Oh, honey. It is *so* much harder to return to school after you've got responsibilities, debts, maybe even a family that you need to support. If all you can get is some dead-end job . . ."

Patsy Lee stopped, realizing from Daisy's averted eyes that her arguments were falling on deaf ears.

"Do you really want to end up like me?" she blurted.

"What's so wrong with that?"

"What's so wrong with—?" Unable to stay seated, Patsy Lee stood up and went to the dresser. Straightening Evening in Paris, she searched for the right words. Convincing words. She finally turned to face her daughter.

"Honey, listen to me. You know I love you—all of you—with my entire heart. My children have enriched my life in ways I never imagined. I've always, *always* been grateful I've had each of you. But . . . when you're young, the world's possibilities are endless. You have this idea that they'll *always* be endless, always there for the grabbing. But they're not. Family . . . responsibilities . . . they shorten your reach."

Daisy frowned. "Is that so bad if that's what you want?"

"And that's *all* you want? What *I* have is all you want?"

"Well," Daisy smiled. "I'd kind of like a husband, too."

"Is that what this is about?" She sat down next to Daisy again. "Did Danny ask you to marry him? You can *have* Danny. But wait . . . just wait until you're both done with school."

"We don't want to wait."

Patsy Lee smoothed back her hair. "I know," she soothed. "At your age, nobody wants to wait, but it's only a couple more years before you finish—"

Daisy drew away. "Danny *will* finish, but I won't. I'll just work somewhere until—" She stopped. "It's not like I wanted to be a brain surgeon. It's no big deal."

She thought of something. "Do Danny's parents know your plans?"

"Not yet. Danny doesn't want to tell them until after Christmas; he doesn't want to spoil their holiday. But I knew you'd guess something was wrong before then, so I said I was telling you right away."

Doesn't want to spoil . . . Danny knew they wouldn't like the idea any more than she did. Feeling a measure of relief, Patsy Lee stood up. After Christmas, all of them could sit down together and persuade these children to wait until they'd grown up to even think about marriage.

"I can tell what you're thinking, Mom. It's not going to work. We *will* get married."

"Oh, Daisy. Please don't do this. Get engaged if you must, but there's no reason to—"

"Mom." Daisy took her hand. "Mom, I'm pregnant."

Patsy Lee went still. Of course she was. There was that "flu" at Thanksgiving. Daisy's recent lengthy silence. And just a few minutes ago, Danny's sideways glance at Patsy Lee. All the signs were there. She just hadn't wanted to see them.

Chapter 25

On Friday evening in the O'Malley dining room, Zeke remembered the last time he'd indulged under this roof. Needing his wits sharp for the confrontation he intended later with Patricia, he bypassed the champagne and ladled a cup of Christmas punch frothy with green sherbet from the bowl nestled among baskets of gingerbread men, pots of fondue, and platters piled high with vegetables, crackers, and dip. His hand shook, slopping some punch onto a crystal pedestal plate topped with a red velvet cake. Surely he'd prevail. Surely she'd see the reason in what he had to propose.

Surely.

Taking a sip, he grimaced as the saccharine brew slid over his tongue. But maybe it wasn't the punch that was making his stomach curdle. Maybe it was fear.

A new fear. Not the one he remembered on that early November day when he'd driven Patricia home from her doctor's and she'd told him she didn't want him to go and he'd thought she'd misread him. That fear had stemmed from memories of the family burdens penned on the pages of his adolescence. Now that he was ready to write a new chapter—hell, a whole new book—the fear was sharper.

Not because he didn't know his feelings.

But because he didn't know hers.

Christine's words had tilted his world. Wanting to make sure of himself, he'd given several days over to reflection after she'd left. And he'd realized she was right.

Somewhere between chickens and donkeys and children and blizzards and Christmas pageants, his yearning for what Lil and Jon possessed had gathered strength; his fears of family had evaporated. Not because he'd suddenly developed new insight, but because he'd found the one person he could share it all with. He'd fallen, and fallen hard, for a pair of doe eyes, a kind, generous nature, and a quick mind.

Abandoning his cup, he surveyed the length of the house, hoping to spot his quarry but failing. Not surprising, since both the kitchen and parlor overflowed with people much like the wastebasket propped in the corner overflowed with paper plates and cups.

Sighing, he resigned himself to more chitchat, just like he had for the last forty-five minutes. He'd circulated every room, made small talk with Rosemary Butz (at least the Ladies' Auxiliary leader had talked while he'd nodded at appropriate intervals), Paddy O'Neill (dawdling suspiciously long near the mistletoe, whiskers atwitter), Phinnaeus Phelps (wearing quiet dignity and Lynette Schroeder on his arm), and Mayor Evelyn Noflinger (who assured him the teeth marks on Eldon's arm had faded to nothing). But he hadn't spotted Patricia.

Maybe—his stomach roiled again—because she didn't want to be spotted. As she'd proven more than once, especially in the last two weeks, she was a master at avoidance.

His gaze raked the crowd again, rather surprised that he recognized more people than not. Growing more conscious of his approaching departure, he'd realized lately that he'd miss the town and it's residents. Honest and upfront and largely hard-working and unpretentious, they were good people, the Ernie Burchams notwithstanding.

Fortunately, that particular resident hadn't made an appearance. Although Bebe certainly had. Now chatting with Finn Phelps, she looked sensational, her slight figure wrapped in a red sarong that set off her silver hair and a sterling choker—and completely unconcerned that Burcham might show. Maybe because gossip, in the form of horizontally striped (red-and-green) Penny Mason, had relayed he was still in a lather over the punch Hank had landed on Skeeter Burcham's nose. Or maybe Burcham was just scared of Bebe's way around a pickled beet.

Hoping Bebe knew where to find Patricia, he headed toward her.

"Hello, Zeke, my friend." Bebe greeted him. They'd spoken more than once over the weeks of pageant rehearsal. "I was just telling Preacher Phelps that I'd have those backdrops delivered to the church in a few days. Two of my students will cart them down for a few bucks and a McDonald's Quarter Pounder. I'll pay them, and you can pay me back."

"No, no," Finn interrupted. "The church owes you the money. And our gratitude. I'll just find Lynette and tell her we'll need a check before I forget."

Watching him wind toward his secretary, looking glad for the excuse, Zeke smiled. "Seems the efficient Lynette has made her feelings known."

Bebe's eyebrows went up. "Ah, romance is in the air?"

"Apparently so. You don't happen to know where Patricia is, do you?"

He tried to keep his voice casual, but Bebe's eyes sharpened.

"Tell you the truth, I'm not happy with her, so I

haven't kept track, but she's here somewhere." She paused. "She said you know about Hank."

"Yes." Out of the corner of his eye, he saw red-and-green stripes bearing down on them. "We'd better find somewhere private. Outside?"

Bebe nodded agreement. Pausing only to collect coats, they pushed through the kitchen and let themselves out onto the back porch. Wrapping folds of red wool close, Bebe sat down at the table where the jack-o'-lanterns had squatted in October. He leaned back into the shadows against the wall, thrusting his hands deep into the pockets of his cashmere jacket. Their breaths condensed, white against the growing darkness. The yard was empty, absent of the color it had worn in the fall.

"So Hank told you?" Zeke asked, glad Hank had finally shared his secret with someone who would fully understand.

She nodded. "I had brunch at Patsy Lee's before we came here. He told me, and she talked to me, too. Sans Hank. Do you know what she has in mind?"

"No." He hesitated. "Bebe, I'm not sure if I should play confidant. Patricia and I have . . . had some differences lately."

"I know. She told me. Idiot. She's always been so busy figuring out how to fit in, she never stops to figure out if she even wants to."

He really did like her. "That's a similar argument to one I plan to make later."

"Yes?" Bebe's eyes lit. "And what argument is that?"

"I'll use her Achilles' heel to my advantage."

"And her Achilles' heel is . . . ?"

"Her children. I'll argue that in San Francisco, Rose will have more opportunities for that brilliant mind of hers, Lily-Too can attend a performing arts school, and while nobody could protect Hank from all the slings and arrows he'll face, he'll find more acceptance on the coast than he will here. And if Daisy doesn't cut it in school, there's more chances for other employment out there." Too nervous for finesse, he rattled off his arguments.

Bebe didn't look enthusiastic.

"You don't think so?"

"They'd go through a period of adjustment, but you're right. They'd all eventually be happy." But she still looked unconvinced.

"Then what is it? You'd miss them?"

"Yes, but there are airplanes. Hell, I'll retire in a few years, anyway, and would be quite happy to invite myself out there. But Patricia . . ."

He'd thought Bebe would champion his cause; that she hadn't wasn't doing much to settle his stomach. He mustered more arguments. If he couldn't convince Bebe, how could he convince Patricia? "Patricia wouldn't need to attend classes she hates, wouldn't need to take over a business she doesn't want. She can do anything. Or nothing. Sugar can come with us; we can board the donkeys in the wine country. We can still summer here, visit here. We can even keep the farmhouse, if she wants. I just don't want to live here. Not year round. And the chickens stay." Sorry, but he'd have to stand firm on that point.

"You've covered all your bases, but I'm afraid—" Bebe sighed. "Patricia's on a tear, Zeke. Making plans. Dropping bombs. On me, anyway. Apparently, the rest of the family get to wait and be bombarded after the holidays have ended."

"What do you mean, dropping bombs? About Hank?"

"For one. And I know she'd buy your argument about him and San Francisco. As a matter of fact, I do, too, if she's with him. Oh, he'll experience bigotry wherever, but it's far easier if there are other kids like you—I was lucky to be raised in Chicago and by parents who, once they peeled themselves off the ceiling, completely accepted me. Patricia's mother wasn't as fortunate. There weren't any other odd ducks in the pool here, so Ruth struggled and lied to herself and denied her feelings up until the time she was pregnant with Patricia. And she always carried around a feeling of shame where none was needed. So as far as Hank is concerned, Patricia would agree he'd be better off in San Francisco."

Zeke felt relieved. "So now all I have to do is—"

"Except she's already made other plans."

His heart stuttered. "What plans?"

"She asked me to take Hank in."

"She wants to kick him out? I can't believe—"

"No, it's not like that. She knows he'd be happier in a more liberal setting. And he would. But not without his family. Without his family, I'm afraid that he'll—"

"You say Hank doesn't know yet?" If not, he still had time to talk to Patricia before any damage was done. After that, it would be a moot point.

"Not yet. She's decided not to tell him until after Christmas. Bah! It seems everyone's keeping secrets until after the holidays. Hank. Patricia. Daisy."

He was nodding, but now he stopped. "Daisy?"

Bebe looked annoyed at herself. "Ask Patricia. That's not my confidence to break. Hank's my concern right now. If Patricia goes ahead with this plan, he'll need someone to talk to. Right away. You'll be here. I won't. I've told her I'd love to have him. But I've warned her he'll feel she's rejecting him, hiding him. Just like she's done with me."

Patricia's voice sounded from out on the patio. "Zeke won't be here after the holidays, Bebe. In fact, he might not even stick around for Santa Claus." Wrapped in her coat and a long scarf, dragging the wastebasket he'd seen in the dining room, she opened up the screen door and hobbled inside. In the light cast from the kitchen windows, her face was tight. "And I'm not rejecting Hank. I can't believe you'd say that."

Bebe looked resigned. "Where did you spring from?"

"I was dumping the trash." She let the door slap shut and plopped down the can. "And I *don't* hide you."

"Darlin,' I know you love me, and you know I love you. But if you could wave a wand and make me straight—make Hank straight—you'd do it and you know it."

"Is that so bad? You'd both have easier lives, wouldn't you?"

"The point is, so would you."

"Me? This isn't about me."

"Isn't it?" Bebe stood up. "I think you'd better give that more thought."

Red with indignation, Patricia started to protest, but was interrupted when the kitchen door banged open.

A squat man with a bald dome crisscrossed by several long hairs combed over and shiny with gel appeared on the threshold. His eyes, aglitter within the folds of his face, landed on Bebe. "Oh, Christ. If I'da known you'd be out here, I coulda waited another *year* for a smoke. But as long as you're here, you can hand over some dough for that floor you ruined at the grocery." Hitching up his pants, he stepped outside. His gaze went to Patricia. "Well, if it isn't the muff divers' daughter, too."

Zeke straightened. This must be Ernie Burcham.

Bebe stood up. "I owe you nothing."

"Skips a generation, eh?" Ernie Burcham smirked, eyes still on Patricia. "Skeeter tells me Hank's growing up light in the loafers. Fuckin' faggot."

Patsy Lee went white. "Seems your son is following his own family tradition: ignorant and stupid as the jerk who raised him."

Zeke almost cheered.

"Why, you . . ." Fists clenched, Burcham took a step toward her.

Zeke stepped out of the shadows. *"And,"* he said smoothly, "with the same disturbing tendency to pick the wrong fight."

Burcham halted, face smoothing into an ingratiating smile. "Why, Mr. Townley. Didn't see ya there."

"I'll bet you didn't."

"No harm meant." Burcham pushed his hands into the pockets of his jacket and rocked back on his heels. "Situation just got me all riled, that's all—you would be, too, they come in and trash your business, beat up your son."

"Beat him up?" Patricia glared. "Hank was only defending his grandmother against the evil your son learned at your knee."

"And a jar of pickled beets, uh, *spilled* on the floor doesn't constitute *trashing*. But give me ten minutes in there and I'll show you what does." Bebe stepped forward, chin raised.

"And I'll help." Patsy Lee's chin hoisted, too.

Zeke shook his head at the man's dissembling. "Maybe we could take this outside?" He nodded toward the door.

Burcham looked worried. "Well, now, I don't know but what I need to take my leave, anyway. I'll just go tell the hostess—" He stepped toward the house.

At the same time, Zeke caught him by the collar of his jacket and steered him the other direction and straight out the screen door. Burcham squawked like a banty hen. When they were outside, Zeke didn't let go until he'd guided Burcham off the patio, around the path on the side of the house, and halfway down the sidewalk to the street out front. "I'll give your regrets to Mrs. O'Malley."

Tugging his jacket straight, Burcham glared. "Now, see here. You can't treat me like—"

"Like the asshole you are?" Zeke pushed his face into Burcham's. "Leave my family alone and tell your son to do likewise."

Burcham looked confused. "*Your* family?"

"*My* family."

"Or what?" Burcham sneered, backing up out of reach.

"Or I'll do whatever it takes to bring you down."

The man continued to step backward. "Oh yeah?"

"Yeah." This felt suspiciously like kindergarten, but Zeke was exhilarated. His family. They were *his* family. Barring an objection from the lovely lady who waited for him inside. "And I have a lot of *whatever* to use."

Burcham stopped, looking stricken. Apparently, the disparity in their influence was—albeit belatedly—registering on his dim brain. He put up his hands, palms out. "Now, Mr. Townley. I won't cause nobody no harm."

Zeke had to admit, there were times when rich and famous felt mighty fine. "You bet you won't."

Zeke waited until Burcham had disappeared toward the street before wheeling around to return to Patricia. He felt like he could conquer the world. One pint-sized woman shouldn't give him too much trouble.

But when he stepped inside, Patricia was sitting ramrod straight on the bench Bebe had vacated, not looking pint-sized at all in her anger. Her face was grim. "Is he gone? Bebe wouldn't let me follow you. Said she didn't want to spend the rest of the evening bailing me out of jail."

Some of Zeke's elation fled. About to relay how he'd slayed the dragon, he suddenly didn't think Patricia would appreciate the extent of his defense—not when she'd just shown herself so able to come to her own. Or at least to Hank's. He wondered if she'd ever cease to surprise him.

He hoped she'd give him the opportunity to find out.

"Where *is* Bebe?"

"Gone inside to celebrate my sudden show of spirit, as she put it. With something, she said, stronger than the fluff in the punch bowl."

"I don't blame her. That was something. *You* were something."

"But it wasn't enough. God! I could *kill* that idiot. I can't *bear* it that Hank—"

"Patricia, it'll hurt, but you can't fight all Hank's battles for him." Zeke would need to remember that neither could he. "Defend him, yes, but he'll need to learn—"

"But soon Hank'll be okay. Better off, anyway. He will; I'll make sure of it." It was like she hadn't even heard him.

"You'll try." He soothed. "And I'll help, if you'll let me. But nobody can—"

"Somebody can. *I* can. Hank's my *child*. It's my job to protect him. To protect all of them. Like—" She hesitated. "Well, you might as well know. Everyone else will soon. Daisy's pregnant. Just past three months."

Apprehension crept up his spine. He didn't know exactly how this news would effect his plans; he just knew that it would.

"Abortion is out." Voice flat, she stared straight ahead. "And even if she'd wanted one, I couldn't have lived with that decision."

"But . . . It's not your decision."

Again, she continued like he hadn't spoken. "And even though it would tear me up, she won't consider what would probably be best; she won't consider adoption. No, she wants to marry Danny. She insists on it."

"Things could be worse." Struggling against a sudden wave of helplessness, he scrambled for an argument against . . . what? "At least he's willing to do the honorable thing."

"It's not honorable, it's stupid. And unrealistic. And shortsighted. They're still children. She thinks she wants my life. Mine! Sleepy, slow town. Marriage to Danny. Lots of children. If anything happened to Danny, she'll end up in some *nothing* job that she hates, trying to support it all. And right now she thinks they can live on love. She has no more sense than a-a *bird*."

"Unlike you, maybe it's a life she'd love."

"Love? She—" Patricia stopped. "What do you mean, *unlike you*? You're as bad as Bebe. This isn't about me; it's about what's best for Daisy."

"Is it?"

"Stop it! Quit judging my life. You live on a mountaintop free of financial concerns. And a couple years taking care of your sisters doesn't mean you know *hellfire* about children."

Her words stung, added a layer of anger to the mound of hopelessness that had settled on his chest. "I know she's over eighteen, so what else can you do?"

But from the jut of her chin, he already knew she'd thought of something. Decided something. And whatever it was, it didn't—couldn't—include him.

"What I can do is raise my first grandchild myself." She glanced at him, defiant. "I know it's drastic, but I've thought it all through. Babies are a lot of work, but Zinnia and Lil and the others will help. Everyone in this family always pulls together. And it won't be for that long. Just a few years. By then . . ."

A few years. His eyes wandered her face, seeing anew the earnestness and honesty in her expression. She believed everything she said, convinced that her way was the right way. The *only* way. Hopes in ashes, he cursed her for her myopic vision. And himself for failing to know his own mind any sooner.

". . . And once they *both* finish school, if they feel the same way about each other, they can still get married. That will be about the same time Lil has said she wants to retire, so the timing is perfect. Daisy can take over her baby; I can take over Lil's stores. I haven't talked with Daisy yet, but I'm sure that between Danny's parents and me, we can convince them this would be best. It's a compromise. One we can all live with."

All except him.

Defeat made him tired. She had dug into Cordelia with a vengeance when she was young, finding something in the O'Malley family that she'd never had, determined to belong. And no matter how ill it suited her now, she was hell-bent on keeping her place. He knew that, but he'd still thought he could convince her that she'd be happier in San Francisco. With him. But even if he could convince her—a stretch in and of itself—she'd never leave. She'd never take a child that far away from its mother. And even if he was willing to remain here those few years . . .

In a few years, he was sure something or someone else would provide yet another reason for Patricia to avoid chancing a happier life for herself.

He couldn't compete.

Not against all the needs of her children.

Not against her own entrenched fears.

She was too timid. Too intractable. Too . . . precious.

A wave of anger and pain swept him. Just like Sinclair's George Babbitt, the character she'd held in such distaste, ultimately, she couldn't escape.

"Well," she said.

He realized she'd stopped talking a few minutes ago and was waiting for him to respond. But for the life of him, he couldn't think of a thing to say. Nothing that he wouldn't later regret.

"Well," she repeated. "I guess I'd better get back inside." She stood up. At the doorway, she looked back. "I haven't mentioned anything to Lily-Too, just in case you decided not to go to New York, but . . . have you made up your mind?"

He had. Just now.

Chapter 26

During her lunch hour on Monday, Patsy Lee turned up the walkway leading to her in-laws' house. Sunshine blinked off windows and turned pale winter grass into spun silver. Sparrows scrabbled at a feeder, scattering chaff in the light wind that had followed her down Maple Woods Drive. Despite the chill, she'd walked (with all the speed of a square tire) from the store, feeling the stretch of reawakening muscles.

But neither the pleasant day nor the walk had lifted her spirits. Over the weekend, she'd told Lily-Too that Zeke would leave for New York two days short of her birthday and the Christmas pageant. When Lily-Too had predictably burst into tears, Patsy Lee had almost done likewise, remembering the way he'd snapped the words out, his face shuttered.

"Mom arrives Sunday," he'd said. "I'll leave with her Wednesday."

"But Lily-Too will be crushed. Are you sure you can't wait until after Christmas?"

Hesitation had flitted across his face, but he'd only said, "I can't. Not even for Lily-Too."

Knowing how much he cared for her daughter, the harshness of his decision had initially surprised her into silence, but later, hugging a sniffling Lily-Too, her own ire had grown. Zeke was a lot of things, but she'd never thought him capable of this kind of selfishness. He'd acted as though her request that he delay his trip by two measly days was heresy. Why had he been so bent out of shape? He was getting exactly what he wanted: his old life back.

Just like I'm getting mine, she thought, mounting the steps to the front porch. Once the chaos of the holidays subsided, she'd pick up the reins where she'd dropped them, redoubling her efforts in school. If she pushed, she could finish before the baby arrived.

That she'd soon be a grandmother still hadn't sunk in. Her worries over Daisy had dampened the excitement she'd once imagined she'd feel. Or maybe it was the blow to what remained of her youthful vanity that was making her so tired. She'd have to stoke her enthusiasm before she talked with Daisy, though, or her daughter and Danny would never buy her proposal.

The door was unlocked as usual and she let herself in. Just like she'd postponed her conversation with Hank about his move to Bebe's until after the holidays, she was delaying her discussion with Daisy, letting her eldest rattle on about her impending Joyful Event without interruption. It wasn't cowardice that held her tongue. At least not much. Fearful Zeke's departure could undo the progress Lily-Too had made, she'd decided to give her youngest daughter her moment in the spotlight before she attacked a different kid crisis.

Hearing voices in the kitchen, she took her time hanging up her coat. Yesterday, Zeke's mother had arrived as scheduled and had taken up residence in Lil's guesthouse. Using the children as an excuse, Patsy Lee had sidestepped Lil's invitation to Sunday-evening supper, but she hadn't been as quick on her feet when she'd heard Zinnia's voice on the phone this morning. "Since you missed meeting Zeke's mama last evening, honeybunch, you just come on over for a bowl of corn chowder and an old-fashioned female gabfest at noontime. You'll just love her; she's a charmer."

Patsy Lee bet. With Zeke's mother worshipping in the same highbrow circles as Christine—and given Zinnia's penchant not to let anyone else get a word in edgewise—her mother-in-law had no doubt mistaken condescension for interest. Sensing Zinnia was making a last-ditch effort to shore up her matchmaking schemes by enlisting Zeke's mother's support, Patsy Lee had rolled her eyes at the absurdity. No way would Patsy Lee O'Malley live up to Marta Tommaso's expectations for her son. But roll them as hard as she could, she still couldn't drum up a refusal Zinnia would accept.

So here she was, fluffing her hair and smoothing the collar on her peach blouse. She made her way to the back of the house, thinking it odd that Zinnia had opted for the casual atmosphere of the kitchen instead of the dining room's decorum. When she reached the doorway, she paused and cleared her throat.

Backs facing her, Zinnia and another woman were standing at the counter in front of a cornucopia of vegetables spread out in front of a large wooden bowl. Zinnia twisted around, waved a paring knife. "Why, there she is. Patsy Lee, this is Zeke's mother."

Setting down a plump onion, the woman next to Zinnia turned on slim ankles—the only thing slim about her—swiped her hand down an apron, and held it out. "Why, how do."

Momentarily confused, Patsy Lee blinked. This woman couldn't be Marta Tommaso. Marta Tommaso would be dimpled and shapely like her daughter. Or gracefully tall like her son. Not short and broad-beamed, with gray curls as tightly wound and redolent of onions as Zinnia's.

She took the proffered hand. "Hello, Mrs. Tommaso."

She got a hearty shake. "I've heard lots about you." About seventy years' time had traced a network on a once fine complexion. Her eyes were beautiful, as intelligent as Zeke's and as merry as Teresa's. And shrewd.

"I'm sorry if Zinnia's been bending your ear about—" Patsy Lee started apologetically.

"Not from Zinnia. From my son." She turned back to her task. "Sometimes he actually keeps his cell phone on so I can reach him. Oh, and do call me Martha."

"Martha?" When Mrs. Tommaso gave her a puzzled look, she blushed. "I mean, I thought Teresa said it was Marta." She moved up to the counter. "Um, anything I can do?" Zinnia pushed a tomato at her, and she picked up a serrated knife.

Mrs. Tommaso's face cleared. "Ah, *Marta*." A smile tinged with sadness crooked up a corner of her mouth. "My dear Ray, bless his Italian soul, called me Marta. . . . *Marta, tesorina mia* . . . my little treasure." She swiped the back of her hand across her eyes. "Dang onions. But it's really Martha, although Terri Sue thinks I should still use the other. Sounds more upper class, you know."

Terri Sue? Patsy Lee looked down quickly.

Martha diced the vegetable into smithereens. *"Teresa."* She snorted. "Like any woman who can't settle down after giving it three tries has a lick of sense when it comes to anything. So is it Patricia or Patsy Lee? I've heard both."

"Patricia," she said, while at the same time, Zinnia said, "Patsy Lee."

The two woman paused and stared at each other.

Feeling stubborn, Patsy Lee repeated, "Patricia,"

then rushed on before Zinnia could open her mouth. "I can understand why, uh, Terri Sue likes Marta. It's a beautiful name. Zeke told me your husband was Italian. How did you meet him?"

As Martha smiled that same sad smile, Patsy Lee could have slapped herself. Cripes. Despite the decades that had passed, obviously reminders of her husband still stirred Martha's emotions.

"On a Caribbean cruise, believe it or not. It was a college graduation present from my whole clan because I was the first girl in the family to get a degree. The ship—*Duchess Fair,* it was—hit a reef when we were coming into Grand Cayman. No real danger except to the reef, but we were stuck. The ferries couldn't handle us all, and Ray and I ended up in the same lifeboat. Poor man. He was terrified. Couldn't swim, wouldn't you know? How we laughed about it later."

But she wasn't laughing now. Her eyes were distant. "So I held his hand. Or rather, he about squeezed mine in two. After we reached solid ground, he bought me dinner and dubbed me his own Unsinkable Molly Brown. Not more than a few months later, this country gal found herself in San Francisco, where she lived happily ever after."

Patsy Lee realized she'd stopped slicing, too, lost in the fairy tale.

Martha swept the onion into the salad bowl. "Except when I lost him, of course."

Despite the matter-of-fact words, Patsy Lee could hear echoes of past devastation. Zinnia must have, too. Sobering, she *tsk*'d. "Always so hard to lose someone dear."

"But I had Zeke and the girls." Martha sighed. "I'm afraid I leaned way too much on my boy, though. I wanted him to stay put in school, but he wouldn't have it. Said he needed to help support us, and God knows the help was needed. All's well now, and he's supported us ever since. But I always wondered if he just wanted an excuse to get out of high school. He hated it."

She gave Patsy Lee a pointed look. "But I guess you know all that. And a lot more."

Still standing motionless, Patsy Lee started. She glanced at Zinnia's small smile and ducked back to her tomato, knowing her face was almost as red. Good grief, what had the two been discussing? It had undoubtedly been a huge mistake to involve Zinnia in trying to squelch the gossip over her and Zeke. She'd probably only encouraged it.

"So . . ." she mumbled, "Where are you from originally?" A safe topic. A neutral topic.

"Vimy Ridge. Not far from Little Rock."

"I'll be," Zinnia said. "I have family in Arkansas. Maybe we've got some in common."

Relieved, Patsy Lee moved to the stove to stir the crock of corn chowder while the older women chattered about family from Fayetteville to Pine Bluff. Martha's speech held the same cadence she'd listened to most of her life. She relaxed with the rhythm, feeling as if she'd known Zeke's mother for . . .

Why, that was it. In an odd way, Martha must be why Zeke had developed such an attraction for Lil so long ago. In all the touring and razzle-dazzle of his career, the small-town girl Lil had been when they'd met had, in some ways, reminded him of home. She'd nudged him into remembering the blessings of family, not just the obligations. Only . . .

Only it hadn't just been Lil. It had been the entire O'Malley family. The way they gathered for celebrations. The way they supported each other when troubled. The way they squabbled and made up and hugged and filled a room—a *home*—with their love . . .

She turned around, spoon dripping. "Zinnia, it's not Lil. It's what she represents."

"Pardon?" Martha turned around.

"Took me a while to see it myself, honeybunch," Zinnia said calmly.

Blushing at her outburst, Patsy Lee turned back to the chowder. But she was right. She knew she was. And it explained so much. Zeke's mind was clouded by conflicting desires. Torn between his past aversion to family and his desire for one now, he'd mistaken his feelings. Twice. He'd believed himself in love with Lil, and maybe he still did. And he'd fancied himself attracted to Patsy Lee. But all the while it had been their families that had really held him captive.

She stirred the chowder. Good thing she hadn't gotten swept into his fantasy.

Hours later, the house sheathed in darkness except for a solitary light over the dining room table, Patsy Lee put the finishing touches on a Christmas present. Wrapping gifts could have waited till her day off on Wednesday, but she'd grab a nap between rising early to see everyone off and working tomorrow afternoon.

She'd felt too restless for sleep. God knew, she had plenty to occupy her mind, but every time she peeked at her thoughts, she was disconcerted to find them busy with Zeke. If escaping his visit with her heart intact was such a good thing—and it was—then why couldn't she put him entirely out of her head?

She flattened a bow on the last present, switched off the lights, and headed for the stairs, forcing her thoughts in a new direction. Except for some uneasiness every time Zeke's name came up, she'd enjoyed his mother today. Like Zinnia, Martha had a penchant for interference plus a disconcerting tendency for penetrating looks. But, also like Zinnia, she had a big heart. Since Teresa had mentioned Patsy Lee's skill with yarn to her mother, Martha had asked a number of questions about her work. Patsy Lee had delighted in answering until talk turned toward shopping her wares in San Francisco. She'd carefully explained the reasons why she couldn't, dropping her gaze when Martha's look turned . . . well, penetrating.

The cats bounded ahead. Upstairs was quiet, the only sound Sugar's snore echoing from Hank's room; the only light a soft splash from a night-light. About to move past the spare room, she stopped. Long ago, she'd promised herself she'd find time for her loom. A few hours each week. The occasional full day. But she'd never kept that vow. And, really, between classes, work, her family, and soon a new baby, who could blame her.

Still . . . why *not* now? Right now.

She opened the door and flipped the wall switch, blinking until her eyes adjusted to the flood of light. The jack floor loom that Bebe had unearthed at an auction still stood in the center of the room, covered in dust, but otherwise looking like Patsy Lee had last risen from its bench yesterday. Up until a few years ago, she'd kept the door locked against childish curiosity, so her work remained undisturbed.

She approached the loom, stopping just short of the breast beam, letting her eyes wander over the harnesses, treadles, beater, reacquainting herself with the equipment that had once held a focal point in her life. Reaching out, she touched the warp she'd threaded so long ago, back when the first of her three children were small and Henry would occasionally cart them off for a day of fishing. Up until Rose was a few years old, she'd tried to make time for the loom, but she'd finally stopped fooling herself that she could complete a project.

This project, whatever pattern she'd intended, was lost to time. But she remembered how the designs used to surface in her mind, as though a muse filled her dreams with color and texture. The brilliance of the yarns had faded, some of the tension had relaxed. They puffed up dust when disturbed by her touch, but with an inner resiliency she wished she could match, they quivered back into place when she lifted her hand. She'd always saved her money; she'd never bought cheap yarn.

Picking up a shuttle from a nearby table and disregarding the smudges she knew the dusty bench would leave on her pants, she settled in front of the breast beam, fitting neatly into the worn valley left to the women that had sat there before her.

Anticipation gathering in her chest, she pushed a treadle. As though it had been used yesterday, several harnesses jingled a harmony as they lifted in response. She let up. They sighed and lowered.

A surge of electricity passed through her. She collected a bobbin wrapped with yarn and loaded it into the shuttle. Sitting again, she took a deep breath, stepped on the treadle, and tossed the shuttle through the shed with one hand. It glided between threads of the warp. She slid to catch it, then beat back the first thread of the weft. Hundreds more beats and fabric would grow under her hands. Choosing another treadle that lifted different harnesses, she repeated the action. Dust motes filled the air, but the motions soothed her. As she found a rhythm, she relaxed and her mind wandered.

Smiling, she thought of the name game played between Teresa . . . Terri Sue . . . and Martha, much as she and Zinnia tussled over her own. It was a silly exercise, really, minor skirmishing carried on out of habit. What difference did it make? A rose by any other name . . . but still they kept at it, the squabble becoming almost endearing, almost like any other family tradition. . . .

Family. Martha. Zinnia. The names kept pace with her movements. The O'Malley sisters were lucky, as were Zeke and his siblings. Zinnia could be maddening at times, but just like Zeke's mother, she was driven by love. Each woman was exactly what a mother should be.

A real mother, she thought, echoing an internal chant that had played throughout her childhood. She beat back the weft. *A real mother in a real home.* She beat back the weft; the chant followed her tempo. . . . *A real mother . . .*

The yearning she suddenly felt was so intense, so *well remembered,* that her motions faltered. She frowned, lobbing the shuttle again. What was her problem? She'd had a real mother. Two. Her mother and Bebe had provided her with a home, love, and anything else within their power to give her. She'd loved them back. Life hadn't always been a rose garden, true, but, just like she did with her own children, they'd tried to shield her from its thorns. And their lives together had been good.

Her rhythm sped up.

Very good. Tears filled her eyes. Always good. She went faster. Except . . .

A thread snapped.

She snatched back her hands as though they'd been slapped and knotted them in her lap. The treadles groaned and fell silent. Distant voices and foggy images filled her head. Things she'd buried as she'd matured while telling herself they no longer mattered: her confusion . . . her *fear* . . . when she'd become aware of how different her family was. She'd introduced Bebe as her aunt. She'd never invited anyone over. She'd refused to accompany them anywhere. And now . . .

Zeke had told her that if she sent Hank away, he'd feel she was ashamed.

Like you are of Bebe.
Bebe had said the same thing to Zeke.
Just like she's tried to hide me.
And she'd told Bebe, *This isn't about me.*
But, oh, God. It was.

Chapter 27

As she hugged Hank good-bye the next morning, holding him just a little longer than she had the others, she whispered, "This *isn't* about me. Not anymore."

Pulling back, he scratched his head, but only made some flippant comment about hormones before heading out the door with Rose. But she didn't care if he understood or not. It was only important that she did. With the words, her heart felt lighter, although she still needed to clear the air with Bebe. Words couldn't undo years of displaying an embarrassment that shared the same spectrum as Ernie Burcham's opinions, but they'd be a start.

As soon as the bus had trundled off with Lily-Too, she checked to make sure Daisy was still asleep, then settled at the kitchen table and dialed Bebe's number. With winter break underway, Bebe should be home.

She picked up on the fourth ring.

"I'm sorry." The apology spilled out.

"That's okay." Bebe yawned. "I just love getting up at the crack of dawn when I have a few days off."

"No, not that. I mean, not only that. It's just, well, you can't have Hank. I've changed my mind; he stays with me."

"Thank God. To what do we owe this newfound wisdom?"

"Because last night I realized that even though you, you and Mom, raised me with the same love as the best mothers in the world, and even though I loved both of you back, I—" She stopped and swallowed.

"Yes?"

"I hated you, too."

Bebe laughed. "Honey, there's no need to apologize. Youth is self-conscious even under the best conditions. No teen loves their parents all the time. In this case—well, it was a tough situation and we completely understood. Even your mom—"

"I know she understood." Patsy Lee had thought about her mother, her lies, through a long sleepless night. She realized that for Ruth, lying to her daughter, creating a fictional relationship with a fictional man, had been far better than running a risk that Patsy Lee would think her mother had once been a tramp out trolling for fun. "It's why she lied."

"I'm glad you understand. She thought the story she made up about your background would give you a feeling of normalcy. She was so young back then. Confused. Especially after she found herself pregnant and unwed and homosexual in a town where tolerance wasn't exactly a byword and tongues could be cruel."

"That's not all of it."

"What do you mean?"

"Don't whitewash for me. She knew her homosexuality shamed me, and she didn't want to give me another reason to hate her more than I already did. The story protected her. . . . From me."

Bebe paused. "Yes. But we both—"

"Wait, there's more." Patsy Lee gripped the phone tighter. "I still do hate you. Oh, not *hate,* exactly, but everything you've said to me before . . . you've been right. I've been ashamed. Of my background. Of you." She dragged in a ragged breath. "Of Hank. Oh, Bebe. I almost banished him from my life."

"Patricia—"

"No. No, it's Patsy Lee."

"It is? But I thought—"

"Don't you see? The only reason I haven't liked that name is because it reminded me too much of things I wanted to forget. When I used Patricia . . . it was like the story Mom told me, or like Lily-Too: hiding behind something—a name, a made-up past, stage paint—because we were afraid to let people see us for what we are. But you know what? I'm okay as I am. Just like Mom was. And just like Lily-Too has already realized she is. She's so much smarter than her mother."

She stopped, struck by a sudden thought. "And there's somebody I need to go tell. Somebody I should have told a long time ago."

She turned her old Caddy onto the street that led to the entrance of the elementary school, looking for Lily-Too among the children racing around at recess, smiling when she finally spotted her daughter and Josephine McGraw walking together on the path that ran along the inside of the chain-link fence that ringed the playground, hand in hand, heads bent together in deep conversation, probably concerning their debut performance on Christmas Eve.

After Sunday night's rehearsal, Lily-Too said Zeke had announced to his young thespians that he had to leave town before the pageant. Harmony Hall had echoed with disappointment, but when the kids had learned Jon was stepping into Zeke's shoes for the last few days before their performance, and would also provide equipment to record their show—with a free DVD for each family—disappointment had turned into excitement.

"Everybody thinks Uncle Jon is way cool." Squaring her slim shoulders, Lily-Too had presented what her mother always thought of as her brave face. "Me, too. I'll miss Zeke, but he needs to be with his own family on Christmas. We can get along without him, right, Mama?"

Patsy Lee wasn't sure if Lily-Too had been referring to the pageant or their family or even to her lessons. To herself—or to her mother. Nor had she asked. She'd simply hugged her, glad to know that Lily-Too wouldn't let Zeke's departure undo her weeks of hard work. Her daughter had grown stronger in the last few months.

Hopefully, Hank had the same inner strength as his sister. Cordelia wouldn't be an easy town to grapple with once his homosexuality was common knowledge, but they'd face it together. As Lily-Too had said about Zeke, Hank needed to be with his own family. Even though she knew he had to learn to deal with things himself, she would show him the support she hadn't given to her mother or Bebe.

Or for that matter, to Lily-Too.

Throwing the gearshift into reverse, she looped an arm over the back, steered into a place at the curb, grabbed her handbag, and got out before she could change her mind.

In Lily-Too's classroom, Mrs. Sherlock stood at the blackboard, printing an assignment. In the fluorescent light, the woman's gold braids gleamed as bright as the buttons on her jacket, a smart military-inspired affair. With epaulets. Before she found herself saluting, Patsy Lee stepped inside and cleared her throat.

Mrs. Sherlock turned. Her eyebrows went up. "Mrs. O'Malley. I certainly am glad you've stopped by, but"—she looked at her watch—"I'm afraid I have a staff meeting in five minutes. If you'd like to take a seat and wait, I can make time for you in a half an hour while the children are at lunch."

"I'm afraid that's not convenient." Patsy Lee closed the door.

Mrs. Sherlock frowned. "I know we need to talk. That is, after all, why I've sent notes home. But if you can't wait, perhaps we could schedule an appointment for a different day."

"I won't take more than three of your five minutes."

Frown deepening, Mrs. Sherlock settled into the chair behind her desk, her spine straight as a general's. She waved Patsy Lee toward a child's desk, but Patsy Lee ignored it and stepped up in front of her. Mrs. Sherlock had to look up. "Um, Mrs. O'Malley—"

Suddenly, Patsy Lee realized Lily-Too's teacher wasn't much older than Daisy. They even shared the same fair, flawless complexions and pastel yellow hair. Patsy Lee relaxed, wondering why she'd ever been scared of this woman. "I just need to let you know that Lily will not be taking ADD tests after the holidays."

"But I thought we agreed that—"

"You're right. But I'm changing my mind. I've been talking to people"—she recalled Zeke's words: *The only time Lily-Too's mind wanders is when she isn't challenged*—"and doing my own research. Lily's inattention and forgetfulness aren't symptoms of ADD. She's shy and sometimes lacks self-confidence, but she has a bright mind and is willing to work hard—"

"That hasn't been my—"

"—*Under* the right circumstances." Patsy Lee kept her voice pleasant. "Unfortunately, those don't include rigid teaching techniques, tight boundaries, and single-focus expectations."

Mrs. Sherlock's mouth dropped open.

Patsy Lee relented. "I know you mean well and you're doing the best you can. Maybe many, or even most, of your students flourish with your methods. My daughter, though, isn't one of them. That's just the way it is. But that's all it is. I'll work with you to keep Lily on track. And no matter what her grades ultimately reflect, I'll know third grade will be a learning experience. She'll be better equipped to handle future challenges once this year is over."

Patsy Lee let her voice take on an edge. "But I won't have her made to feel that because she doesn't fit your definition of the perfect student that there is something wrong with her. Okay?"

Mrs. Sherlock swallowed and nodded.

Around nine that night, while Daisy was out with Danny and their friends, and her other children were bent to end-of-semester homework, Patsy Lee settled on the bench in front of her loom after nudging Blinken and Nod out of the room. She'd tied off the break in the thread—this was only practice, after all—and wondered if she'd lost her mind. Only three nights away, Christmas Eve loomed. Lily-Too had ultimately made the decision to appear as herself, the soloist at the pageant's end. No headdress, no veils, no heavy makeup.

Which meant there was a hem to sew on the confection of a dress Lily-Too had chosen when her grandmother had taken her shopping last week. Along with the rest of the presents to wrap, pumpkin pie to bake for the after-pageant potluck, party favors to package for the third-grade winter party, and a few last-minute cards left to get in the mail. But the lure of the loom, so long at rest, had been too strong to resist.

She shrugged her shoulders and picked up her shuttle. Enough time tomorrow to regret how she'd squandered her time tonight.

In a few moments, she'd relaxed, letting her body take over in remembered rhythm. Weaving for short periods like this created uneven tension that showed in the finished material, but until she felt her skills had fully returned, until she could figure out when to grab the blocks of time she'd need to create something worth keeping, she'd continue to use the abandoned warp for practice. For therapy.

Her upbeat mood this morning after she'd seen Mrs. Sherlock hadn't withstood the rush of shoppers in the store this afternoon, but the hectic pace had kept her fears for Hank, her anxiety over Daisy, and her thoughts of Zeke at bay. But as soon as she'd left Merry-Go-Read, they'd all crawled back into her head. Paramount among them was the fact Zeke would leave tomorrow. He'd picked up the children after school today and taken them to an early supper at Phillip E's, where he'd given each one a gift. For Rose, a laptop. For Hank, a telescope. And Lily-Too had returned bearing his beloved Hofner.

Clutching it like she'd once clutched her dolls, she'd looked up at Patsy Lee. Tears dampened her lashes, but her smile was a sunbeam. "It's my birthday present. Birthday and Christmas. He said when he comes back to visit Uncle Jon, we can play together again."

The Hofner case pressed between them, she'd hugged Lily-Too and wished—no matter how much she tried to bury it—that he'd left something for her.

But he hadn't. Nothing more than a neutral farewell message left on her answering machine and carefully timed for when she was at work. She chose to ignore that she could have returned his call.

Wondering why in hellfire she just couldn't let him go, she beat back the weft with more force than necessary, then twisted around as the door opened, half expecting to see him lounging against the jamb. But it was only Daisy, her cherry red sweater aglow against the dim hallway. With the matching ribbon she'd used to tie back her curls, she looked five years old.

Dismissing Zeke from her head, she beckoned Daisy in. "You're home early."

Daisy shut the door and wandered around the room. "God, it's been eons since I saw you do this." She paused to watch a few minutes—actually, fidget for a few minutes—then flopped on the old armchair in the corner. "I'm home early because I'm tired. I'm always tired. All I want to do anymore is sleep. And, man"—she yawned—"are my boobs ever sore." Her voice was overly casual; the yawn looked forced.

Patsy Lee let the loom still, swiveled around on the bench. "It goes with the territory. Sleep all you can now. Later on, it will be a different story."

It wasn't until the words had left her mouth that she realized her error. If she had her way, after this summer, it wouldn't be Daisy who would get up to soothe a baby back to sleep; it would be her mother. Expecting to feel a trill of anticipation similar to what she'd once felt before the birth of each of her children, she was dismayed that the only feeling she could summon up was a creeping tendril of exhaustion.

"So I've heard." Daisy paused, plucking at a hole in the chair arm.

"Daisy . . . what's up?"

"Um, well. You won't like this, but . . ." Daisy took a deep breath. "Oh, balls. We're moving. He's been accepted at the University of Kansas next year."

"Oh, honey." Patsy Lee felt shaken. A different state? How could she wrap that into their plans? MU wasn't a long jaunt from here, not like it was to Lawrence, Kansas. She pushed aside her concerns. They'd make something work. "Why?"

"Once we're residents, KU's law school is cheaper than MU's, and more graduates pass the . . . whatever those tests are they take."

"The bar exams?"

She nodded. "We've already applied for married

student housing beginning this summer. If we get it, our rent will be low enough that Danny can support us for a few months. Except . . ."

"Except?"

"Oh, it's nothing. Not really. It's just when school starts next fall, he'll be so busy. We don't want to use day care the first year if we don't have to, but if I can't find a night job . . ." She sighed. "And if I *do* find a night job, that means we won't have much time together. Which I guess we can stand until Danny's done, but . . . well, I just want everything for our baby to be *perfect.*"

Patsy Lee was surprised to find Daisy had thought things through so thoroughly—and glad to hear they'd already tripped over some of the realities of their situation. It might make her proposal easier for them to swallow. She hesitated. Then, with her recent success over Mrs. Sherlock floating through her head, she decided to dive in without thinking it to death.

"Why don't you leave the baby with me?" She kept her tone casual.

"What?"

Patsy Lee raised her hand to forestall the objections she saw trembling on her daughter's lips. "Just hear me out. I don't know that we can make things *perfect,* but I can at least provide an alternative plan for you to consider. I've done a lot of thinking and . . ." For the next few minutes, she mustered all her arguments, explaining how the arrangement would benefit all of them, allowing Danny to concentrate on his studies, Daisy to finish school, both of them to save money, and render day care a moot point. "You can live at home in the summers—"

"And not marry Danny?" Daisy's face had paled.

Patsy Lee didn't want to tackle that question yet. "And when you return to school, I know your Aunt Lil will let me take the baby to Merry-Go-Read."

"And what happens when the baby is crawling?"

"We can set up a playpen; or the baby can stay with Gran and Pop."

"Gran can't keep up with a baby anymore."

Patsy Lee feared the same thing, but was once again surprised. Daisy and logic didn't usually go hand in hand. "You might be right, but Rose and Hank could help after school. It would only be a few years, not a lifetime."

"No way." Daisy pushed herself out of the chair and took a turn around the room. "Why am I even talking about this? This is *insane*. For God's sake, *I'm* raising my child, me and Danny, certainly not Rose or Hank. *Or* you."

"But, Daisy, *think*. You're so young. This would give you time to know your own mind before you throw yourself away like I—" Patsy Lee stopped.

Daisy halted. "Like you did?"

Patsy Lee looked away, hesitating to give voice to the truth that had grown in her since Zeke had walked into her life, knowing that in saying the words, she'd no longer be able to hide from herself. "Yes," she finally murmured. "Like I did."

The words settled gently between them. Daisy swallowed.

"Oh, honey, don't get me wrong. I'd do it all again in a minute knowing that I'd end up with you four. But . . ." She thought of the look on Martha Tommaso's face when she'd spoken of Ray. "I—I didn't love your dad when I married him. Not the way a wife should love a husband. I think I mostly just wanted to create a home and family like the one I'd never had. But once I had everything I thought I'd wanted, I no longer had any time to think about how I felt. It took all my energy just to keep us all afloat." She looked up, found Daisy's gaze still on her and held it. "Don't you see? I want more for you than I've had. I want things to be easier."

"Oh, Mom. I do see." Kneeling, Daisy slid her arms around Patsy Lee and laid her head on her chest. Patsy Lee could feel the small, solid bulge of Daisy's stomach pressing against her calf. "But I'm not you. I *do* love Danny. I want him. And I want this child."

Patsy Lee smoothed Daisy's hair. The curls sprang back, refusing to be tamed. "I know you think you love Danny, but—"

"No, I don't *think* I do. I *know* I do." Daisy pulled back. Her eyes held a wisdom Patsy Lee had never seen there before. "And if you never really loved Dad . . . well, maybe you don't know much about love."

As intent on convincing her daughter as Daisy was on resisting, Patsy Lee let the remark pass. For another half an hour, they talked in circles. Patsy Lee finally decided to shelve her arguments for a later day, not the least because the more unshakable Daisy's resolve grew, the more uncertain Patsy Lee felt. Maybe she was wrong; maybe Daisy was right. And maybe this child would be the making of her daughter.

That night, as she lay awake with restless worry, the echo of Daisy's remark returned to ring through her mind. Once she'd finally dropped off to sleep, it murmured in her dreams. And when she woke up the next morning, just a few days shy of Christmas, it was the first thought that entered her head.

Maybe you don't know much about love.

Maybe she didn't.

While the cats still slept curled near her side, she studied the shadows shifting on her ceiling as dawn swam through the murk of a cold December morning. But over the course of the last weeks, some things had become clear, growing from ephemeral suspicions when Zeke had first walked into her life to a shape with substance during that brief chat with his mother.

Just like Zeke, she'd been drawn to the O'Malleys' warmth. Just like Zeke, she'd allowed that attraction to lull her into the belief she loved someone she didn't. She'd confused the security of belonging to a family like the O'Malleys with . . .

She blinked in the growing light. With love, yes. But she'd also confused it with *life*. Her own life. Not Henry nor her children nor her growing responsibilities had limited her. At least not the way she'd indicated to Daisy, like they were circumstances beyond her control. She'd made the decisions herself.

Herself.

She was precisely where she was because this is where she'd chosen to be.

And she could still choose. At forty-three, she still had time, decades of time. And while she was uncertain what form she wanted her future to take, she suddenly knew without doubt what it was she didn't want.

She threw back the covers and clambered out of bed. The cats scattered like tumbleweeds.

Chapter 28

Patsy Lee stood on Lil and Jon's front porch, eyes watering in the wind scouring the top of the hill. The day was an unbroken blue, crisp as a wafer. Moments ago, Lil had buzzed her in through the gates at the bottom of the drive.

She looked across the acreage to the guesthouse, then realized she was looking for Zeke, wondering if he'd already left. She turned resolutely back to the door, a heavy glass affair elaborately etched like the upper panes of the multitudes of windows. The yards of glass were framed by heavy timbers, contemporary yet warm. The house was big, but not huge—Lil hadn't wanted huge—but no expense had been spared on detail. She saw Lil hurrying down the stairs in the two-story atrium.

She opened the door and motioned Patsy Lee inside. "I was just getting ready to leave. I thought you'd already be at work." Her voice held no censure, only concern.

"I would have, except . . ."

"Is something wrong? At the store?"

"Kind of . . . can we sit down somewhere?"

"Sure." A slight frown creasing her brow, Lil led the way to the kitchen, an inviting combination of smooth cherrywood, sun-kissed brick, and pale yellow walls. She waved Patsy Lee to the table. "Do you want some tea?"

"No, thanks." She sat down; she wanted to get to the point before courage failed her.

Frown deepening, Lil settled herself across from Patsy Lee, folded her hands, and waited.

Patsy Lee licked her lips, then plunged in. "I know we agreed that when Michael left for college, you'd retire, and I'd take over the stores, but . . . Lil, I can't do it. I'm so sorry."

Lil took a moment to catch up. "Is it the terms? When it's time, I'm sure we can—"

"No, what you've proposed is more than generous. As always. And I'm grateful. Really. Maybe I'd make a lot of money if I owned them. There's also the chance I'd bankrupt them, too. I just—"

"Is that what you're afraid of?" Lil's face cleared. "Believe me, it's not brain surgery. You're more than up to the task."

"It's not that. Or at least, not only that. I like working there. I like being around children and playing with the merchandise and helping the customers. Part ownership in the Cordelia store is wonderful. . . . *You're* wonderful. You saved me from food stamps and the night shift at PicNic after Henry died." A note of bitterness had crept into her voice and she swallowed, ashamed. With four children to raise, she would have been crazy not to accept Lil's help, so accept it she had. It wasn't Lil's fault if it was a decision that she could never entirely stomach. "But I don't want the responsibility of full ownership. I hate doing all the things you love—the vendor negotiations, the bookkeeping, the legalities, the payroll. To be honest, I'd rather spend less time there, not more. I want more time with my family. And more time for . . . for other things."

Her ideas were still too new to stand up to skepticism, so she didn't want to elaborate. But somewhere between meeting Zeke's mother and now . . . no, that was dishonest. Somewhere between meeting *Zeke* and now, she'd decided that the hours she now spent on school, she should spend on weaving.

Or at least on textile classes, not accounting. As long as she was taking leaps, the idea of moving her family to Columbia was gaining ground. Bebe was there. Daisy could live at home with the baby and continue her classes. (Danny could, of course, visit them whenever he could get away from Lawrence.) Hank would fare better. Rose could go to a larger school with more opportunities. And the university had a well-respected music department where she could find instructors for Lily-Too.

The children would balk at first; of course they would. But maybe less than she thought. Rose's infatuation with San Francisco might signal she'd welcome any change, Hank had no close friends here, and Lily-Too would be absorbed in her music. Daisy already had friends there. Besides, it wasn't like they'd never return. The O'Malleys were family; they'd be here often. The children would adjust.

They had to, because she needed to do this. The more she thought about it, the more certain she was. She needed to do *something*. Instead of clutching the coattails of the O'Malley sisters and bowing to Zinnia's will, no matter how well intentioned, it was time—*past* time—for her to create her own future. The path she was choosing might be wildly impractical, but it was her path. *Hers.* It had very little to do with what she *should* do and everything to do with what she *wanted* to do. It was the obligation she owed to herself.

Lil continued to sit quietly. Patsy Lee couldn't read her expression.

"You've been so generous, Lil, and I'm so thankful. I feel like a toad letting you down."

She did feel like a toad—balancing her own desires and her knowledge of what she owed Lil was like trying to juggle water—but the stores had been Lil's dream, not hers. Surely, even with all Lil had done, it didn't mean she owed Lil the rest of her life. She certainly didn't believe Lil owed her a living for the rest of her own.

"Somehow . . . somehow, I'll pay you back, I promise. Just not that way."

"Pay me back," Lil repeated, then shook her head. "It's not just your dislike of the work, is it? You're afraid you'll feel even more indebted to me if you take the stores."

"It's not that, it's—" She stopped. "Yes. That's part of it. Not all of it, but a big part."

"I humiliated you, didn't I? Oh, not recently," she added when Patsy Lee frowned, not following. "Back when Henry died. I took over like I was responsible for the world. Maybe I managed to keep everyone afloat back then, but I didn't take your feelings into account. I should have at least consulted you before I rode to your rescue."

"Please, Lil. Don't apologize. You've done so much."

Just like Zinnia, Lil let her heart drive her, often past the boundaries of what people wanted. It was one thing to offer help, another to insist on it, or offer it up like a done deal just like . . .

Patsy Lee sucked in her breath—just like she'd almost done to Hank.

And just like she was doing to Daisy.

Startled, she put the insight aside for later thought and forced herself to concentrate on what Lil was saying.

"I was afraid I'd offended you then. That's why I let you think that I was giving you the stores because

I wanted to preserve them as some kind of family legacy."

"But . . . don't you?"

"Oh, it would be nice if it happened, but . . . well, I just thought it was a reason you could accept. Just like before, I wanted to insure your future—your family's future—as much as I could. And just like before, I didn't consult you first." Lil's expression turned rueful. "I guess I've got a lot of my mother in me. If you don't want the stores, I'll sell them when the time comes—or pass them down to one of the children, if someone wants them. I never meant you to feel beholden to me. I'm sorry you did. And you—" She smiled gently. "You need to apologize to me for feeling that way."

"Apologize? Why?"

Lil leaned forward and reached for her hand. "I love you. I love your whole family. And when something's offered in love, it doesn't create obligation. Or maybe I should say it shouldn't."

All the energy and time Zeke had put into her family while he'd lived with them flitted through her head. She realized that he'd never asked anything from her in return.

Patsy Lee settled back into the Cadillac. Her talk with Lil had lifted a burden off her shoulders, so she was surprised to find her heart still felt heavy. Blaming the thoughts of Zeke that had just crossed her mind, she started the car. She hadn't asked Lil about Zeke. She hadn't really wanted to know where he was.

Or so she'd told herself.

But now she glanced at the guest house. If he hadn't left yet, she supposed she should stop and thank him for the gifts he'd given the children, say good-bye. Anything less would be childish.

She followed the drive over a couple of sloping acres and stopped under the portico that spanned the guesthouse entrance. No movement was visible on the other side of the glass doors. Just as she was about to open her door (or leave, she hadn't decided which), someone tapped on her trunk. Eyes flying to the rear-view mirror, she saw Jon. She ignored a stab of disappointment.

Opening the passenger door, he slid in and shook back the upturned collar on his sheepskin jacket. "Brr. Give me a ride back to the house, would you?"

She put the car into drive without comment, embarrassed that he'd caught her lurking.

"Looking for Zeke?" He didn't wait for her answer. "The limo to St. Louis picked up him and Martha an hour ago. I was checking if all the faucets and lights were off."

The stab of disappointment became an ache. *Of guilt,* she told herself. And only because after all he'd done for her family (disregarding his desertion of Lily-Too), she hadn't made more (any) effort to thank him before he'd left.

She felt Jon's gaze resting on her, but didn't look at him. Finally, he spoke. "You and Zeke are worse than I was with Lil, you know it?"

She frowned. "What are you talking about?"

"Early in our relationship. At least she kept fighting for us even when I was ready to give up. But with you two . . . sheesh, both of you threw in the towel before you'd even squared off."

"I don't understand what you mean. We're here," she said brightly, as if he wouldn't notice that she'd pulled to a stop in front of his house.

He didn't move. "Look . . ."

"No, you look," she burst out, "he doesn't love me, he thinks he loves L–" She chomped down, almost biting off her tongue. She should just wire shut her jaw and be done with it.

Jon's eyebrows went up. "Lil?" He laughed. "Is that what you think?"

She was glad he was laughing, but he probably wouldn't be once he'd thought things through.

Jon still sputtered. "Him and Lil? One of them would kill the other before a week was out. They both think they know everything." He sobered suddenly. "Shh. Don't tell her I said that."

Patsy Lee could tell from the merry dance in his eyes that Lil's occasional high-handedness didn't really bother him a bit. "I shouldn't have said anything, because he's wrong."

"You are, too." Jon was still grinning.

"No, let me explain. He's not in love with Lil, he's in love with what she represents. . . . What you and she represent."

"Hell, I know that."

"You do?

"Which is a good thing, because if I'd thought like you . . . well, I like him, you see. I wouldn't want to have to kill him." He gave a gusty sigh. "Patricia—"

"Patsy Lee."

"God, make up your mind . . . Why do you think Lil and I threw him at you? Because," he answered himself, "he wants what we have. But, poor guy—" Jon's voice turned confiding. "People think he's smart, but he's really stupid, you know."

"Well, now he'll have it. With Christine."

Jon rolled his eyes. "You're both stupid. It's not any family he wants. It's yours."

"I know." That didn't make her feel any better. "He's not attracted to me. He's attracted to my family. Just like—"

Jon snorted. "If he loves your family more than you—"

"Loves? *Me?*" She felt her insides go tight.

"—Then tell me why he's letting down Lily-Too."

Her mind was still reeling. *Zeke . . . loves . . . me?* Even a little? "I don't know, but—"

"Because he's in too much pain over you to stay even one more day."

She sat stunned.

"When Lil told me she wanted to try to get the two of you together, I thought she'd have better luck trying to mate a dog with a duck. . . ."

"Gee, thanks."

"Oh, you know what I mean. And she was right. Lil is, as she loves to remind me, always right. The man was so hangdog when he left here, it's a miracle he didn't trip over his drooping ears. He is completely nuts about you."

"No, he isn't."

"Is, too."

"Then why didn't he say anything?"

Jon opened up the car door. "From what he said, you've been very busy making plans. And none of them included him." He got out and shut the door.

Jaw slack, Patsy Lee watched him take two steps toward the house. Then he pivoted, returned to the car, wrenched open the door, and bent down to peer in.

"I thought I'd add that their flight to New York doesn't depart until three o'clock this afternoon. American Airlines. Flight six ninety-eight. From Lambert Field. You still have time to catch him."

"But I can't. . . . I-I'll call him."

Jon dug in his pocket. Aghast, she watched him pull out his cell phone, flip it open, and push a button. "Speed dial's one of the world's best inventions." He tossed it in her lap. "Put your money where your mouth is."

Hesitating, she finally picked up the phone and put

it to her ear, heart stopping at the sound of Zeke's voice. His recorded voice. Relieved, she handed it back. "He—it's off."

Slipping the cell phone back in his pocket, Jon kept her gaze pinned with his. "But it's not really something you want to discuss on the phone, anyway, is it?"

"Yes . . . well . . . maybe. No." Then she repeated, more emphatically, "No." She needed to see his face if she was going to tell him—She shook her head, trying to clear it. Tell him *what*? What was she thinking? What was she about to *do*? This was all happening too fast. "I'm not . . . the children . . . I mean, how could I—"

"Oh, for God's sake, woman. Lil and I will see to your offspring. Go."

When she still hesitated, Jon looked ready to stomp his feet. "Patsy Lee O'Malley, listen up. You survived an oddball childhood, your mother's early departure from this planet, and marriage to a—pardon-me-and-don't-ever-tell-Lil-I-said-this—bum. You're a single mother of four, you've handled (really well, I think) women like Zinnia and Lil and her two sisters for years, which is more than I can do, not to mention the Rosemary Butzes and even Ernie Burchams of the world—yes, I heard what happened at the party. You live in the middle of nowhere with—with chickens and donkeys and other four-footed things. You are, my dear sister-in-law, really, *really* brave. Now go."

He slammed the door shut again. For a moment Patsy Lee sat stunned. Jon's words resounded in her head. Then Daisy's.

Maybe you don't know much about love.

She put the car into drive, suddenly laughing like a loon. The hell she didn't! She knew enough. She knew she loved Zeke Townley. The knowledge walloped her right in the gut, scaring her to death while at the same time making her feel she could fly. And she knew she'd wasted too many precious moments telling herself all the reasons why she couldn't do exactly what she wanted rather than examining all the possibilities still spread ahead of her.

She glanced at her watch. It was nearing ten. If she drove straight through, with only a quick stop for gas and maybe a doughnut—okay, okay, maybe a piece of *fruit*—she could buy a cheap puddle-jumper ticket to get her past the security checkpoint to the concourses and make Zeke's gate with an hour to spare. Maybe Jon was wrong about how Zeke felt. But she knew for sure how she did.

And she owed it to herself to let him know, too.

She punched on the accelerator and the Cadillac fishtailed down the drive. Behind her, she heard Jon's shout of encouragement.

Within minutes, Cordelia had disappeared in her rearview mirror; miles later, she whisked past Columbia. Sayonara to both. She knew exactly where she wanted to go.

And it was exactly where she belonged.

Chapter 29

At Lambert Field, except for the occasional ring of a cell phone and the rustle of a paper or two, it was quiet inside American Airlines' Admirals Club. The plush carpeting and upholstery swallowed the din at the intersection of concourses that lay just outside the club's double doors.

Yet Zeke's spine refused to relax. He pushed it back against the chair anyway, hooking an ankle over his knee, pinching the crease on his black trousers to a knifepoint, and snapping open his complimentary *Wall Street Journal.*

He'd read only three paragraphs, without comprehending any of it, before his mother nudged his foot. He looked up to see her standing in front of him, bearing two cups. The rising steam disappeared against the gray of her silk jacket. Combined with her silver hair and the steel in her eyes, the tailored suit made her look invincible. Appropriate.

"Coffee?" she asked brightly.

He grunted and took a cup from her, setting it on the table beside him, not giving her the satisfaction of seeing him touch it to his lips. She settled into the chair that flanked the table's other side and hummed to herself. He pretended not to hear.

So far during his mother's visit, he'd successfully

kept her and her curiosity at bay, shunting her off into Zinnia's willing company while he busied himself with Jon, the Vreeley Home Boys' Band, pageant rehearsals, and anything else that would distract him from his dashed hopes. He'd almost climbed out of his skin waiting for the opportunity to escape Cordelia, especially when he'd seen the disappointment in his young troupe's faces. He'd never felt like such a coward in his life.

But he hadn't been relieved once the limo was finally rolling down Jon and Lil's drive. How could he? From the moment they'd climbed inside, his mother had started shooting questions, trying to put holes in his guard. He'd fended her off by burrowing into a sheaf of papers concerning nonprofit organizations that his business manager had sent him, just like he was burrowing into the *WSJ* now.

Her humming grew louder. Knowing he was only postponing the inevitable, he stiffened the paper in front of him. She stopped humming, kicked his foot with her own. He raised the white flag of surrender by lowering the paper a few inches.

"Why are you so irritable? You haven't said two words all day. In fact, you haven't said much more than two words since I got to Cordelia. And it doesn't look like you've slept more than that many minutes. With those circles under your eyes, we should call you Rocky."

"As in the boxer?"

"Hardly. As in the raccoon. You haven't shown much fighting spirit of late, at least not so's I've seen it. Before I got here, your phone calls—at least the few there were—had convinced me you'd found something to cure whatever's ailed you since the band broke up. But now . . ." She examined him, and infinitesimally, he snuck the paper back up. "Well, you do seem less restless than when I last saw you, but your mood this week has been distinctly unpleasant." When he didn't immediately reply, she shoved at his foot again.

He wasn't sorry he'd left Cordelia, but he heartily wished he'd headed in the opposite direction from his mother. He'd felt the need, though, for family ties. Obviously, he'd forgotten how quickly his mother could lash a square knot.

Ceding victory, he sighed and folded the paper. "You're right. I'm less restless; I've found new purpose." He motioned at the briefcase containing the nonprofit information beside the chair. "Happy?"

"Ah, new purpose. But what about a new *person*. Seems to me—"

"But," he interrupted, "right now I don't feel like talking."

"And this is because—?"

He gave her a look of disbelief, and she returned a bland one.

"Because—?" she repeated encouragingly.

"Oh, for God's sake." He slapped the newspaper down on the table, narrowly missing his cup. She didn't give him the satisfaction of jumping. "If you must know, I'm irritable because I'm letting down a group of children. In particular, one very special young lady."

He looked away, his throat suddenly tight as he remembered the brave smile Lily-Too had given him on his last night in Cordelia, and how she'd hugged his guitar like she'd never let it go. He'd be back, he reminded himself. They hadn't said good-bye forever.

He looked back at his mother, whose gaze was way too sharp for his own good. He shrugged. "So even though I'm certain—certain, did you hear that?—that leaving Cordelia, and leaving it *now*, is the best—"

"You don't sound so certain."

"Mom."

"Sorry. Continue."

"I'm done."

She fell silent. After a moment, he blew out a breath and unfolded the paper.

"You know, you could keep Christine at a distance; in fact, that's how she preferred things. Once upon a time, you did, too. But not anymore. She's not right for you. She never was."

He felt his eyes cross. "I *know* that."

"Then *why* are you going to New York?"

"I'm not going so I can spend the holidays with Christine. I'm going because I don't want to spend them alone. You and Teresa are part of my family, remember?"

"I do; I'm glad you do, too. And I'm very glad you've found out that shouldering burdens for your family—which I never should've let you do at that young age—doesn't always have to feel like you're dragging around some ball and chain. Still . . . it doesn't seem to me Cordelia lacks for folks who would make sure you wouldn't be alone."

"Mom."

Quiet descended again.

But not for long. "I'm just saying, your normally impeccable logic doesn't sound so . . . peccable . . . at this point."

He dropped the paper. "I would very much appreciate it if you would make *your* point."

"Christine isn't right for you."

"You said that."

"*But* there is someone in Cordelia who is."

Zeke snorted. "Maybe. But just you try to pull all her baggage off her."

"I believe that's your job, not mine. I'm surprised at you—the son I raised wasn't a quitter."

"The son you raised knows when to stop tilting at windmills."

She opened her mouth again, but a quiet announcement interrupted. "American Airlines flight six ninety-eight for New York will board shortly on concourse C, gate two."

Shouldering their carry-ons, Zeke stood up. "Let's go."

But his mother wasn't one to let anyone else get the last word. As he escorted her down the concourse, she filled his ears until they rang. Again he wondered if it was too late to change his flight reservations. While his other sisters undoubtedly had their holiday plans already set, one of them probably wouldn't mind adding him to the mix. He picked up his stride, childishly letting his mother puff along in his wake. Then he stopped dead. A familiar woman stood up ahead.

His mother halted beside him. "What?"

"Just someone I didn't expect to see."

Outside gate four, standing next to a man he didn't know, was Maisie Ann Phelps. She held no baggage. Just the arm of her escort. The man gazed down at her and she looked up at him with a smile that was so blindingly brilliant, Zeke's heart suddenly ached. He was whisked back to that night he'd shared a seat with Patricia at the football stadium in Cordelia, to the night he'd first heard the story of the choir director and her pharmacist.

From Patricia. And as she'd talked, her face had been briefly struck by the same kind of naked emotion he now saw on Maisie Ann Phelps'. Longing. And barely concealed envy.

Five hours after leaving Cordelia, Patsy Lee hurried over the asphalt toward Lambert Field's main terminal, her hair whipped by the wind, her gait an awkward half skip, her spirits finally flagging. Despite heavy traffic (and a dollop of fear at her unaccustomed daring), exhilaration had fueled her as she'd wound north out of Cordelia, jumping onto I-70 near Columbia, where she'd pressed the Caddy up to speeds it hadn't ever seen. She'd been certain she could make the airport in plenty of time and equally, certain that she could find Zeke once she did. Until an accident west of O'Fallon had halted her headlong rush.

A tractor-trailer had jackknifed across the highway. Once she'd crawled through that mess, she'd still held out hope, but it had faded to only a flicker when she'd finally arrived at the airport, just to be confronted by cars packed into the parking lots like so many sweet pickles jammed into a jar. It had taken her too many precious minutes to find a place.

And now it was after three.

Bursting through the terminal doors, barely hearing the cacophony that pressed against her ears, she loped around suitcases and strollers and multitudes of people, her eyes glued on the arrivals-and-departures screen up ahead.

Stopping just short, she scanned the list for a three o'clock to New York. There. Flight six-ninety-eight. Her eyes leaped to the right side of the board. ON TIME.

He'd already left.

Heart plummeting into her shoes, she gritted her teeth against the urge to sink to the floor and bawl like a baby. She wouldn't give up. Not yet. If there was space on a plane, she'd hightail it to New York, pride and practicality be damned. If she had to track down Zeke in the middle of an airport four times the size of Cordelia, she'd do it. And if she had to throw herself at his feet in front of Christine's curled upper lip, so be it.

Although she wouldn't see New York before Sunday. She found the American Airlines line and joined it. She'd charge a ticket to New York before common sense had a snowball's chance to crush her determination, but she couldn't leave for New York before Christmas. Lily-Too might be able to survive Zeke's absence at the pageant and from her birthday on Christmas Eve, but she wouldn't forgive her mother's. This was one instance where obligation did outweigh personal desire—maybe she was finally learning how to balance the scales.

Digging through her purse for a wallet, she jumped a foot when a voice sounded near her ear.

"It's not a good day for travel."

Hand still in her bag, she froze, swallowing around a suddenly tight throat. "It's . . . it's not?"

"No. Way too many people."

She blinked back the tears that had sprung to her eyes, but kept her voice steady. "I'm disappointed. I'd hoped to find a flight to New York. You see, I recently realized there's nothing stopping me from going anywhere at all. Even . . . even San Francisco. Except my own fears."

There was a beat of silence.

Then, "You know what? I have a ticket to New York that I don't plan to use."

A sob caught in her throat. She turned around and looked up into Zeke's dark eyes. "I'd buy your ticket, but I've just changed my mind."

"You're going home?"

"Yes, at least for now, but . . ."

Then the words spilled out before she could stop them. "I know what home is now. It's not a place. It's . . . it's me . . ." She pressed one of his hands to her chest where he could feel the beat of her heart; then placed her palm on his. "And it's you."

Zeke had gone completely still. She reached up, touched his face, then let her hand drop to her side. Blinking back tears, she whispered. "Don't you agree?"

Love and relief flooding his face, he swept her into his arms. "Ah, my love . . . darn tootin,' I do."

DON'T MISS JERRI CORGIAT'S OTHER HEARTWARMING ROMANCES FEATURING THE O'MALLEY FAMILY

Sing Me Home

Country music star Jonathan Van Castle has had his ups and downs. Right now he's back on the road—and back in the spotlight. While traveling through his home state of Missouri, Jon ducks into a bookstore to flee some adoring female fans—and comes face-to-face with a woman whose china blue eyes sing out to him. . . .

Lilac O'Malley Ryan doesn't even recognize the world-renowned celebrity who bursts into her store. And she's bewildered by what seem like tongue-tied attempts at charm. She just wants to make a sale—and get him out the door. But it's a lot harder to get that to-die-for smile out of her mind.

Once they put their rocky start behind them, Jon and Lil will discover what happens when two unlikely lovers hit the perfect note. . . .

"The unforgettable characters resonate long after the last page is turned."

—*Romantic Times BOOKclub* (Top Pick)

"Filled with joy and laughter, pathos and challenges."

—*Midwest Book Review*

Follow Me Home

Serving eggs at the local diner is not where Alcea O'Malley Addams expected to wind up. But a divorce from her cheating husband wore out her bank account and her self-esteem. Now Alcea finds her plate full of problems: foreclosure on her house, a difficult fourteen-year-old daughter, and a well-meaning—yet infuriating—family.

So it's just one more problem when she accidentally runs Dakota Jones—her old high school crush—off the road. And it gets even more complicated when he veers straight into her heart. Dak is the kind of man who can turn a woman's knees to jelly. And though he doesn't want to be tied down, spirited Alcea is almost too tempting to pass up.

These crazy feelings might just be leftovers from long ago. But then, some people can make miracles from leftovers. . . .

"If a reader is very lucky, sometimes a new author will come on the scene and steal her heart. . . . Jerri Corgiat is that kind of author. . . . An incredible book."
—*Affaire de Coeur*

"Jerri Corgiat's second novel is as delightful as her first . . . a talented mix of plot, characters, and emotional discovery. Fast paced. . . .You won't want to miss either."
—Readers and Writers Ink

Home At Last

After shaking the Ozark dust from her designer stilettos for the last time, Marigold McKenzie O'Malley headed to Kansas City to find fame and fortune. But now, eight years later, Mari is unemployed, broke, and brokenhearted—and in no shape to resist her older sisters when they drag her back to Cordelia, Missouri, to help their mother after her heart attack.

Though she's still clinging furiously to her big-city dreams, Mari finds she has a disconcerting tendency to go weak in the knees around No-Account Andy Eppelwaite, her best childhood chum and the former town troublemaker. But even though Andy has gotten his life back on track, he has no desire to leave the backwater Ozarks—and he may not be the kind of man who can forgive Mari's past mistakes.

If Mari can trust Andy with her darkest secrets, she just might be able to trust that home really is where the heart is . . .

"Cordelia, Missouri, is a wonderful down-home town to visit and make new friends, ones you will want to visit again and again in this keeper of a series."

—Romance Reviews Today

"Corgiat skillfully interweaves the lasting legacies of child abuse, alcoholism, and infidelity and adultery into this hard-hitting contemporary Southern romance."

—*Booklist*